The Upward Way

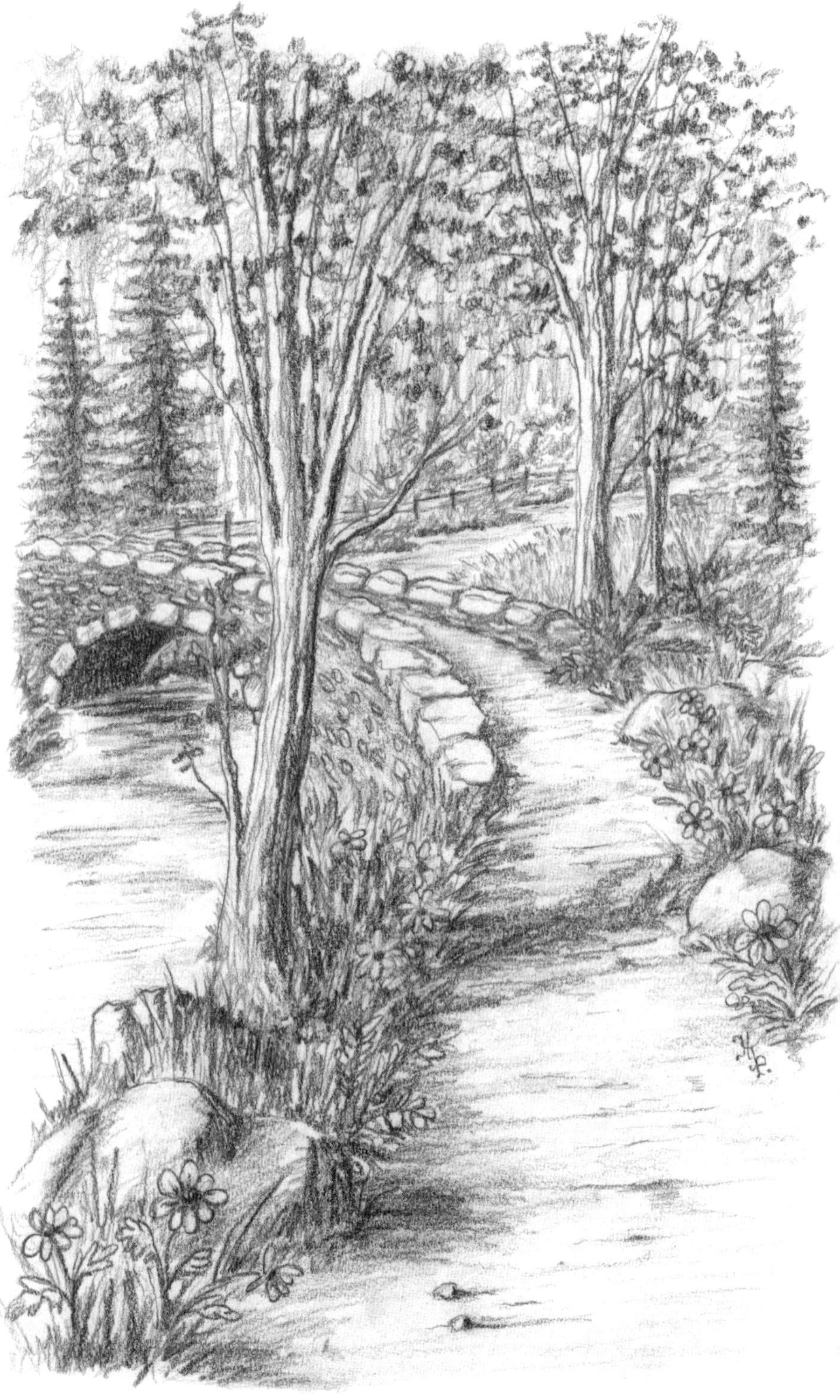

The Upward Way

Written by Audrey Siegrist

Artwork by Hannah Putt

Rod and Staff Publishers, Inc.
P.O. Box 3, Hwy. 172
Crockett, Kentucky 41413
Telephone: 606-522-4348

Copyright 2009

By Rod and Staff Publishers, Inc.
Crockett, Kentucky 41413

Printed in U. S. A.

ISBN 0-7399-2410-9

Catalog no. 2456

2 3 4 5 — 18 17 16 15 14 13 12 11 10

Preface

Much of this story is taken from "Ruth's" journals and diaries. Of course, many details and conversations have been reconstructed to carry the story along. In a few cases, I have changed actual dates of unimportant historical occurrences to help them fit better with the flow of the story. The names of the main characters have been changed, but I have kept the real names of many other characters. By doing this, I trust I do not cause offense in any way to anyone. I have tried to retain as much of the color of the time and the actual happenings as seemed possible and practical.

This book is not meant to be a book of history, but rather the story of one woman's struggle to follow Jesus in the midst of much conflict and opposition. Her sole desire was to "know [Christ] and the power of his resurrection, and the fellowship of his sufferings." She was not perfect, as people who were close to her well knew, but she had—as saints of all ages—a "passion for perfection."

Jesus states that we cannot serve God and riches. "No man can serve two masters: for either he will hate the one, and love the other; or else he will hold to the one, and despise the other." How willing are we to leave our earthly accumulations and associations for the sake of the Gospel or, as in this story, for the sake of our families?

"For what shall it profit a man, if he shall gain the whole world, and lose his own soul?"

–The author

To those who have left
"houses, or brethren, or sisters,
or father, or mother,
or wife, or children, or lands,
for my name's sake."
Jesus said that such
"shall receive an hundredfold,
and shall inherit everlasting life."

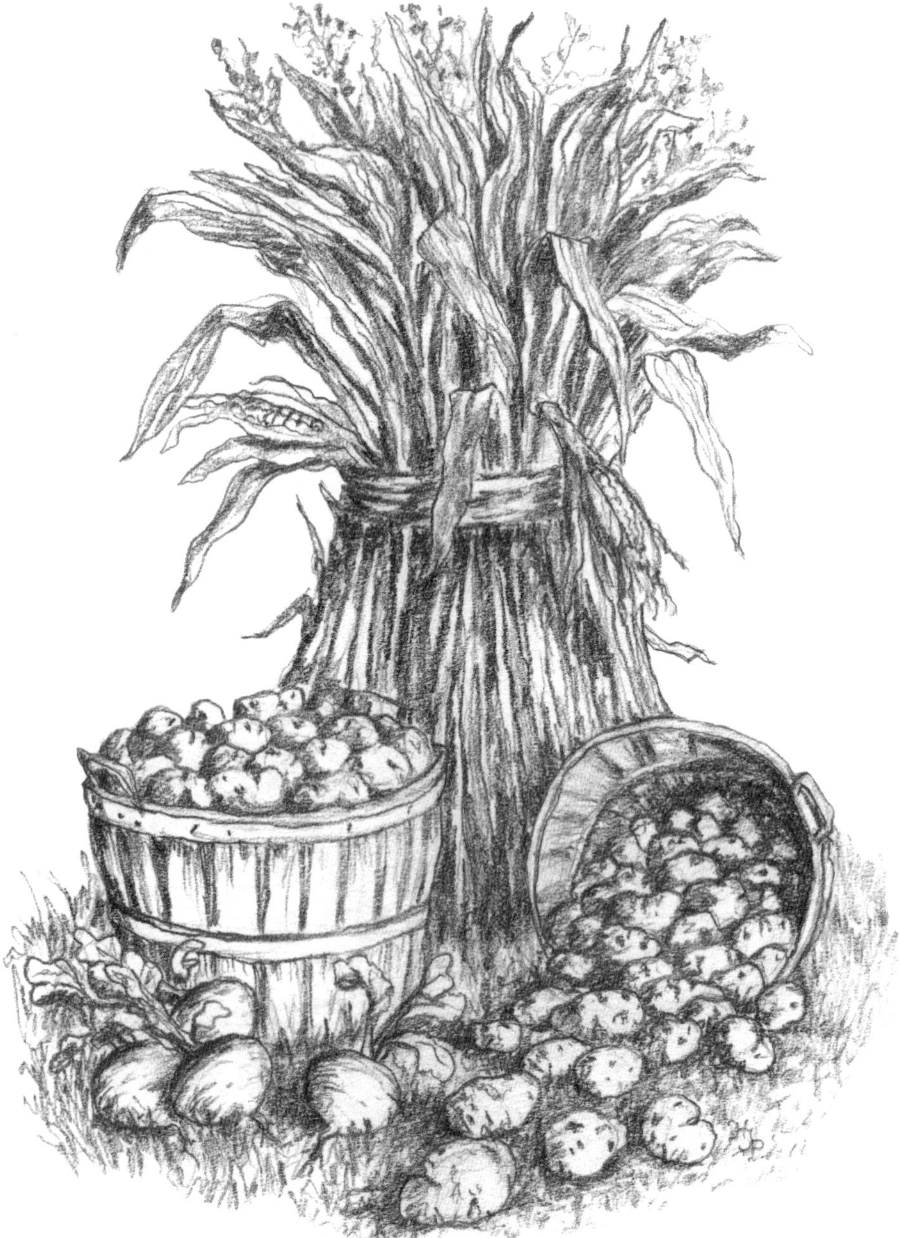

Chapter One

October 4, 1933, Wednesday. Today I am nineteen years old, and what a birthday! I received a special card from Charles, as well as one from Grace G., which was very thoughtful of her. I cut corn for the cows all morning and picked up potatoes all afternoon. In the evening, Kore and I brought in a load of turnips. We worked till late. Was a mild fall day but got cloudy in the evening. I am very tired.

Virginia Ruth Clemmer, better known as Ruth, stretched wearily and reached to turn off her clattering alarm clock. It was four-thirty in the morning and still very dark outside, but darker still in her little garret bedroom.

Ruth sat on her bed and thought. She liked everything about her little private sanctuary. She liked her old, black iron bed, which had once belonged to Grammy Clemmer, even though the ancient springs creaked dreadfully whenever she got into bed or out of it. And even though she could only feel it now, she liked the shades-of-purple patchwork quilt that covered it, which Mama and Dorcas

The Upward Way

had made for her several years before. She liked her two long windows out of which she could watch the blue hills appear to greet the rising sun, and the long, ruffled, purple curtains that bordered them both. Dorcas had made the curtains as well.

Yes, she liked her own little bedroom. But it was almost too lonely here now without her sister Sarah, who had gotten married almost three weeks ago. Her oldest sister, Dorcas, was crippled and slept in the regular upstairs, in a bedroom by herself. It would have been hard for Dorcas to climb the winding, narrow stairway that led to Ruth's chosen room over the kitchen. Besides, to be quite honest, Ruth would rather not share this haven with Dorcas. She was not a kindred spirit, as Sarah had been. Perhaps that was mostly because Dorcas was nearly nine years older than Ruth. Perhaps too it was because they did not share a lot of common interests. While Dorcas liked nothing better than sewing and housework, Ruth loved the vast out-of-doors and reveled in any work that took her into the open air and sunshine.

A raw breeze from the east was blowing in the open window. Ruth quietly groped her way to the window and stood there, breathing deeply of the fresh morning dampness and gazing into the vastness of the starlit sky. Besides the points of light that the stars made, millions of light-years away, all was black darkness outside. No city lights lit up the horizon. No dusk-to-dawn lamps turned the humping hillsides into half-day. It was so dark that Ruth could not even see her hand in front of her face. *As dark as this seems, I wonder how Egypt's darkness could have been darker,* she mused. But she knew that

The Upward Way

the Bible called that plague a darkness so thick that it could be felt. She shivered, not that she was afraid of the present darkness, but thinking about the kind of darkness that offered no ray of light or hope.

Feeling for her matchbox, she lit her oil lamp and proceeded to dress in the early-morning hush. Nobody else was stirring. Dorcas and Mama would not get up for another hour and a half, but Papa would be up at five-thirty, and then she would need to help him with the milking. Until then, she would spend the time in Bible study and prayer, as was her usual practice.

Sometime later, Ruth awoke with a start. She must have fallen asleep on her knees. "Ruth!" Papa's impatient voice echoed loudly up the garret stairway. "Virginia Ruth! Are you getting up this morning, or do you intend to sleep all day?"

"Coming," she responded calmly in spite of the quick hurt that rose up inside her. Oh, why must Papa have such a quick temper and make such scenes in his anger? What a way to start the day—her birthday at that! She should never have fallen asleep, and now she was the cause of a racket that no doubt awakened the whole household. She quickly blew out her lamp and set it back on her bureau—she would not need it downstairs this morning if Papa had already lit a lamp in the kitchen. Then, feeling her way, she scuttled down the garret stairs and out into the washhouse, where she quickly splashed cold water over her face from the bucket sitting under the pump. Ah, that felt bracing! After drying her face on the feed-sack towel that hung from a rod behind the door, she hurried into her barn jacket.

The Upward Way

Papa must have gone out ahead of her; she could see the lamp he carried bobbing across the road to the barn. She hurried after him, hoping he was not still angry. Probably he was not; usually his temper flared quickly and cooled just as quickly. But by then, the harm was done. Papa was the deacon at Grove Hill Mennonite Church—had been for as long as she could remember. In many ways, Papa seemed like an upright, faithful Christian, and he was well respected in the church community. He was also, as far as she knew, appreciated and held in high regard by their many neighbors and business acquaintances in and around Grove Hill. But why could he not, by the grace of God, have victory over such a sinful habit as displaying his temper?

Papa had been born and raised right in that township, coming from a long line of Clemmers who had also been born and raised there. They were able to trace their lineage in America back to 1707, when the first Clemmer set foot in Philadelphia, coming from Wolfsheim, Switzerland. Though poor in earthly goods for many years, they had given themselves to the Lord's work, producing a progeny of ministers, teachers, and lay leaders. Ruth had heard the story many times from Mama, who very much enjoyed keeping genealogies.

One thing she had not heard from Mama, though, was how Papa had been a cheerful and considerate brother in his home as he was growing up. Ruth thought now, as she stepped briskly to the barn, about the time recently she had been sharing with her cousin Grace about how quick-tempered Papa could be and how she did not know how to respond to him at times like that. Aunt Emma had

The Upward Way

overheard her and rose in defense of her brother. "Your papa was never like that as my brother in our home," she had said. "Why he would be since he is married, I do not understand!" Aunt Emma had gone on to elaborate on how thoughtful and kind he actually had been then, ending with the question again of why he would have changed so.

Ruth wondered about that herself. Was it from all the responsibility he had as a father in hard financial times? Was it because of all the trying situations that he faced in church relationships? Was it maybe because Mama was sometimes snappy to him? Or was it a combination of these and other things? *Dear Father in heaven, whatever the reason, please help me not to become like that as I grow older,* she prayed fervently as she dashed into the barn. Nearly a dozen cats of assorted sizes and colors rose sleepily from their nests on a pile of straw by the door. They yawned and stretched, fore and aft, as she stopped to watch them with amusement. This was nearly always their ritual when she entered the barn each morning. She stooped to pet her favorites and then hurried on.

Mark, Ruth's only brother, had brought their fifteen cows in from the pasture. "Good morning," he greeted her cheerfully when she entered the cow stable. "And happy birthday." She could see the gleam of white teeth, and she knew, in the semidarkness, that he was smiling.

"You remembered my birthday?" Ruth asked in amazement as she grabbed a bucket and her milking stool.

"How could I forget—with a good wife to keep me reminded about such little matters!" he returned. Then he

15

The Upward Way

too disappeared behind a cow, and soon the steady stream of milk hitting the buckets spoke of the diligent efforts of the milkmaid and milkman. Papa fed the horses and the cows and the other animals while Mark and Ruth milked.

The feeding was usually Papa's job, but Ruth did not mind. She enjoyed the more intimate contact with the cows that milking them afforded, and she treated them all as pets. The cats too. She had always pampered the cats and had a name for each of the dozen that prowled around the barn in search of mice, or dozed on the doorstep on sunny days, or—as now—waited expectantly near her as she milked, hoping for a shot of milk now and then. With a chuckle, Ruth directed a stream of warm milk to Nellie, who caught it expertly in her mouth. "There you," she said, "now go catch a mouse in payment for that treat." Nellie just blinked and meowed, not interested in leaving at the moment, but obviously interested in more milk.

The milking was finished by six-thirty. Papa finished straining the milk and washed up the buckets. Mark had gone to his house up on the hill for his breakfast, and Ruth hurried to their house across the dirt road. She hurried, but not too fast to observe the morning sky. Shafts of light in shades of pink and orange shot over the horizon, but scudding clouds threatened to block out the emerging sun at any moment. Was rain on the way? Probably, with the wind from the east. The creaking windmill blades were whirling high above her head, turning the lively wind currents into water for the cattle and horses in the barn and the pigs and chickens in their pens and sheds on the hillside.

She rushed around the side of the house to the

The Upward Way

washhouse. Pumping a basin full of water, she scrubbed her hands thoroughly but hurriedly with Mama's good homemade lye soap. Papa would soon be in, and his patience wore thin pretty quickly if meals were not on time. Mama was always happy for help to finish the last-minute details.

When Ruth entered the kitchen a few moments later, Mama, short and stout, was bustling about from cookstove to table. Dorcas was setting the table methodically, her lameness making her movements slow and deliberate. Ruth poured a bowl full of breakfast food[1] out of a tin molasses pail. "Everything smells wonderful!" she said as she set it and a platter of fried mush on the table. Dorcas had already gotten the molasses to go on the homemade bread. "And chicken gravy to go on the mush! You must've gotten up early, Mama, to get all this ready."

"I heard Papa call you at five-thirty," Mama returned. "So I did get up earlier than what I usually do." Mama turned to smile at her from where she was cutting a fresh ground-cherry pie into four pieces. Her mouth was busy with some morsel. Ruth smiled as she noticed. Mama was a good cook and loved to eat food as well as prepare it. She nearly always served pie for breakfast, and she set it on the table now. She gathered up bits of flaky crust that had crumbled onto the cupboard top and stuck them into her mouth. Then she stood back to peer at the table. "What else do we need?"

"The coffee," Ruth said.

"It's been perking for a while. You may pour it," Mama directed. "Papa will soon be in."

---

[1] This was possibly something like Grape-Nuts cereal.

The Upward Way

Ruth poured coffee into Papa's and Mama's oversized mugs, debating briefly if she herself wanted a cup this morning. No, she would rather have milk, just plain, cold milk, she decided.

"Is there milk in the icebox, or do we need to bring some up from the cave?" she asked, looking around.

"Oh, I used the last of what was in the icebox. Run quickly and get a jug, please," Mama requested hurriedly. "And while you're there, bring another jar of cream for Papa's coffee too."

Ruth darted down the back path to the cave, a dugout along the stream bank behind the house. As she hurried, she thought of Mama, now stout and graying, and wondered about the days gone by of which Mama spoke sometimes—the days when she had been popular among the young people. Mama had grown up near Harrisonburg, Virginia, and had had access to all the culture that her time offered. She sometimes seemed to feel, Ruth thought now, that she had been a cut above others, having had extensive musical training as well as the opportunity to work in the homes of some of Virginia's elite—the Robbs and the Byrds. *I wonder what good Mama feels those "advantages" do her now,* Ruth mused as she stood for a moment at the heavy wooden door of the cave. She thought of pictures that Mama had of herself from that time—she had been a beautiful brunette and dressed in the styles of the day. *But outward beauty fades. And besides, now Mama is married to a conservative Mennonite deacon and cannot be dressy anymore, even if she would like to be,* which Ruth did not really feel she would.

The Upward Way

Slowly Ruth entered the cool darkness of the cave, feeling her way around. *Why, as children of God, do we tend to take pleasure in what the world considers important?* she pondered further. *We who are not to love the world or to value what it does. If we do, we are not children of God—1 John 2 states that plainly . . .*

She lifted a glass jug of milk and a smaller one of cream from the trough set in the cool mountain stream, and carefully lugged them back up to the house. She hurried, trying to make up for the moments she had stood thinking, knowing as well as Mama did how impatient Papa got if breakfast was not ready when he got there.

"Well, we'll need to keep at silo-filling today," Papa stated as soon as the prayer of thanks was over. He looked directly at Ruth. "Can you cut corn this morning?"

"I suppose. Will Kore be back to help?" *If only Sarah were here yet to help me with such work,* her thoughts added impetuously. *How I miss her since she is married! Of course, Dorcas is not able to help—and probably wouldn't want to if she could . . .*

Papa looked at Mama. "Did you say Kore is coming back right away this morning?"

Ruth thought of Kore Plank, the foster boy who had lived with them for several years. His father had died some years before, and his mother, a member in a church in their district, found as her son grew older that she could not handle his rebellious tendencies. And so, at the tender age of ten, his lot had somehow fallen with the Clemmer family. In many ways he seemed like part of the family; but in other ways, it was a blessing when he was not around for a few days. He could be

19

The Upward Way

so temperamental! Since Ruth worked outside so much, she was usually the one who worked with him. And she never knew when he would get upset about something and go into a moody spell, not talking for hours—or even days. He still attended the Spring City school during the week, so he was mostly around just after school and weekends—except during the summer, when he was usually there every day.

Mama nodded in answer to Papa's question. "Yes, Uncle Claude will bring him back from his mother's place on his way past this morning."

"Good," Papa stated. "Then he and Ruth can start cutting corn right away. Mark will run it through the chopper, and I can do the odd jobs."

"But Kore needs to go to school today," Mama interposed.

"I made arrangements for him to be at home the rest of the week. And he knows about it already," Papa returned emphatically. "There's all the fall work to be done; and I need his help here today, as well as Ruth's."

Ruth groaned inside. She was so tired already, and the day was only beginning. But she knew there was no hope of any sympathy from Papa. He was hale and hardy and expected everyone else to be able to keep the pace he did. "Quit your brutzing[2] and get busy," Papa had told her more than once. Furthermore, he thought she looked strong and rugged enough to do a man's work—she had heard that quite often too, if she dared to complain.

O Lord, she breathed, *will You please give me special*

---

[2] Brutz is a Pennsylvania Dutch expression that means "to fuss or complain."

The Upward Way

strength again! God was always faithful, she rejoiced inwardly, meeting her needs and giving her daily strength.

Uncle Claude drove past while the Clemmers were still eating breakfast, letting Kore off at the yard gate. Ruth watched him through the window as he ambled up the front walk. *He might make a good-looking man someday*, she thought with an inner chuckle, *but right now he is simply a gangly thirteen-year-old.* Kore brushed through the door, said a half-hearted "good morning," and skulked on through the kitchen on his way to the sitting room and stairway.

Dorcas looked after him. "Hey, young fellow, no dirty shoes upstairs!" she reminded him.

"Okay, okay!" He grudgingly returned to the kitchen, dropped down in a chair by the cookstove, and untied his work shoes. Stocking footed, he carried his satchel upstairs to his room and soon reappeared, dressed in his work overalls. Again he sat down and pulled his clumsy shoes back on. Without many words, he was out the door again, on his way to hitch up the horse to the wagon.

Ruth hurried outside too, first grabbing her barn jacket from the hook in the washhouse. She seldom helped with the dishes; that was one job that Dorcas could easily do.

By the time old Dick, hitched to the express wagon, was on his way to the cornfield, the intermittent sunshine had warmed up the autumn day. Ruth lifted her face, letting the brisk wind ripple the dark waves of her hair. "Oh, I forgot my sunbonnet," she suddenly moaned to Kore, who was driving the horse to the cornfield.

"You're already brown as a mulatto," he returned. "Why worry about a sunbonnet?" He laughed good-naturedly.

21

The Upward Way

"I know I'm suntanned and brown—not white and ladylike like the other girls my age. But a sunbonnet *does* help to keep my unruly hair in order!" Ruth laughed with him, glad he was in a good mood. But maybe he was glad to have a break from school. He made it no secret that he preferred farm work to schoolwork, hard though it was.

Steadily Dick plodded out the lane behind the buildings, past the cow pasture and the creek on the left, and up a grade to the fields on the side of the hill. The wagon rumbled along behind. Ruth bumped with it, glad for the brief time to sit, even though it was not the softest seat she could wish for. She glanced back toward the barn and saw the black-and-white Holsteins crowding through the barn door, heading for the lane to the pasture along the creek bank. Mark had let them out of the barn as soon as his breakfast was over, and now he was closing the gate behind them.

Ruth watched the cows coming down the lane. They stepped solemnly along, heads nodding up and down. Big Horny was in the lead as usual. She was a kicker, and Ruth was glad that one of the men usually milked her. The cows plodded on, kicking up little puffs of dust behind their feet. At least today they would be inside a fence, Ruth was thinking, so no one needed to be the cowherd. But sometimes Papa wanted them to graze another field where there was no fence, and then someone needed to be on guard to keep them where they belonged. Ruth did not mind that job—the hours alone with nature and God, the time to meditate and dream . . .

"Whoa, boy," Kore called out, and Dick stopped readily.

Ruth reluctantly slid off the bench at the front of the

The Upward Way

wagon, picked up her corn knife, and started the long job of cutting off the corn. Kore shuffled through the rustling stalks and started on a row nearby. After the wagon was full of the long brown stalks, old Dick pulled it back to the barn. There Kore hitched Dick to another wagon, and he and Ruth filled it while Mark fed the first load of stalks into the chopper.

Cut and carry, cut and carry . . . By noon, Ruth was dirty and totally weary. How would she ever be able to keep cutting corn through a long afternoon?

"Whew!" Kore sighed as he stuck his corn knife back in its special place on the wagon. "I'm tired! And hungry enough to eat a whole cow, horns and all!"

"I'm tired too," Ruth agreed. "It will feel good to sit down awhile to eat." She found a place on the wagon to sit among the cornstalks and rode along in with the load, glad to relax a bit.

Papa had other plans for the afternoon. "We had better dig some of the potatoes this afternoon," he stated at the dinner table. "We could soon have a hard frost, and we don't want all the potatoes in the ground till the last minute."

Papa walked behind the potato plow as Dick pulled. Mama held Dick's reins while Kore and Ruth picked up the potatoes.

"Can't you keep that horse in the row better?" Papa called sharply up to Mama. He was wrestling with the plow, trying to keep it on the potato row.

Mama's tones came back just as sharp. "I'm doing the best I can. The brute can't understand English, you know."

The Upward Way

"Well, then, tell him in German!"

Kore glanced at Ruth and made a grim face, which hurt her heart. *If only Kore would not need to hear such interchanges. He struggles spiritually himself, and how can Papa and Mama expect to help him if their own lives fall short of what they profess?*

Sometime later, Mark and Ellen came to help. "I put Roy and Robert down for naps," Ellen stated with a smile. "Now I can help with this big job. Looks like you can use every available pair of hands to gather all these." She bent over to fill the basket she had pulled off a stack at the edge of the field.

Ruth glanced gratefully at her kind and capable sister-in-law, thankful again to have such a friend in the house up the hill. Mark had gotten a treasure when the lovely Ellen Snader consented to be his wife four years before, she thought. But then, Mark was pretty special himself. Ruth's thoughts ran on for a time as she filled her basket with creamy-white Irish Cobblers. Mama would not grow any other kind. They were big and nice after a summer of adequate rains.

Soon the potato-picking crew was singing as they worked. Even Mama joined in, and Papa as he could with his exertions at the plow. Both had rich voices and had always enjoyed singing, and they had passed their aptitude and appreciation for music on to their four children.

" 'I'm pressing on the upward way, / New heights I'm gaining every day . . .' " That was one of Ruth's favorite songs, and the sentiments fit her spiritual aspirations well. Steadily she picked on. Singing did not go so well with this kind of bending and stooping, she thought with an inward chuckle. Maybe she should crawl along the row as both Mark and Ellen were doing—that was easier on the back, but harder on the knees. She plopped to her knees, grateful for the change. And singing did go better.

How much she enjoyed working with Mark and Ellen! They made every task seem lighter by their constant cheerfulness. How often Ruth dreamed of a happy home as Mark and Ellen appeared to have! Why could not Papa and Mama work together like that? Should not professing Christians be able to get along peacefully and work out any differences in a rational manner? She thought again of Papa's quick temper and Mama's tendency to respond with either sarcasm or self-pity. Such carnal traits did not seem to contribute very much to happy marriage relationships. Although she was sure her parents loved each other and that they wanted to serve the Lord, it seemed to her that real love would not respond as they often did to each other. At least 1 Corinthians 13 would suggest that there was a better way. But could she ever hope to rise above their example, if the Lord would lead her to marriage? Then she thought of Mark, and her hopes were raised. He seemed to be growing beyond the example of his father and taking his role as leader and father in a godly and respectful manner.

"What a good crop of nice potatoes this year!" Ellen remarked as she filled still another basket. She stood to carry it to the wagon.

Kore grunted as he stood up. "We will soon have the second wagon full."

"Next we won't have room in the cave to store them all," Ruth stated, gathering her thoughts to the present.

The Upward Way

"Then what will we do with them?"

"Why, sell them at market," Papa emphatically reminded her from the other side of the wagon. "And we can store them in the hayloft until we sell them. We'll only store ones in the cave that we plan to keep for a while."

Of course, they always sold their extra produce. Ruth knew that well enough—she had just forgotten for the moment. Papa and Mama went to market at Amityville every Friday for much of the year with any fresh produce they had, as well as cheese, eggs, and—during the colder months—fresh meat. Probably right now, Dorcas was scalding cheese for market. Often they had as much as eighty pounds to sell at market on Fridays. Many customers also came to the farm for fresh produce and other things, as well as to patronize the little store that Mama had kept for years in the upstairs hallway. There she stocked shoes and boots and rubbers, dress material and various sewing notions, as well as all sorts of candy.

As the afternoon passed, Ruth picked up potatoes more and more mechanically. No one seemed to feel like singing anymore, and so Ruth retreated into her thoughts. She thought back to when she was in her mid-teens and Papa had started growing produce for market. Milk prices and other farm prices, Papa had often said, had dropped to half or less of what they were in the early 1920s. Then the stock market had crashed and the Great Depression had begun, sending many local farmers into a financial tailspin. But Papa, with his natural savvy for finances, had managed to stay afloat. Ruth thought they had even seemed to get ahead during the past years—at least by

The Upward Way

the buying and building that Papa had been doing. *But we sure have worked hard,* Ruth thought with a grimace as she continued to shuffle down her row, gathering potatoes to fill another basket.

By late afternoon, the largest patch of potatoes was all dug and picked up. "This patch is finished at least," Mark said, emptying his and Ellen's baskets for the last time. "That many less to dig another day."

Ruth surveyed the field, now just a bumpy plot with odds and ends of discarded potatoes lying here and there where they had been tossed. Yes, it was a good feeling to have this much finished!

Mama had walked down the hill to help some customers, and Papa was hitching Dick to the wagon again. "Must be at least one hundred bushels," he gloated, "with what we've already unloaded in the barn."

"Thank the Lord," Mark remarked.

"That's right," Papa agreed fervently. "Thank the Lord."

He started Dick down the hill to the barn. "By the way," he called back to Ruth, "I want you and Kore to get a load of turnips in as soon as I have the wagon unloaded. We'll need them for market on Friday."

"Don't I need to help with the milking?" Ruth called back.

"Not this time. Mark and I will do it."

Ruth forced her aching legs into a run as she hurried to the house. She had seen the mailman's Willys[3] rumble

---

[3] The Willys-Overland Company, an American manufacturer that produced cars and trucks during the early twentieth century, manufactured the Willys, the Overland, and the Willys-Knight.

27

The Upward Way

past an hour ago, and surely there would be some mail for her today. Maybe, if she hurried, she would have time to read it by the time Papa had the wagon unloaded.

Two envelopes addressed to "Miss Virginia Ruth Clemmer" waited on the kitchen table. "Oh, wonderful!" she exclaimed, resisting the urge to open them before she scrubbed her dirty hands.

Dorcas, who was standing at the cookstove, stirring cheese in a large kettle, did not bother to turn around or make any comment. She always had been, Ruth knew, slightly jealous of her two younger siblings who were married, while she, at twenty-eight, still was not. And now that Ruth, the youngest in the family, had a special friend, Dorcas struggled with even greater feelings of resentment.

But Mama responded. She had just come in from helping a customer with produce and was looking over the mail. "Looks like another one from Charles," she stated with a pleased grin in Ruth's direction. Ruth was hurriedly shedding her outdoor wraps. "At least it is a Harrisonburg, Virginia, postmark," Mama added.

"Oh, Mama," Ruth chided in fun, "you know it could be from any one of our many cousins too." But in her heart she did hope that Charles had remembered her birthday. They had had a couple of visits in the summer, before Charles went off to Eastern Mennonite School in Harrisonburg, Virginia. Since then, they had been writing. Charles Derstine was the boy of her dreams, gentlemanly and nice-looking as well as sincere and godly. God was good to her, she often felt, to give her such a fine young man for a special friend. She knew Mama was

The Upward Way

pleased about it too, just as she had been with Mark's and Sarah's choices.

There *was* a card and a letter from Charles, and also a card from her favorite cousin, Grace Good. Her tiredness vanished in an instant, and she felt ready to tackle bringing in *two* loads of turnips! *Thank You, dear Lord, that somebody thought of me today to help make my birthday special. You know I don't expect anything from Papa and Mama, because Papa wouldn't hear of such a thing—not even of having a decorated cake and bought ice cream, like many others have on their birthdays. He says there isn't time for such fuss when there's work to do.* Ruth's thoughts continued. *But Papa is breaking down when it comes to the grandchildren—or so it appears. And it is so much fun to do special things—sometimes at least!*

By suppertime, Ruth and Kore had a load of turnips on the trailer. After supper they cut off the tops with knives. "Good!" Ruth stated as she flung the last turnip into a crate. "I think that gives us"—she counted the bushels quickly—"forty bushels."

"Well, forty bushels barely make a dent in your papa's two acres!" Kore reminded her gloomily. "And tomorrow, and tomorrow, and tomorrow, there will be many more forty bushels to bring in, to top, to wash, and to store." He sighed, seeming to exhale all the accumulated sorrows of his thirteen years.

Ruth burst into laughter. "Well, at least tomorrow is another day," she returned gaily. "And by then, I hope I'll have a new store of energy!"

After going to the house, Ruth spent time singing before going to bed. The first song she turned to was

The Upward Way

"I'm pressing on the upward way." She sang all the verses and meditated on the message of the words. She always thought that singing like this was a wonderful way to draw her mind to spiritual things after a busy day. But as the others one by one went upstairs, she too plodded wearily up the garret steps to her little room. It was nearly ten-thirty now, and she was almost too tired to undress and go to bed. But she did, and she wrote a brief entry in her journal as well.

Chapter Two

October 6, 1933, Friday evening. Papa and Mama went to Amityville today as usual. They had lots of stuff to take—turnips, cup cheese, fresh chickens, potatoes . . . They brought home several bushels of apples—I don't know why, when we have plenty of our own!—and a whole bunch of bananas. How good bananas will taste again. I mowed the yard this afternoon. It was a beautiful fall day. In the evening, after the milking, I helped Mark change the pigs. I think I am developing a carbuncle on my right knee—at least a very painful boil. My knee has bothered me some most of the week, but feels the worst yet today. Rather uncomfortable when I walk!

Ruth stood at the picket fence and watched the Overland drive up the dirt road, *putt-putt-putting* along to the top of the hill. What a load of goods that truck was hauling to market today, along with Papa and Mama to sell them. The back end was almost dragging on the gravel. And even then, not nearly all of the turnips had fit into the limited space. Probably Papa would come back for the rest later. She watched until the truck dropped over

The Upward Way

the crest of the hill, on its way to Route 724 and Amityville. She turned away with a sigh of relief. Much of the morning so far, ever since a little before five o'clock, had been spent butchering chickens for market. Now at least the regular day's work could be gotten to without needing to think anymore about getting ready for market.

"Are you going to stand there daydreaming the rest of the morning?" Kore called impatiently from the machinery shed. "Your papa said we have to cut a load of corn for the cows."

"I'll be out soon—by the time you get Dick hitched to the express wagon." Ruth turned and hurried into the house. Dorcas sat as usual at her sewing, the treadle beating out a fast rhythm with her methodical foot movements. *If only she could be more useful around here!* Ruth sighed under her breath. As soon as the thought came to her, her conscience smote her, and she regretted it. Dorcas could not help it that she was born with one leg shorter than the other, which made walking more difficult for her. At least she could run the treadle machine, and expertly at that. In so doing, she was able to contribute something to the family's finances, or her own support—whatever the case (Ruth did not know how that was)—sewing bonnets and coverings and aprons for many people in the surrounding churches. She could also take care of the store customers and most of the produce customers that came when Mama was away.

Remembering to grab her sunbonnet off the hook by the washhouse door, Ruth sailed out the door, just in time to catch a ride on the wagon. "I'd have gone on without you if you hadn't come soon!" Kore said grumpily as

The Upward Way

Ruth hopped onto the wagon.

"Sorry!" Ruth said, hardly able to keep from laughing at the grouchy look on Kore's face.

"You sound sorry!" he returned, the grouchy look deepening. "Get-up!" he called out, slapping the reins on Dick's back.

Ruth looked on, comprehending in part at least how Kore was feeling, as the wagon rattled along. No doubt he was tired already too, just as she herself was. Fridays were always such long days, getting up an hour earlier in order to finish all the work before time to leave for market.

Working with a will, the corn cutters soon had the wagon piled high with corn. Ruth walked briskly back to the house, eager for the rest and relaxation of dinnertime. Hopefully, Dorcas had dinner ready. She was hungry after a morning of hard work!

Um-m . . . Ruth sniffed appreciatively as she washed up. The smell of something good frying came from the kitchen. Ruth burst in the back door from the washhouse. "Oh, good! Fried chicken!" she exclaimed, peering into the frying pan on the cookstove. "And mashed potatoes. You went to a lot of trouble for just the three of us, but it will sure taste good!" Her eye also caught the row of pies cooling on the side counter. *Yum! When did Dorcas make those? Or did Ellen bring them down?*

Dorcas returned a pleasant smile, her deep dimples showing and her dark eyes sparkling. *She's so pretty when she smiles,* Ruth thought to herself. *What a shame that she is crippled.* But even as the thought came to her, she remembered that God had allowed it, and who

33

The Upward Way

was she to question His purposes. If only Dorcas could always be so pleasant. So often she was saucy and sharp, probably due in part to the fact that she had never fully accepted her crippled condition.

As soon as dinner was over, Ruth hurried back outside. She pulled the mower out from where it was stored under the high side porch and began to push it purposefully around the yard. The cutting blades spun, and the grass flew. How thankful she was for the coolness of the day and the brightness of the blue sky above her. *Probably soon will be the last mowing for the season,* she thought as she continued to shove the mower up the inclines close to the house. Zinnias, cleomes, asters, snapdragons, verbenas, and an assortment of other flowers still bloomed profusely in all the flower beds, because there had been no killing frost yet. Each time she passed the grape arbor, the tangy sweetness of ripe grapes teased her senses. She would have been glad to pick a bunch and eat it while she mowed, but it took all her energy to keep the mower blades spinning.

Each time she rounded the corner of the house, she could see their white Muscovy ducks down at the creek. Soon they would bring the ducks up to one of the chicken houses for the winter. Then gradually most of them would be butchered to sell at market. They would keep just enough stock to hatch more young, come spring. Most of this summer's pigs were also running free in the meadow by the creek. They feasted on the acorns and hickory nuts that dropped in abundance from the oaks and shagbark hickories along the edge of the creek, and wallowed with pleasure in the mud along the banks.

The Upward Way

Before long it would be time to bring them up to pens in the barn, where they could finish fattening on corn for the winter's butchering.

She could see Kore and Mark, cutting corn in the field behind the barn. Probably they would soon bring a load in, and Mark would run it through the chopper while Kore started cutting another load. She probably should be helping, but Mama wanted the yard taken care of too—"regardless of what Papa said about the fieldwork," she had said.

Ruth put the mower away gladly after more than two hours of vigorous work. She broke off a bunch of grapes and sat on the side porch steps, enjoying the smell of newly mown grass as she savored the grapes one by one. Her gaze swept across the neat yard, bordered below her by a white picket fence. The picket fence was also the upper border for one of the pastures, which swept down across the meadow to the creek. Hand-split locust posts lined their road on either side, and to them the barbed-wire pasture fencing was attached. Ruth laughed as she noticed how crooked the posts had gotten over the past years. *It's time to work at those fences,* she decided. *It's a wonder Papa hasn't already—the eyesore they're getting to be!* Both Papa and Mama were very particular about such details.

In the field lane came Dick pulling a load of corn. Kore sat on the bench at the front of the wagon, loosely holding the reins and chewing a piece of grass. *Mark must not have gone back to the field after chopping the last load. He's probably working around the buildings somewhere*, Ruth thought. *Anyway, it will soon be time*

35

The Upward Way

to start milking.

"Aunt Rufie! Aunt Rufie!" A voice suddenly burst into her cogitations, and a small boy came bouncing along the sidewalk and flung himself at her.

"Well, Roy," she said as she grabbed him, "are you all done sleeping already?"

"Oh, yes. Me all done. Robbie still sleep though. He a baby. He sleep long time."

Ruth gazed lovingly at the small, towheaded, dark-eyed boy who looked happily up at her. How she loved her two small nephews, Mark and Ellen's boys. How thankful she was that they lived only a hop away, up the hill, so that she could see them almost every day. And they seemed to love her just as much as she loved them. She gave Roy a squeeze.

"I need some berries, Aunt Rufie," he stated, looking very interested in the grapes in her hand. "Can you get me some too?"

"These are grapes. Sure I can get you some. But you mustn't try to pick them yourself. Okay? Grammy and Aunt Dorcas want to make lots of good juice and jelly from these grapes after a while."

Roy nodded soberly as Ruth picked him a ripe bunch. Together they sat back down on the porch steps while Roy ate his coveted grapes. As he ate, he stared purposefully at the maple trees around the house. "Aunt Rufie, why the feathers coming off the trees?"

Ruth thought back to cleaning chickens that morning, realizing that the leaves fluttering down from the trees no doubt reminded him of the many feathers he had helped to pick. "Those aren't feathers, Roy; those are leaves.

The Upward Way

God made trees that way."

"Why God make them that way?"

"I don't know for sure. Maybe because . . ."

"Where is God, Aunt Rufie?"

"God is everywhere. He is here with us right now. He can see us, but we cannot see Him."

Roy looked around half in fright. "What God look like?" he asked next.

"I don't know for sure, Roy. I have never seen God. But the Bible says that God made us 'in his own image,' so He must look something like we do."

Roy stared up at the sky. "Aunt Rufie, how high is the sky? Why does the sun hurt my eyes? Why can't I feel the sky?" He reached out probing fingers.

Ruth had to laugh in spite of herself. How was she expected to answer all his little-boy questions? "You should ask your papa such things," she suggested.

"Oh, I ask him lots 'n lots. Mama too. And she says—"

"Ruth!" Kore's crackly adolescent voice echoed across the road from the area of the barn. "Hey, Ruth, do I get any help tonight?"

Ruth stood up quickly, standing Roy on the walk beside her. "Sounds like someone is calling me. It must be time to go milk the cows again."

Roy grabbed her hand and danced along beside her. "Me help too," he stated importantly. "Papa says I getting to be his little man."

Suddenly Roy stopped and gazed at Ruth. "Why you walk so funny?" he asked.

"My leg hurts," Ruth explained with a laugh. "I have a sore on my knee." The boil that she had first noticed on

37

The Upward Way

her knee a couple days before was now hurting tremendously. She must have aggravated it with all the walking while mowing. Oh, well, maybe it would open up and start getting better.

"Come. You come to Mama. She put a tape on it for you. Then your knee feel better." Roy pulled on her hand, trying to coax her up the hill to his house.

"Maybe after the milking is done, Roy," Ruth told him, knowing she had better hurry now and help Kore before he was helplessly put out with her. But maybe she ought to go to Ellen. She had great skill with doctoring nearly anything. And this boil was beginning to worry her, the way it continued to swell. It made her whole knee stiff and very sore. She thought about it even more as she bent to milk the first cow. Sitting on her low milking stool, she could have screamed for the pain.

It was not until late that evening that she was able to go up to Mark's house and ask Ellen to take a look at the boil. After the milking, she and Kore had helped Mark move some of the pigs up from the meadow to pens near the barn. She had been glad the pigs went willingly and that she did not need to run after them. Ellen took one look at her swollen knee and told her she must soak it in hot Epsom salts water.

"How can I soak my *knee?*" Ruth asked. "I can't *kneel* in a pan of water!"

Ellen considered for a bit. "You'll have to sit in a tub, I guess. But you really should do that, regardless of the bother."

After a good soaking, her knee did feel better. She was just crawling into bed when she heard Papa and Mama

The Upward Way

come home from the market. She would have liked to run downstairs and find out how the day went, but she guessed she had better stay in bed now that she was there.

The next morning at breakfast, the first thing Ruth noticed was a hand of bananas on the table. "Bananas!" she exclaimed happily. "They will taste good again. Did you get them at Amityville yesterday?"

"Yes," Mama said as she bustled about with last-minute details. "Papa got a whole bunch. They are hanging behind the washhouse door and should keep awhile there, in the cool."

Ruth eyed the hand hungrily, eager to eat her fill once again. "It's a wonder I didn't see them when I went to the barn this morning," she added. "Or at least *smell* them. I would have already had a sample!"

"It's good you didn't," Dorcas returned. "Or there wouldn't be many left for the rest of us." She primly poured the coffee.

"That's for sure," Kore joined in as he yanked out his chair and sat at the table. "She eats bananas like a pig!"

It was not that bad, and Ruth knew it; but maybe she did eat more than she should. *I had better try harder to control my appetite, so the family won't have such things to say about me!* she thought soberly.

As the family ate breakfast, Papa had a good report of market the day before. "We sold all the turnips for forty cents[4] a basket," he said, leaning back in his chair. "And the eggs sold for twenty cents a dozen. We sold all the cider too, and could have sold more chickens."

---

[4] These were actual prices received, according to records kept in Ruth's diary.

39

The Upward Way

"Thank the Lord," Mama reminded him.

"Yes, yes, thank the Lord," Papa echoed. "But it takes a little know-how on our part too," he added with a knowing nod.

Ruth noticed how Kore sat and looked at Papa with an unreadable expression. Her heart hurt for him. He was a precocious teenager, with wisdom and experience beyond his years. More than once, he had exploded to Ruth that Papa's religion didn't reach much further than Sunday. "He may be a deacon," he had said one time, "but he doesn't do much more than 'deak.' " Ruth had not known exactly what he meant by that, but she thought she caught the gist of his meaning by the way he said it. At times like that, she especially tried to speak respectfully of Papa, for Kore's sake.

Ruth was not inclined to be like Mama, who, when Papa lost his temper, would afterward shrug and say, "Oh, that's just Papa's weakness." Did not the Scriptures offer victory through the power of Christ to live above the weaknesses of the flesh? *But who am I to criticize,* Ruth thought ruefully, *when I face the same struggle so often myself.* Her own temptation came sooner than she thought.

After breakfast Papa took Kore home for the day. Ruth, with Roy's "help," brought in a wagonload of turnips, topping them and storing them in the cave. When she went to the house, Dorcas was sitting at the sewing machine.

"Why aren't you doing the cleaning?" Ruth asked, frustration boiling up inside of her. "I don't have time to do that too."

The Upward Way

"Well, I have these coverings to finish for Swartz's," Dorcas replied, turning back to her sewing.

Sudden anger flared up inside Ruth. *Sometimes I think I could slap her!* she thought desperately. With great effort, she resisted the urge to retort sharply.

Mama looked up from where she was crocheting a rug. "I will do the cleaning this week," she intervened, laying her rug aside and puffing to get out of her chair. "If you would, bring leaves up from the wood lot and mulch the raspberries and rhubarb, Ruth."

Ruth shrugged resignedly, her anger melting as suddenly as it had come. She would surely enjoy hauling leaves any day much better than cleaning. But the way the pain throbbed in her knee, all she felt like doing was sitting down with her leg propped up.

"And if you have time," Mama continued, "I'd really like the dropped apples picked up so that we can make cider and apple butter the beginning of next week."

"I do have a sore knee, Mama," Ruth protested. "I think it's a boil." She proceeded to show her mother the swollen knee.

"You poor child!" Mama exclaimed. "You've got a carbuncle! How long have you had this?"

"Oh, I don't know. Since early in the week sometime."

Mama nodded knowingly. "Did this swelling start after you ran the needle through your foot? What day was that?"

"It was Monday, when you and Papa were at the Souderton Home for a board meeting. After Ellen helped me get the needle out, I soaked my foot right away in Epsom

The Upward Way

salts to get out any infection."[5]

"Well, this is obviously infected," Mama said in a worried voice. "Oh, what shall we do?"

"Mama, it's just a boil. Don't worry about it," Ruth said, trying to comfort her. "After all, I've had lots of them in my life before!"

"I guess you have," Mama agreed. "But this seems more like a carbuncle."

"You should remember," Ruth said tersely, "because Papa usually assures me it's my meanness coming out!"

Mama looked sad, and Ruth right away regretted the hastiness of her assertion. "Oh, well," she said, trying to bridge the situation, "I'll go out and do what I can."

"Why don't you go lie down?" Mama suggested, belatedly, as Ruth hustled noisily out the door.

I guess I'll work till I fall down dead of something. She pitied herself with all her heart as she vigorously pulled great piles of leaves together down at the wood lot, forgetting to Whom she should be turning for help. *Nobody cares about me. All I do is work, work, work around here. Mama loves me,* she conceded finally as tears began to spill down her cheeks. *But Papa—seldom do I hear anything from him but criticism. Oh, I surely do understand how Job must have felt!*

After loading the truck full of leaves and tramping them down, she drove the truck up to the yard and backed close to the large raspberry patch. It did not take her long to throw the leaves on a pile. Then she repeated the process before beginning to spread the piles of leaves around the lush bushes.

---

[5] This was before the days of antibiotics and tetanus shots.

The Upward Way

Soon Roy joined her in the garden, happily jumping in and flattening her piles. "Aunt Rufie, this is so much fun!" he said delightedly. Her dark mood passed for the time as she enjoyed the antics of her little nephew.

"If you want to help me, Roy," she suggested, "you may carry buckets of leaves and put them around those plants over there." She pointed to the section of rhubarb stalks that stood at the edge of the garden.

Roy very importantly stuffed his bucket full of leaves and carried it to the rhubarb, dumping them out there. By the time Ruth had carefully mulched all the raspberries, it was time for dinner. After dinner, she took the wheelbarrow to the apple orchard. There she filled the wheelbarrow time after time with the best of the dropped apples, hauling them to the garage and putting them into boxes and crates, ready for processing on Monday. Again her thoughts turned morbidly to her situation at home, and the tears came again. *All Papa thinks about is work—"do this," "do that," "go here," "go there," "hurry up," "no time to waste . . ."* But before she had had much time to wallow in her self-pity, Ellen came to help her.

"The boys are taking their naps," she explained, "so I thought I could help you with this job. You look like you aren't feeling the best. Is your boil bothering you?"

"Quite a bit. Mama says it's a carbuncle."

"Well, you look sort of glum. Is it worse?"

Ruth just shrugged, wondering if Ellen had seen her crying.

Apparently she had. "You are bothered about something, Ruth," she probed after a while. "Why don't you tell your sister about it?"

The Upward Way

Trust Ellen to get everything out of me! Ruth thought with more humor than grimness. "I guess I was pitying myself," she admitted.

Ellen looked up questioningly.

"I mean, all I do around here is work, work, work. And nobody appreciates it. Nobody cares about me."

Ellen held up a hand. "Stop right there," she said. "Are you really being truthful? Sure, you do a lot of work. But are you working harder than anybody else? And why do you say nobody appreciates or cares about you? You know better than that!" Ellen's tone was gentle, as she always was. But her frankness cut Ruth. She would not need to be quite so hard on her!

When Ruth did not say anything for a bit, Ellen went on, "Ruth, I think most of the problem is that you think too much about yourself." When Ruth turned a dumbfounded gaze on her, she explained, "I don't mean to make you feel worse, but you need to forget yourself and think of how others may feel. Get yourself absorbed in the needs and feelings of others. The Lord will help you if you ask Him."

Ruth could not help it; the tears came again. Such a sermon from her beloved sister-in-law! And especially at a time when she needed encouragement rather than advice! But Ellen did not back down at the sight of Ruth's tears. "Think about it, and pray about it, Ruth," she encouraged her.

"Maybe I'm just missing Sarah," Ruth ventured after a while, when she could speak again. She picked up apples under the last tree with great diligence.

"I know you miss your sister," Ellen agreed. "But just think about how happy she is with her new husband.

The Upward Way

Rather than thinking about yourself and your loss, rejoice in her joy!"

For a time, Ruth worked in silence as she thought of Sarah, now Mrs. Norman Breckbill. Certainly she was happy for them. And she was happy for a fine, new brother-in-law. But how much she missed Sarah's help with all the outdoor work. She missed Sarah's closeness too. They had been close in a way that she and Dorcas had never been. Sarah, with her wavy blond hair and brilliant blue eyes, looked a lot like Papa; but unlike him, she had a sweet and cheerful disposition. Ruth felt sure she would never have a friend as close or who understood her as well as her own dear sister Sarah.

Ruth thought back to September 12, the day of Norman and Sarah's wedding. What a bittersweet day that had been for her. It had been a very pleasant day, and even Charles had been there. But "coming events cast their shadows before," as the saying went, and she had wept her heart out that night in her lonely garret bedroom. By the time the happy couple had left for Virginia with a chauffeur two days later, she was beginning to accept the changes that their marriage had brought. But life would never be the same without Sarah. Never.

"There! The pigs can have the rest of these apples," Ellen concluded, looking over what still lay on the ground. "I think we've gotten all the good ones."

"Thanks for your help," Ruth said as Ellen turned to go back to her house.

"You're welcome. Glad to help!"

After emptying her wheelbarrow one more time, Ruth limped to the house. Maybe she would have some time

The Upward Way

to rest before needing to help with the milking. But that was not to be.

Papa looked up from reading the *Mennonite Quarterly Review*[6] as she walked into the kitchen. "It's time to start milking if you want to go along to Norristown this evening." He picked up his magazine again, and Ruth turned to Mama for explanation.

"Dorcas is planning to go, and you may too, if you wish," Mama offered further. "Aunt Emma called, and she and Uncle Jonas offered to take you girls along. Kore needs a way back here too this evening."

And so, very soon, Ruth followed Papa to the barn. Her leg still ached dreadfully, but she knew better than to complain to him.

Later, Ruth was almost able to forget the pain in her knee as she spent a happy half-hour driving to church with Uncle Jonas's. She and her cousin Grace chatted almost nonstop, glad for this unplanned opportunity to visit. But at church she faced a crushing disappointment. There was Kore with a tie on again. He never wore one if he thought Papa would catch him, but it seemed any other time he thought it was all right.

"Now don't you tattle on me," he said behind his hand as he crawled into the car after church. "I'll take it off before I get back to your place." And he did, hiding it in the cave, where he had often hidden his cigarettes and other contraband.

"I don't need to tell on you," Ruth responded. "The most important One already knows what you're doing."

---

6 *The Mennonite Quarterly Review* was then published in Goshen, Indiana. Harold S. Bender was the editor at that time.

The Upward Way

Kore shrugged with unconcern. He *knew* better than doing many of the things he was doing, Ruth was sure, but he could not seem to *do* better. *Maybe it is because he doesn't really want to,* Ruth concluded realistically. She knew too that his school chums were no help to him, nor were some of the boys at his home church.

That night as she lay on her bed, waiting for the pain in her knee to subside enough for her to sleep, many thoughts filled her mind. She thought of Kore and his many spiritual needs; if only he would give his heart to the Lord. She thought of Papa, wondering how he could be so holy at church and yet often so unkind in his dealings with the family. If only Papa would tell her just once that he loved her and that he was happy she was his daughter. Or if he would have the grace to apologize when he lost his temper. Or if he would just *act* as though he appreciated her help—he would not even need to thank her—how much easier it would be to keep going at times.

Then like a stab in the heart came the remembrance of Ellen's rebuke that afternoon. Who was she to criticize others when she had such a definite need, at least in Ellen's eyes, in her own life?

Her thoughts then turned to the things Ellen had said, and she rolled them around searchingly in her mind. Was it really so, that she thought too much about herself? *Dear heavenly Father,* she prayed sincerely, *You know I want to live for You. Please show me my needs and help me to live in daily victory.*

She lighted her oil lamp by the dim light of the new moon and then opened her Bible. It fell open to

47

The Upward Way

Philippians, and she began to read hungrily. *Everything for the apostle Paul was joy and rejoicing,* she thought. *What was his secret? Was it that he had learned to be content in whatever situation he found himself? Was it that he had learned not to worry about anything but to give it to the Lord in prayer? Was it that he purposed to think only on true, honest, just, pure, lovely, and virtuous things? Was it that he had the faith to believe that God actually would supply* all *his needs?*

For some time, Ruth read and meditated, the Word bringing comfort to her troubled heart. *Lord, please help me to live in victory over a self-pitying spirit. Help me to see it as a sin that You hate, even as much as You hate any other sin. And, Father, help me to truly love Papa and to be a good daughter to him. He is a good papa in many ways—he provides well for us and he gives us good teaching in many areas, . . .*

Finally the throbbing in her knee eased, and the pain in her heart was also released to her heavenly Father. She extinguished her lamp and settled herself for a good night of rest. And she thanked God that tomorrow was a day of rest.

Chapter Three

October 8, 1933 Sunday Went to Grove Hill this morning. Could scarcely bend my knee. Came home and nursed my sore knee. Planned to sleep all afternoon, but gladly gave that up when Sarah and Norman showed up! Norman read to us for a while from the Gospel Herald. *Went to Weaverland to hear Dr. Eshleman in the evening. Cletus P. had Ruth S. there. It showered some in the afternoon.*

Ruth rolled over happily after turning off her alarm clock. *Squeak, squeak,* went her bedspring, but she barely noticed it. She was thinking instead of the wonderful gift of Sunday. *How luxurious not to have to hurry out of bed for once,* she thought with a smile into the darkness. *God knew how much we needed Sundays. How thankful I am for them!* Papa and Mark usually did the milking on Sunday mornings without her help, which was so nice. Rather than the usual four-thirty, she had set her alarm for a little after six o'clock. *For once I feel rested,* she thought as she sat up in the darkness and felt for her lamp. Lighting it, she settled back

49

The Upward Way

on her bed with her Bible.

At church several hours later, Ruth looked around eagerly as she found her place with the youth girls. A few of her Clemmer relatives attended Grove Hill, and then there were the Macks, the Swartzes, the Goods, the Planks, the Sheelers, the Kolbs, and all the rest. She noticed their bishop, Brother Warren Bean, was also at church this morning. He sat on the ministers' bench along with Papa and their ministers, Brother Henry Bechtel and Uncle Jacob Clemmer. In the amen corner on the men's side of the church sat many of the older men. Most of their wives sat in the corresponding amen corner on the women's side.

Then Ruth's attention was drawn to the stranger sitting with the youth boys across the aisle from her. *Hm-m, I wonder if that is Uncle Claude's new hired man. What did they say his name was? David Peachey, I think, from somewhere in North Carolina. He looks shy and kind of shabby . . .* Her thoughts rambled on until the service began a few minutes later. *That hired man—there is something attractive about him, even though his clothes look like he is poor. I wonder why he came all the way to Pennsylvania to work.* She had heard Mama and Papa talk about him—that his father drank and his godly mother had a hard time providing for all the children. They had said that David himself seemed to be a very sincere and spiritual young man, a little younger than Dorcas.

Ruth smiled inside, remembering the response Dorcas had given when Mama had made a remark to her about David Peachey being only four years younger than she. Mama did not think that was very much of an age

The Upward Way

difference, as Papa was six years younger than she was. Dorcas had responded emphatically that she would not have any tramp that nobody knew anything about, and from the boondocks at that!

Suddenly, Ruth's favorite cousin, Grace Good, nudged her, and she came quickly back to the present. Grace was pulling a *Church Hymnal* out of the rack as her father walked to the front. Uncle Jonas announced the number and took the pitch from the tuning fork he struck on the side of his hymnal.

I'm glad the church voted to get the new Church Hymnal*s*, Ruth thought, finding the page in her book. She remembered well when they had replaced the old *Church and Sunday School Hymnal*s with these recently published hymnals. *I like the majestic worship hymns in these new songbooks.*

Ruth was glad too that for Sunday school the song leader led from the front. She always thought the singing went so much better for Sunday school than it did for church, when the leader stayed at his seat to lead. *I guess I should just be glad we have had Sunday school here at Grove Hill for as long as I can remember,* she thought happily. Some of the other churches in their conference had only recently accepted having Sunday school in the actual church building. She remembered, as a little girl, visiting a few of the churches in their conference where Sunday school was held in an adjoining building. *And we have church every Sunday, not every other, like some of the other churches. And we have Communion twice a year, rather than just once a year. And nobody makes a fuss at Grove Hill about having the services in English*

51

The Upward Way

rather than in German. They've been that way, Papa says, for more than thirty years, while some others have only recently changed to English.

Our congregation is more progressive in some ways, and yet in other ways, we're one of the most conservative. . . . Ruth continued to muse over the past as she joined in with the lusty singing. But soon she recalled herself to the present, caught up in the beauty of the four-part singing. She was thankful for the strong support for four-part singing in their conference and for the many singing schools to help everyone learn the simple rudiments of music. Because she so thoroughly enjoyed the singing, she hoped that it was not sinful to appreciate the fine, strong blending of voices in harmony. Had not God given the voice, and the wonderful ability to produce the harmonious tones of worship in song?

The youth girls' class was at the back of the auditorium, taught by Aunt Mary Guntz. Later, during Brother Bean's sermon, she noticed some of the girls whispering behind her, which was a fairly usual occurrence during most services. Ruth felt sorry for them, thinking about all the good spiritual truths they were missing by their inattentiveness. Not that she had never been guilty of the same! She had been, especially in her earlier teen years. *Maybe if we girls would sit further up front, we wouldn't have such temptations to visit during the services,* she thought, remembering that at some of the churches in their conference the youth did sit in the front. But when their Sunday school class was held in the back of the auditorium, it made it easy for the girls to remain sitting there.

The Upward Way

At the conclusion of the service, Brother Bean made several announcements. One was that Brother Paul Clemmer (that was Papa) had asked for deacon help. Ruth knew he had more deacon work than he could keep after comfortably—so many people to look after, meetings to go to, finances to handle. Brother Bean further stated that they were looking at November 26 as the possible date for an ordination. Ruth thought soberly about the prospect, wondering who would be called to fill the place in their congregation of one hundred fifty people. She glanced across the church at the assembly of men gathered there, marveling at how God would work to choose one of them.

Mama had put a plump duck to roast and her wonderful oyster filling into the cookstove oven for dinner. "Aren't you having company for dinner with such fixings?" Dorcas asked as she set the table for the usual five. She always enjoyed company. And it was not often that they did not have company for Sunday dinners.

"I didn't plan for any today," Mama answered from where she was dexterously carving the duck. "We've had a busy week, and a busy one to come," she added, forming her words around a mouthful of fatty tail meat that she had just popped into her mouth. "Today will be a good day to rest up."

"It was amazing that there were no visitors today," Dorcas said as she poured water. "Well, except for Brother Bean and his wife. And they were going to Uncle Jacob's, Aunt Climena said."

Mama nodded. "I had thought about unexpected visitors. And we would have invited such, if there had been

53

The Upward Way

any. But I'm glad for a day to rest."

Dorcas laughed. "It will be *very* unusual if this day passes and nobody comes! How often people drop by just before suppertime and expect us to give them supper!"

"Oh, well, we do that too," Mama returned, her mouth busy once more with a piece of duck meat. "And we don't mind doing it for others."

Ruth was just climbing her stairway to the garret after the dishes were done when she heard a car coming slowly up the road from the bridge. *Toot, toot, toot,* went a horn. Bounding back down with more energy than she had felt going up, she exclaimed, "Somebody's coming, and it sounds like Norman's Willys!"

She was out the door in a flash, sore knee notwithstanding, and at the end of the walk almost before the engine quit. Opening Sarah's door with great fanfare, she greeted her dear sister as though she had not seen her for three years instead of three weeks. "Oh, Sarah, it's so good to see you! How is everything? How long can you stay? For supper?"

Mama and Papa and Dorcas came out too. But soon the nippy fall air drove everyone back into the house, where they all settled comfortably in the family sitting room. Soon Kore also joined them, coming down the stairs and seating himself unceremoniously on the arm of Ruth's chair.

She stared up at him with embarrassment. Usually he treated her with near disdain. Why such familiar behavior today? "Find your own chair, sir," she stated when she had collected her thoughts sufficiently. She nudged him firmly with her elbow.

The Upward Way

"Aren't you going to be my girl today?" Kore returned with artificial sweetness.

Papa looked across the room and noticed the commotion. "Behave yourself, Kore," he said, his blue eyes flashing ominously.

Kore heaved himself up and slouched into a nearby stuffed chair, glowering toward where Papa sat. Ruth watched with a troubled heart. She did care for Kore, as a sister would for a wayward younger brother. And somehow she sensed that Papa was not good for Kore.

Mama also gave them a troubled look; but the rest were visiting, and she soon joined them. Ruth was just happy to sit and gaze at her dear sister, trying to absorb enough of her presence to carry her through the days to come till she would see her again, whenever that would be. Hopefully it would not be too long, since they had found a house to rent only ten miles away. *Huh,* Ruth thought, *if we would do like the "Old Orders" in Lancaster County, we'd have Sarah living at home with us until spring. That would be better yet!*

After a while there was a lull in the conversation as everyone sat in companionable enjoyment. Outside, a fall rain was dropping steadily, and little courses eddied lazily down the windowpanes. "I brought along the last copy of the *Gospel Herald*. I thought you all might enjoy it," Norman suddenly began. "Shall I read aloud awhile for you all?" Ruth had noticed he carried a magazine in with him, but—bookworm that he was—she had thought little of it.

No one voiced any objections, so Norman reached for his paper. "There were some especially good articles this

The Upward Way

week, I thought. Daniel Kauffman is an inspiring editor and writer. He has an article in that a John Martin wrote about the Kansas Dust Bowl, which I thought was very interesting. I thought you might enjoy it too."

Norman paged a bit and then began to read. " 'Christians have been so busy producing abundant crops that God sent dry years to give time for spiritual matters.' " He continued to read, finishing the article. "Then Daniel Kauffman comments, 'Covetousness lies at the bottom of this world's poverty.' " [7]

Papa looked up, not totally pleased, Ruth thought. But he did not express at once what he might be thinking.

"I guess Daniel Kauffman was suggesting," Norman went on, "that Christians should be more diligent in giving rather than in spending money 'for that which is not bread.' "

With that clarification, Papa's face seemed to brighten, and he sat up eagerly. "I read in the Souderton paper a report about that sale at Franconia Square that I was to the other week," he began. "Whoever wrote the article sure made some startling observations!" He heaved himself out of his chair. "Let me find that paper."

He rooted for a little through the magazine holder. "Here it is," he said, sitting down again and rustling the paper open. "The writer talks about how the women's clothes and bonnets, although subdued in color, were as expensive as any from a good tailor or hat maker. 'Over their plain dresses', he writes, 'they draped expensive black shawls'. He also talks about the men

---

[7] Paul Toews, *Mennonites in American Society, 1930–1970* (Scottdale, PA: Herald Press, 1996).

The Upward Way

in their 'lapel-less' coats, paying fancy prices for Mary Bechtel's[8] gilt-edged securities—and then leaving in expensive cars."[9] Papa shook his head. "I tell you," he stated indignantly, laying the paper back down, "I didn't buy a thing that day. Things went ridiculously high! But that isn't all. We've got to address some of these issues as a ministry. Our sisters with their expensive shawls instead of a traditional coat! And some of the brethren are far too reckless with their money."

Ruth noticed Kore make a hopeless gesture and roll up his eyes. Again, hurt rose in her heart. Kore would readily accept Papa's conservative views, she felt quite sure, if Papa also lived a life of cheerfulness and daily contentment to complement his Biblical convictions.

Not knowing how to answer Papa, Norman simply nodded in agreement. Ruth wondered if Norman and Kore were thinking about the same thing she was, that people sometimes said of Paul Clemmer that he was so tight with his money that he squeaked!

Norman started reading another article. After some time of listening, Ruth found herself drifting off to sleep. She jerked herself awake; the article about ways to help those affected by the drought *was* interesting. And Norman had a way of reading that made it even more so. But she was tired, and the room was so warm, made cozy by the coal-oil stove next to the closed-off fireplace. Soon she gave up and propped her feet on the hassock sitting near her chair, and then laid her head against the back

---

[8] The estate sale was for this person.
[9] Paul Toews, *Mennonites in American Society*, 1930–1970, p. 43

The Upward Way

of her chair. Outside, the rain continued to drip steadily down from a lowering sky.

When she awoke, the room was empty and the women were talking and banging around in the kitchen. Apparently Papa and Kore and Norman had gone to the barn. She glanced at the chime clock on the fireplace mantel. Could she possibly have been sleeping for two hours! It must be the infection in her body that was making her more tired than usual. She hurried to the kitchen, sorry to have missed any of the afternoon, but feeling more rested after such a good nap.

Mama was turning an omelet, Sarah was putting tea leaves in a kettle of boiling water to steep, and Dorcas was cutting cinnamon buns. Mama looked up at Ruth. "Have a good nap?" she asked with a smile. "We need the pudding from the cave yet. Can you run down for it?"

Ruth glanced quickly out the window. Yes, it had stopped raining, though no doubt it would be muddy running down the bank to the cave. But, oh well . . .

"Sure," she said, but then Sarah started speaking, and Ruth waited to hear.

"We thought we'd go to Weaverland this evening," Sarah was saying. "A Dr. Eshleman is to be preaching there tonight."[10]

"Oh, he is a missionary to India," Dorcas said.

Sarah nodded. "The Eshleman's are home on furlough right now. His topic this evening is to be 'The Christian Standard of Social Purity.' At least that's what was announced this morning at Towamencin."

---

[10] In Mama's diary, she had recorded the name as 'Dr. Eshe'. It has not been established with certainty that the name was Eshleman.

The Upward Way

"Oh, Mama, could we go too?" Ruth asked, thinking how interesting the topic sounded.

"Don't you have a letter to write today?" Sarah asked.

Ruth nodded with a satisfied feeling. "I should have. But maybe I'll have time to write this week." She turned again to her mother. "Could Dorcas and I go too, Mama?"

Mama looked uncertain. "We'll have to ask Papa. But are you sure you're up to it, Ruth, with that carbuncle on your knee?"

"It feels some better today, since I'm not using my knee. I had my leg propped up for a couple hours, and sitting at church shouldn't hurt it."

"And you had such a good nap," Sarah added teasingly.

"Well, we'll ask Papa when he comes in," Mama said as she carefully lifted the omelet onto a platter.

Ruth went quickly for the pudding, half sliding down the bank to the cave. She climbed back up the bank more carefully, not wanting to spill the covered dish she was carefully hanging on to. Soon the men came from the barn, and they all sat down for supper.

Papa gave his permission for the girls to go along with Norman's, and they happily headed out with them when they left a short time after supper.

Ruth's night of rest seemed extra short, but she began her day purposefully the next morning. The challenge of the message the evening before was still with her, and she was determined by the help of God to keep her life clean and pure before Him. She continued to muse on the message as she pumped buckets of water to heat in the caldron over the washhouse fireplace for the Monday washing.

The Upward Way

Then she got the washer engine going. For a while the blessings of the day before almost made her forget the pain in her knee. When the water was hot enough, she dipped it out of the caldron into the wringer washer. A belt from the nearby gasoline engine ran the washer. How thankful she was for this relatively new invention, replacing the washer with a hand crank that turned the agitator, which Mama had used for many years. But even with such a convenience and the added convenience of the long clothesline on a pulley from the washhouse to a tall pole in the far corner of the yard, her knee soon began to hurt dreadfully. She soon realized she would have to beg off from the washing to go sit down.

When Mama came to the washhouse with an armload of bedding some time later, she pitied Ruth limping around and sent her off to prop up her leg. "I know Papa won't like your sitting around, but you've got to take care of that knee!" Mama exclaimed.

Using the time to an advantage, Ruth wrote a letter to Charles. The outside door in the kitchen opened and Ruth tensed, wondering if it might be Papa. But, no, Papa was at a sale today, she remembered. She brightened when it was Ellen who appeared.

"Look at this lazy lady," Ruth quipped.

"I wouldn't say lazy," Ellen returned. "It's about time you took care of yourself. Let me take a look at that carbuncle."

Soon Ellen had wrapped a hot Epsom salts poultice around Ruth's knee. "There, that ought to draw the poison out," she said optimistically. "And now, you just rest."

"Thanks, sister dear," Ruth said gratefully. "That does

The Upward Way

feel so comforting!" Ruth reached for her box of stationery. "Would you mind dropping a letter off in the mailbox for me?" she asked as she stuffed her letter hurriedly into the addressed envelope.

"I'll be glad to," Ellen assured her. "Especially if you let me read it first," she added with a grin.

"It's a deal—if you let me read all the pink-ribbon-wrapped letters stowed away up at your house," Ruth returned quickly. "By the way, where are the boys?"

"Roy is with Mark in the chicken houses, and Robert is taking a nap. I thought I could run down quickly while he is sleeping. Actually, I came to borrow some baking powder, if Mama has some to spare," she added as she hurried to look in the cupboard. "Mark ordered apple dumplings for dinner, and I was out of both baking powder and saleratus."[11]

By evening, Ruth felt well enough to help with the evening milking. Papa was back from the sale too. He had come home just before milking, pulling a fodder cutter behind the Overland.

Almost as soon as Ruth walked into the barn, Papa asked, "Well, what did you get done today?"

"Not too much," Ruth admitted hesitantly.

"What do you mean? Were you loafing while I was away?"

"I didn't mean to be," Ruth said slowly. "But I do have a bad carbuncle on my knee."

"A carbuncle? What's that? Nothing worth brutzing over!"

---

[11] A baking leavening consisting of potassium or sodium bicarbonate, much like the baking soda that we presently use.

61

The Upward Way

Ruth chose to be silent rather than to talk back to Papa. Soon she was sitting to milk her regular cows, thankful that the pain and stiffness in her knee had lessened somewhat through the day.

By the next morning, her carbuncle had opened in two places; and by the next day, two more heads had opened, discharging great quantities of puss at each head. Ellen insisted that Ruth wash it carefully several times a day with Mama's good, strong lye soap. Then she would tie a fresh cheesecloth bag of mashed garlic on it to continue to draw out the drainage. "We can't have this infection getting into your blood," she explained. "Then you would be in real trouble."

On Thursday Sarah came home for a couple of days. "I told Norman I get awfully lonesome around our place, one person bumping around in that big house all day alone! And I don't have enough to do, just keeping house for two, and no outside work," Sarah explained, plopping her satchel and another bag on the floor. "Norman said he doesn't care if I want to come home and help out a couple of days, if that's what I want to do. So here I am, bag and baggage!" She laughed her jolly laugh as she crossed the kitchen to look at Mama's blooming African violets.

"I wish I could get mine to bloom like yours do," she said wistfully. "Your flowers are always so pretty."

"I think a lot of the secret is to have them in the right light," Mama returned. "They have always done best for me at that east window."

"Our house doesn't have the deep windowsills like you have here. I guess I could set a table at a window. Oh, well, I don't have so many flowers yet." She picked

The Upward Way

up her bags. "Where shall I take these?"

"To your old room, of course," Ruth injected happily.

"If I can still make it up those stairs," Sarah returned, starting for them. "I'm an old married lady now, you know!"

Ruth was thankful to feel well enough to be out again. She spent the morning in the field, husking corn with Ellen and Sarah. Ellen had left the boys in Grammy's and Dorcas's care this time.

"This is like old times!" Ruth exclaimed happily as they rustled down the rows together. Nearby, patient Dick waited with the wagon, pulling it along to stay even with the girls' flying ears of yellow corn.

"A hen party!" Sarah suggested with her hearty chuckle.

"We sound like hens when we cackle," Ellen added, joining her merry laugh with the others.

Ruth reveled in the precious hours of working together, singing and visiting. She was glad that Norman and Sarah were back from their trip south and renting a house close by—close enough, at least, that they could come home as often as she hoped. In the afternoon, Ruth needed to pull and top turnips for market the next day. Sarah helped Mama and Dorcas in the house. They were canning pears and making catsup.

On Friday, Papa and Mama went to market as usual. After the Overland was out of sight on the hill, Ruth helped Sarah pick up walnuts and glean the potato patch for potatoes to use at their new home. Sarah left when Ruth went to the barn in the evening, wanting to be home in time to get supper for her husband. How dismal

The Upward Way

everything seemed suddenly, Ruth thought. After supper, when no one suggested anything that had to be done, Ruth slipped out the back door and took a long walk along the creek up to the woods. Near where the creek had its beginnings in a small, gurgling spring, there was a large rock and a fallen tree that she called her own special haven.

Settling herself comfortably on the rock and leaning her back against the tree trunk, she turned her thoughts to God. Off to the west, the sun was disappearing below the tree line as streaks of orange and pink and red shot up from the horizon. Darkness would soon follow. But for now, all was quiet and peaceful and calm, except for the warbling of a lone bluebird somewhere nearby. The brook murmured softly as it fell over the rocks in its path. In the distance a blue jay screamed, and farther away, probably in Spring City, she heard the minor chord of the late train's whistle.

But those noises did not intrude on her peace. How she loved these stolen hours for meditation and prayer, all alone with God. *Lord, look upon your handmaid. See the earnest longings of my heart to love You truly. Lead in my life, and make of me what You want me to be. Give me grace to be loving and kind to those around me, even when they may be spiteful to me. Help me to grow into Your own holy likeness, and use me, Lord, in Your service.*

Darkness was deepening as Ruth followed the meandering creek back through the pasture and climbed over the fence to the yard. Her spirit was refreshed and strengthened in the Lord to face the days ahead.

Chapter Four

October 19, 1933, Thursday. Ellen and I were butchering nearly all day. Brought in a load of turnips late afternoon. Received a letter from Marie Burkholder. Meetings started at Limerick this evening, with Aaron Mast as speaker. Very discouraged with Kore today. He helped me hardly at all with the evening work. Very beautiful day. Millers here this evening.

But back to Saturday . . .

Early on Saturday morning, October 14, Papa and Mama left for a trip to Maryland. This trip had come up quite suddenly, and Henry Bechtel's planned to go along. Mama had not told Ruth much about the trip, other than that there was some church work to attend to.

Now Ruth stood at the barn door and watched them head off, several cats curling and purring about her legs. In the front seat of Papa's Buick sat Papa and Henry Bechtel. Henry's wife and Mama sat on the back seat. Ruth waved as the car started out the lane; and dimly in the moonlight, she could see Mama waving her

The Upward Way

handkerchief out her open window. Finally the Buick disappeared over the crest of the hill, on its way to 724 and other routes south.

Now we're on our own for several days, Ruth thought, but not unhappily. She enjoyed seeing how much she could accomplish, and she enjoyed such interludes with her only "boss" her brother Mark. The gentle *moo* of one of the cows recalled Ruth to the present, and she reached down to retrieve her milk bucket. "Get out of my milk bucket, you nosy cats!" she scolded, shooing Nellie and several of her progeny away from the bucket. "Now I need to go wash this bucket before I can get back to work."

She hurried to the milk house. Mark was coming from that direction, an empty milk bucket in each hand. "So Papa has church work to take care of in Maryland now," he stated, rather than asked.

Ruth nodded. Then, realizing Mark could not see such an answer in the semidarkness, she said, "That's what Mama said. But she didn't tell me what sort of church work."

"I know they're planning to visit Bishop Aaron Mast and bring him back for meetings in our district, but I don't know what else they have in mind," Mark returned as he squatted to milk his first cow. Ruth hurried into the milk house.

Milking finished and breakfast over, Ruth got busy with the duties of the day. Dorcas kindly offered to do the weekly cleaning, which left Ruth free to work in the barn, husking corn. All morning, she and Kore separated the long brown stalks from the huge piles, broke off the

The Upward Way

ears and husked them, throwing the stalks one way and the yellow ears onto another pile. When they had a great pile of ears husked, Ruth left to mow the yard, sweep down the barn—and finally to do evening chores again. How different the day seemed without Papa and Mama there. But it was comforting to know that Mark and Ellen were just up the hill, near enough to help if she and Dorcas had any trouble. Kore was staying with Mark's too, which left her and Dorcas a lonely twosome in their big house at mealtimes.

Sunday dawned as bright and blue and beautiful as any fall day could ever be. Ruth pined to walk the four miles to church, along the country roads through the tranquil woods with their coloring leaves and calling birds. But knowing Dorcas would not be able to walk that distance, she gave up her wish and drove the Overland instead.

She slid into her usual spot beside her cousin Grace. Grace immediately leaned over and whispered, "Who are those visitors ahead of us?"

Ruth looked and then whispered back, "Is the family the Vernon Swartz family, from Ohio? And I met the strange girl in the vestibule. She is a Good, and she said her brother and two cousins are also traveling with them."

Grace watched the visiting girls as suddenly they laughingly stood up and exchanged seats. Then she whispered behind her hand, "Humph! They look kind of dressy, don't they! We'll soon have young girls here making their dresses with those real long waists! I wouldn't mind doing it myself, except I know Papa and Mama wouldn't let me."

The Upward Way

Ruth did not respond; she just looked on soberly. Personally she thought those very long-waisted dresses looked quite foolish, but she knew they were the fashion in some Mennonite circles.

Ellen, with her love for hospitality, invited all the visitors for lunch, along with Dorcas and Ruth. The afternoon was jolly, filled with lots of fun and laughter, and Ruth enjoyed it while it lasted. But when they left and she went to do the milking, a feeling of sadness overwhelmed her. "It just doesn't seem right to be so silly," she said aloud to the pigeons in the rafters overhead as she forked corn fodder down the funnel for the cows' bedding. "Spending an afternoon like that leaves me feeling so empty."

Dorcas went to Limerick with Mark's that evening, but Ruth chose to stay home and go to bed early. It was lovely, she thought, to have a quiet evening at home alone, time to pour out her sorrow for the misused day to her heavenly Father and then to spend time reading and singing before she finally climbed the garret steps to her own bed.

When Ruth awoke early Monday morning, the wind was blowing briskly in her east window. *Doesn't appear like a very good wash day,* she thought as she stood at the window and felt the dampness of the air.

Later, as Ruth and Dorcas ate their lonely breakfast of mush and hamburger gravy, Dorcas suggested, "If you would get the wash water for me and start the washer engine, I think I could do the washing." Then, as an afterthought, she added, "Papa wanted you to help cut corn today, you know."

The Upward Way

Sudden resentment boiled up inside Ruth as she thought about Dorcas's "easy" life. Ruth always had almost more work to do than she could hope to accomplish in a day, while Dorcas more often than not sat around sewing or doing fancy work. "Yes, I have corn to cut, and Mark suggested that the pigs should be bedded," Ruth retorted. "And no doubt I'll have a couple dozen other jobs that have to be done before the day is out!"

"Well, you don't have to be so snappy about it!" Dorcas returned.

Instantly Ruth felt ashamed. Dorcas was surely doing what she could to share the burden of work in the family. "Sorry," she responded. She was truly sorry for her meanness. But, on the other hand, Dorcas would not need to act so prim and proper—as though she never said or did anything wrong.

"What a pain to have the pigs all penned up again!" Dorcas declared then. "It's so much nicer when they can be running in the pastures. Makes a lot less work!"

"I know," Ruth agreed.

Dorcas broke off a small piece of bread and daintily wiped out the last bit of gravy from her plate. Ruth grinned inside. *Dorcas is so ladylike! I probably ought to be more so! I am more of a farm "boy" than a lady,* she admitted to herself. She scraped her plate with her fork, gathering the last of the gravy and mush together that way, while Dorcas looked at her across the table with her eyebrows pulled together.

"Did I do something wrong?" Ruth asked, grinning. "Is it unmannerly to use my fork to clean my plate?"

"Well, maybe not," Dorcas conceded, returning her

The Upward Way

grin. "But it screeches so! And you sound just like the men do!"

Ruth shrugged and laughed. "I guess I should try harder to be a lady," she admitted, getting up from the table and beginning to gather the few dishes.

While Dorcas did the dishes, Ruth carried buckets of water to fill the boiler for washing. *This is going to be a long day,* Ruth thought, *with just Dorcas and me here.* Loneliness for the familiar faces of her parents made her feel a little sad. Later as she filled the washer and washtubs, she suddenly heard a horn. *Toot! Toot! Toot!* Dropping her buckets on the washhouse floor, she rushed to the door in time to see Norman's Willys laboring up the hill. She waved happily out the open door, her doldrums vanishing instantly.

"What brings you today?" she greeted Sarah as soon as Sarah parked at the end of the sidewalk.

Sarah got out and gathered her baggage. "I came to get my bantams," she said.

"What do you want your bantams for now?" Ruth asked.

"I want them at home so we can use the eggs," Sarah said with a jolly laugh.

"What eggs?" Ruth asked, laughing with her. "They don't lay many this time of year."

"Oh, I know."

The girls walked to the house together. Ruth returned to the washhouse, and Sarah went to greet Dorcas. All that morning Sarah helped where she could, first with the washing and then she went to the cornfield with Ruth to cut a load of corn for the cows. After she helped bed

The Upward Way

the hog pens, she and Ruth worked together to find and catch the bantams.

All day Monday, the weather was cloudy and unsettled, and a chilly east wind blew. When the wash did not dry outside, the girls finally reeled it all back in to finish drying on lines in the washhouse.

The rain held off all day. "I'm so glad we could get the corn in before it rains," Ruth said as she told Sarah good-bye late in the afternoon.

Sarah nodded. "We'd have had to work in the rain, that's all," she said. "And we've done that plenty of times before."

When Ruth awakened on Tuesday morning, the rain was pouring in torrents across her window, driven by an east wind. "No outside work that has to be done today," she said happily into the darkness, climbing out of her squeaky bed.

How Ruth enjoyed that day, a day to work in the house—at least when the barn chores were done. Dorcas spent the day sewing for orders, busy at her treadle all day long. Ruth brought the wash from the washhouse lines, folded it, and put it away. Then she did the huge ironing. Finally, while Dorcas got dinner, Ruth sat down, propped her feet on Mama's special footstool and embroidered on some quilt patches for a quilt she hoped to sometime put together.

After dinner, Ruth was trying to decide what to do next. "We don't have anything baked around. Shall I bake pies?" she asked Dorcas as they worked together at washing the few dishes.

"Sure. Mama would be happy for that. Why don't you

71

The Upward Way

make some apple and some ground cherry? You know, we have lots of both of those to use."

"And some vanilla pies—they're my favorite! But apple and ground cherry—will you help me peel apples and husk the ground cherries? It'll take me most of the afternoon to bake pies if I have to get everything ready too."

Dorcas considered a bit. "I guess I can spare a little time to help you."

"Good! I'll get a pan of apples from the washhouse and a box of ground cherries from the garage." Ruth flew out the door.

Soon she was back with her goods, depositing them on the kitchen counter, where Dorcas could easily take them from there. "Now to roll out the crusts."

Before too long, there were twelve pies—four apple, four vanilla, and four ground cherry—cooling on the range top. Ruth looked at them with a sense of fulfillment. *Hm, that should be enough to last a week, at least if we don't get too much company,* she thought. After she had cleaned up the kitchen, the pies had cooled enough to cover and put away. She carried them to the shelves above the basement steps. It was cool there, and pies kept well. The only problem with having them there was that whenever Ruth ran to the basement for jars of canned things, it was quite tempting to grab a piece of pie, especially if a pie had been cut. Other good things were often stored there too, especially in cool weather, when those shelves became a sort of refrigerator.

"What are you doing down there so long?" Dorcas asked suddenly from the top of the basement steps.

The Upward Way

Ruth jumped, startled. Then she laughed. "Just thinking," she returned. "Wishing I wouldn't have inherited so much of a weakness for good food."

Dorcas humphed. "Yes, from the Good side of the family. They all like to eat too well!" she said. Then she added, "Just wanted to tell you there is a customer out at the garage."

"Okay." Ruth bounded back up the steps and closed the door behind her, shutting out the present temptation at least. But it would take more than a closed door, she knew, to keep her from the pies in the days to come. It would take the Lord's help to control her appetite.

Papa and Mama came home that evening, blown in with the rain. Bishop Aaron Mast was with them. He and the Bechtels stayed for the good supper that Dorcas had prepared. "I'm glad you made pies," Mama said with a smile when Ruth carried one of each kind to the table for dessert. "I don't know what we'd have served otherwise." Mama could not serve a company meal—or any meal, for that matter—without dessert. Papa left to take the Bechtels home and to take Brother Mast to the Limerick area, where he was to begin a week of meetings on Thursday evening. Ruth curled up by the stove in the sitting room and finished reading her book, *The Trail of the Conestoga*.

It was a joy and a relief to have her parents back home again, Ruth thought as she prepared for bed that night. With a sense of gratitude for God's care, both for her parents and for herself and Dorcas while their parents were gone, she settled into bed for a night of rest, lulled to sleep by the rain on the windowpanes and the constant

The Upward Way

pouring from the eaves.

By Wednesday morning, the rain had stopped. That meant returning to the fields again. "What a wonderful reprieve Tuesday was!" she quipped to Mark as they cut corn together.

Mark laughed. "It surely was. I don't know when we last had such heavy rain, so that I didn't even feel guilty to sit around the house catching up on my reading and bookwork." He lifted one boot after the other out of the sucking mud as he went to guide Dick and the corn wagon forward. "I just hope we don't get the wagon stuck out here in this awful *mud*!"

Ruth giggled, already wet to her skin from the dripping cornstalks and muddy to her hips from the "swamp" that they were slopping through. "I was thinking that I hope we don't get stuck in this mud," she called after him.

Load after load they hauled to the barn floor. There it was dumped, to be husked out later during the long, cold days of winter. Then the corn would be fed to the hogs and the fodder would be stuffed down the straw funnel for bedding for the cows in the stable below.

Twice during that morning, Mark needed to bring Harry and Gerry out (two other workhorses) to help pull the wagon out of the mud. When Ruth went for dinner, she was covered with mud nearly from head to foot. One look at her and Mama ordered her to stay out in the washhouse and clean up while Mama went and got her clean clothes.

Ruth and Mark laughed together later as they shared tales. "I was turned out of my own house too—by my own wife, mind you!" Mark said. "She handed me clean

The Upward Way

clothes out the back door and sent me to the milk house to wash and change before she would give me any dinner!"

The women were planning to help with church cleaning in the afternoon, and Ruth hoped to help. But Papa had other plans. "Can you watch the pigs this afternoon?" he asked Ruth at the dinner table.

Ruth glanced at Mama for her reaction. "Ruth was planning to help Dorcas and Ellen clean the church this afternoon," Mama said. "But I guess she can do that if you would rather."

"Well, I would rather!" Papa responded emphatically. "Or I wouldn't have mentioned it. And Ruth will need to, unless Dorcas can. I turned the pigs into the orchard to clean up the dropped apples, and we don't want them digging up the yard or anywhere else they take a notion to."

Mama looked at Ruth, and then at Papa. "Ruth can do that. I can help the girls clean this time. But why don't you fence the orchard? We go through this all summer when you have the heifers in there—"

"I'll put up fence when I've a mind to," Papa broke in. Then he turned to Ruth. "And you don't just sit out there with a book," he continued. "Pick the rest of the Delicious apples while you're out there."

"I would like for you to go over the pole beans one more time too before they freeze," Mama suggested to Ruth. "You would still be close enough to the orchard if you are picking the pole beans."

"Well, whatever. As long as she isn't loafing," Papa agreed, nodding at Ruth.

And so, Ruth spent the afternoon watching the pigs as they grunted and rooted happily among the half-rotten

75

The Upward Way

apples under the apple trees. She enjoyed picking apples, and she enjoyed picking the pole beans. But she knew all along that she would also still need to get a load of turnips in sometime that day for an order the next day. With Ellen's help, she got that done too—forty bushels of them.

Work, work! There surely does not seem to ever be an end to it! Ruth shook her head soberly as she washed for supper, feeling an ache in nearly every bone. But her day was not finished at suppertime. As soon as Papa finished his last bite of apple pie, he leaned back in his chair and said, "You know we want to start our winter butchering for market this week. That means a hog must be killed, scraped, and hung up yet this evening."

Ruth shook with an agonized feeling. Surely Papa did not expect *her* to shoot it! She did not mind the butchering, or even scraping the hair off, as long as someone else did the actual killing. But Papa *was* expecting her to kill it, so shoot it she did! *I can't understand why Papa doesn't want to shoot the hogs when he loves to go hunting. Maybe they are too much like pets.* Ruth nodded comprehendingly. *That is probably why. I suppose Mark would do it, but they went to Boyertown to visit Ellen's parents for the evening.*

Ruth hung the caldron in the milk house over the fireplace there. Then she pumped it full of water from the windmill cistern and got a roaring fire going beneath it. Papa helped her then to scrape and hang up the hog in the shed. She was glad for that; sometimes he expected her to do such things herself. And so the busy day finally ended, and she could go to her garret for some much-needed rest.

The Upward Way

The sun was already over the horizon when Ruth headed for the house on Thursday morning. *Looks like a lovely day,* she thought happily. *I'm glad because it is always nicer to butcher when the weather is nice.* Ruth always wished the walk across the road from the barn to the house would be a longer one. The eastern sky was brightening with the rising sun as she left the barn. She ran across the short yard beside the milk house, across the dirt road, and up the walk to the house, thankful that her healing carbuncle no longer pained her at all. *Ellen is a good nurse,* she thought as she burst into the washhouse.

The caldron of water was steaming from where it hung over the fire in the washhouse fireplace. Quickly Ruth hung up her outdoor wraps and waited for Papa to finish washing up. She always had to laugh inside as she watched his washing procedure. First, he thoroughly scrubbed his hands, lathering them well with homemade soap, and then rinsed them carefully. Then he scooped up a handful of the cold water, splashing it onto his face and scrubbing with his large hands while he spluttered and snorted to keep the water out of his nose and mouth. Finally he was finished, and dried his face and hands carefully on the feed-sack towel hung behind the door. It was always quite a ritual! Then it was Ruth's turn. She washed quickly, pretty much repeating his process— except for the face wash. She preferred using a washcloth! Then she hurried into the kitchen.

"Butchering days have come again," she quipped to no one in particular.

"Yes, and that means lots of good bacon, ham,

The Upward Way

scrapple, pork chops, and—" injected Kore with a smack of his lips. He was already in the house, sitting in the corner of the kitchen, reading the *Farm Journal*.

"Are you ready for school, young man?" Papa asked, glancing at him.

"I'll be, as soon as I have eaten," Kore responded, laying down his magazine and going to the table.

Papa had cut the hog four ways—left, right, and hindquarters—and laid it out on a table in the washhouse by the time the girls were ready to help after breakfast. Ellen helped cut up meat for a while, as long as Roy and Robert cooperated. When she went up to her house to take care of them, Dorcas also said she had other things to do. So she limped to the kitchen. Ruth knew that Dorcas's physical condition did not allow her to stand for long periods of time, so she did not resent her leaving. And Ruth did not really mind working alone. She enjoyed cutting the meat off the bones, and she enjoyed times of quietness with her thoughts.

After a while, Ruth carried a full dishpan of trimmings to the sausage grinder. Then she plopped the cleaned bones into the caldron of boiling water in the fireplace. After the meat on the bones cooked soft, she would pick the meat off and put it back into the broth. Then Papa would thicken the broth with cornmeal and flour and season it just right to make the delicious scrapple that sold so well. Papa did make good scrapple.

Soon he would grind the sausage—as soon as all the meat was trimmed off the bones. Right now he was getting the smokehouse ready to begin smoking the hams and bacon, Ruth thought. She had seen him cleaning it

The Upward Way

out after the summer of disuse, and then hauling wood in that direction. But he wouldn't start the fire in the smokehouse for several days yet, not until the hams and bacons had soaked in a salt brine to marinate first.

Grabbing an empty dishpan, Ruth went back to her meat-cutting table. She would soon be finished. One hog did not take so long. Later in the season, they would cut up three or four on Thursdays for Friday's market.

Just then Ellen and Roy burst into the washhouse. Ruth looked up happily. "Oh, you're nearly finished already!" Ellen exclaimed. "I wanted so much to get back down here and help with this, but Robbie would not cooperate and go to sleep. And I didn't want to leave him up there alone until I knew he was sleeping. Anyway, here we are now, in time to help you clean up!" She stopped short with a laugh.

"Oh, we'll still have the meat to pick off the bones for the scrapple, but it isn't done cooking yet. And the intestines to clean for the sausage—unless Mama is doing that. Sometimes she does."

Mama was not cleaning the intestines; she was sewing and mending. So Ellen and Ruth did that. After dinner, Ruth helped Papa grind the sausage and stuff it. Then the stewing bones were ready to be picked clean. Mama helped with that, so the broth was soon ready for Papa to finish the scrapple.

"Are we finished?" Ruth asked as she emptied the last pan of meat into the boiling broth.

"I guess for now," Mama answered. "Papa will need help later with the scrapple. I think he is working with the hams and bacons now."

The Upward Way

"Are you going to make soap today with the lard?" Ruth asked.

"We probably should. Our soap is about all gone from what we made last winter. But I need the lard for baking. I suppose we can buy some of that Lava soap to hold us over. Papa likes using that."

"If we sell some lard, we'll likely get more for it than what the soap would cost," Ruth observed, remembering how well lard sold other years.

Mama nodded, as though that was a new thought, and then hurried into the kitchen.

Ruth scrubbed up and also went into the kitchen. Maybe if she hurried, she could quickly mix up a cake and ice it before milking time. Finding Mama's receipt[12] box, she started paging through the cake receipts. She decided to try a four-layer cake.

"Won't this be good with icing between all these layers?" She laughed as she later put the four pans into the wood-stove oven.

"It will be quite a fancy cake," Mama said, looking up from where she was cleaning the pig feet for souse. "And it's not even anybody's birthday!"

Ruth laughed again, but a little guiltily. She probably should not make such good things to eat—they always tempted her to eat too much, and Mama too.

There was a stomping at the back door and Papa came in. "I got the hams and bacons all in the brine. Should be ready to hang in the smokehouse in a couple of days, and then be ready to sell in a couple of weeks. Now I must get to the scrapple." He glanced quickly at Ruth. "What

---

[12] Recipes were called "receipts" in those days.

80

The Upward Way

are you doing in here? Don't you know you've got to get turnips for market tomorrow?"

"I'll go now," Ruth said meekly. *Oh, how could I have forgotten to get turnips! I knew it had to be done.*

"Kore is supposed to be hitching up the wagon. So hustle yourself out if you want a ride to the field."

"I'll watch the cakes," Mama offered kindly.

"And, Vena"—Papa looked at Mama—"the Benners stopped by and said Abe Miller's are planning to be here for supper."

"Abe Miller's?" Mama looked uncertain for a moment. "Who are they?" she asked. "Oh, are they the people from Greenwood, Delaware?"

Papa nodded as he helped himself to an apple from the bowl. "They said they'd be here around six. So we don't have time to dilly-dally." This he said to Ruth, who was still standing at the kitchen door, listening.

Ruth hurried out the door. *Hm-m, the Millers. They have a son about my age, I think, but no girls. Maybe I won't have to help entertain anybody. I might not feel like it anyway by the time I get turnips in and do the milking.*

Kore was waiting at the field lane as Ruth went puffing up the barn hill past the machinery shed. "Come on, slowpoke," he said. "Next time you can walk. I've been waiting up here half an hour at least—ever since I got home from school. Where have you been?"

"I forgot about turnips till Papa just reminded me," Ruth said honestly. "Sorry."

As she sat near Kore on the wagon, a strong smell of tobacco blew over her. "Were you smoking again, Kore?" she asked, looking at him intently. "You know better."

81

The Upward Way

"Oh, hang off. I'm not hurting anybody."

"Just yourself. And the Lord," Ruth reminded him. "You know it is a dirty, sinful habit."

"No worse than some things some others do," he remarked smartly, cracking the whip over Dick's back. Old Dick plunged forward, and the wagon creaked along behind. Ruth chose to be silent. It never did any good to talk to Kore when he was in such a mood.

After the load of turnips was in, Ruth went to do the barn chores. Kore fed the cows and young stock and then disappeared. Mark came to help with the milking, but Ruth had the rest of Kore's chores to finish as well as her cows to milk. The Millers were already in the house when she rushed in, later than usual, to clean up and change her clothes. It was only Mr. and Mrs. Miller, Ruth noted with relief; none of their family was with them. Kore came in, after she was back in the kitchen, washed up quickly, and slouched in his chair at the table, just in time for prayer.

Everybody was visiting congenially around the table as they enjoyed Mama's good supper of sausage and fried potatoes and homemade noodles and pole beans—everyone except Ruth and Kore. Ruth watched Kore silently. *Where was he during the milking?* she wondered. She wished Papa would always be in the barn to see what was going on. But would that help? If she told what she knew, Kore would get upset with her and probably would not talk for days. But this time she really did not know where he had been—other than that he had been smoking before they got the load of turnips in.

Discouragement wanted to settle on Ruth's heart. It seemed so impossible to help Kore. Silently she breathed

The Upward Way

a prayer for help to rise above her feelings, and the refreshing peace of her heavenly Father again strengthened her heart.

Ruth came suddenly back to the present when she noticed everyone looking at her. "What—did you ask me a question?" she asked.

Sister Miller smiled understandingly. "I just asked if you have any plans to go to Eastern Mennonite School?" she repeated.

Ruth looked quickly at Papa, but his face was unreadable. "I would like to sometime," she began, "if Papa and Mama can do without my help here."

"Our Daniel is there this year," Sister Miller went on. "He is really enjoying the studies. He says he enjoys Brother J. L. Stauffer's classes as well as any." This last she addressed more to Papa, since J. L. was Papa's brother-in-law.

So that is why Daniel is not along this time, Ruth realized. *If only I could go to EMS too. How can I ever teach school if I'm not allowed to get teacher training?* Discouragement threatened to overwhelm her again, but with a prayer for help, she turned her thoughts to the conversation around her.

For dessert, Mama brought in the four-layer cake that Ruth had baked that afternoon and a big dish of warm tapioca pudding. Yum! Tapioca was one of Ruth's favorite desserts. The cake looked nice too. Mama had spread icing liberally between each layer and on the top.

"Oh, that cake looks lovely," Sister Miller gushed. "But your supper has been so good, I declare I can't eat another bite!"

The Upward Way

"Nor me," Brother Miller added.

"Not even a taste?" Mama urged. "Ruth baked this one, and she makes good cakes."

"Well, maybe just a taste," Sister Miller conceded as Mama handed her the cake platter.

Ruth looked on with interest. Maybe that was how Sister Miller stayed slim. *Why do I have such a sweet tooth?* she inwardly chided herself. It seemed next to impossible for her to turn down good desserts or any other kind of sweets. *Maybe this is something I need the Lord's help with. I know the Bible calls overeating sin.* . . .

After supper, Ruth went out to top the load of turnips. Again, Kore was not around to help. But Mark and Ellen and the boys came down for a while. As they stood around the wagon and cut off tops, they sang and told stories and entertained the boys, making the work fly. Little more than an hour and a half later, there was nothing left but crates of purple turnips on the wagon, and piles of green tops on the ground.

"Good night, and thanks for the help," Ruth said sincerely as she began gathering up the piles of turnip tops to give the cows.

She was glad to retreat to her own room earlier than usual that evening. It had been a long day, and a tiring one. She wrote in her journal to the drone of the visiting voices downstairs. She did not know when the Millers left. She heard them still visiting, when, after a time of Bible reading and prayer, she extinguished her lamp and lay down to sleep.

Chapter Five

I haven't written in here, you dear old Journal, for a couple weeks. So will try to catch you up on a few days and the things that I remember about them!

October 25, 1933, Wednesday. We gathered in a lot of garden things as it was getting so much colder—beans, tomatoes, and dahlia bulbs. Sarah had been here a couple days, but she went home that evening with John and Ruth Kolb. Letter came from Charles. Sarah insisted that she should read it, so I said she may! Then she didn't really want to after all! Papa made me shoot a hog to butcher the next day. Thermometer was already at 32^0 at bedtime, so we knew it would get cold during the night. Was 24^0 the next morning. Winter—br-r-r! Went to Limerick several evenings during the week to hear Aaron Mast from Maryland preach. His message Wednesday evening was "Midnight Scenes From the Bible." Very inspiring and challenging. Kore seemed to have been challenged too, by the messages that week.

October 29, 1933, Sunday. We were at Towamencin for church that morning. Then we went to Norman and Sarah's for dinner and supper. How delightful to be with my sister for the day. Ate ripe

The Upward Way

persimmons off their tree in the afternoon. Sure were good! In the evening we went to the Finland Mission for church. Linford Hackman and Llewellyn Groff have surely begun a wonderful work there. Two black couples who are members, Clara and Will Anderson and James and Rowena Lark, were at the service, along with many other community people from several different nationalities. What a blessing it was to visit with new converts and catch their fresh enthusiasm for the Lord. How I would love to be able to serve the Lord in some special way like in a mission!

November 1, 1933, Wednesday. First day of gunning. Mark shot three rabbits, and Papa, several squirrels. I skinned them all, and then husked corn for part of the day. It was cold in the field, but I had the fun of chasing out a beautiful pheasant cock. Looked for a special letter, but it did not come until Thursday this week. Papa does not allow me to write more than once every two weeks, but I'm glad for Charles's letters a little more often than that. Kore caught a skunk in the garage that evening, and oh, what a smell! We killed four hogs to butcher the next day. Mama got Roy a tricycle for his third birthday. He was so happy with it!

November 7, 1933, Tuesday. We were at Pottstown for church in the evening. Mrs. Sterling and her children were there. Those poor people. Her husband chased them from home on Sunday night, threatening to put them all "out of the way." He carries a revolver with him all the time. That night he was waiting outside in his car during the service. Everyone was "worked up," and much sincere prayer was offered up for the situation. Brother Henry's were able to get them safely out and take them to Uncle Amos's again, where they had been staying since Sunday. The next day Papa and Mama went for a meeting with some other deacons to decide what to do for Mrs. Sterling and her children.

November 10, 1933, Friday. And now I am caught up again! Papa

The Upward Way

and Mama went to Amityville to market today as usual. Mark took meat to Parker Ford and sold it. Helped to finish cutting corn this afternoon. Then baked a cake. This evening I went along with Kore to set his traps. The first thing he caught was his fingers—twice, in fact! It was a lovely walk, but very cold.

Breakfast over, Papa pushed back his chair from the table. "Well, it's high time to get the garden things all in. Sure feels like we could get a hard frost tonight."

Mama nodded soberly, while Sarah called out, "I'll help!"

Norman had dropped Sarah off Monday morning on his way to his painting job. So she had been home for two days, helping to get the corn in, as well as doing other jobs around the farm. She had told them once more how lonesome she got when Norman went off on his job every morning, and Norman had encouraged her again to come home to help her very busy family.

Very generous of him! Ruth thought happily. Papa only smiled slightly at Sarah's enthusiasm, but Ruth's heart was light. It had been so nice to have these days like old times again—days to work and chatter with her sister.

"I'll do the dishes," Dorcas offered as she daintily wiped her mouth with her handkerchief.

"Maybe you could dig the dahlia bulbs too," Ruth suggested, thinking she would have enough to do to get the rest of the garden crops in.

"Oh, I doubt I'll have time for that," Dorcas returned quickly. "I have three aprons to make, and Swartz's have a big order of coverings to be done by next week. And I also have bonnet orders waiting."

The Upward Way

"We have cheese to melt too," Mother reminded her. "And Papa has two more cans of milk sitting in the washhouse to be heated for cheese today."

"I'll help you," Sarah injected quickly, looking at Ruth. "We'll get all the work done. We'll just make it fly!"

Ruth smiled at her gratefully. Although she loved her sister Dorcas, she did prefer the blessing of a sister who could work with her.

When the mailman's Willys went soon after dinner, Ruth was helping Dorcas stir the kettles of cheese while Mama rested. So it was Sarah who rushed out for the mail. She came back into the house, waving an envelope in one hand. Quickly she laid the rest of the pile on the table. "See what the mailman left for me?" she teased, flaunting the envelope before Ruth's face.

Ruth quickly washed her hands and dried them on her apron. "Does it have your name on it?" Ruth asked, trying to decide if she should grab for it.

Sarah held it close to her eyes. "I can't quite read the name, but I think it says 'Sarah Clemmer Breckbill.'" She pulled out a hairpin and pretended to slit the envelope. "I guess I'll go ahead and read it," she stated.

Ruth decided that to play along was better than to protest. "Sure, go ahead. Just read it aloud so that I can hear it too," she agreed, feigning unconcern.

Sarah grinned at her and tossed the letter her way. "I wouldn't read your mail, sis. Take it and enjoy it."

Grabbing her letter, Ruth dashed up the garret stairs to her own room. *Squeak, squeak,* protested her bed as she flopped across it. Quickly tearing open the envelope, she hungrily devoured the letter.

The Upward Way

Harrisonburg, Virginia
November 2, 1933

Dear Ruth,

Greetings in our blessed Lord and Master's Name.

Thank you for your letter again. I am always so glad to hear from you. (You'll have to excuse my writing paper, but I can get more of this kind easily. Besides, it's the words that count and not the paper!)

I hardly know where to start. Last Thursday evening, I went to see Bro. Chester Lehman about some of my subjects. I hoped to be able to drop Biology and take Old Testament History instead. He told me the next morning in chapel that he had arranged that for me.

My roommate, Ezra Landis (you probably remember that), and I went to Natural Bridge yesterday. That is well worth seeing, but it would have been a lot more interesting if you could have been along too.

Last Sunday I went with Isaac's to Bethany, a little mountain church where my Uncle Francis has charge of the Sunday school. He drafted me to lead the singing, which I didn't mind too much. Then a visiting minister preached. I was at Uncle Francis' for dinner and supper. In the afternoon we walked up over the hill behind the school. I was at Bethany this morning too and went with Uncle Francis' to J. L. Stauffer's for dinner (a very special time for me, especially when they talked about their niece!) and to A. D. Wenger's for supper.

On Saturdays we may do whatever we want except for from 10:00 to 12:00, during which time we must study. On Sundays we have quiet hour (if we are in the dormitory) from 2:00 to 4:00.

I am enjoying my studies very much. I think I will especially enjoy Old Testament Bible Studies. A.D. Wenger teaches that class, and everyone says how he tells a lot of stories about his travels in the Holy Lands. I have some catching up to do in that class, since I didn't begin with it at the beginning of the year. The rest have memorized Abraham's plea for Sodom, from Genesis 18:23–33, as well as the

The Upward Way

Ten Commandments. I have been working on memorizing both passages and almost have them done.

Yesterday some of us fellows went in a big truck to Massanutten Peak. We had a nice time climbing over rocks! We ate our lunch out there—three sandwiches apiece, half a pickle, two wieners (which I'm not so fond of), a piece of cake, an apple, and an orange. That all tasted right good after so much climbing! On the way home, we were singing in the back of the truck, and people surely did look at us. Noah Mack and some other boys left Friday evening and walked to another mountain peak and then to the Massanutten Peak.

This morning the message text was from 2 Peter 1:1 "To them that have obtained like precious faith with us." It was a message addressed to us as Gentiles, and how blessed we are that the message of salvation is for us as well as for the Jews. They have YPM[13] here, but I like ours at home the best.

One evening someone rang the fire alarm for fun, to scare the girls. (It was not me.) Later that evening, during study period, I went down to the library to do some reading for my English class. While there, the lights went out. I figured somebody did it for a joke again. But they were out all over town. Some of the students went for their flashlights, and the librarian brought some candles. So I read for a while by candlelight. Then Bro. J. L. Stauffer came into the library, and all at once the lights came on. He shook his head and looked just as if he knew they would, but said not a word and went out again. It all was sort of funny. . . .

That reminds me—I have Bro. J. L. for my Bible study classes. Right now we are studying the Book of Daniel—an extremely interesting study, especially the prophetic part, and an extremely interesting instructor.

I often wish you could be here too as a student. How nice that

---

[13] Young People's Meetings

The Upward Way

would be! I doubt that I will be able to make it home before the Christmas holidays, if even then. Funds are just too tight. Maybe you can come down sometime for a visit, or for short-term Bible study . . .

It is almost time for church, and I must close. Wishing you the best!

Your sincere friend,
Charles Derstine

Ruth finished reading with a sigh, partly of contentment and partly of longing. She wished as well that she could be at EMS. Ever since she was a little girl, she had longed to be a schoolteacher. But how could she teach without a college education? College seemed a remote possibility though, since Papa had no time for higher education. He thought it made young people proud, which no doubt it did for many[14]. Well, she consoled herself, perhaps next year Papa would let her go for a short-term Bible study at least. That would be better than nothing.

She laid the letter beside her Bible, a feeling of longing enveloping her. How she wished that she and Charles could be together and visit every weekend as most couples did. It seemed so long since she had seen him last. And now Charles was saying that he doubted that he would get home before Christmas vacation, if even then.

---

[14] At that time, higher education was viewed differently than what it is today, even by many conservative Mennonites. There was not the secular, humanistic approach to education then as there was by the latter half of the twentieth century. Also, for many Mennonites, higher education was seen as the way to acquire the training for service to the church. In the 1930s and 40s, Eastern Mennonite School was a fairly conservative institution and considered a safe place to go for a college education.

The Upward Way

Ruth could understand why he did not come home often. It was a long drive from Harrisonburg, more than eight hours, even with good traveling. And gas prices were high because of the Depression. Why, a gallon of gas cost more than most people could earn in a couple of hours! But understanding why did not make his not coming home oftener any easier. She bowed her head on her arms, praying for a submissive heart to the circumstances of life.

Slowly she went back downstairs to the kitchen. Mama was up from her nap and bustling about the kitchen again.

"Bad news?" Sarah asked, eyeing Ruth carefully.

"Oh, no," Ruth returned. "Just that he says he can't come home sooner than Christmas, if even then."

"Oh, well, if he was in the military in another country, you wouldn't see him often either," Dorcas said. "So why brutz about that?"

Ruth felt like retorting, but bit back the words. *Dear Father, where is the submission I prayed for? Why does Dorcas say the kind of things that make me feel like getting angry at her? But probably it is my fault—what she said is true enough! Please do help me to accept rebuke!*

She smiled at Dorcas, and then turned to Sarah. Sarah and Dorcas were still stirring the kettles of melting cheese. "I guess we should go back outside. At least if you plan to help me," she said. "Papa still has work in the truck patch for us girls."

"Sure," Sarah agreed. "If Mama can take over my oar here." Sarah leaned her wooden paddle against the inside of the kettle so Mama could conveniently reach it, and then followed Ruth to the washhouse for her jacket.

The Upward Way

"Dorcas hasn't lost her sharp tongue yet, has she?" Sarah said as they walked to the garden together.

Ruth shook her head. "She can be sweet when she wants to be. And I really enjoy her at times like that."

"Well, I suspect she thinks if she had a man, it would solve all her problems," Sarah went on. "But if she is sassy now, she would be sassy then too; and no man would be very happy with such a woman, you'd better believe! She's going to have to submit to her lot before she'll be happy, whether single or married."

Ruth only nodded. She did not know too much about married life, she conceded to herself. Sarah ought to know a lot more, being married for all of six weeks! But still, married or not, she understood the spiritual principles—that being contented in whatever situation of life she found herself was crucial to true satisfaction.

"Well, I know I can do better at being kind to Dorcas," Ruth admitted as she picked up a basket at the edge of the garden. "She doesn't have an easy lot—and I'm not always very sympathetic."

Sarah nodded with understanding. "Same here."

That evening, it was a wonderful feeling to know that all the beans, tomatoes, squash, cabbage, and other things had been gleaned from the garden. The cave and the cold room in the cellar were both full and running over with the remainders of the summer's bounties. *How good God has been to us, to give us so many blessings!* Ruth thought as she sat at supper with the others, enjoying Mama's wonderful fried chicken, homemade noodles, fresh beans, and coleslaw. *Now let winter come!*

After supper, Sarah left to go home to her Norman,

The Upward Way

loaded with bounties that she had helped to gather that day. She caught a ride with John and Ruth Kolb, who stopped in for a short visit after supper.

True to Papa's predictions, the thermometer showed twenty-four degrees the next morning. "Let's get the rest of the late potatoes in today," Papa stated at breakfast. "They have to come in before the ground freezes."

"Well, you can't dig potatoes now!" Mama said. "They'd freeze and so would we!"

Papa looked irritated. "Do you think I don't know that? We'll wait until the sun warms things up."

They waited to start with the potatoes until ten o'clock, but the potatoes were all dug and picked up before a later-than-usual dinnertime and stored in crates on the barn floor with straw as an insulator. Then Papa, Ruth, and Mark started the butchering. By evening, Ruth had helped to butcher several hogs and twenty chickens for orders and for market the next day.

On Friday, she stayed busy with selling meat and other goods to the various customers that showed up at the farm, baking for the weekend, bringing in a load of grass for the cows—all that along with the regular chores. By suppertime, Ruth was so tired that all she could think about was going to bed early for a change.

"Well, I would like to go to Limerick this evening," Papa announced as soon as supper was over. He cleared his throat noisily as he scraped his chair away from the table. "Anybody else want to go?"

Ruth sighed inwardly. She felt awfully weary! And yet, she did not like to miss an opportunity to hear Brother Aaron Mast, who was having special meetings

The Upward Way

there. She had gone with some of the family one other evening, and that time had been so inspiring.

Mama shook her head. "I'm too tired, but the rest of you may go if you wish."

"I'd like to go," Kore said. "I like the way that man preaches."

"I'll go too," Dorcas said, getting up slowly. She began to clear a place on the table to set her dishpans.

I may as well too, Ruth thought as she also got to her feet. *They'll all think it strange if I stay home, especially if Dorcas and Kore go.*

After the challenging message of the evening, "The Crisis, the Cry, and the Chorus," Ruth was glad she had gone. *I need that kind of spiritual refreshment, especially for these busy, busy days,* she mused, alone in her garret room that night.

Saturday dawned cold and bright, and Ruth awoke early for her morning devotions. Her reading that morning was from Ephesians 5: "Giving thanks always for all things unto God and the Father in the name of our Lord Jesus Christ; submitting yourselves one to another in the fear of God." Ruth thought about those verses for a time as she knelt by her bed, reading by the light of her oil lamp. *Give thanks; . . . submit . . .* Her conscience smote her as she realized the many times that she inwardly rebelled at some direction her father gave her. *Dear heavenly Father, I'm sorry for my unthankful, insubmissive spirit. Help me to be humble and helpful and submissive, even if I may think some things are unfair. I do thank You for good health and for strength for the duties that are my lot.*

The Upward Way

Sometime later, feeling spiritually strengthened to face the day, she hurried to dress. Below her in the kitchen, the stove plates clanked and banged as Papa put wood into the wood stove. Then she bounded down her stairs to follow Papa and Kore to the barn. The cold nipped her nose, and she was glad to step into the barn, filled with the warmth of the cows, and the smells of cows and hay and silage.

"Right after breakfast," Papa said to Kore as he passed him in the stable, "I want you to haul a load of hay and a load of corn from the other farm. Use the express wagon. Ruth can help you if you need help."

Ruth heard from where she sat at her cow, busily directing the warm streams of milk into the bucket. *As though I don't have enough to do already—with all the normal Saturday work,* she fumed. No doubt, she would have all the cleaning to do too, and all the oil lamps to clean, because Dorcas would be busy with sewing orders that she *had* to finish for next week.

Give thanks; . . . submit . . . Recollections of her morning reading suddenly smote Ruth, and she could not believe she had forgotten so soon. *Forgive me, Father, for failing my first test! Give me grace to accept whatever comes, and to trust Thee to give me the strength . . .*

The day passed quickly as Ruth finished one chore after the other. Mama had stayed busy with extra customers throughout the day, and true to Ruth's predictions, Dorcas stayed close to her sewing machine. So they gave her little help. But it seemed the Lord gave extra strength, and by midafternoon, most of Saturday's regular work was finished, even *with* helping Kore in the morning.

The Upward Way

Ruth put the dust mop and the cleaning rags away in the washhouse. Then she trimmed the wicks on all the gathered oil lamps and put back in place their now-sparkling globes. Bursting back into the kitchen, she exclaimed with sudden realization, "And we don't even need to get food ready for tomorrow."

"Oh, that's right!" Mama exclaimed happily. "We have a dinner invitation tomorrow!"

"Supper too!" Ruth added.

When Sarah had been home through the week, she had invited the family for dinner and the afternoon on Sunday. "I forgot about that," Dorcas said, looking up from her sewing. "That will be nice."

"Nice! I should say so!" Ruth returned happily.

"But you'd better get the lamps put back where they belong," Dorcas reminded Ruth. "I need mine here at the sewing machine again. It's getting too dark to see this fine work."

Sunday dawned a lovely fall day. Papa had planned to go to Towamencin that morning because that was where Norman and Sarah had been attending. Papa enjoyed getting to the other churches in their conference, and he made a practice of taking in special meetings when possible, as well as visiting of other churches on Sunday mornings. They drove up to the church, a new stone building. Ruth remembered Papa's talking about how expensive it had been to build such a fine meetinghouse. She thought he had said it cost over $13,000.00,[15] which,

---

[15] J.C. Wenger, *History of the Mennonites of the Franconia Conference* (Telford, PA: Franconia Mennonite Historical Society, 1937), p. 150.

The Upward Way

according to Papa, would have bought several farms! But she guessed the people could afford it as she looked around at the parking lot full of late-model cars. Not that that made it right, she concluded. She did not understand about such things, only that when she heard about the many poor people all over the world, and even in their own country, it seemed a sin to spend so much money on things that did not really matter.

Brother Warren Moyer preached, but Ruth had to rein her thoughts in more than once. *Oh, why am I so addlebrained this morning,* she scolded herself. She did appreciate the day of rest and worship, but perhaps, she confessed to herself, she was looking forward more to the afternoon and being with her sister than to the spiritual nourishment coming over the pulpit.

After dinner, she and Sarah and Norman took a walk around Norman's small property while Papa and Mama and Dorcas rested.

"Oh, a persimmon tree!" Ruth exclaimed, noticing a tree with gnarled branches at the edge of the yard, hanging full of little yellow-orange fruits.

"Hey, you don't want to eat any of those," Norman said as Ruth stood on tiptoe to pick one off a low branch.

"Why not?" Ruth asked. "They look perfect—soft and red-streaked."

"But they'll give you a pucker you won't lose for a month!" Norman exclaimed.

Sarah burst into gay laughter. "What do you know about it?" she asked.

Norman looked at her with a grin. "I tried one, the day we moved in. They tasted absolutely terrible!"

The Upward Way

"But if they freeze first," Sarah offered knowingly, "they're delicious. Try one now."

Norman shook his head decidedly. "Not me, ladies. Go ahead if you like."

Ruth picked one and took a careful nibble. "Um-m-m. Delicious! They're just perfect."

Soon she and Sarah had eaten their fill. Gathering a couple more for the rest at the house, they slowly followed Norman back to the yard. After spending time looking at the remnants of various flowers in the beds around the house, they went back inside, where they found Mama making coffee for them all.

"Oh, Mama, I'm sorry," Sarah apologized. "I should have been here to make Papa's coffee. But look"—she held out her hand—"see what we brought for you to eat."

"Oh, persimmons!" Mama observed happily. "I haven't had any of them for a while." She and Papa each had one, but Dorcas politely declined.

Later, as they ate an early supper together, Norman asked, "Would you all like to go to the Finland Mission this evening? Sarah and I were hoping to be able to go."

Ruth looked at her brother-in-law with admiration. She knew he was very concerned about missions and about getting the Gospel out wherever he could. He often spent free evenings with other young men, passing out tracts in some of the larger towns, or in nearby Philadelphia. He also spent a lot of time helping with the Norristown Mission.

"Well, now . . ." Papa stalled. "I guess we could go.

The Upward Way

Can't say though that I'm too keen about those two young fellows trying to run a work by themselves."

"You mean Linford Hackman and Llewellyn Groff?"[16] Norman inquired. "I admire them and think they are doing a wonderful work. Besides, Elias Kulp is in charge there now, and he is an older, ordained man."

Papa nodded gravely. "Still, it's for the older, seasoned leaders to go ahead with such mission work, not the young upstarts. What do they know about the right way to do church work?"

Norman was not one to be put down, even by such pointed remarks. "Sometimes it takes the enthusiasm of young Christians to be able to reach out and get things accomplished," he said. "It was hardly two years ago that those two young men started having prayer meetings at the 'Devil's Potato Patch,' on that mountain ridge north of Souderton. Soon they were mingling with the people in the poor areas of Finland and Rocky Ridge, working with them, doing things for them, living among them as Christ did when He was on earth. They won their confidence, so the people were willing to listen to the Gospel. On Sunday mornings now, the community attendance is in the eighties, and souls are being saved." Norman sounded as enthusiastic as the young men he was defending, and Papa must have sensed it too, as he had nothing more to offer.

"I understand what you are saying, Papa, about needing the direction of older men," Norman added thoughtfully. "We need the wisdom and experience of years. And

---

[16] John L. Ruth, *Maintaining the Right Fellowship* (Scottdale, PA: Herald Press, 1984), p. 482.

The Upward Way

I think we young men want to be sensitive and sensible about that. We need older, seasoned leaders to keep our enthusiasm balanced."

"I would like to go," Mama stated after a bit. "I always enjoy Clara Anderson and her quaint southern ways so much."

"I do too," Sarah agreed. "And Rowena Lark too. They are both such faithful Christians, and their husbands are faithful too."

So all of them went to Finland for the evening service. Brother Elias Kulp preached a message entitled "Eternity." It was late when Ruth crawled into bed, but the joy in her heart for the wonderful day compensated for the late hour.

Monday was the beginning of another busy week. Ruth began the week, full of eager ambitions. It was so nice to feel well and rested after a refreshing Sunday, and so wonderful to have the companionship and support of her loving Saviour.

She went to the turnip field early, as soon as she had helped Mama get the washing process started. It was cold, and some of the turnips were frozen; but they would be all right, she knew. Soon Roy joined her, carrying pulled turnips to the wagon for her to cut off the tops.

Suddenly a strange noise came over the horizon, and then a big, round, silver dirigible began a slow traverse across the sky. Roy clung in fear to Ruth's skirts. "Come, Aunt Rufie. Let's go home quick!" he gasped, his face hidden in her skirt.

Ruth hid a smile as she tried to explain to the terrified child that it would not hurt them. It was something like

The Upward Way

a car in the sky—only it made more noise than a car. Finally, he uncovered his eyes to watch it with interest.

Wednesday, November 1, was the first day of hunting season. Papa and Mark went out early in the morning, while Kore and Ruth did the morning chores. Kore stayed home from school that day, so after breakfast, Ruth went to the field to help him husk corn. Suddenly a pheasant rooster flew up, startling them both by his noisily beating wings and his raucous cackle.

"Oh, I wish we had a gun to get that fine fellow!" Kore exclaimed. "Oh, well, I guess we get enough chicken, without having to shoot wild ones."

"We likely couldn't have hit him anyway," Ruth added, "as fast as he was going."

"Probably not," Kore conceded. "At least not you," he added with a tormenting grin.

Ruth just laughed, knowing there was no point in taking offense. She knew she was not the world's best hunter, and she had a notorious track record when it came to hitting rabbits or groundhogs in the garden.

The morning passed too slowly for Ruth, who was especially eager to get to the house at noon. She hoped there would be mail for her today. Usually Wednesdays were special mail days. But this day the mailman's Willys rumbled on past their mailbox, not leaving a single piece of mail.

"Oh, well, maybe tomorrow," Mama attempted to comfort Ruth when she saw how crestfallen she appeared.

Mama was happy when the men came back to the house in late afternoon with some game to show for their time. But it was Ruth who needed to skin and clean the

The Upward Way

rabbits and squirrels while the men ate a late dinner.

Mama fried the game for supper, and invited Mark and Ellen and the boys down.

"Fried rabbit always tastes so good in the fall," Mark declared as they all enjoyed Mama's spread. "And no one can make it taste quite as good as Mama," he added. Ellen nodded in agreement.

Ruth was thinking about Roy's birthday that day and wondering if Mama had made him a cake.

Just then Mama spoke. "Well, Roy, is today a special day for you?"

Roy nodded his blond head. "I'm three today, Grammy," he told her with a smile, making great effort to hold up three pudgy fingers.

"Tut, tut! So you are getting to be quite a big boy now, aren't you?" she complimented him.

Dorcas got up slowly from her chair. She limped to the pantry and soon returned with a big, iced cake. Mama brought a canister of homemade ice cream from the washhouse, where Ruth had seen it earlier, seasoning in frigid brine. Making ice cream was nearly a weekly chore year round. It took less effort in the wintertime though, when all the ice they could use was free-for-the-taking from the creek below the cave. But they had their ice in summer too. There was an icehouse in Limerick where they could buy a hundred-pound block of ice for thirty cents. Papa often stopped for a block on the way home from the auction. In the summertime, the ice was used to keep the icebox in the kitchen cold. But a hundred-pound block was also enough to declare plainly to the womenfolk that Papa wanted ice cream!

The Upward Way

Ruth could remember the time in the long-ago past when every winter that the ice was thick enough, Papa and Mark would harvest ice. They cut huge squares of it from a dammed area in the creek and stored the blocks in sawdust in the icehouse, where it held well throughout the following summer. The ice then kept the icebox cold during the summer. It was much easier now, being able to buy ice.

Roy looked up with delight as Dorcas carried in the cake. "Yum!" he declared. "I like cake, Grammy. And is that ice cream?"

"Yes, it is, sonny." She dipped some onto his plate, and Dorcas served him a piece of the layer cake. "Can you eat all that?" Mama questioned him.

Roy nodded eagerly, but his mother looked doubtful. "Don't give him too much now," Ellen warned. "He's already eaten a big supper."

After Roy had finished his dessert, Mama disappeared into the storeroom. Soon she returned, dragging something with her. It was a bright-red tricycle. "Is there a boy around here who would maybe like this?" she teased.

Roy perked up on his chair, looking very interested. "Is it for me, Grammy? Is it?" he asked with great excitement.

"I guess it's for the birthday boy," Mama affirmed with a chuckle.

"That's me!" Roy hopped off his stool and hurried to the tricycle, totally fascinated.

"Tell Grammy thank you," his mother reminded him.

"Thank you, Grammy," he said brightly as he tried the seat. Soon he was riding the tricycle around and around the kitchen while Mama came back to the table to finish her cake and ice cream with the rest.

The Upward Way

"Now, tomorrow, we need to do a lot of butchering," Papa declared after supper was over. "Seems we can't butcher enough meat to satisfy all our customers."

More butchering . . . How can we ever do more than we've been doing the last couple of weeks? Ruth wondered. *And yet, we always do sell out. People come here for meat too, and we don't have enough to fill the orders. O heavenly Father, give strength . . .* Mama looked sympathetically at Ruth, understanding the things Ruth did not say.

Butchering tomorrow meant killing the hogs yet that evening, heating plenty of water in the caldron to dip and scald the hogs, scraping the hair, and then hanging the scraped hogs up in the shed to bleed out overnight. Ruth knew she would need to help with all that too. Grimly she followed Papa out after supper. He and Mark took care of choosing the hogs to kill and the actual shooting. *At least Mark is here to do the shooting tonight!* she thought gratefully as she carried wood and built up the fire. Then she hung the caldron on its hook above the fireplace and pumped buckets of water to fill it. *I do not like to see the hogs die any more than Papa does,* she thought as she completed her process.

After the water was boiling, Papa and Mark dipped the hogs into it. After hanging the carcasses on hooks, Ruth helped with the scraping. "Four hogs for tomorrow," Mark said. "That should be enough to keep our womenfolk busy."

"Well, I hope it will give enough meat to sell," Papa injected. "Prices are high now, so we may as well sell as many of our hogs as we can."

"And we may as well sell them now while we still

The Upward Way

have fresh produce to sell too," Mark added.

Papa nodded, but did not speak as he industriously scraped and dipped his knife. Usually, after the fresh produce was all sold, Ruth knew, Papa would stop going to market for the winter. But still they would have some sale for fresh meat with all the customers who came to the farm every week.

As Ruth walked back to the house in the darkness, she saw a light in the garage. As she got closer, the overpowering odor of skunk coming from the garage almost choked her. Suddenly Kore burst out of the garage, holding his nose, and with tears streaming down his face.

"Oh, Kore!" Ruth cried out. "Are you all right? It smells awful. What happened?"

"I'm okay. But my eyes are burning like fire! And the smell!" Kore sputtered out. "I was in there working on the Buick, and a skunk came out from under some boxes along the wall. I opened the door and tried to chase it out, but it wasn't minded to go out of the warm garage. It ran back under the boxes, and the next thing I knew, it was caught in a rattrap. Then it sprayed, and, oh, what a smell!"

"How will you get it out of there?" Ruth asked.

"I guess I'll have to shoot it, and then carry it out. Do you want the job?"

"Oh, no! Not me, please!" Ruth gasped. "I probably couldn't hit it anyway, remember?"

While Ruth hurried on to the house, Kore ran for his rifle. Soon they heard the shot. After allowing time for Kore to get rid of the skunk, Mama sent Ruth to the garage with clean clothes and instructions for Kore, along

The Upward Way

with a bottle of homemade catsup. He was to wash in the barn, using the catsup first, and then plenty of the strong lye soap and water. And the clothes he had on were to be buried or burned! They were not to show up in the washhouse for her to wash.

"What does she want to do? Skin me?" Kore asked good-naturedly when Ruth passed on Mama's instructions. He did smell better when he appeared back in the house sometime later, but the smell lingered around the buildings for days.

The week passed, and Sunday came again. Ruth was glad to be at Grove Hill once more, especially after having missed the past Sunday. She rode to church with Mark and Ellen and the boys in Mark's brand new Buick.

"What a nice new car! And you have a new suit too," Ruth said. "Ellen couldn't have made that one for you, or I would have known about it."

Mark shook his head. "She didn't, but she would have liked to."

"Since I didn't have time," Ellen offered, "Della Sauder made it."

"It looks nice," Ruth complimented. "Della must do nice work."

"I was satisfied," Mark agreed. "Although I like better when my wife can do the sewing. Maybe after the boys are bigger and can help outside, she can do such things again." He turned toward Ellen and gave her a fond smile.

At church, Ruth took Roy's hand, leading him to the bench beside her cousin Grace and setting him primly beside her.

107

The Upward Way

"Hi, there, sonny,[17]" Grace whispered, chucking the small boy under the chin. Then she looked across Roy's head to Ruth. "Where were you last Sunday?" she asked quietly. "We missed you!"

"We went to Towamencin, since we were going to Norman and Sarah for dinner," Ruth whispered back. "Then we went to Finland in the evening."

Grace nodded. "You missed a good topic here at Young People's Meeting on Sunday night. Guess who had it."

Ruth tried to think. She had not heard any announcement about who it would be. "I don't know," she returned after a bit.

"It was David Peachey. You know, Uncle Claude's hired man. He did really well. I think he seems like a really fine young man, regardless of how poor he looks."

Ruth glanced across the church to where David Peachey was sitting, several benches ahead of the other youth boys. He surely did look shabby. Why didn't he wear better clothes? Her eyes quickly went to her brother Mark, sitting on the bench in front of David, with his fine new suit. She thought of the even finer new car sitting out in the lot and wondered absently if David Peachey even owned a car.

On Tuesday evening, Ruth and Dorcas went along with Papa to Bible study at the Pottstown Mission. Ruth enjoyed going to the small mission outreach and often caught a ride with someone who was going. She especially had enjoyed learning to know Alice Sterling and her family. Mrs. Sterling was a sincere seeker who had been

---

[17] Many close relatives called Roy "sonny."

The Upward Way

coming to church faithfully for many months, despite her husband's protests. Just on Sunday night, when she and the children had gotten home from church, he had been waiting for them and threatened to kill her and the children if she did not get out of the house immediately. She had fled in fear and then had contacted Brother Henry, who had come and taken her and the children to safety with one of the church families.

Papa had the topic that evening, bringing a splendid message on the need for temperance in the Christian life. How Ruth's heart ached as she realized how much Papa himself needed the teaching he was giving to others. But the admonition was good, and she took it to heart.

There was some coming and going while Papa was speaking, and Ruth wondered about the commotion. Suddenly Brother Henry Bechtel stood up, and in an unprecedented move, interrupted Papa, calling the whole congregation to prayer. "We have a special situation here this evening," he said soberly. "You have noticed that Mrs. Sterling and her children are here. I have just been made aware that her husband is waiting outside for the service to end, hoping to take the children from her by force when she leaves the building."

So, in the middle of Papa's topic, they all dropped to their knees and began to pray. After some time in prayer, a measure of peace was restored in many hearts, so that they went on with the service. Immediately after the service, Brother Henry ushered Mrs. Sterling and her children out by a side door, and hurried them away to Uncle Amos's, where they had been staying since Sunday.

Ruth was relieved to get home to the safety and

The Upward Way

security of her own home after such a traumatic evening. It was only after the service that she had learned that Mr. Sterling was armed and ready to do violence if his wishes were not granted. "Dear Father," Ruth prayed as she fell by her bed, "thank You for keeping us all from harm this evening. Be with Mrs. Sterling and the children, and keep them in Your care as they seek to know You more perfectly."

The rest of the week was full of a variety of activities for Ruth—husking corn in the snow, cutting and splitting wood for Ellen, lots of butchering, and pulling more turnips. Last but not least, she helped Kore set his traps on Friday evening. She had been looking forward to a quiet evening in the house, but—wonder of wonders—Kore invited her to go along to help him.

"Hey, Ruth, want to go along to help set traps?" he asked after supper.

"Well"—Ruth thought a bit—"I guess I could." She knew he always appreciated help to carry all his paraphernalia on the long walk. And maybe it would be a time to have a confidential chat with him. He had seemed more open the last week, and Ruth was always glad for an opportunity to show a sisterly interest in him.

After Kore gathered his things together, Ruth offered to carry the lantern and part of the load, to which he cheerfully agreed. "Kore," she began after he had set the first trap, "I've been so thankful to see you more cheerful the last while. Are things going better for you spiritually?" Ruth hoped he had seen his need for a Saviour and given his life to Him. But she was afraid to ask specifically, as that topic was not something freely discussed in

The Upward Way

their church circles at that time. Many young people did not respond to the call of salvation until their late teens.

Kore shrugged, but a pleased grin lit up his face. "I want to live right, Ruth. I really do. It's just so hard!"

"It is hard in our own strength, Kore," Ruth admitted. "In fact, it's impossible. We have to have the help of our heavenly Father. And He is always ready to help us when we call on Him."

Kore pondered that for a time. Then he said, "I know. I wasn't reading my Bible for a while, like I should have been. But now I am taking time every day to do that. And to pray. It does help me to be more cheerful, I know. And it helps me not to get mad about things too."

Ruth's heart was happy as she tramped along. She had prayed so long for Kore, that he would choose to follow the Lord. Would this effort last? She knew it would if Kore would do his part. "Keep on reading your Bible and praying and trusting the Lord for help. It is only by God's help that you will be able to defeat your enemy," she encouraged him.

Kore nodded. "It would help if I wouldn't need to go to public school and be around those boys all the time," he said. "And then when I'm home, I'm working all the time. It's hard, when you're so tired, to take the time to read and pray—when you'd rather be sleeping!"

"I know, Kore. I wish too that you wouldn't need to be with the evil influences at school. But God will help you. And He'll give you extra strength too, for all the hard work here at home. I've found that the Lord blesses with extra strength when we call upon Him. It isn't your doings that we are so busy. And I believe God sees all

The Upward Way

that and meets our needs because of it."

Kore stopped to place another trap. Ruth held the lantern high enough for him to see to drive in the stake and then set the trap. Suddenly the trap sprang shut, catching his gloved fingers.

A swearword escaped Kore's lips. He stopped short with a guilty look as he carefully released his fingers. "I'm sorry, Ruth. That word just popped out. I didn't mean it!"

"That's right, Kore," Ruth encouraged him. "If you do fail, confess it right away. But you had better tell the Lord you are sorry too." Her heart cringed, even as she spoke. It was at school that he heard such words. If only they had Christian schools.

Kore nodded as he reset the trap, more carefully this time. "I can be glad I had gloves on at least, or I might be missing a couple fingers!"

Several sets later, another trap sprang on Kore's fingers. But this time, he did not respond by swearing. He simply grimaced until his fingers were loose, and then he gave Ruth a crooked grin. Ruth noted and appreciated the difference. *Dear Lord, please help Kore as he tries to live a life that honors You. . . .*

Ruth enjoyed the long tramp through the snow up to the spring where the creek began, helping Kore set traps all along the creek banks. Wildlife was plentiful, and Kore hoped to harvest many pelts to sell. But most of all, she appreciated the heart-to-heart talk that she had been able to have with him.

Instead of walking back to the house with Kore after the trap line was finished, Ruth crossed the creek and

The Upward Way

went up the hill to visit Mrs. Cook. Kore took the lantern, so she had a dark walk. But the moon was bright enough on the snow cover that she was able to see to reach the little house set back off the road in a coppice.

Mrs. Cook welcomed her happily. "Well, well, if it isn't my Ruthie," she said. "How are you, my dear?"

"I'm good, Mrs. Cook. How are you? Are you able to keep warm these cold winter nights? Do you have enough wood cut, and everything?"

"My boy, he comes home sometimes to split wood for me. Yes, yes, I'm getting along about as well as an old body can."

Ruth glanced at the woodbox. "Why, Mrs. Cook, your woodbox is about empty. It's going to be a cold night! May I fill it for you?"

Mrs. Cook nodded gratefully. "I didn't know how I would get that done. I'd be much obliged, dear. While you're doing that, I'll brew some tea." She hobbled to the sink and filled the teapot. Then she stirred up the fire in the cookstove and added a few more pieces of wood. "There now, as soon as it boils, we'll add some dried mint." Ruth noticed the mint hanging in bunches from the rafters above the stove, along with strings of dried and shriveled hot peppers and green beans.

After carrying in armload after armload of wood from the woodshed behind the house, Ruth finally felt satisfied that Mrs. Cook would have enough wood to last for a few days at least. "There," she said, "now you should be able to keep warm till I can come and fill it for you again."

"Thank you so much, dear. Now, would you have a cup of tea with me?" Mrs. Cook was already pouring

113

The Upward Way

some of the pleasant-smelling mint tea into two cups.

Before she knew it, an hour had passed and Ruth knew she must get home, or her mother would be worried about her. "Thank you for the tea, Mrs. Cook," she said. "I'll try to bring a dressed chicken up for you tomorrow. Then I can fill the woodbox for you again for over Sunday."

"And I'll send a pumpkin home with you. My pumpkins did so well, and I don't know what to do with them all."

"That's nice of you. Mama will be happy for one. We all like pumpkin pie," Ruth said, resolving to bring a small pie up for Mrs. Cook after they were baked.

"God bless you for coming, Ruthie dear." The old lady hobbled to the door and said a fond good-bye as Ruth started out the snowy sidewalk.

The walk down the road to the creek, over the bridge, and up the hill to their own farm was a cold one, but the night was bright with moonlight and starshine. Ruth, as always, enjoyed the night sky, finding and identifying the constellations, and thinking about the great Creator of it all.

Mama was sitting on the kitchen rocker, reading her Bible when Ruth came in. With a good-night, Ruth headed for her stairway. Mama sat up straighter. "Where are you going so fast, Ruth? I know it's after ten o'clock, but I hardly get to see anything of you anymore. You're outside all day, and when you do come in, you're ready to go to bed. Where were you this evening?"

Ruth came back to stand beside her mother's chair. Impulsively she leaned over and planted a big kiss on her forehead. As she straightened up again, she said, "Sorry, Mama, that I didn't tell you. I went along with Kore to set traps, and then I walked back by Mrs. Cook's." Ruth

The Upward Way

went on to tell her mother about the time spent there. "She seemed so glad for company. We should go over more often," Ruth finished.

Mama sighed. "Ach, yes, we're so busy that we don't take time for the neighbors as we should."

"Well, you and Papa are busy with church work too," Ruth told her. "It seems almost every day you either go somewhere in relation to church work, or someone is here. Or we have other visitors."

"That may be. But we work too hard, and we wouldn't need to do all the things we do." Mama sighed again. "But—well—you know how Papa is."

A workaholic! Ruth thought, but did not say. She already knew how Mama felt about all the work projects that Papa was into. And she also knew how very weary she herself so often was due to their intense work schedule. Would they really have to work so hard to pay their bills and have to give to others? She knew that Papa gave liberally to needs in the church, but he was very careful with how he spent money himself or with how much he paid the family.

She knew also that some families had daily worship together. But, even though Mama had suggested it at times in the past, Papa had felt too busy for that. She wished they would have such times of sharing spiritually together. She did not remember ever having heard her mother pray, though of course she knew that she did in private.

"Well, go on to bed, Ruth," Mama went on finally. "You need all the rest you can get. Good night."

Gladly Ruth went, grateful for the love and concern of her mother.

Chapter Six

November 25, 1933, Saturday. *How can I describe the burden that is resting on my heart tonight? We had special services at Grove Hill this afternoon in relation to the ordination for deacon tomorrow. There were a number of visiting ministers and bishops. Brother John Dressler from Richfield had a topic and so did Brother D. A. Burkholder from the Lancaster area. They had very inspiring messages, mostly relating to the work of ordination, but it was hard for me to concentrate as I should, wondering who would be chosen from our congregation. Believe me, dear Journal, if I had known who it would be, it would have made it all the harder! After the nominations were taken in the counsel room, Brother Howard Bean announced that there were two who had received enough nominations—John Gants and Mark Clemmer! I was so shocked to think that my brother may be ordained. I know Papa is, and many of my uncles, but somehow it is different when it is my own generation. I tried to encourage my dear Ellen in the Lord, but I doubt either of them will sleep much tonight. For that matter, neither will some of the rest of us!*

How the days pass when one is busy, Ruth thought one Friday morning as her alarm clock wakened her at the

The Upward Way

usual four-thirty. She did feel more rested than sometimes. Maybe it was better after all that she had stayed home last evening rather than go to Uncle Henry's for the young people's singing. Ruth thought how that often there was more foolishness than actual singing anyway. Her mind flitted back unexpectedly to the previous summer when she and her cousin Nancy had ridden to the singing on horseback, wearing scarves instead of coverings, and how convicted she had felt later for it. Remorse hit her again that she could have done such a thing, but she had asked forgiveness and vowed never again to dishonor her Lord in that way. Even if she tried to do right, Ruth thought now, she often felt guilty and depressed after coming home from an evening spent with the young people. Many of them did not seem to take life very seriously. And was she really any better?

But, Lord, You know my heart. I want to please You and to be a godly example to others as well. She dressed for the day and turned to her Bible reading with anticipation. Kneeling beside her bed, she opened her Bible to 1 Timothy 4: "Let no man despise thy youth; but be thou an example of the believers, in word, in conversation, in charity, in spirit, in faith, in purity." *Thank You, Lord, for this Scripture,* she prayed in her heart. *It is just what I was thinking about!*

For a time she propped her chin on her hands and stared off into the darkness beyond the glow of her oil lamp. *Timothy was but a youth, and yet God could use him in His service. How good of the apostle Paul to take such an interest in him and give him so much encouragement.* She thought of the young minister and wondered

117

The Upward Way

how he had the courage to face the antagonism of unbelievers, and finally physical persecution. *Lord, help me to truly be strong for Thee, and to be faithful, even though we don't face physical harm for our faith in our day.*

For a long time she knelt there, her mind full of many thoughts—thoughts of service for the Lord, thoughts of the future and what it held for her, thoughts of the coming ordination at Grove Hill, and wondering who would be called to fill the place and help her papa.

When she heard Papa filling the wood stove downstairs, she quickly got up from her knees, put out her oil lamp, and hurried down her garret stairs, before he could call her. "Good morning, Papa," she greeted him, but he only grunted in reply as he pulled his work shoes from beside the cookstove and sat down to put them on. A sadness came over Ruth. She so often wished for a better relationship with her father, but she did not know what to do about it. Bravely she determined to be a more faithful daughter and not give him cause to find fault with her. *With God's help, I will be "an example of the believers,"* she thought as she hurried into the washhouse for her barn coat.

Mark was letting the cows into the barn from the barnyard when she ran in the front barn door. He returned her good-morning, but not with his usual vim, she thought. Was something bothering him?

The day seemed very busy, even though Papa and Mama did not go to market in Amityville. Papa did deliver several orders of turnips and meat, and Mark and Ellen took meat to Parker Ford to sell. Ruth spent much of the day cleaning up around the barn—gathering trash,

The Upward Way

pulling and cutting down dead weed stalks outside the barn, washing windows and sweeping down cobwebs inside the barn—as well as the regular Friday work, such as baking, trimming the oil lamps, and cleaning the house. Dorcas left her sewing to help with the baking.

When Friday's work was finished, Ruth started with Saturday's regular chores, knowing that Saturday would be busy enough with only a half day for working. She washed and simonized[18] theirs and Mark's cars and filled the straw and hay funnels in the barn. When Mark and Ellen came home, she wished they would give her some help, but she did not see much of them. After his nap, Roy came out to help her wash the cars. He was all dressed up in his little coat and hat. "I like to wash the car, Aunt Rufie," he said happily, scrubbing diligently with the rag that Ruth gave him. Ruth laughed at him, wet to his elbows, and hoped he would not catch a cold.

By Friday suppertime, Ruth was ready to quit and spend the rest of the evening reading. She hoped Papa would not decide to go somewhere for church in the evening, as he often did on Friday evenings. But she was failing to reckon with his unflagging energy! Supper over, he pushed back his chair. "I heard that J. B. Smith is to be at Frazer this evening to speak on prophecy. From the Book of Revelation," he explained further. "I thought I would like to go and hear him. Anyone want to go along?"

Mama shook her head no. "John Dressler's will be coming here overnight, Papa. Did you forget that?"

---

[18] A local expression used for waxing. Possibly the term came from a brand of wax that was used.

The Upward Way

"They likely won't get here until late," Papa returned. "We should be back before they get here. Brother John said they wouldn't leave until after supper out there, and it takes a good four hours to drive here from the Richfield area."

Dorcas was looking eager. "I'll go with you," she said.

"Count me out," Kore said. "I'm ready to hit the sack."

Ruth was not sure what she should do. Oh, well, she guessed she could sit in church as well as she could sit at home. And she would enjoy hearing the topic—prophetic discussions always greatly interested her. And she might even see her good friend, Emily Brackbill, who often attended there. "I'll go too," she said. "Unless you need me for something, Mama. Are the beds ready?"

Mama nodded. "Dorcas got the spare room ready this afternoon for the Dresslers. We'll need to get some more beds ready tomorrow night, since Uncle John's are planning to be here then too. And maybe Uncle Amos's—depending who is named in the service tomorrow." She looked at Ruth fondly. "I think everything that needs to be done this evening is done. Go along if you wish."

Papa glanced at the clock. "Well, we should leave in a half hour. Can you be ready in time?"

Ruth was not sorry she had gone when she got back to her own garret bedroom that evening. Many thoughts of God's wonderful works through the eras of time filled her heart as she prepared for the night. *And all that still awaits us in the future . . .* she pondered further. *Dear heavenly Father, may I be counted worthy to be part of Your glorious plan for the church.*

The squeaky springs sounded wonderfully welcoming as Ruth crawled wearily into bed, and she relaxed

The Upward Way

with a thankful sigh.

The afternoon service at Grove Hill began the next day at two o'clock. Gravely Ruth rode with her family along to the service. Mark and Ellen had arrived just before them and were walking soberly toward the meetinghouse. Mark carried Robert, and Ellen led Roy by the hand.

Ruth hurried to catch up with them as soon as she was out of the car. "Shall I keep one of the boys?" she asked as she fell in step beside Ellen. She often did during Sunday services because Mark had a regular Sunday school class, and sometimes Ellen taught too.

"Maybe we should keep them today," Mark said. "But thanks anyway." He smiled at her, but it was then that Ruth noticed how drawn and tense he appeared.

"Are you all right, Mark?" she could not help blurting out.

"Oh, I think so," he returned, forcing a smile.

But as she slid onto her regular bench, Ruth thought back to that drawn look. Surely he did not expect to be included in those nominated! Her thoughts pitched and tossed tumultuously. Mark was so young—only twenty-six, and seldom was anyone ordained in their conference who was under thirty. But did he think he would be? Neither Mark nor Ellen had suggested feeling that way, at least not that she knew about. A heaviness settled upon her heart that she could not dispel, not even by telling the Lord about it.

The messages by the visiting ministers were challenging and intense, and many in the audience were shedding tears as the afternoon progressed. Ruth glanced at Mark

The Upward Way

from time to time and could not help but notice his somber attitude. Ellen sat in front of her, busy with meeting the needs of her little son, but with an anxious, tearful face. *Dear Lord, please give them strength,* Ruth prayed earnestly, hardly knowing how to pray for them.

Finally the local ministry and visiting bishops went out into a small side room to receive the nominations from the congregation. Everyone waited in prayerful silence as one by one the brethren went out to give their nominations. After what seemed like a very long time and no more brethren went out, the ministers all returned. Brother Howard Bean took his place behind the preacher's stand. The entire congregation seemed to be waiting in breathless anticipation until Brother Bean made his announcement.

With the announcement, Ruth noticed Ellen's chin drop till it rested on the top of Robert's head. Then Ellen's tears began to flow, and Ruth's flowed with hers.

As soon as the service was over, Ruth hurried to Ellen, taking Robert from her arms. Then Ruth squeezed Ellen's hand, and they shed tears together. "God will give grace," Ruth said softly as soon as she could speak. "Just trust Him. He will not call you to anything that He won't give you the strength to carry out."

"Oh, I know all that in my head," Ellen returned humbly. "But right now it is hard to feel it in my heart."

The barn seemed quiet that evening as Kore and Ruth did the milking and other chores. Neither Papa nor Mark were there to help them. Ruth was deep in thought, and Kore seemed content to give her plenty of space. Finally the work was finished, and Ruth went to the house, eager

The Upward Way

to go to her room and spend time in prayer. Dorcas had fixed a pot of potato soup, but Ruth did not want to eat. She started for the stairs, but Dorcas called her back.

"I don't care if you don't eat, Ruth," she said. "But could you help me get ready for Uncle John's and Uncle Amos's? They will be here for the night, you know. And John Dressler's will be here again too."

Ruth thought about Uncle John Stauffer's. And Uncle Amos Burkholder's. Both were from the Harrisonburg, Virginia, area. How could they get to their area so fast? And would any of their children be along? When she asked Dorcas, she had a ready answer.

"Neither of them brought their families along this time. They traveled up to Lancaster yesterday to be with friends. So they are just traveling from there this evening."

"Oh," Ruth responded. Then she added, "I would have been happy to see Lois again. But it will be fewer beds to make up if none of the children came with them. Even so, where will we put the third couple? Dressler's can have the room they had last evening, and Uncle John's the other spare room. But what about Uncle Amos's?"

"Mama said to fix the parlor for them to sleep in. We'll have to get that mattress down from the attic—or rather you will have to. And we'll have to start the coal-oil stove in there to get it decently warm."

Dorcas offered to stay up until Mama and Papa got home and the company came. "Thank you, Dorcas," Ruth said. "I feel so tired. And I'll need to get up early to milk tomorrow morning for Mark again, I suppose."

After spending time in prayer, Ruth was able to lie down in peace and sleep.

123

The Upward Way

It was very pleasant the next morning to sit down to breakfast with their visitors. Ruth had always greatly admired Uncle John and Aunt Lydia for their spiritual convictions. They seemed like such a godly couple, deeply interested in and concerned for the future of the church. Uncle Amos's were different in that respect. Uncle Amos was a piano tuner by trade, and they attended a more progressive church than what Uncle John's did. But still they were a pleasant couple, and Ruth enjoyed visiting with them.

"So Ruth is here! We missed seeing you last evening," Uncle John said to her after prayer.

"I'm sorry. I wasn't trying to be unsociable—I was just very tired and decided to go to bed," Ruth said with a smile.

"Oh, that's okay. I'm sure you had a busy and stressful day," Aunt Lydia consoled her. "Lois was sorry not to be able to come along, but she sent a letter for you."

"Oh, good! I should try to get one written to send back with you for her."

"By the way, when are you coming for a term of Bible school at EMS?" Aunt Lydia asked.

Ruth looked expectantly at Papa, but he was busily conversing with Uncle Amos and had not heard the question. "I don't know," Ruth answered. "I would like to come next winter if Papa allows me to."

"John says he appreciates Charles Derstine in his Bible classes," Aunt Lydia continued with a knowing twinkle in her eyes.

Ruth smiled with satisfaction at this mention of her special friend. Charles had mentioned in a letter that he had Brother J. L. Stauffer as instructor for his Bible study

The Upward Way

classes and that he really appreciated him as a teacher. But she had not known what Uncle John thought of Charles. "It must work both ways," Ruth said. "Charles says he really enjoys his Bible classes!"

The ordination was planned for the afternoon. Of course, Sarah and Norman came to the service. Sarah seated herself beside Ruth, giving her a look that set Ruth's tears to flowing again. Robert, sitting on Ruth's lap, looked up at her and gently patted her face. Ruth had to smile in spite of herself. She squeezed him and then sat quietly, watching the crowds of people gathering in, filling the Grove Hill meetinghouse full to overflowing. People were standing along the walls, and the vestibule and inside entrance steps were also crowded full.

Uncle John Stauffer preached the message, and Ruth listened with open heart. He had such a way of making truth live, and she rejoiced for the opportunity to hear him speak again. Robert sat quietly on her lap, seeming to sense the solemnity of the occasion. Then it was time for the books to be chosen; and just as Ruth had feared from the start, the lot was found in Mark's book.

How solemn and dignified Mark looked as Brother Jonas Mininger gave the charge. Many thoughts also filled Ruth's heart. But she did not think about how much Mark's call to leadership would affect life at home and on the farm. Those realizations did not come until the months that followed.

Chapter Seven

January 1, 1934, Monday. *The beginning of another year! The old year is past, and we are one year nearer to our eternal destiny. Which destiny will it be? Oh, that I could live closer to Christ. I pray for more faith and a greater infilling of the Holy Spirit. I have made only one resolution—to try harder to "press toward the mark for the prize of the high calling of God in Christ Jesus." The past weeks have been so cold—temperatures below zero, and windy, but yesterday and today have been much warmer. The snow is going fast. Today we fed a wayfaring man and had a good talk with him. He took tracts along and promised to read them. The story had a wonderful ending! Mark's were here for dinner, and we were at their place for supper. I wrote to Charles and thanked him for the lovely bureau set that he sent for Christmas.*

"Good morning, beautiful world, on the first day of a new year," Ruth said as she stood at her window. She gazed out into the blueness of the moonlit snow. All was quiet in the house. But she lit her oil lamp and proceeded with her morning routine.

The Upward Way

Sometime later she stepped out of the washhouse and into the new morning. "Oh, it's so warm out here!" she exclaimed under her breath. She stomped through the snow to the thermometer hanging on the washhouse wall and held up the lantern to it—forty degrees! Little wonder it felt so mild, after several weeks of below-zero weather! She looked at the thermometer again, hardly able to believe she was seeing it right. But it had to be above freezing, she concluded, as she heard the distinctive sound of dripping from the rooftops around her. With joy in her steps, she hurried across the road to the barn.

"Did you see that it's above freezing?" she asked Mark, who was just then coming from the back of the barn.

"Feels like spring!" he returned with a smile.

"I'm so tired of carrying water for the cows! Maybe their water bowls and the trough will finally thaw out."

"And maybe the snow will melt so we won't have to take the milk out with the horse and sleigh," Mark added. "But you think that is fun, don't you?"

He added that to tease, Ruth knew, after her mishap the past Friday. The train had passed noisily, picking up steam, as she was coming back to the buildings after taking out the milk. The horse had spooked and taken off running, with her bouncing along on the sleigh and hanging on to the reins for dear life. Finally she had been able to get control, but not until she had had a frightful scare. When Papa had heard it, he had just been thankful that she had already unloaded the cans of milk so that they had not gotten dumped all over the countryside. *He seemed to have had no thought for my safety,* Ruth

The Upward Way

thought now, *and didn't appear thankful at all that I was unharmed when I got home!* But it *was* funny, she had to admit as she thought back on it now. No doubt the neighbors were watching out their windows, wondering why she was tearing home at such a rate!

"Mrs. Watts asked us about it yesterday," Mark went on as he got his milk stool and pail, "when Ellen and I took a chicken over. She thought the horse was running away, and she hoped you got home safely."

"I figured the neighbors were all watching," Ruth said, able to laugh now. "No doubt it looked hilarious!"

Mark began milking the first cow while Ruth sat down to hers. "If the snow melts, I'll miss going everywhere in the sleigh," Mark continued after a bit. "We'll have to get the cars out of the garage again."

"I've enjoyed using the sleigh too," Ruth conceded. "But it was awfully cold going places. Like Thursday evening when we went down to Milton's to the singing, it was four above when we came home, and windy. Dorcas and I were about frozen. Kore said he was just fine and couldn't figure out what we were complaining about, but then he was all wrapped up in the wool blanket."

"By the way, where is Kore?" Mark asked.

"I haven't seen him," Ruth said. "Maybe he is out feeding the hogs. He isn't feeding the cows, because I saw Papa at the silo." Ruth thought soberly about how Kore's resolutions of some weeks before had seemed to evaporate into thin air. Still, she continued to pray for him.

"I wonder if he is even out of the house yet. He hasn't been doing so well at getting out the last few days, has he?" Mark got up, carrying his pail of milk to empty it

The Upward Way

into a can in the milk house.

Ruth's thoughts turned to the milk house as she watched Mark go. As they filled cans, they set them in a trough that had fresh water running through it, to cool the milk quickly. A coal-oil stove in the milk house kept the water in there from freezing. The cream separator was in the milk house too. Papa often separated the milk when prices were low. Then Mama made butter to sell from the cream, and the buttermilk she used to make some of her different kinds of cheeses. What was left, after all the uses Mama could possibly put the cream to, was put out for the hogs. And how they loved those milky by-products!

Right now milk prices were fairly good, so they sold most of the milk from their fifteen Holsteins. That was what prompted the sleigh rides every morning out to the pickup station, where the train passed to pick up the farmers' full milk cans and return the empty ones.

Ruth carried her full pail to the milk house to empty. Then she sat down to the second cow. Mark was already on his third one. "How can you milk so fast?" she asked.

"I've been at it for more years than you have. And have stronger hands," Mark returned with a smile.

Just then Kore appeared, still looking very sleepy. "What am I to be doing?" he asked Mark, none too pleasantly.

Mark looked at him with yearning in the look. "I don't know how much of the feeding Papa has done. Why don't you check with him?"

"I don't want to talk to the old man!" Kore burst out in subdued vehemence. "He'll give me an earful for not

The Upward Way

being out earlier."

Always eager for peace, Mark sent him up to feed the pigs.

"But it's as dark as a wolf's mouth up at the pigpens," Kore complained. "Can I take a lantern?"

"Take the one hanging up there by the barn door." Mark stopped his milking long enough to point to the front barn entrance.

When Kore and the lantern had disappeared out the door, Mark said, "What's wrong with that boy lately?"

Ruth shook her head. "He hasn't been very pleasant, has he? I had high hopes for him after he shared with me back in early November his desire to do right, but it seems he is resentful ever since you were ordained. He said something about it to me afterward, something about having two hot-headed deacons in the family. I told him he knows that isn't true. And also, doesn't he think that God planned this? I know that underneath his thorniness, he is a boy under conviction, and I just wish I knew how to help him."

"I'm glad for the stronger teaching on the new birth that we are getting in our churches lately," Mark said. "It has bothered me for years that not many of our youth respond to the call of God until they were older. For that matter we didn't either."

"And our ministry has gotten more open about having revival meetings and things like that," Ruth added. "Papa has said that such services were frowned upon as belonging to worldly churches not many years back."

Mark nodded. "I know. I can remember a little of that feeling. And so many of our youth left the church because

The Upward Way

their spiritual needs were not met, it seemed. Now, with good evangelistic preaching, and more teaching in our homes, young teenagers are recognizing the call of God sooner, and responding to it."

"I'm glad. But still there is Kore . . ." Ruth stopped, trying to think through what she really felt. "He knows what he ought to do, I think, and he would like to be a Christian. But he is so confused about what, or who, is right."

"Well," Mark said thoughtfully, "we can keep praying for him. He does have some deep spiritual needs. It would help if he wouldn't go home to his mother so often. And yet, it isn't fair to deprive them of seeing each other—they do belong together, you know. But he goes to some of the more liberal churches on weekends when he is home too, and ends up not knowing what he ought to be doing."

"Why is there such a difference among our churches?" Ruth asked, voicing a question that had been bothering her for some time.

"You mean . . ." Mark began.

"I mean, our discipline[19] states that women are not to wear hats or fashionable clothing. But some do. And it says that we should wear a plain devotional covering with strings used for tying and not for ornament. But some don't wear any covering at all except for church. I've seen the 'cap boxes' in the anterooms in some of our churches, where the women store their coverings from

---

[19] J.C. Wenger, *History of the Mennonites of the Franconia Conference* (Telford, PA: Franconia Mennonite Historical Society, 1937), p. 433.

The Upward Way

Sunday to Sunday, like at Blooming Glen. And many of the women who wear strings let them dangle down their backs rather than tying them." Ruth's hands were still as she thought for a moment, and the cow she was milking turned to look at her. "If we have a discipline, why don't we keep it?"

She could have added that the discipline forbad costly or stylish cars, but many—including her own brother Mark—had a car that she would place in that category.

"Well, Ruth, there are things that the leaders will need to address. But sometimes I wonder if we will ever get people back in line where they ought to be. There are just so many worldly influences that bear on what we do. And another thing we face is the affluence of many of our people, even in spite of the Depression. They have the money to buy fancy things that they would otherwise not be tempted to have."

"And some of our churches still use wine at Communion!" Ruth shook her head. "I can't believe it when even the world has so much to say about prohibition."

"I know," Mark agreed. "I'm thankful that Grove Hill changed to grape juice. But I wish all our churches would. I'm afraid using wine is an offense to some."

Ruth appreciated the talk with Mark and pondered on it off and on through the day. She was glad she could talk with him in a way she would not have felt free to talk with Papa.

"What do you girls want to do today?" Mama asked after breakfast. She would go along with Papa to the Souderton Home as she usually did on the first Monday of every month. While he met with the board, she spent

The Upward Way

the time visiting relatives or friends, either in the home or nearby.

"I was thinking of doing some baking," Dorcas said. "Iona suggested some of our families could do some baking for the Philadelphia Mission."

"Why don't you bake some graham cookies?" Mama suggested. "They appreciated them the last time we sent some."

"Some of the girls were saying last week at the singing that they were doing sewing for bundles to go to Canada."

"Oh, yes," Mama said. "That was brought up at the last deacons' meeting, Papa said. Most of all, they need children's clothing and blankets. We should have things ready for when some of the ministering brethren go for their visit later this month."

"Sounds as though we'll have enough to do today," Ruth quipped. She was glad for the colder weather that brought an end to most of the fieldwork. How nice to spend some time in the house with baking and sewing, chores which she very much enjoyed but seldom had time for during busy times of the year.

Ruth was sitting at the sewing machine in the sitting room near noon, busily sewing the seams on a little girl's dress. She pushed the treadle purposefully, hurrying to finish before dinnertime. Dorcas had offered to get dinner, and Ruth heard her now, stepping around in the kitchen. They had invited Mark's down to dinner, since Papa and Mama would not be there. Suddenly, someone walking on the road drew her attention. She stood up for a better look out the gable windows. It was a man, and he

The Upward Way

looked like a tramp with a huge pack on his back. Now he was turning toward the house. After peering intently at it for a while, he started hesitantly up the sidewalk.

Ruth turned and hurried noiselessly to the kitchen. "Dorcas!" she hissed. "There's someone coming up the sidewalk right now, probably someone wanting dinner. What shall we do?"

Dorcas limped to the window. "I'm sure I don't know. He surely does look like a tramp."

"I think we have basically two choices—pretend nobody is home and let him go on (which wouldn't be kind or Christian), or invite him to come in and give him dinner."

By the time Ruth had finished saying this in a loud whisper, a knock sounded on the door. Giving Dorcas a helpless look, she went to the door. "May I help you?" she asked politely.

The man looked at her hopefully. "Mind if I sit by your fire a minute, miss? I'm frightful cold."

"Come in and warm yourself," Ruth said, truly feeling sorry for the helpless-looking old man. "Here, I'll set a chair by the wood stove for you."

Carefully scraping his dirty feet on the mat, he came in. "Aw, miss, this is wonderful," he rasped out as he dropped his pack wearily beside him and sat down.

"I'm sure you must be cold and weary," Ruth sympathized. "You just sit there and rest a bit. Soon we will have some dinner ready, and you can have a plate of warm food."

Dorcas was eyeing Ruth skeptically from the table, where she was adding an extra plate. But Ruth ignored

The Upward Way

her. She was caring for the hungry and cold as Jesus commanded, and she felt no compunctions whatsoever about it.

Soon Mark and Ellen and the boys came down the hill. Kore rushed in, after his run home from school, planning to eat lunch at home that day. Acting as though nothing was out of the ordinary, they all sat down together with their unexpected guest.

They did not act strange, Ruth thought later, but the man did. She thought he seemed as though he were listening for something or somebody as he gazed around in a searching manner. He surely was not a robber, or anything like that, was he? The thought troubled her a bit, but what else could they have done for a wayfarer?

She was happy that Mark did most of the talking. He treated the man, who said his name was Randall Sheets, as any other guest. Mark kept up a pleasant conversation through most of the meal, finally coming to spiritual issues. No, the man did not go to church. And, no, he did not read the Bible, even though he had one in his possession. "Would you like to go along with us to church on Sunday?" Mark asked as the man was scraping his plate clean.

"Well, now, can't say that I ever thought much about going to church," he returned.

"We would be happy to have you go with us," Mark went on. "Where could we pick you up on Sunday mornings?"

Mr. Sheets acted as though he did not know how to respond. "Well, I live up Pottstown way," he hedged. "But let me think about it."

The Upward Way

Mark nodded. "You said you have a Bible. I would encourage you to read it and learn how to follow the Lord Jesus. That is the only way to true happiness and peace."

Ruth got up and went to Papa's desk, sorting out a selection of tracts. "Here," she offered the man, coming back to the table, "take these along with you and read them."

"Thank you," Mr. Sheets said. "And thank you for your kindness. If you don't mind, I'll be off now."

Ruth watched him as he gathered his pack and arranged it over his back again. Something about his face did not match the grayness of his hair, Ruth thought as she studied him more closely. His face looked young. And he did not look like a seasoned tramp or like someone who spent his time outdoors, wandering the countryside.

They watched the man trudge out the walk and turn down the road to the creek.

"Well, what do you think of that?" Dorcas finally burst out. "Something didn't ring true about that man, I don't think!"

"I didn't think so either," asserted Kore, who had not said a word during the whole meal. "He was a fake, if you ask me!"

"Now, now," Ellen said. "Don't jump to conclusions. He did seem to have a genuine spiritual interest."

"I thought so too," Mark agreed.

Ruth was beginning to wonder if she had done the right thing to invite him in. "Well, if he's a burglar and comes back to burgle us tonight while we're all sleeping in our beds, it will be all my fault!" She felt half foolish and tried to speak lightly. But still she was troubled.

"I wouldn't worry about it," Mark comforted her. "You did the best you knew. The Lord expects us to help out wherever we can and whatever the need."

Ruth helped Dorcas do the dishes and then brought in the laundry. "It isn't going to dry outside, damp as it is," she said. "I may as well hang it on the lines in the washhouse."

"You could fill the big clothes rack and put it here by the wood stove. It would dry fast in here," Dorcas suggested. She was emptying cheese curds out of cheesecloth bags into pans on the cookstove to melt.

"I'm hungry for ice cream," Ruth asserted as she hung wash on the wooden rack. "Shall we mix up the pudding for it?"

"I don't care. Maybe Kore could break up some ice from the creek, and then turn the ice cream for us after school this afternoon."

After Ruth mixed a kettle of pudding for ice cream, she carried it out to the washhouse to cool. Then she got her coat and boots and went out to where Mark was working on a new chicken house. He was hoping to have room for several hundred more laying hens when he got the house finished. Getting a hammer and a molasses bucket half full of nails, she walked to where he was nailing boards up onto the frame. "Got a job for me?" she asked.

Mark nodded. "I was hoping you'd show up again today," he said. "The more nailers, the faster this house will be finished."

Ellen came out to help too, after the boys were down

The Upward Way

for naps. "Why don't you eat supper with us?" she asked. "We have all that venison from the deer Mark got the other week. If it gets warm, it won't keep. I guess I could can the meat—and might need to can some anyway. But we may as well use up fresh as much as we can; I already have more meat canned than we'll use in the next year!"

"I can't speak for Dorcas," Ruth said, laughing, "but I'll be glad to come for venison roast."

Kore joined them at the chicken house soon after he was home from school. Ruth thought of the ice cream waiting to be frozen. "Oh, by the way, Kore, if someone turns the freezer, we can have fresh ice cream for supper."

"I'll be glad to!" Kore agreed with more enthusiasm than was his wont. "That would be better than milking any day. I might even get to sample the ice cream!"

"Well, you don't need to run off yet," Ruth said laughingly when Kore dropped the hammer he was using and looked ready to fly away. "It will be time enough if you go to turn it when we go to do the milking."

"What about the ice?" Kore asked.

"Oh." Ruth thought a bit. "You should probably go and cut some out of the creek while it is still light." Kore whisked off his nail apron and was already galloping off down the hill when Ruth called after him, "But be sure to hurry back!"

"Sure! Sure!" floated back to them. And soon Kore disappeared into the garage, where he would find a wooden tub, the ice pick, and the coaster wagon. He was soon back with the ice and again nailing.

"I'd like to stay at this till dark," Mark announced. "We can milk after dark. We may as well work as long

The Upward Way

as we can on a mild day like this."

It was growing too dark to see by soon after five o'clock, and Mark and Ruth began cleaning up to quit for the day. Before long, Kore too had shed his carpentry tools. "I'll go turn the freezer now," he said, and was soon loping down the hill toward the house. Ellen had gone to their house earlier to start the roast and to tend the boys.

Ruth felt famished by the time the milking and feeding were finished. After washing up, she and Kore each took a handle of the tub, where the frozen ice cream was seasoning in its brine, and carried it up the hill. Dorcas followed more slowly after them.

Mark's were ready and waiting, the boys eagerly watching for "Aunt Rufie." After their silent prayer at the table, Ellen looked at Roy. "Why do we bow our heads before we eat?" she asked him as she passed the homemade bread to Mark.

"To thank Jesus," Roy said soberly.

"What do we thank Him for?" Ellen prodded kindly.

"We thank Jesus for the gravy," he said, just as soberly.

Ruth burst into hearty laughter, and the others joined her. They all knew that gravy on bread was one of Roy's favorite dishes. Roy just looked on innocently, appearing not to understand what was so funny.

After all was quiet again, Mark comforted his little son. "Of course we thank God for the gravy, sonny. And we thank Him for all the other good food too. God gives us so many good things."

A smile lit Roy's face, and he dug happily into his gravy bread.

Before they had finished their late supper, Papa and

The Upward Way

Mama came in. Ellen jumped up. "Did you have your supper yet?" she asked kindly, ready to set dishes on for them.

"Oh, we ate at the home," Papa answered.

"Why are you eating so late?" Mama asked. "Why, it's after eight o'clock!"

"The house was dark, so we came up here to find out what everyone was doing," Papa added.

"Oh, we were working at the chicken house till dark, and then had the milking to do yet," Mark said.

Then Papa went on, "We stopped at Henry Bechtel's just a little bit ago and learned some news that you might be interested in." Ruth was looking at Papa eagerly as she finished her mashed potatoes and venison. Often they had interesting community news when they came home from somewhere. "Henry Bechtel says that different ones were telling about a tramp that was showing up at their doorstep the last several days. He had heard first about it at church yesterday, I guess. Anyway, this afternoon the tramp showed up at Amos Kolb's place, and Amos right away recognized him—in spite of his disguise."

"His disguise?" Ruth burst out. "Who is he?"

"Well, Amos realized it was Mr. Sterling. You know, Mr. Sterling has been trying to find out where his wife and family disappeared to. He knew they were finding refuge with a Mennonite family in this area, but he didn't know with whom."

Mark nodded. "That's right. He showed up at the school where his children are attending one day a couple weeks ago, but the teacher locked him out."[20]

---

[20] This was a public country school with a non-Mennonite teacher.

140

The Upward Way

Ruth could not wait any longer to hear more. "But what did Uncle Amos's do? Did Mr. Sterling find out that his family was there?"

"No. He came just at mealtime, and they were all at the table eating. You know they eat supper early, before they milk. But Amos kept him occupied on the porch until Lizzie got the family all into the washhouse and then through the buggy shed to the barn. When that was accomplished, she quickly cleared the extra dishes off the table and set it with one more plate for him."

"Then she went calmly to the porch where Amos was still visiting congenially," Mama broke in, "and asked him if he wouldn't like to invite the man in for some supper. I wouldn't have had the grace—or the nerve—to do what that dear lady did!"

Ruth was looking at Mark, wondering if he was going to speak or if she should. But it was Dorcas who blurted out, "And we had that impostor in our house for dinner today! I had a feeling that something was wrong about it all."

"I'm sorry. It was all my fault," Ruth apologized. "I was the one who pitied him and invited him in."

Papa shook his head and for once took Ruth's part. "You did the only right thing to do in the circumstance, Ruth. Besides, there is more to the story."

Feeling not a little comforted, Ruth sat up and listened closely. "Brother Henry said Mr. Sterling stopped at his place, after he left Uncle Amos's, and told him who he is and what he had been trying to accomplish," Papa went on. "He said that he was at 'the Clemmers' and how kind they were to him. Brother Henry said he broke down

The Upward Way

and cried, saying that he no longer blames his wife for leaving him to identify with the Mennonites. They are a godly people, he said, and he wants to find out more about the Mennonite faith himself. Brother Henry was able to lead him to salvation. Mr. Sterling was in the living room yet when Henry was telling us about this out on the side porch."

"Well, that is an astonishing ending to the story!" Mark burst out.

And Ellen added sweetly, "You just never know how soon the 'bread' that you 'cast on the waters' will return to you, do you?"

"Or the seed that you sow," Mark concluded. "This was one time when it seems there were immediate returns!"

Ruth did not say anything. But her heart was full of joy. To think that she had had a little part in helping an ungodly man like Mr. Sterling to find salvation!

That evening she sat in her garret bedroom, finishing a letter to Charles. After writing in her journal, she knelt at her windowsill, her heart bowed in thanks. *Dear Father, thank You for this day. Thank You that You hear and answer prayers. Thank You for such a wonderful manifestation of Your interest in us as You have sent today. Help me to press onward in faith, seeking to follow You all the way!*

Chapter Eight

March 21, 1934, Wednesday. The first day of spring, and am I ever ready for it. We have had snow on the ground almost all the time since Christmas. But the snow is melting enough to make high water some places, and mud everywhere else! Today was a beautiful day. Trimmed grapes, cleaned chicken houses, and made ice cream. Helped Ellen make some cold frames to start some early lettuce and other vegetables. Cut out a dress—which when Kore saw, he said he hated! Lots of customers today, some for dry goods, some for lumber. Men hauled logs from Pottstown. We went to Uncle Amos's for the evening.

"Is spring coming after all this year?" Ruth sang out as she came into the house for breakfast. "It really is lovely out today, despite the snow and the mud underfoot."

Mama smiled at her as she scuttled about the kitchen, busy with breakfast preparations.

"Um, scrapple! And mush with gravy," Ruth said, peering into the assortment of pans on the cookstove. "This kind of weather gives a person an appetite."

The Upward Way

"Well, Papa will be hungry too when he gets here," Mama said. "Can you give us a hand to finish up here?"

"Yes, please do. Spring comes every year, so why let it make you addlepated," Dorcas added sarcastically.

Ruth bit back a reply. Maybe if Dorcas needed to work in the snow and the cold . . . maybe if she wouldn't sit in the house all day by the fire . . . maybe if she needed to carry water from the spring for the animals every day because their water cups were frozen . . . maybe if she ruined her lovely white hands shelling corn upstairs in the frigid barn . . . maybe if she needed to scrape hogs and pick chickens in the frigid shed every week—maybe then she would appreciate spring too! *I must not respond like that. Lord, give me grace to be sweet,* she pled inwardly. *Besides, maybe Dorcas would be happy to trade places with me sometimes, if only she were able!*

Then Mama broke into her thoughts. "Will you pour the coffee, please, Ruth?" she asked. "Then I think we are ready when the men come."

"Sure!" Glad for something to do, Ruth poured the mugs full of the pungent, freshly brewed coffee.

Papa left for a sale as soon as breakfast was over. "Does Papa want something in particular?" Ruth asked Mama as she helped to clear the table.

"I think he wants to get some shoats," Mama said. "And maybe another cow or two. Milk prices are good right now."

Ruth nodded. A couple of their cows were dry, and they were not getting as much milk now as sometimes. She had heard Papa say that he hoped to get a few more.

"I think he wants to get another horse too," Kore spoke

144

The Upward Way

up from where he was sitting reading the *Farm Journal*. "He wants to sell Harry and Gerry. They're getting too old for fieldwork, he says. But I like those old fellows. I hate to see them go to the dispatcher!"

"Me too," Ruth agreed. She always got attached to the animals and hated when any of them were sold.

"We have to get rid of Danna too," Mama added. "She tested positive for tuberculosis. Thankfully none of the cows did."

Ruth nodded. She was thankful too.

"By the way, Kore," Mama said, looking at him, "you'd better get ready for school."

"Paul wants me home today," Kore returned from behind his magazine.

Mama nodded. "I forgot—he did tell me that. And he told me too that he wants you to bring ensilage over from the other farm. He said to fill at least 36 bags."

"Uh-huh. He told me," Kore agreed reluctantly. "I guess I had better get at it." He looked at Ruth as he stood up slowly. "Are you going to help me?"

"Well"—she looked at Mama—"I was hoping to do other things. Like trim the grapes. And Mark wanted me to help clean chicken houses."

"Okay then. If I don't get any help, I don't get any!" Kore slumped out of the kitchen and into the washhouse.

Mama shook her head at Ruth. "Don't mind him," she comforted softly. "He can easily haul that ensilage before dinner, *and* have time to spare!"

The day was beautiful for trimming grapes, even with spots of snow underfoot. Bluebirds were warbling on the fence, killdeers were calling, a robin lighted near her,

145

The Upward Way

trying to find a bare spot to listen for worms. The sky was a blue bowl of beauty turned over her, and she gazed in never-ending fascination at the marvel of it.

By dinnertime, the grapes were trimmed as well as one chicken house cleaned. Ruth rushed to the house, eager to see what was happening there. A canister of fresh ice cream was ripening in icy brine in the washhouse. "Oh, yum!" she said under her breath. "I hope that's for dinner!"

"Where's Kore?" Mama asked when Ruth came into the kitchen.

"He's eating at Mark's this dinner. Said he didn't want to eat down here with just women."

Mama laughed with Ruth. "That's okay. I just wondered why he wasn't in yet. Usually he's here first!"

"So, when will Mark's be getting a new set of chickens?" Mama asked as the three women enjoyed their hot tomato soup.

"I think he said he wants to go to Souderton for some today or tomorrow."

"With their new chicken house filled up and the new chickens they will be getting now, they will have a nice amount of laying hens."

Ruth nodded. "Ellen really enjoys her hens, she says."

"And eggs sell well," Mama added. Ruth nodded again. She knew customers who came to the farm were taking all the eggs that Mark's chickens produced, for twenty cents a dozen. And they were not even going to Amityville now, where they could sell many more dozens each week.

"Ellen would like to put up some cold frames this

The Upward Way

afternoon to start some early vegetables," Ruth said later. "I told her I would help her."

Mama shook her head with a grin. "She is one ambitious lady!"

"Too ambitious," Dorcas retorted. "Maybe her children would behave better if she would spend more time training them instead of working all the time!"

"I think they're normal children," Mama responded mildly. "And if you had some of your own, Dorcas, you'd realize that too."

"Well, I don't have any. And I wouldn't want any as wild as theirs."

Mama rarely stood up to Dorcas, but this time she did. "I think you need a little more grace in your attitudes," she said pointedly.

Dorcas shrugged and pinched her mouth shut, the way she often did when irritated. Ruth wondered why she was feeling so out of sorts today. Had something happened that she did not know about?

"I hope Papa gets back before so late," Mama went on. "There have been so many customers."

"Yes, and that's all I got done this morning," Dorcas inserted. "Fetch and carry, wait and dawdle, fetch and carry. Up and down the stairs, back and forth to the cave . . . When I have all this sewing to do, I have to wait hand and foot on people that can't make up their minds or do anything for themselves."

"I noticed a lot of cars and trucks coming through," Ruth said. "I didn't know how many had stopped in for something." She felt sorry for Dorcas, knowing how hard it was for her to be on the move so much.

The Upward Way

"We had a lot of customers for lumber too. Mark came down to help some of them, but ones with small orders I could help. Anyway," Mama added, "we need to get more logs here to saw up for lumber." She sighed. "I really do wonder why Papa got into cutting lumber yet!"

"Didn't he start doing it for other people after our barn fire several years ago? You know, he bought the sawmill to do our own lumber for rebuilding, and then figured he may as well make it worthwhile to keep."

Mama nodded. "I know. And I'm thankful we had it to cut our own lumber. It saved us a lot of money and bother. But now it just makes us busier than we ought to be, trying to keep up with all the demand for sawed lumber."

Papa came home before Ruth went back outside after dinner. "Well, I got us some shoats, two horses, a cow, and a mule, and all for good prices," he informed Mama and the girls.

"Good," Mama said. "Will someone be bringing them yet today?"

Papa nodded. "A fellow with a truck will be bringing them out later this afternoon, maybe around milking time." He sat down to eat some soup, and Ruth headed up the hill to Mark's to see if Ellen was ready for help.

It did not take long to fashion several cold frames out of blocks so that old windows would fit to cover them. Ruth turned the dirt over with a shovel and then carefully raked it while Ellen went to the house for seeds.

In a short time, the beds were all planted. "Thank you so much for your help, Ruth," Ellen said. "I get so hungry for fresh things in the spring."

The Upward Way

"We've been finding some dandelion in some protected places," Ruth stated. "And in the straw where the snow is melted off the strawberry patch. Soon there will be watercress ready too, from the creek below the cave."

"I'll have to look for dandelion. I didn't know there would be any yet."

Soon Ruth hurried back to the house. She was hoping to start sewing a dress for herself yet that day. Maybe if she hurried, she could cut it out before milking time.

She had it all cut out and was starting to sew when Kore came to the house. He walked by the sewing machine on his way upstairs. "What's that?" he questioned her, eyeing the material.

"A dress for me," Ruth returned.

"A dress! You call that ugly stuff a dress? I thought it must be curtains for the outhouse, or maybe the barn!" he remarked tartly.

"Thanks," Ruth said as cheerfully as possible. "But for your information, I like the material."

"Well, I don't."

"You won't have to wear it."

"But I'll have to *look* at it!"

Ruth only laughed, while Kore dashed up the stairs.

While he was still upstairs, Ruth heard a truck coming slowly up the gravel road. *Papa didn't think that truck would deliver the animals till milking time,* she thought. She glanced at the clock. *Well, it is about that time!* The truck stopped at the barn. Ruth knew that she or Kore had better go out and tell the driver where to unload, since Papa and Mark had gone for lumber. Going to the stairsteps, she called, "Kore."

The Upward Way

"What do you want now?" came an irritated voice.

"The cattle truck is out here. Somebody had better go out and help unload."

"Well, go then."

"Okay."

Ruth quickly donned her coat, pulled on her boots, and hurried out to the truck. After opening the gate, she directed the driver to back around the lower side of the barn to unload in the barnyard.

The driver backed the truck in without any problem and unloaded the animals. But when he went to pull out, the truck just spun in the mud. *Oh, no! Now what shall I do?* Ruth wondered.

Kore came on the scene then and looked the situation over. "That was a rather dumb thing to do," he said degradingly. "Having that truck back in here in all this mud!"

"I'm sorry. I didn't think very far, I guess," Ruth said.

The driver jumped out of his truck and stepped gingerly on high spots through the mud to where they were standing. "What do we do now?" he asked.

"Get the horses and pull you out, I guess," Kore responded. Grateful for his help, Ruth let him take over. Soon the horses were pulling and the truck engine roaring. Mud flew everywhere from the spinning tires while the truck pulled slowly onto solid ground.

It was nearly time to start milking, so Ruth decided to get started. Papa and Mark were not back, and they did not get home until she and Kore were nearly finished with the chores.

When Ruth went in for supper, she noticed a newspaper

The Upward Way

that Papa had brought back with him. On the front page was a picture of a large building on fire. "Look at this," she said to Mama, after scrutinizing the paper for a few moments. "This is that box factory in Souderton that I was telling you about that burned Sunday while I was at Souderton for church."

Mama came to look. "I see. That was a big place."

Ruth nodded. "It says here that the estimated loss was around $75,000. We went to look at it after we left church." Then Ruth remembered something else. "Oh, Mama, I never told you what else happened Sunday. When Norman's and I got back to their place, someone had broken into their house."

"Had broken into their house?" Mama repeated. "Were things missing?"

"Not that we could tell," Ruth went on. "My satchel was ransacked, and there was cream smeared all over the dishes, and other things were scattered around—things like that. Norman and Sarah figured it was somebody who resented Christians living in the area. Sarah said, 'Oh, well, this sort of thing has happened before, and we are used to it.'"

"Poor children," Mama sighed. "But I guess they live in a low-class area. And such things are more likely to happen in places like that."

Soon Papa came in, and they all sat down to supper. Mama had made pigeon potpie for supper, in the way that only she could make it. Ruth had caught and cleaned the young pigeons the day before. Mama used only the tender breast meat to make her delicious potpie.

"Well, I should go over to Pottstown this evening.

151

The Upward Way

They are having a special service in their new building," Papa stated. "Anyone wish to go along?"

"Amos's invited us over this evening," Mama said. "Uncle Will's are around. Oh"—she looked at the girls—"that reminds me, they will be here for the night. Aunt Martha called and wondered if it would suit, and of course I told her it would."

"We were at Pottstown last night for church," Dorcas said, "in case you forgot! I don't feel like going again tonight."

Papa looked undecided. "Well, I didn't know about Will's being around. Guess we wouldn't need to go to Pottstown, if everybody would rather go to Amos's."

And so they spent the evening at Uncle Amos's. The young people sang much of the time while the older ones visited. Ruth enjoyed the evening very much and came home feeling that it was an evening well spent.

Chapter Nine

April 8, 1934, Sunday. Went to Grove Hill with Mark's this morning. Papa, Mama, Dorcas, and Kore went to Souderton to their special meetings. I should have gone with them! Superintendent John Gants asked me this morning to teach the class of teenage girls. It nearly floored me, especially as just two weeks ago, Brother Elmer Kolb asked me to take a class of young girls Sunday afternoons at the Pottstown Mission. I have prayed to be used of God, and now, if this is how He is answering my prayer, I want to lay down my own will. Today was my second time teaching at Pottstown. There were only three students there today, but it was interesting. One little girl couldn't come, I learned, because she is Catholic and she has been forbidden by her church to go to other churches. Charles and Mildred Gogle took me over this afternoon to Pottstown. Revival meetings started at Pottstown this evening with Brother A. W. Weaver as evangelist. I went with Uncle Jonas and some of the cousins.

It was a mild, rainy Sunday morning in spring. *April showers bring May flowers,* Ruth thought as she headed for the barn. In spite of the rain, she stopped to check the

The Upward Way

flower beds beside the walk. "How things grew since the rain!" she said aloud. "Most of the crocuses are blooming, finally, and the daffodils and hyacinths are coming into full bloom." They were later than usual this year, but the warm rain would bring everything fast now. She always loved to see the first flowers each spring, and she bent now to observe their perky purples and yellows more closely. "Oh, how I love spring!"

A robin sat on the fence, alternating between singing its "cheer-up" song and fluffing its feathers in the drenching rain. Ruth noticed it and laughed happily. Spring was truly here.

"Hey, get over to the barn and give me some help!" came a sudden call from the barn door.

"Coming," Ruth responded. Kore and she would need to do the milking alone as Mark had begged off to study this morning. He needed to preach at Grove Hill. And Papa had the chickens and pigs to tend besides the horses and cows.

She slopped through the rain and mud to the barn, thankful for the warm temperatures that had finally thawed out their water and drain lines to the house. Those lines had frozen during an especially cold spell in February and had stayed frozen all through March. How tired she had gotten of hauling all the water for their house use up from the spring in the cave, and then needing to haul the waste water back out again!

Kore was waiting for her in the barn. "What do you think you are? A duck?" he asked. "Standing out there in the rain like you'd lost your senses."

"Maybe I have," Ruth said cheerfully. "It's spring!

The Upward Way

Haven't you noticed? And even the rain has a cheerful sound as it hits the ground."

"All I've noticed is that it's wet. And it makes lots of mud. We sure have plenty of that underfoot!" Kore grouched.

Ruth grabbed her milking stool and pail and was soon busily milking her first cow. As she milked, her thoughts ran over the past weeks. They had been busy catching and selling the old chickens, and then cleaning the houses to get ready for new ones. Mark had finished not one, but two new chicken houses and had gotten layers in both of them, giving him seven hundred more laying hens. It all made more work at a time when Mark and Ellen were becoming more and more involved with church work. *Work that we really don't need!* Ruth thought.

Then there were the days she spent sorting turnips down in the cave. They would soon start sprouting with the warm weather, and the good ones had to be gotten out and sold. Papa had taken the saleable ones to Philadelphia and gotten a good price for them. The dehydrated ones they had hauled up to the barn to feed to the horses and pigs.

On sunny days she had spent her time outside, trimming raspberries and the fruit trees. That was the work she enjoyed the most—being out in the bright sunshine. She smiled to herself as she thought of Kore's comment, that she was already getting brown, and summer was not even here yet! She supposed she should always wear a sunbonnet, and stay white and ladylike. But then, she could not feel the fresh breezes or the warmth of the sunshine on her cheeks.

The Upward Way

But I shouldn't be thinking about these things on Sunday, Ruth suddenly thought as she squirted a stream of milk to a waiting cat. Then her thoughts shifted to the new responsibility that had come to her so unexpectedly. Brother Elmer Kolb had asked her two weeks ago if she would teach a class of girls Sunday afternoons at the Pottstown Mission. At first she had hardly known what to say, and so she went to Ellen for counsel.

"You love children," Ellen had told her. "And you have confided to me that you have felt a special call from the Lord for some service. Perhaps this is it."

"But I feel so young and . . . and unable," Ruth had burst out.

"I think you would make a good teacher," Ellen had assured her. "But you can't do anything of any worth in your own strength. Trust the Lord to give you the wisdom and the words. Have you talked with Papa and Mama about it?"

Ruth had admitted she had not.

"I think you ought to," Ellen had continued. "Your parents, especially Mama, should be your closest confidants. I know that many young people don't want to talk to their parents. But ones who want to please the Lord should surely start there. That's what God gave parents for. Be thankful you have them."

Talk to Papa and Mama? Ruth had grimaced at the thought. Papa would probably laugh and ask her when she thought she'd have time to study. But Mama would want to hear about it; she was always deeply interested in what her children did.

Ruth had talked to Mama at the first opportunity. Her

The Upward Way

counsel had been much like Ellen's. "You enjoy children, and I think you would make a good teacher. Pray about it. The Lord will not fail you, if you are faithful to Him."

Ruth had known the Lord would not fail her, but could she be faithful to Him? That was the question. After wrestling and praying about it for several more days, she had driven over to Brother Elmer's and talked with his wife, Emily.

"I just feel so unworthy to stand before young girls in this way, and try to teach them," Ruth had confessed. "I fail so often in my own Christian life. How can I help others to learn to walk with God?"

"Do you have any specific failures in mind, Ruth?" Sister Emily had probed. "You know, none of us is perfect. And the Lord doesn't wait until we are perfect before He calls us to areas of service. If He did, there would be very few available Christian workers." Sister Emily had chuckled a little, but Ruth's thoughts had been too deep for humor.

She remembered now how humbled she had felt as she confessed to not always having pure thoughts. And she had confessed too that she often struggled to love her sister Dorcas as she should. And her papa too. If Christ was really in her heart, would she not find it easy to love? And easy to live in victory in her thought life?

"Would it help if you confessed your desire to be more loving, to your sister and your father?" Sister Emily had asked her.

Is that really what I should do? Ruth had wondered at the time. *How can I? They might just mock me.*

"And if you are having other struggles," Sister

The Upward Way

Emily had gone on, "confess it to the Lord and ask His special help."

"I have," Ruth had assured her, thinking now how such requests were so much a part of her daily prayers. "And if you think I should confess failure to Dorcas and Papa, I will do that." She had broken into tears then and could hardly finish what she had wanted to say—that she did not want anything to be in the way of serving the Lord as she should. And that she would try to teach the class, with God's help, if they felt she was able.

"Elmer would not have asked you if he felt you couldn't do it, Ruth," Sister Emily had told her. "We'll be praying for you." And Ruth knew that she had been sincere when she said it.

As Ruth finished milking each assigned cow and moved to the next, she mused over how the Lord had given her the courage to go to Dorcas, and then to Papa, confessing a desire to be more loving to them. Dorcas had looked at her strangely, and then answered with characteristic tartness, "Well, we'll see how long this lasts!" Papa had spoken almost kindly. "God bless you, Ruth," he had said.

She thought of her walk up to the spring in the woods one evening soon after that, where she had spent a good part of the tranquil evening in communion with the Lord, confessing her failures and seeking God's help for the unknown future. *How good it is to meet God out in the open, where there is nothing to disturb or distract. And how good God has been!* she thought now. Such peace had come to her that evening, and a new power for service that she had not known before.

The Upward Way

Getting up stiffly, Ruth carried her last pail of milk to the milk house. Her seven cows were milked for another time. She was eager to get to the house and study for her class in the afternoon. The past Sunday had been her first time of teaching, and she had thoroughly enjoyed the six little girls from the community who had showed up for the class. But it took a lot of study to prepare a lesson interesting enough to hold the attention of children not used to hearing Bible stories!

She started for the barn door, but Kore called her back. "You aren't running off yet, are you?" he demanded. "Who's going to wash up the milk house?"

"I thought you would," Ruth returned.

"Well, I have a lot of feeding to finish. I don't think Paul has even finished the chickens yet, much less the pigs and horses. At least he hasn't shown his face down here in the barn yet."

"Okay. I'll wash up," Ruth conceded. It would not take long if she hurried, and she would still have enough time to study if she skipped breakfast.

Two hours later she was on her way to Grove Hill with Mark's. Papa and Mama had taken Kore and Dorcas and gone to Souderton to an all-day conference. She slid into her regular place beside her favorite cousin Grace.

"You have a new dress," Grace whispered. "I like it."

Ruth would rather not have discussed that right now, but she nodded. "I like it too," she whispered back, "but I didn't know if I wanted to wear it this morning."

Grace looked at her with puzzlement on her face.

"When I came downstairs with it on this morning, Kore clutched his face with both hands and said he sure

The Upward Way

was glad he wasn't going to church with me."

Grace shook a little with merriment. "I take it he doesn't like it."

"You're right. He said he hates it. He thought it would make nice curtains for the outhouse," Ruth whispered with a smile.

People were still walking in and finding their places. Ruth glanced to her right and noticed David Peachey slowly making his way up the aisle. He looked uncertainly at the youth boys as he passed them, but he continued toward the front of the auditorium, finally finding a place to sit on the fourth bench from the front.

"Did you see that?" Grace leaned closer to Ruth as she whispered.

Ruth nodded. "Our boys could learn something from his example. For that matter, so could we," she returned softly.

She glanced again at him. He was looking neater. Maybe Aunt Eva was helping him get some better clothes, she thought. And his hair was neatly trimmed and combed. He turned slightly and glanced back her way. She had noticed him before at some of the young people's singings; but other than that, she had never paid him much attention. Why should she? He was not anybody she would ever be interested in, even if she didn't already have a special friend. But maybe her sister Dorcas . . .

Grace nudged her. "What are you thinking about?"

"Nothing worth mentioning," Ruth returned with a smile. "But we'd better be quiet and ready for worship, don't you think?"

As she was visiting after the service, Ruth was

The Upward Way

suddenly aware that some man was saying, "Sister Ruth." She turned quickly to see Brother John Gants standing near her.

"I would like to speak with you a minute," he said as Ruth stepped nearer to where he stood.

"Okay." Ruth trembled in her heart. What could he want? Brother John was the Sunday school superintendent, but surely he would not be asking her to take a class.

"Sister Ruth," he began, "we need a teacher for the teenage girls. Sister Mary Guntz feels she cannot take the class another year." He paused briefly, and Ruth thought again that surely he would not want her to teach a class that she was barely out of! But she knew that Sunday school had just reorganized, and no doubt they were looking for teachers.

"As I was saying, we need a teacher for the teenage girls, and your name was given. Would you be willing to take the class?"

"B-but," Ruth stammered, "I am only a youth myself."

"I know," Brother Gants agreed with a nod. "But you have substituted for the class, and some felt that you would do a good job of teaching."

Ruth felt devastated. How could she ever take on another class? And at her age? *Lord, what shall I say,* she breathed fervently.

"I just feel so young," she said again. "Isn't there anybody older who could do it?"

"I'm sure there would be. But the girls need someone like you, who can be a good example as well as a teacher," Brother Gants encouraged her. "Think about it,

161

The Upward Way

and pray about it. Let me know next week. All right?"

Ruth nodded dumbly, hardly trusting herself to speak again. He had said she could be a good example—she who had so many struggles herself!

For the rest of the day, she rolled the idea around in her mind. She thought of it as she ate dinner with Mark and Ellen. Charles and Mildred Gogle were there too for dinner, so she tried to follow the conversation enough to at least be sociable. She thought of it as she rode with them to Pottstown soon after dinner.

"You're surely quiet today, Ruth," Mildred laughed as they drove along in Charles's Willys Knight. "Are you feeling well?"

"Just scared about your class?" Charles teased.

Ruth did not want to tell them about John Gants's request, so she simply agreed. "I was thinking about the class some, and wondering how many students I would have today."

She was thankful they did not press the issue further. As her cousin, Mildred had also been a good friend for many years. But this teaching business was one thing she did not feel inclined to talk about to just anyone.

She thought of it as she taught her little class at Pottstown in the afternoon. But she could not think of it very much then—not with a class of live wires such as she had, even if there were only three of them that day.

"Where is Lucy today?" Ruth asked as she took the roll.

Edna rolled her eyes. "Dunno, Miss Ruth. I reckon her priest foun' out she were comin' here and he tol' her she hafta stop. But specs she might come agin next week.

The Upward Way

She say she likes to come."

Ruth smiled at her. "Well, you tell her that I asked about her, and that I really would be happy for her to come again next week."

Edna nodded her head happily. And Ruth launched into the story of Daniel in the lions' den.

Revival meetings started that evening at Pottstown with Brother A. W. Weaver as evangelist. Papa and Mama were not back from Souderton, but Ruth would have really liked to go as many evenings as possible, especially to the first meeting. Some of her students had promised to bring their parents, and already she was feeling a deep burden for the work there.

After a lonely supper, she ran up to Mark's house—to find that they were not home. "Oh," she remembered as she retraced her steps more slowly back down the hill, "they were going to visit Ellen's parents after the milking was finished." What should she do? She supposed she could just stay home and go to bed early, but somehow that did not seem like a right thing to do this time.

"I know—I'll call Grace and see if she would go with me. I don't think Papa would mind if I drove over." She was thinking aloud as she stood on the doorstep, several cats brushing about her ankles. Absently she bent to pet her favorite yellow one, Teddy. He arched his back and purred as Ruth continued to think aloud. "I'll go call her. If she can't go, then I'll figure I'm to stay home this evening."

Soon she stepped into the kitchen and went to the telephone. Taking down the mouthpiece, she waited for the operator to say, "Operator." Then she gave Uncle Jonas's

163

The Upward Way

number and waited while the operator connected her to their line. Soon Aunt Emma answered. "This is Ruth Clemmer," Ruth said. "May I please speak to Grace?"

They chatted awhile about everyday things, and then Ruth stated her reason for calling. "Oh, Papa and some of us children had planned to go too this evening," Grace told her. "I'm sure we won't mind taking you along."

"Good!" Ruth replied. "I did really hope to go this evening, and now I won't even need to drive." They planned a time when Ruth should be ready for them to stop for her, and then she hurried to get ready.

Only in the last year, Papa and Mark had installed a bathroom downstairs. Ruth appreciated that, especially now as she prepared for church. No more carrying heated water upstairs for a sponge bath. Now she could take a full bath in the modern tub sitting proudly in the bathroom on its claw feet! The water fed into the house by gravity from the reservoir up the hill near Mark's house. Their new kitchen cookstove had a hot-water reservoir, where some of the cold water stayed long enough to get heated and then it continued its gravity flow, when needed, to the bathroom. Ruth did not understand how it all worked, but she was glad for Mark's native ingenuity to figure out time-saving innovations and put them to practical use. Many people in the towns had electricity, and they had electric pumps to pump water, and electric heaters to heat the water. But Papa said he doubted electric lines would get to the farmers for another five or ten years. But this was almost as good!

The service at Pottstown was well attended. Uncle Claude's came, and with them their hired man, David

The Upward Way

Peachey. David said a shy "hello" to Ruth and Grace as they happened to meet at the church door. Ruth smiled at him, noticing again the humility of his character. But she promptly forgot him in the joy of seeing some of her students there with their parents. Before Ruth went to sit down, Hazel's mother, Mrs. Root, came to talk with her. Mrs. Root was dressed in stylish clothes and bedecked with jewelry, but she spoke sincerely. "I just want to tell you, Miss Clemmer, how much our Hazel is enjoying Sunday school," she said. "We're happy she can come to this Sunday school. It sure is cheaper than the movies! And it helps to keep her off the streets on Sunday afternoons."

Not that such words were great encouragement, but they cheered Ruth's heart and gave her hope that the seed she was sowing would produce fruit for God's glory. Fervently she prayed throughout the service that the many unsaved people there would receive some nugget of truth and respond to the call of the Gospel.

There were no responses that evening. But that did not dampen Ruth's determination to continue to pray for the week of meetings to follow.

Chapter Ten

June 1, 1934, Friday. *Sorry, dear journal, for not writing in here for the last week. The fact is, I was in Virginia and forgot to pack you in my suitcase! I went with Jonas Swartz's, partly to visit relatives, but partly also to see Charles. What a week of strange experiences it was. . . . At least now I have some answers, such as they are. God help me!*

Rain! Ruth thought with a groan, looking out her window early one Tuesday morning in the middle of May. *That's all I need this morning to help my dismal spirit!* For days, Ruth had been feeling discouraged. And she just could not get on top of it. Was it because she had not heard from Charles for more than three weeks? Was it because her class at Pottstown seemed to be a failure? Was it because there was never any letup in the work at home? Was it because no matter what she did or did not do, nothing seemed to please Papa—or Kore either, for that matter?

She sat at her window, brooding in silence over the

The Upward Way

past weeks, her Bible lying unopened on her nightstand. The east-driven rain splattered against her windowpane and then coursed in eddies down it. *Rain!* she thought again. *Sunshine would help at least a little.*

Outside in the dim light, she could see the greening hillsides, the leafing trees giving new life to the barren landscape. All across the meadows were the blues and yellows of early-blooming wildflowers—cowslips, buttercups, violets, and spring beauties. And the grass everywhere was lush, sparked to new growth and green by the falling rain. But the signs of returning summer gave her no joy this morning—nor had they for some days.

Had it all begun two Sundays ago when she had only three students in her class at Pottstown? And then, her depression had deepened when she heard the rumors among the young people that Ruth Clemmer thought she was really somebody, teaching two Sunday school classes every Sunday. Then some whispers had drifted to her ears that Charles, her own special friend, had found a girl in college that he was seeing on the sly. Was it true? Could she believe such things? And if it were true, what was she to do about it?

The sad fact was, Ruth had good reason to believe the rumors were true. For the last several months, the time between Charles's letters had gotten longer and longer. And the letters that did come did not sound like the Charles she had always known. She had continued to write in answer to his letters when they came, but no oftener. As much as she wanted to reassure herself, she had not dared to ask him about the truth of the rumors that were floating around. Perhaps it was because she

The Upward Way

was afraid of what she would hear!

Her clock ticked steadily on, but Ruth did not open her Bible or fall on her knees beside her creaky bed to pray. Soon she heard Papa in the kitchen, and she drearily pulled her clothes on to go out to begin another day.

Papa was just about to call up the stairs when Ruth started down. "Come on, girl. It's time to get out," he stated when he saw her on the winding stairway. "I didn't hear anything up there, and figured you overslept." He turned then and strode into the washhouse for his barn jacket. Ruth morosely followed him. What was the use of trying to be cheerful? God did not care about her. His blessings and promises were for others, not her.

The day passed just as it had started. Horny, the first cow Ruth milked, kicked the bucket over, spilling milk all over her and leaving very little in the bucket to show for her efforts. With the ensuing scolding Papa gave her, she burst into tears. Kore walked by and looked at her with a smirk, seeming to enjoy her unhappiness. She felt like screaming at him, at Papa, at the whole world. But she knew that would do no good. Nothing would do any good. She may as well be dead for all anybody cared.

Later she tended her chickens, her own little flock that Papa was letting her care for and keep the money from. When she bent to check Biddy's nest, the hen suddenly reached out its long neck and pecked Ruth on the lip. Angrily she yanked her favorite setting hen out of her nest, scattering and breaking several of the eggs in the process.

"Oh, now what have I done?" she moaned, noting the nearly developed chicks in the broken eggs. Again

The Upward Way

she burst into tears, sobbing out all the frustration that was seething inside of her. Finding an empty tin can, she scooped up the broken eggs and took them out for the cats to eat.

The rest of the morning and part of the afternoon, she spent cleaning the cave. When Mama called out to tell her they were all waiting for dinner, she called back that she was not hungry, and they could go ahead and eat without her. How her heart ached as she cleaned out spoiled produce and hauled it in the wheelbarrow to the pigpens. Many times the tears spilled over. She wished she could talk with the Lord, but He seemed far away and uncaring.

And so the day passed. Kore gave her a wide berth, and even Mark and Ellen stayed out of her reach. But Papa did not scold as much as usual, and Mama looked after her with tender concern. What Ruth did not know was that Mama and Papa had also heard certain rumors and had reason to believe they were true. But how did a mother go about telling such things to an already heartbroken daughter. She could have offered sympathy, if she only would have. But, like many other mothers in those times, it was hard to enter into the emotional needs of her children.

That evening, as Ruth trudged slowly upstairs to her lonely room to begin another night of tossing and turning, she heard flying footsteps on the sidewalk. Then someone burst into the kitchen. "Oh, please, Mama, call the doctor quickly," she heard Ellen panting out. "Roy is having convulsions."

She heard Mama hurry across the floor to the telephone and the soft sounds of Ellen's sobbing. Flinging

The Upward Way

her own hurts aside, Ruth dashed back down the stairs. "What's the matter, Ellen?" she asked in distress.

"Oh, Ruth," Ellen cried, "we're afraid Roy is not going to make it."

"Make it?" Ruth echoed in disbelief. "What do you mean? He's not sick, is he?"

Ellen nodded, catching a sob in her throat. "He's had high fever all day, and I was trying to treat him with willow bark tea.[21] And I sponged him off with cool water often through the day, hoping to get his fever down. But the last time I took it, it was still 105 degrees, and now he is acting strange—sometimes like he's having convulsions and sometimes like he's delirious. I'm so scared!"

Forgetting her own sorrows, Ruth hurried to Ellen and put her arms around her. "I didn't know he was sick, Ellen. I'm sorry. I would have come and helped you, had I known!"

"You looked like you had troubles enough of your own, and I didn't want to bother you with ours," Ellen returned, tears still coursing down her face.

Mama came from the telephone. "Dr. Simpsom will soon be out," she said. "When I told him the symptoms, he seemed quite concerned." Mama looked on sympathetically with tears in her eyes, but she did not seem to know what else to say.

"Shall I go back up to the house with you?" Ruth asked Ellen.

---

[21] Willow bark tea, scientists have since learned, is rich in salicylates, which are aspirin-related compounds. Some naturalists still consider willow bark "nature's fever medication" when brewed into a tea and drunk in small doses.

The Upward Way

"Oh, that would be kind," Ellen returned, not appearing the strong and capable lady that she usually was.

As they hurried up the hill together, Ruth asked, "When did Roy get sick? He seemed okay yesterday."

"Well, he's had a little cold for the last week, but I wasn't concerned about it. Then during the night last night, he kept crying out and begging for me. He said his head hurt. I thought he had a little fever then, but I wasn't concerned about it until this morning. Then he really seemed warm, and he had no appetite or ambition."

"And that is very unusual for Roy!" Ruth returned.

"That wouldn't concern me so much," Ellen went on, "but he minded the daylight this morning and wanted his shades all pulled—"

"And it was a dark, rainy day," Ruth inserted.

"And when he bent over to try to pick his blanket off the floor, he said his neck hurt him so much." Ellen shook her head. "All of these symptoms make me think of meningitis."

"Oh, no!" Ruth gasped. She thought it, but did not say it, that Nancy Sheeler had died from that very same condition only last December!

Ruth stood by quietly while Dr. Simpsom later examined the small boy. "I think he should be hospitalized," was his verdict. "I can't be sure, but I think he may have spinal meningitis." Ellen, now quieted and submissive, with Mark beside her, nodded with understanding. "I will call the hospital and tell them you are coming," Dr. Simpsom offered. "But get him there as soon as you can."

While Mark went out to bring the car to the door, Ruth helped Ellen to gather a few necessary articles. Then she

The Upward Way

carried Roy, wrapped in a light blanket, to the car, laying him gently on the back seat. "Go with me, Aunt Rufie," Roy murmured slowly.

Bursting into fresh tears, Ruth backed away from the car and gently shut the door.

"It will be okay," Ellen comforted her. "Whatever God sees as best, it is all for our eternal good!"

"Oh, Ellen," Ruth cried, "I can hardly bear it. Our dear little Roy . . ."

"Just take care of Robbie until we get back, if you will. And please, pray for us," Ellen said as she climbed into the car. Mark took off with as much speed as was safe, and soon his Buick disappeared over the crest of the hill.

Ruth stood still for some time, her heart lost in sorrowful regrets. How much time for prayer had been lost the last while by her self-pitying discouragement! *Oh, dear God, I'm sorry,* she burst out in an agony of tears. *Please forgive me for my selfishness and my ingrownness!*

Walking slowly in the darkness back to Mark's quiet house, she slipped into Mark's bedroom to check on Robert. He lay in his little crib, sleeping peacefully, his chubby arms flung above his head. Softly leaving the room and pulling the door closed behind her, she fell beside the living room sofa. There she wept her heart out—tears of remorse and sorrow for her failure, tears of pity and petition for her beloved nephew, and tears of understanding for the grief and uncertainty her brother and sister-in-law were experiencing.

Hours later, in the blackness of the early-morning hours, she crept back to Mark's room, the heavy burden

The Upward Way

of the past days completely gone, and replaced by a meek submission to the will of the Father in relation to Roy. A lamp was still burning there. She carried it, and Ellen's Bible, to the spare bedroom, where she sat on the bed to read. *Oh, you dear friend,* she thought, caressing the Bible fondly. *And to think how I have neglected you the last while!* She opened it to where Ellen's marker lay—to Isaiah 42: "Behold my servant, whom I uphold; mine elect, in whom my soul delighteth; I have put my spirit upon him: he shall bring forth judgment to the Gentiles. . . . A bruised reed shall he not break, and the smoking flax shall he not quench."

A bruised reed . . . smoking flax . . . Ruth sat deep in thought for a time. "This is wonderful," she finally murmured aloud. "Bruised reeds are not good for anything, but God will not discard them if there is any hope they can be restored to usefulness! And rather than put out the smoking flax, He stirs the fire into flame again! My wonderfully caring Jesus. Oh, dear heavenly Father, how could I have thought You do not love me or care about me anymore?" With wonderful peace again in her heart, Ruth undressed and crept into bed for a few hours of sleep.

The next morning passed slowly as Ruth cleaned out the back cow stables. Physically she was very weary, but her heart was free of the burden that had depressed her for days, and she often burst into song.

"Well, well, so we are bright and perky again, are we?" Kore teased as he passed through the barn.

"I'm sorry I've been so gloomy, Kore," she apologized with a smile, forking another load of manure onto the cart.

"Well, now you can't be so hard on me if I'm not

The Upward Way

always feeling on top of the world," he shot back as he disappeared out the barn door.

What a poor example I've been! Dear Father, please keep me from such an experience again, no matter what comes to me, she prayed.

"Any news from Mark's yet?" she asked when she went to the house for dinner. She picked up Robert and cuddled him tightly, wishing Roy would also be there to ask her his usual scores of questions.

Mama nodded. "Mark called from the hospital not long ago and said Roy seems to be better. The doctors feel it is meningitis, but that it may not be the kind that is life-threatening."[22]

"Oh, thank the Lord!" Ruth said.

She worked with a will that afternoon, planting carrots and lima beans in the garden and weeding in the strawberry patch. Often Robert toddled along in the rows beside her as she worked in the strawberries. He seemed to enjoy walking in the clean yellow straw, or sitting down in it to play with a little gray kitten that persisted in staying in the garden all afternoon.

Sunday came again. Ruth had spent several evenings in study, but still she did not feel ready for her two Sunday school classes. "Dear Father in heaven, give me Your grace and wisdom today, that I may speak only Your words," she prayed as she walked along on her way to church.

---

[22] Now we know there are two kinds of spinal meningitis—bacterial and viral. Doctors did not know that at that time. They only knew that sometimes it was fatal—which was likely the bacterial type treated nowadays with antibiotics.

174

The Upward Way

It was a lovely May morning, and Ruth had decided to walk the four miles to church. The birds had a symphony of songs going in the wooded areas as she passed. Various neighbors saw her pass and called out cheery *good mornings*. She wished she had the time to stop and chat but knew she would need to keep going in order not to be late. As she neared Grove Hill, various members on their way there passed and then stopped to ask if she needed a ride. But she assured them each time that she had chosen to walk and was enjoying the invigorating freshness of the morning.

As she sat down after Sunday school, a feeling of deep thankfulness passed over her for the Lord's faithfulness in giving her the words to speak. And now she could relax and enjoy the morning message, which she did. A visiting minister, Brother Claude Meyers, was there and preached a message entitled "A Peculiar Treasure, a Royal Priesthood." *What a wonderful sermon!* she thought when he finished an hour later.

Brother Claude was at Pottstown in the afternoon as well, and preached the same sermon there. "But it was still fresh and inspiring, even the second time around," she told Sister Emily Kolb after the service.

"How is your class going?" Sister Emily asked.

"I was feeling sort of discouraged about it," Ruth admitted slowly. "But I felt encouraged today by what seemed like the special presence of the Lord with me. And today I had seven students instead of the three that have been there the last few weeks. That blessed my heart too."

"We are praying for you, Ruth," Emily encouraged

The Upward Way

her. "I know it isn't the easiest class to teach."

"I enjoy the girls very much," Ruth said. "It is just discouraging to me when what I try to teach seems to have so little affect on them."

"Just give them the Word," Emily said. "God has promised that it will bring forth fruit. 'My word . . . shall not return unto me void, but it shall accomplish that which I please, and it shall prosper in the thing whereto I sent it,' God told Isaiah."

The next morning, Mark and Ellen brought Roy home from the hospital. Ruth saw their car and left her wash basket to hurry up the hill. Mark was carrying Roy to the house.

"How's our boy doing?" Ruth asked breathlessly as she caught up to them at the kitchen door.

"Much better, thank God!" Mark responded. Ellen held the door for Mark as he carried Roy into the house. Ruth followed, eager to talk with her precious nephew again.

He looked white and weak as Mark deposited him on the living room sofa. "He's not well yet, but much better," Ellen said fondly, brushing the blond hair off Roy's forehead. "We'll soon have you all well at home; won't we, sonny-boy?" Ellen said to him.

Roy nodded, with a weak smile. Ruth made a move to caress Roy, but Ellen warned her off. "You know, Ruth, meningitis is quite contagious, and I'm not sure he's past the contagious part yet. Maybe you shouldn't touch him."

"Okay," Ruth agreed. "I should have thought that far myself!" She could not hold him or hug him, but at least he was still with them, and she thanked the Lord again for that.

The Upward Way

That evening, Jonas Swartz's stopped in for some dress material and sewing notions from Mama's little store. "By the way," Jonas began as they were leaving, "we plan to go to Harrisonburg this week, leaving early Saturday morning and coming back the next Friday. We'd have room for one passenger. Maybe one of the girls, if they'd like to go along."

Ruth was sitting at the kitchen table, stemming a few strawberries she had picked after supper. She sat up with a start. Would she possibly be allowed to go? But what about the rumors . . . ?

Then Mama said, "Well, Paul and I had been talking for several weeks that it would be nice if Ruth could find a way down for a visit. Paul and I will talk it over, and we'll call you with what we decide."

As soon as the Swartz's were out the door, Dorcas spoke up from the sewing machine. "Ruth go? I thought it was about my turn! What will she want down there anyway if Charles . . ." She stopped suddenly when Mama gave her a warning look.

Turning to Ruth, Mama said, "What do you think, Ruth? Would you like to go?"

Would she? Ruth nodded eagerly, her doubts about Charles having been left with the Lord. "I would like to visit Grandma again, and all the rest—if you think you can spare me around here for a week. But I don't care if Dorcas wants to go." She turned to Dorcas. "I'll stay home if you would rather go this time."

"Oh, that's okay," Dorcas said, turning to look almost with sympathy at Ruth. "You need an opportunity to talk with your boyfriend, I know. And I don't want to deny

The Upward Way

you that privilege." She turned back to her sewing and began to work the treadle again. But Ruth was touched by the unusual show of understanding from Dorcas.

"Well, if Dorcas doesn't care, I would be glad to go," Ruth said.

"Okay." Mama smiled. "I'll talk with Papa when he comes in."

Papa gave his consent, and the rest of the week passed quickly. Ruth tried to work ahead as much as possible. She harrowed the truck patch and gave it a thorough weeding. She finished weeding the strawberry patch. She cleaned out and scrubbed down the chicken houses, getting them ready for a new batch of chicks that Papa planned to bring home from Amityville on Friday. She dusted the watermelon and cucumber patches. And she did some necessary sewing.

She also made a special trip to the house up the hill each day to check on Roy. How thankful she felt to see him improving each day. By Friday, Ellen was not able to keep the normally active little fellow in the house anymore. She allowed Ruth to carry him out in the warm sunshine for a short time, where he chattered happily, almost seeming like his usual healthy self.

After her work was finished Friday evening, Ruth knew she really should go to bed. She would need to be ready to leave soon after four o'clock the next morning. But instead she walked along the creek up to the spring in the woods. There she petitioned the Lord for special grace for her stay in Virginia. *Lord, You know all about Charles. You know if the rumors are true or not. Please, give me wisdom to know how to relate to him, and give*

The Upward Way

me the grace to accept it if he wants to end our relationship. . . . To express the thought hurt her. But she knew it would need to be faced.

They were off by four-twenty the next morning. Ruth slept much of the way. She was thankful for that privilege, as she was very tired.

Soon after one o'clock, they arrived at Uncle John's place, with the old-fashioned, stucco house that Ruth had always so much admired. Aunt Lydia came to the door with young James hanging onto her apron, surprised and happy to see them.

"Why, is it our dear Ruth!" she exclaimed happily. "Do come right in, all of you." She stepped aside and welcomed Jonas and his wife in as well.

"We can't stay long now," Ruth said after a warm greeting. "But we'd all be glad for a drink."

"Of course you would!" Aunt Lydia picked up James and hurried to get them all fresh drinks of water while they caught up on the general news. "I'm sorry your cousins aren't here, Ruth," Aunt Lydia inserted after a bit. "They won't get back from school until after four o'clock, at least the older ones."

"I realized that Lois and Paul would be at EMS at this time of day," Ruth assured her. "But I'll get to see them later, the Lord willing, when we stop back."

After visiting a short time, they left for Aunt Josephine's. Then they drove to Grandma Good's at Waynesboro.

Dear, lovely, and godly Grandma came to the door at Ruth's knock. "Why, if it isn't Ruth Clemmer!" she exclaimed with her sweet southern charm as she shook Ruth's hand. "Are your parents here too? Or who brought you?" Grandma peered out at the car just then backing around in the driveway.

"Mama and Papa aren't here this time. Jonas Swartz's brought me," Ruth said, setting her suitcase down on the porch. "They plan to stay around for nearly a week. So I was hoping you would be happy to see me!"

She smiled at Grandma, who responded sincerely, "Yes, I surely am. And I will be glad to have you stay here. I see so little of you!"

On Sunday, Ruth went to church with Grandma to Hildebrand Church. There her uncle Philip Harner gave her a class to teach, much against her protestations. She spent the day with Uncle Philip and Aunt Maymie, where Uncle Emanuel's and Uncle Amos's also came to visit, with their families. Often throughout the day, Ruth found herself wondering why there seemed to be so little spiritual interest among these Virginia relatives. Rather than discussing spiritual things, they laughed and teased and fooled around—in ways that left Ruth feeling embarrassed and ashamed. She could not help thinking of the verses in Ephesians 5: *"Neither filthiness, nor foolish talking, nor jesting, which are not convenient: but rather giving of thanks. . . . Let no man deceive you with vain words: for because of these things cometh the wrath of God upon the children of disobedience. Be not ye therefore partakers with them."* She was very thankful that her cousin Roy Harner offered to take her to Valley View in the evening, where John Grove preached a very uplifting sermon.

As she went to her room at Grandma's that evening, Ruth's heart was heavy with thoughts of the day. But

The Upward Way

amid those thoughts always arose the question, where was Charles? When would he learn she was in the area? And would he want to see her? She had not written to him of her plans, mostly because she had not heard from him for several weeks. But also because she did not want him to feel that she expected him to see her while she was there.

The days passed, with invitations to this uncle's place and to that one. "All I do is eat and sleep," she moaned to Grandma on Tuesday evening as they visited together on Grandma's porch before retiring for the night.

Grandma chuckled. "I guess none of these good Virginia cooks want to be outdone," she surmised, "and so they all put out a feast for you."

"They surely do," Ruth agreed. "And if I refuse to eat something, they are sure to notice and suggest that I ought to try just a little!" She sighed, recalling her frustration just that evening at Uncle Amos Weaver's.

"You can't say you don't do anything," Grandma remonstrated gently. "Why, you mowed my yard today and cleaned up all my flower beds and the garden. That meant a lot to me."

"I was glad to do it, and wish you'd have more for me to help you with," Ruth returned. "But the time goes so fast!"

"It surely does!" Grandma agreed. "Why, tomorrow already you will leave me to go to Emanuel and Ella's. I have surely enjoyed these few days learning to know you again."

"It has been good to be here!" Ruth assured her.

Ruth enjoyed the more spiritual atmosphere at Uncle

The Upward Way

Emanuel Burkholder's. She especially enjoyed the times of family worship the two mornings she was there.

It was on Thursday that Charles called to talk with her. "Ruth," he said, after they had chatted awhile, "is there somewhere we could visit by ourselves, if I came out to your aunt's this evening?"

Ruth's heart trembled, but she answered calmly, "I plan to be at Uncle John's for supper this evening, but I'm sure there would be."

"Good. They're closer to my boarding house. I'll be there around seven o'clock," Charles promised.

One of the cousins drove Ruth to Uncle John's in time for an early supper. The whole family was home this time, and she enjoyed visiting with the cousins near her own age. Lois and Paul had many interesting details to share about life at EMS, while J. Mark and even eleven-year-old Ruth had tidbits to share from their school days.

"Now," began Uncle John when supper was over, "Mother and I would like a little time to visit with Ruth. Why don't you children see how quickly you can do the dishes while we have Ruth to ourselves for a bit."

Ruth protested about getting out of doing the dishes, but she really was looking forward to a private time of sharing with this uncle and aunt whom she appreciated very much. They ushered her into the study. "So, your mother writes that you are teaching two classes on Sundays," Uncle John said, leaning back in his desk chair. "That's quite an undertaking for one your age."

Aunt Lydia, a little woman, sat up straighter. "But I hear you are doing well," she encouraged Ruth.

"If I am, it is only by God's help," Ruth admitted.

The Upward Way

"I just want to wish you God's blessing in your service for Him," Uncle John added. "I wish we could convince your father to let you come to EMS for schooling. But he doesn't seem to feel you need that. So you just keep studying the Word, and apply yourself at home to learning all you can. Perhaps that is the best way anyway." Uncle John seemed deep in thought for a bit. Then he said, "It disappoints us very much how so many who come to EMS seem to lose out spiritually, rather than grow as we think they should." He shook his head.

"We're sorry to hear about Charles," Aunt Lydia began gently. "We thought he came here so sincere, but he seems to have changed." She seemed ready to say more, but Ruth was almost glad when she appeared to change her mind.

"As have many others," Uncle John added sadly. "I do not understand the reason, with all the careful instruction and good Bible teaching . . ." His thoughts seemed to drift off, and after a time Aunt Lydia began asking about things at home.

After a time of sharing, Ruth and Aunt Lydia joined the cousins in the kitchen. From there, Ruth kept a watch out the kitchen window, waiting anxiously for Charles to come. Promptly at seven o'clock, he came striding up the sidewalk to the door. Aunt Lydia gave her a look of understanding and support, and Ruth returned a grateful smile. Then she hurried to open the door, hardly knowing how she should respond to him.

Charles looked as good to her as ever. *My Charles*, her heart wanted to say. But was he? He smiled at her as they shook hands, but Ruth noticed that his eyes seemed evasive.

The Upward Way

"It's so good to see you again, Ruth. It's been a long time," he said, giving her hand an extra squeeze.

She gently withdrew her hand, wondering why he was doing something he had never done before, especially since their relationship seemed uncertain.

"It's good to see you too, Charles," Ruth said sincerely, and then added, "and I have missed your letters."

"I'm sorry about that. I've been sort of busy," Charles excused himself. "By the way," he went on, "where could we talk?"

"Shall we take a walk down to the orchard?"

"Sure."

As they walked along in the softly scented May evening, Charles made small talk—about the weather, about the beauty of the season, about what was happening at school. But Ruth listened with only one ear. Her heart was too heavy for light conversation as she pondered what she should say about their relationship. Should she confront Charles with the things she had heard, and if they were true, tell him they were through? *Oh, Lord, help me!* she prayed silently more than once.

She decided to be open with her feelings. "Charles," she began when he became quiet, "I have heard rumors that you are courting a girl from this area. I would like to give you the opportunity to clear yourself before I believe such things."

Charles did not say anything for some time. But Ruth had noticed that his chin dropped, and her heart dropped with it. Finally he spoke. "I can't be honest, Ruth, and say I'm not. But it's not because I don't care for you. It's just that I got so lonely down here, so far away from you. I was hoping when I come home for the summer that things can be as they always were." He was speaking more and more rapidly.

"Suppose, Charles," Ruth began earnestly, feeling a keen sense of hurt, "that I told you I was courting a boy from home. And I told you it was because I was lonely, not because I didn't care for you. Would you accept that? Would you trust me? Would you want a girlfriend like that, who might find another man to comfort her while you were gone? Would you?" She stopped to look into his face.

But he averted his eyes and gazed fixedly at the verdant fruit trees.

"Would you, Charles?" she repeated softly.

Turning back to look at her, he said, "It doesn't make sense, looking at it that way."

"No, it doesn't make sense." Ruth started walking slowly again, and Charles walked with her. "But what concerns me the most, Charles," she went on, "is that you appear to be failing to seek the Lord as you once did. Is that true?"

Suddenly Charles's attitude changed. "Hey, I'm only young once," he said. "And youth is for fun. I've found lots of that the last few months, fun of all kinds—away from my parents and from probing preachers. I'm tired of living strait-laced all the time." He looked a challenge at Ruth. "Can't a fellow have a little fun?"

Ruth met his challenging stare without faltering. "Tell me, what happened to the Scripture that says that without holiness no man will see the Lord?"

"Who believes that old bunk anymore!" he said

belligerently. "I believe the stuff that says grace gives us freedom to enjoy ourselves."

Ruth could hardly believe her ears—that Charles, faithful sincere Charles Derstine, would talk in such a manner. Surely he could yet be touched by Scripture! " 'For, brethren, ye have been called unto liberty; only use not liberty for an occasion to the flesh, but by love serve one another.' Or 'Be not deceived; God is not mocked: for whatsoever a man soweth, that shall he also reap,' " Ruth quoted softly, her heart torn nearly in two, but determined not to cry in front of Charles.

"Ruth," he began again, more subdued, "you always were too good for me. But let me get home for the summer, and I will try to do better if you stick by me."

They had left the orchard now, and were walking back toward the house. What was the point of this interview, Ruth was wondering. Something had sadly shattered their relationship. How could she ever trust Charles again? "Charles, I think you should turn to the Lord. He is the Friend who sticks closer than a brother. If you can prove yourself for several months—that you are truly sorry for your failures and really desire to walk with the Lord once more—then I would consider writing again. But until then, I think our ways must part." She spoke firmly, but her lips were quivering before she finished. How could she say such things? But they had to be said. She could not continue a friendship under such circumstances.

"Very well," Charles stated resolutely. "Then I'll just forget the church stuff!" He started determinedly across the lawn, but then he turned to say, "Well, then, I guess this is good-bye."

The Upward Way

Ruth's tears came then, but she answered bravely, "I will not stop praying for you, Charles."

When she walked into the house shortly afterward, she was thankful no one was around except Aunt Lydia, who met her and clasped her tenderly. "God bless you, dear," she said. "I know you didn't have a pleasant time out there."

Ruth sobbed into her shoulder, thankful for an understanding motherly figure just then. After she could speak again, Uncle John joined them, and Ruth shared the details of their talk. "Oh, do try to help him, Uncle John," she pled after she had finished. "He still seems to have a tender spot for spiritual things."

"We will do what we can, Ruth," Uncle John assured her.

Ruth was thankful for the foresight that prompted Aunt Lydia to give her the spare room that night, rather than putting her in Lois's room as she usually did. It proved to be a long night, and she heard Aunt Lydia's chime clock strike midnight before she got off her knees and crawled into bed. She had shed many tears for Charles and for their broken relationship. But even more than the heartache for her own loss was the burden for Charles's spiritual condition. Fervently she had prayed, asking the Lord to bring conviction and renewal to this young man whom she had so lately loved.

After barely two hours of sleep, she was up again, knowing that Uncle Jonas's would be there to pick her up at two-thirty to leave for Pennsylvania. She was glad the Swartz's were not feeling overly talkative as they drove home. Part of the time she tried to sleep, part of the time

The Upward Way

she spent in petition to her heavenly Father for grace to face the ones at home as well as the coming days. It was exactly twelve o'clock noon when the Swartz's dropped her off at her front door.

Glad to be safely home, Ruth hurried up the sidewalk. Papa and Mama were at Amityville, but Dorcas was there to welcome her home.

"So you made it," Dorcas said, turning from the cookstove with a smile.

"Yes," Ruth responded, thankful for a kind welcome from Dorcas, "and so thankful to be home." She dropped her satchel and peered at the pans and bowls on the counter. "Um-m, strawberries. Lots of them, but what else good do you have for dinner? I'm so hungry!"

"Didn't you get anything to eat down there?" Dorcas asked. "Usually those Virginia cooks feed company very well!"

"Oh, I got plenty. Too much. All we did was eat and sleep! But I haven't had anything today since a bowl of oatmeal when I left Uncle John's, and a couple of cookies while we were driving."

"I didn't know when you'd be home, so I didn't make anything for myself. There's cold beef in the icebox, if you want some for a sandwich. I was just planning to eat some bread soup with strawberries."

"Okay. That sounds good enough. But maybe I'd better change my clothes first." Ruth dashed upstairs, so happy for the sweet familiarity of her own purple room with its bright windows—and, yes, even her own familiar squeaky bed. She sat on it with a sigh, feeling that she could have lain down and slept the rest of the day.

The Upward Way

Ruth hurried up the hill almost immediately after eating dinner, eager to see how Roy was doing since she saw him last. He came racing out the walk as she entered their yard. "I was watching for you to come, Aunt Rufie. Mama say she see you come home!" He flung himself at her and embraced her legs with all his three-year-old strength.

"Why, Roy, aren't you sick anymore? Did you get all better again?" Ruth asked as soon as she could get the breath to speak.

"Mama say God make me all better again," he said, peering up at her happily. "Mama not let me go out to play a lot, but she say soon I can. I can hardly wait!" He now took Ruth's hand and pulled her toward the house.

Ellen was washing dinner dishes, but welcomed her eagerly. As soon as Ruth had properly hugged her little Robert, who was so happy to see her, and Roy had gone off to play, she began to tell Ellen all about the trip, especially the part about Charles. Ellen sympathized, just as Ruth knew she would. But she also gave the encouragement that Ruth knew she needed to go on from here. "Remember, sister dear, that all things work together for good when we love God," she said. "And that the steps of a good man are ordered by the Lord. Nothing just *happens* to the Christian. God has everything planned, and He will work everything out in the best way possible."

Ruth nodded, tears filling her eyes. But they were not sad tears. She had given her desires to God.

"We have seen God's mercy and care during the last weeks," Ellen went on, "in a way we never had before." She paused briefly. "You know, Roy could be in his grave,

189

The Upward Way

but God in mercy allowed us to keep him. But it wasn't until I submitted totally to God and was able to say from my heart, 'He's Yours, Lord. Do with Him whatever You feel is best' that Roy made a turn for the better."

"Slowly I'm learning that truth, Ellen, that there is no peace unless we give up our own will and submit to whatever God brings into our experience. It is easy to say that—and I have said it glibly to others, I'm sure—but now I think I understand the truth of it in a new way."

Ellen nodded with understanding.

When Ellen went to put the boys down for naps, Ruth hurried back down the hill. There were so many chores waiting, and she was so eager to do something once again besides sit around!

Chapter Eleven

August 15, 1934, Wednesday. How the summer days fly, and I hardly find time to keep up with you, dear Journal. But today is quite a notable day. Sarah was feeling fine when she got up this morning, but soon after noon, she presented Norman with a dear little daughter. Her name is Ella Mae. Norman seems so happy! Of course we all rode over to Norman's this evening to meet this new member of the family. I picked corn beans and limas this morning. Several customers were here and bought limas for 25 cents a half peck. Also put up stakes to the tomatoes—there are a few getting ripe. The men were making hay all day. Helped saw wood this afternoon. Made a freezer of raspberry ice cream and served it for supper to the hay crew. Had a hard thunderstorm this evening, and it got so cool afterward that the men almost shivered eating the ice cream. It is clear again now.

But back to June . . .

The June morning was very warm, and Ruth dropped wearily beside the raspberry patch, wiping the dripping sweat from her face. "What a hot day!" she exclaimed to the bluebirds sitting on the pasture fence nearby. Already

The Upward Way

she had picked ten quarts of raspberries off the prickly branches, and she still had one row to finish. She gazed hopefully at the sky. Might those be thunderheads coming up over the western horizon? She hoped so. They needed rain. But the men were cutting wheat, and a hard storm would not be good right now when the wheat was so ripe.

On top of the hill, she could see Papa driving the horses and binder through the yellow wheat field. Behind the binder appeared the sheaves of golden wheat. Mark and Kore, Uncle Jonas and cousin Harold followed the binder, setting the yellow sheaves upright in shocks, ten sheaves to a shock. Some days she helped with that job, but today Mama had begged off for her, saying there was plenty of garden work to do—which there was. Here it was the twenty-second of June already, and they still did not have their late planting of potatoes in. Of course, there was lots of picking too—like the raspberries. And when she was finished with them, there were peas and string beans to pick. *But I won't get anything done very fast, just sitting here,* she thought with a chuckle. Feeling refreshed from her short rest, Ruth jumped to her feet again to finish her job.

Sometimes Sarah still came home for a day or two to help with some of the work. *I wish she were here right now,* Ruth thought. *How much faster this raspberry picking would have gone.* She sighed wistfully, still not fully accustomed to her sister being a housewife in her own home. *And soon Sarah will be a mother too, the Lord willing.* That thought rang joyfully in Ruth's mind, and she could hardly wait for the time to pass until she was.

The Upward Way

The raspberries were finished, and the peas and string beans picked, when Ruth hurried to the house for dinner. Dorcas and Mama had prepared an ample dinner for the harvest crew. There was fried chicken, smoked ham, cup cheese, fresh potatoes, noodles, peas, green beans, red beets, pickles, homemade bread and preserves, pie and cake, and ice cream. The men ate first while the women served. Then, while Mama and the girls ate, the men went outside to lounge on the grass for a while before going back to their work in the fields.

"Do you think we could plant the potatoes this afternoon?" Mama asked as she chewed the meat off a tailpiece of chicken.

"I would, if someone would help me," Ruth responded.

"If we have someone to lead Nuke, he can pull the planter," Mama went on. "And then we need a couple of people to ride the planter . . ."

"Count me out," Dorcas said. "I'll clean up all this food and put things away. And then I have plenty of sewing to do."

"Maybe Ellen could help," Mama decided. "The men are too busy, and will be for the next couple of weeks."

Ruth nodded. "As soon as the shocking is finished, they will have hay to make. I'm glad I got most of the dock pulled out of the hay fields." Ruth thought of the many days that she and Kore had spent hours at a time going through the hay fields, pulling the stubborn dock weeds. Papa did not like any dock in the hay fields for a couple of reasons—the seeds, if they got in the hay might poison the cattle, and the heavy stalks clogged the cutting teeth when he went through with the mower.

The Upward Way

The potatoes were cut and waiting in the cave, and as soon as Mama and the girls had eaten dinner, Ruth went out to hook Nuke to the planter. By the time to milk, the women had the acre planted that Papa had saved for late potatoes. "Good! This job is off the list," Ruth rejoiced to Ellen as they put the empty crates back in the shed.

The threatening rain held off until evening, after the milking was done. Then it came in torrents as the family sat at the supper table, enjoying guinea soup. The road past the house looked like a river as the water rushed downhill to the creek, and the creek rose several feet, spilling over its banks into the pastures.

"Well, we needed the rain," Papa stated as he stood at the kitchen window after supper. "But we didn't need it all at once!"

"At least we got the potatoes planted before it rained," Ruth said.

"And the wheat field cut," Kore added from where he still lounged at the table.

"Well, if the potatoes don't all rot in the mud, and the shocks don't all wash over and the wheat mold!" Papa exclaimed, not appearing very happy.

Mama attempted to soothe him. "All things work together for good when we love the Lord, Papa," she said.

"Can't see much good in so much rain at one time. I could manage better than that," Papa insisted, but his voice was more subdued.

Ruth cringed at such a reflection against the omnipotence of God; but not daring to stand up to Papa, she meekly kept still. *Can't Papa realize that material things are not all that important in the light of eternity?* she

The Upward Way

wondered again, as she often did.

It was Thursday a couple of weeks later, and Ruth was busy hoeing in the potato patch. Most of the potatoes were up, in spite of the heavy rain earlier, but the weeds were coming faster. As she hoed, her thoughts ran to various things. Her mind went to Charles. He had not come home at all for the summer but had found a job in the Staunton area. As far as she knew, he was still seeing the girl he had taken up with in the spring. But worse than that, reports coming home were that he was losing out spiritually and often did not go to church anywhere. *What had caused him to leave his love for the Lord?* she wondered again as she had dozens of times before.

On a brighter note, she thought of her Sunday school classes. Often now she had eight or ten in her class at Pottstown on Sunday afternoons. She was enjoying that class very much as she endeavored to implant seeds of truth in the hearts of those community girls. She thought also of her Sunday morning class at Grove Hill. Many of those girls were only two or three years younger than she, but they applied themselves to study, and she was finding the class very fulfilling. *Thank You, Lord,* she breathed. *It is only as You work through me that my teaching can amount to anything!* Ruth rested on her hoe for a bit as she looked around the patch. Soon she would be finished with this job!

In the afternoon, after Ruth was finished hoeing, she hooked Nuke to the cultivator. Mama walked up from the house to help her, and with Mama leading the horse, Ruth carefully cultivated between all the rows.

"Now, that patch looks better again!" Ruth stated as

The Upward Way

she guided the cultivator out of the ground at the end of the last row.

"Yes, it does," Mama agreed.

"Thanks for your help, Mama," Ruth called after her as Mama started back to the house. Ruth unhooked the cultivator and guided Nuke back to the barn, happy to be finished with that job.

Often Ellen helped with garden work, but today she and Mark had gone to fix the sewing-circle sewing machines at Pottstown. They had taken the boys along, since they planned to go over to Ellen's parents afterward. Ruth missed Ellen's help, and she also missed the towheaded little nephews following her around in the garden and yard. Robert was just beginning to talk, and with the two of them, Ruth was always amply entertained!

"Well, it's time to go milk," Ruth said later as she rested in the house for a time, looking at the mail.

"Papa likely won't be back to help," Mama reminded her from where she was vigorously mixing something in a bowl. "And Mark and Ellen aren't here."

"Where's Papa?" Ruth asked.

"He needed to meet this afternoon with the bishops and with Abe Gross and Elmer Mack, to decide what's to be done at Rockhill."

"Oh." Ruth would have liked to ask questions, but she knew from past experience that it was no use to try. And she supposed that was best. The deacon and his wife learned many things that the family had no reason to know. "I guess I'll try to find Kore and start the chores."

After the milking and supper were finished, Ruth

The Upward Way

worked in the barnyard, making a pen for the guineas. She had hatched several clutches that spring, but they were still penned up in an empty room in a chicken house.

"There," she said as she lifted the half-grown guinea chicks into their new surroundings. "Now you can peck to your heart's content!" Later she would need to clip their wings, but for now they should stay put inside the fence, at least with the wire over the top. She watched them for a while as they scurried about, exploring their new surroundings. "I hope you fellows are too big to arouse the cats' interest," she stated to them wryly.

That job done, Ruth walked down to the creek, now a harmless trickle compared to the torrent it had been several weeks earlier following a couple of hard rains. A bullfrog jumped into the water as she neared the edge. Then several more. How she would love to catch a few of those big ones! What was better than fried frog legs! Sometimes they were able to catch some that ventured into the cave, especially if they got into a dish of pudding or applesauce!

She listened to the songs of the birds in the shagbark hickories and the oaks bordering the creek. Squirrels scurried up and down the rough bark of the hickory trees, peering curiously around the trunk at her as she neared their tree. She laughed to herself as she recalled how her younger cousins liked to climb the trees to make the squirrels come down. Soon she reached the spot where the cows had bedded down for the night. They lay in silence in the thick thatch under the oaks, solemnly chewing their cud. Then she crossed the fence and walked up the hollow to her own special retreat.

The Upward Way

There she listened to the murmur of the birds, and the chirping of crickets and tree frogs as she watched the night fall softly about her.

Many thoughts filled her heart. Thoughts of the future, thoughts of Charles, thoughts of church life and the lack of spiritual interest in so many of the young people—and the older ones as well, for that matter. All that mattered to some good church members, it seemed to her, was getting ahead financially and staying abreast of current world trends. Was that what the life of a stranger and pilgrim was all about?

As the darkness deepened, she slowly retraced her steps back to the farm buildings. The others had already gone to bed and she followed suit, not even taking time to write in her journal.

The next Tuesday, Ruth was picking raspberries when a car stopped at the sidewalk. She did not think much about it, assuming it was one of the frequent customers. Then the familiar forms and faces of dear Uncle John and Aunt Lydia suddenly became clear to her. They saw her and waved, and she waved happily to them as they walked to the house. "I wonder if Mama and Papa knew they were coming," she said aloud to the cats napping in the mulch under the raspberry bushes. "If they did, they didn't tell me about it."

That evening at Pottstown, Uncle John had the message. He preached a message entitled "The True Church." As Ruth listened intently, she remembered her thoughts of the week before. Uncle John's clear exposition answered many of her questions. Carefully she jotted down his main points, purposing to go over them again and again.

The Upward Way

The church is a living church. It consists of a group of born-again believers, made alive by the life of Christ. He emphasized Christ's condemnation of the church of Sardis, who had a name that they were alive when they were actually dead. "It takes a living church to go against the current of the world to live an overcoming life in Christ," he said.

Uncle John went on to enumerate conditions that make a living church: (1) It is a holy church. God has commanded that His people be holy, even as He is holy. (2) It is a humble church. God hates pride. Satan was cast out of heaven because of his pride, and pride is still an abomination to God. (3) It is an enlightened church. It is made of people who study the Word, and by the aid of the indwelling Spirit are able to discern truth from error. The entrance of God's Word into hearts gives light. (4) It is a loving church. Jesus said, "By this shall all men know that ye are my disciples, if ye have love one to another." God's love abhors what is evil and cleaves to what is good. (5) It is a separated church. One of the reigning thoughts of Scripture is the separation between God's people and the world. God's people are to come out from the world. They are not a part of it, even as Jesus was not a part of it. Furthermore, when we follow the teachings of Scripture as we should, the world will not want anything to do with us. (6) It is an obedient church. Those who do not keep Christ's commandments cannot be a part of His church. (7) It is a nonconformed church. God's people do not follow "the god of this world," nor does the god of this world deceive them. The world is the enemy of God; and if we are friends to the world, we are

The Upward Way

also enemies to God. Pure religion is to keep ourselves unspotted from the world. (8) It is a peculiar church. We are a royal priesthood before God; but we are made as the filth of the world, and are the offscouring of all things. (9) It is a glorious church. It is a holy bride, without spot or wrinkle. We are washed from our sins in His own blood, a purified people, zealous of good works.

Uncle John closed the message with an evangelistic appeal: how can one get into this glorious church? (1) He must recognize that he is a sinner and in need of the cleansing power of Jesus. (2) He must look by faith to Christ for cleansing and forgiveness. (3) He must trust Christ to make him a new person by the power of the Holy Spirit. (4) He must seek Christ as the only hope of salvation, for there is no other name under heaven by which we can be saved. (5) He must hear the voice of Christ and faithfully follow in obedience, denying the worldly lusts that war against his soul. Then he can be part of the glorious church, the bride of Christ, not having spot, or wrinkle, or any such thing.

An invitation was given, inviting a response from the congregation. Ruth rejoiced to see the mothers of two of her Sunday school children stand to their feet. Bowing her head, she humbly prayed, *Thank You, dear Father, for these responses. Please grant them Thy strength to commit their lives wholly to Thee, and then to live faithfully in service to Thee. And more than that, I thank Thee for Thy faithfulness to me this evening, for meeting the needs of my own heart. . . .*

Uncle John's stayed overnight and then left to visit other relatives in the area after breakfast the next morning.

The Upward Way

Before they left, Ruth had an opportunity to visit alone with Aunt Lydia as she and Aunt Lydia walked in the yard, looking at flowers.

"How are things going for you, Ruth?" Aunt Lydia asked kindly.

"I think well, at least in relation to Charles. I have given to the Lord my desire for his friendship. But I have been having questions about a lot of things. I appreciated Uncle John's message last evening. It seemed sent just for me!"

"What kind of questions?"

"Well, I've wondered why there is so much difference between professing Christians. I'm not only thinking about all the different church groups but also about the differences within our own conference."

Aunt Lydia bent to sniff the fragrance of a pink dianthus. "Um-m-m. They always have such a delightful scent," she said as she stood up. "Well, Ruth, people will never think exactly alike. There is room for some variation of opinion and application. But there is never room for disobedience to the Word. We certainly draw the line there. And when the church we are a part of decides on certain standards and discipline, and they are in accordance to the Word, then we have a responsibility to faithfully respect and keep them."

Ruth nodded. "I understand what you are saying, and that is the way I feel, I think. But I can't understand why so many of our church people do not keep the standards that have been established by our church. And they often speak disrespectfully about some practice that they don't like—or make fun of some who want to keep the standards."

The Upward Way

"Such disrespect," Aunt Lydia began softly, "is the forerunner to open apostasy. It is very sad, but it is the way Satan works, and we have seen it many times already in our short lifetime. Always respect and appreciate the safeguards that the faithful church has set for you."

"People call it bondage, or they say it is Old Testament Law, and that we as New Testament saints are under grace. We are liberated from the Law. I hear people say this kind of thing all the time."

Aunt Lydia gently shook her head. "The sad thing is that very soon such 'liberated' people find themselves slaves to the world's system. Certainly we are liberated from Old Testament Law—we understand that. But we are called to a higher law—the law of love to God and man that draws a clear line of separation between the saints of God and the servants of sin. Never, never allow anyone to confuse you with such theology. I'm afraid that those who claim liberation are like those about whom Jude wrote: they turn grace into a license to live according to the flesh. Appreciate a faithful church and strive to support it, Ruth. You will find the blessing of God resting on your life in a way that you will never experience in any other way."

Uncle John, Papa, Mama, and Dorcas came out of the house then, and Ruth and Aunt Lydia walked to meet them. With many exchanged well-wishes, Uncle John and Aunt Lydia were soon off.

Ruth spent the day helping Kore and Mark clean up the barn and whitewash it. But while her hands were busy, so was her mind. *Lord, I thank You for the wonderful help Uncle John's visit was to me just now,* she prayed

The Upward Way

often and fervently as she meditated on the message from the night before as well as on Aunt Lydia's encouragement. How good her heavenly Father was to provide for her needs at just the right time!

Papa had gone to Amityville for a load of cedar posts. In the afternoon, he and Mark worked at putting in new posts and fixing the pasture fences along the road. Ruth stood at the barn window to watch them briefly. "What a wonderful improvement!" she exclaimed.

"What improvement?" Kore questioned from where he was sloshing whitewash on a back wall with a broom.

"Well, the barn for one," Ruth returned as she looked at the fresh whiteness of the barn walls. "But just now I was thinking about the pasture fences. They've been sagging so sadly for a couple of years. The men don't have many posts in yet, but I guess I was seeing in my mind the finished product," she finished with a laugh.

"I'd like this job in here to be a 'finished product,' " Kore muttered. "Maybe if you'd quit mooning there at the window and come help me, it would be."

"I have been helping you," Ruth protested mildly, going back to her bucket and beginning to apply whitewash again. "All day in fact. And you ought to be grateful for that."

"Sure! Sure!" Kore made an exaggerated bow, flipping his whitewash broom in the air like a wand. When he straightened up again, he stepped backwards, knocking firmly against his bucket of whitewash. "Yow-ee!" he exploded as he fell over the bucket and sprawled on the floor behind it, the bucket neatly tipping and whitewashing him and everything around him.

The Upward Way

Ruth could not help it—she burst into hearty laughter at the hilarious sight of long legs flying in the air and white water streaming all over an indignantly flailing boy. Finally Kore got on his feet again, whitewash dripping off him. At first there was fire in his eyes, but as Ruth continued to laugh helplessly, he finally saw the humorous side too and joined in.

"It was all your fault!" he sputtered when they had both calmed down. "You made me do it." But he was not angry at her, and Ruth laughed again.

"Well," she began after she got her breath, "I guess you can go clean up. Or you can stay in those clothes till you dry, and be a truly 'white boy.'"

"Where am I supposed to go to clean up? Vena will take one look at me and send me to the creek!"

"There you go!" Ruth said. "Go down to the creek for a swim. Or else I can throw buckets of water on you till the whiteness washes out," she added, laughing again.

"All right! Ho-ho! To the creek I go." Kore stomped out of the barn, leaving a trail of whitewash as he went. Ruth ran to the window, where she could watch him marching resolutely down the road, his very white and wet clothes sagging and clinging to him. His white-splotched face and hair added emphasis to his whole ragtag appearance.

She laughed till the tears ran down her cheeks as she watched him go. Papa and Mark turned from their post-hole digging to see the sight coming down the hill. Soon she heard an eruption of hearty laughter, and then Kore's remarks to them—although she could not hear what he was saying.

The Upward Way

Ruth watched until she saw Kore plunge into the deep part of the creek. Then she returned to the whitewashing.

It was then that a guilty feeling washed over her. Had she been too foolish? But then the Scripture verse came to her: "A merry heart doeth good like a medicine." That was a verse Ellen had quoted one time when she and Ellen were discussing when to laugh. "I laugh too much when I'm with the young people," Ruth had said. "Then I feel bad when I come home and think about how silly I was."

"There are times to be sober, and there are times when it is right to laugh," Ellen had told her. "Someone who is laughing all the time, or trying to be funny, is out of their place. And often that happens when a group of young people are together in a social setting. But it is right and proper to enjoy humorous situations, especially in the family setting." That was when she had quoted the verse, and Ruth had felt she understood better when humor was all right.

Ruth felt comforted now as she thought of that conversation, and she worked with a happy heart. Soon it would be milking time, but until then she could finish the back wall of the barn.

Later, when she passed the silo on her way to wash up her bucket and broom, she heard a funny squeaking sound. "What is that?" she said aloud, stopping suddenly to listen. Then she heard it again. She peeped into the empty silo, not sure what she would find. Then she spotted it—a little downy-white creature huddled against the wall, its big eyes in a heart-shaped face staring at her.

"A little barn owl!" she exclaimed. It pecked and

The Upward Way

hissed at her as she went to pick it up. "It's a wonder that the cats didn't find you," she told the half-grown bird. She looked up the forty feet to the top of the silo, where she saw a strawy nest on a crossbeam. "You must have tried walking around on the beams and fallen," she said, caressing the little bird. "Now how do we get you back up there?" She stood and looked up. The top of the silo looked much too far away for her to climb. Maybe Kore or Mark would take the little bird back up. But until then, what should she do with it? She found a box and tucked the bird in with some straw.

When Mark came to the barn to start the chores, he put the owl in his pocket and climbed up the ladder, depositing the little bird back in the nest. "Now, hopefully it will stay there," Mark said when he was back down.

"Thanks!" Ruth said. "I surely didn't want to climb up there."

"I wouldn't either, for just any reason. But barn owls are nice to have around. They eat lots of mice." Mark looked around. "By the way, is Kore around yet?"

"I haven't seen him since he went to the creek," Ruth said.

"Well, he came back up," Mark said with a chuckle. "Probably went to the house for dry clothes."

"Wasn't he a sight?" Ruth laughed again at the thought, and Mark joined her. "It looked so hilarious when it happened."

"I can imagine! I was glad he could take it well," Mark returned. "I just hope the lime on his face and in his eyes won't do any permanent damage."

The Upward Way

"Oh, I didn't think about that," Ruth said, suddenly sobered.

"I doubt it will, since he got it washed off as soon as he did."

More beautiful summer days passed. July ended and August came, bringing with it the steamy heat of summer's dog days. Ruth stayed busy with sweet corn, tomatoes, beans, and all the rest of the gardening, heat or no heat. When the vegetables were taken care of, she helped with the barn work—cleaning the stables or chicken houses—and with the fieldwork—picking up stones, fixing fences, or cutting grass for the cows. The men were building a lumber shed, and Ruth often helped with that too, as she had time. In the evenings, she often visited one neighbor or another, enjoying the opportunities for helping others and sharing the Gospel.

On Sundays, she went to Grove Hill in the mornings and to Pottstown in the afternoons. How Ruth enjoyed her classes. She rejoiced in the ten that were her usual number now in the afternoon service at Pottstown.

Wednesday, August 15 dawned a fair and warm morning. Ruth bounded out of bed at four-thirty, happy for the light that was already starting to break over the eastern horizon. "What will today bring?" she murmured, gazing out her window at the shadowy hills. Soon she had dressed and was kneeling by her bed, alternately reading her Bible and talking to the Lord. Her thoughts often strayed to Sarah, and she prayed for her. She thought also of Mrs. Cook, and others of the neighbors, who had seemed open to the Gospel on recent visits to them. She thought of Lloyd Black, who had gone along to church

The Upward Way

with her family several times recently.

Her room grew more and more light as golden beams shot up over the horizon. Too soon her hour with the Lord had passed, and it was time to begin the day of work.

Breakfast was over, and the men had gone back out. Mama and Dorcas were doing the dishes while Ruth quickly finished some mail before going to the garden. "There, that's done now," she stated, sealing a letter to her cousin Anna and one to Grandma Good in Virginia. "What do you want me to do first, Mama?" she asked. "There are corn beans ready, I noticed yesterday. And it's time to pick the limas again too."

"You'd better wait to pick the limas until the dew is gone," Mama suggested. "But they should be picked as soon as possible because several people are hoping to get some today."

"What are you and Dorcas going to do?"

Dorcas spoke up from the table where she was washing the dishes. "I want to bake cookies. We need some around again. I thought I'd bake black walnut cookies, since we have those walnuts in the cellar that need to be used."

"It will take a while to crack them!" Mama said. "Do you have time for that?"

"Oh, I guess. It doesn't take so many to flavor cookies."

Mama wiped the table and cupboard tops. "Papa wanted to go to Worcester to the Harvest meeting," she said. "I think he is planning on that yet this morning. Probably we'll go to Jacob Landis's for dinner, unless he decides to come home for dinner so he is here when the men want to make hay this afternoon."

The Upward Way

"It would be nice to go along," Ruth ventured, coming from the sitting room with stamps for her letters. "But I know there's work to do, so I don't mind staying home to do that."

Through the morning, Ruth worked in the garden. She picked nearly a bushel of corn beans, and then started on the limas. There were nearly three baskets of those by the time she was finished. She took them to the washhouse and told Dorcas about them, in case someone came for some while she was out.

"How much are we supposed to sell them for?" Dorcas asked. She was lifting cookies off a baking sheet and putting them on the table to cool.

"Didn't Papa say they were selling for twenty-five cents a half peck at Amityville?" Ruth answered, helping herself to a cookie. "Good!" she said, savoring a bite. "Black walnut cookies are a favorite!"

"Okay. Twenty-five cents for a half peck sounds fair enough," Dorcas returned. "I'm glad the cookies are finished. It's not fun to try to bake cookies and wait on customers at the same time."

Ruth chuckled, remembering some "burnt offerings" that such experiences had produced for her in times past. "Well," she said, "I'll go put stakes to the tomatoes. Mama doesn't like them lying on the ground when they get ripe. They surely are growing."

"No wonder!" Dorcas retorted. "All the manure Papa piles on the garden."

"I saw a couple of ripe of tomatoes," Ruth returned as she picked up another cookie and bit off a piece. "I'm sure hungry for tomato sandwiches."

The Upward Way

"Well, they'd be better for you than so many cookies," Dorcas suggested knowingly.

Ruth shrugged and grinned. "I know. But I worked hard this morning. I'll work off the calories!" She glanced at Dorcas, her usual slim and neat self, as a laugh rippled out.

"And what's so funny, if I may ask?" Dorcas asked, turning from the stove.

"Nothing, really." Ruth headed for the door. "Just a thought that came to me. But I had better get busy."

"Yes, you were laughing at me, weren't you?" Dorcas demanded. "You may as well say so! If you were still young, I'd give you a good kopfschneller[23]!"

Ruth stopped at the door, regret surging through her. Dorcas was so sensitive to anything that might be misconstrued as mockery. *How can I be so insensitive!*

"I was thinking that I am a bit overweight, Dorcas," she admitted, wanting to keep peace if possible, "and how I'll probably never be slim like you."

"Well, all right. If that was all." Dorcas looked relieved and happy again as she turned back to her work.

Ruth sauntered out to the garden to work at the tomatoes, her thoughts on Dorcas. *Why is she so sensitive*, she wondered once more, as she often did. *If she could just accept her physical condition as from the Lord, what peace and rest she could experience—instead of her continuing battle with bitterness. Dear Father in heaven, please help Dorcas,* Ruth prayed in her heart as she gathered stakes from where Papa had placed them alongside the garden.

---

[23] A *kopfschneller* is a Pennsylvania Dutch word meaning a snap on the head with the finger.

The Upward Way

Papa and Mama were home soon after dinner. "I should go out to the hayfield and see how things are going," Papa said. "Then I should saw some wood. Can you help with that, Ruth?"

Ruth glanced at Mama. "I suppose. The garden work is pretty much caught up."

"Good." Papa changed immediately and hurried to the hayfield where Mark, Kore, Uncle Jonas, and Harold were already busy with the hay.

"May I sew until Papa comes back in, Mama?" Ruth asked, eager to finish the dress she had been working on for the past month.

"I suppose you could. Dorcas can work at her own machine if she has sewing to do."

"I hope someone else can help customers this afternoon," Dorcas inserted. "I did my share of running this morning."

Mama nodded. "Well, I'm here now, and should be able to take care of that."

Mama had just come in from helping a customer get some lumber when the telephone rang. Mama answered it, and soon her voice became quite excited. "Tut, tut! So, a little girl. How nice!" she exclaimed. "Is everybody doing all right? . . . Very good. We'll be eager to see her!"

As soon as the receiver was back on the hook, Ruth and Dorcas besieged Mama with questions.

"Was that Norman?"

"Is it a boy or a girl?"

"What's the name?"

"How much did it weigh?"

211

The Upward Way

"When was it born?" . . .

Mama collapsed into a chair, laughing. "You two are worse than your nephews!" she exclaimed. "Let me get a word in, and I'll tell you all about it. Yes, that was Norman. They have a little girl, born at twelve-thirty. Her name is Ella Mae, and she weighs seven pounds and three ounces. Baby and Mother are doing fine. Any more questions?"

"One more question. The most important one," Ruth burst out eagerly. "When can we see her?"

"Well, I don't know. But maybe we could drive over this evening. I can hardly wait either," Mama assured her.

Ruth collapsed with a happy sigh on the kitchen rocker. "A dear little niece! How delightful! Oh, I can't wait to hold her!"

The three delighted women did not have much time to dwell on the exciting event until a truck went chugging past the house up to the sawmill. Mama went to the window. "Looks like somebody else for lumber," she said. "I hope Papa soon comes in. I think we'll soon need to cut more lumber, and I can't run the sawmill."

"I don't mind helping Papa," Ruth said. "But I don't want to start that engine and handle those logs myself."

Mama was still looking out the window. "Good. There comes Papa now, on Nuke. He can help the customer. But you had better go out too, Ruth, in case Papa needs to cut some lumber."

Until time to do chores, Ruth helped Papa saw lumber. They got a nice pile of rough lumber sawed and ready for customers. Over the noise of the engine and sawing, Ruth had managed to tell Papa about his new granddaughter.

The Upward Way

Ruth was glad to see the happy light in his blue eyes and knew he had a soft spot for the little ones.

The men had just come in with the last load of hay at suppertime, when a hard thunderstorm hit. Lightning flashed and blazed across the darkened sky, and thunder rumbled. They all sat in Mama's kitchen—Mark and Ellen and the boys too—enjoying her delicious supper while the storm raged outside.

"I'm sure glad that hay is in," Papa stated, spearing a forkful of fresh lima beans.

"That's for sure," Uncle Jonas added. "It looked threatening for the past couple of hours, but the Lord held the storm off till we could finish."

Papa nodded. "We did get a nice pile of lumber sawed too."

Mama got up to close the outside door. "The weather is changing," she said. "It feels colder."

Kore shivered. "I was dripping with sweat all afternoon, and now I feel like I need a coat!"

Mama laughed. "Dorcas made a freezer of raspberry ice cream for supper, but maybe nobody wants it."

Cousin Harold spoke up from where he was still eating industriously. "Hey, bring it on. We can eat ice cream anytime, no matter what the weather."

Ruth grinned at him. She knew he had often expressed that one major reason he liked to come to Uncle Paul's was for the never-failing homemade ice cream.

Supper was eaten leisurely as the rain continued to pound down outside. But Ruth, usually welcoming such an interlude in a busy day, was on edge this time. She wanted to go to Norman and Sarah and see that new baby.

The Upward Way

And if they did not hurry and finish supper, Papa would think there was not time anymore that evening.

But she was failing to reckon with Papa's love for going away—along with his love for the grandchildren. As soon as Uncle Jonas and Harold were chugging up the road in their old truck, Papa said, "Well, what was I hearing about going to see Sarah and the new little one this evening? Is anyone still wanting to go?"

Ruth was already scurrying around cleaning up the supper dishes, but now she stopped dead in her tracks. "Me!" she burst out.

"And me too," Mama added with a chuckle.

"And me," Dorcas added.

Kore shrugged. "Count me out. I'd rather get to bed early than go see a new baby. They all look alike to me anyway—red and wrinkled."

"This one will be beautiful," Ruth said teasingly. "Just you wait and see!"

And Ella Mae was. Ruth stared at the tiny bit of humanity in her arms with hungry eyes. She had light hair, a fair complexion, and the promise of the pure blue eyes of her mother. "What a dear, lovely little one you have, Sarah," she finally said.

"I never knew how precious and special our own baby could be," Sarah returned warmly. "She is a little miracle from God, and I'm already her devoted love slave!"

As they drove home in the clear night, rain-washed and bright in the moonlight, Ruth's heart was filled with many thoughts. Would she ever have the privilege of motherhood? How she longed for it, if that was God's will. But somehow, the probability of such an experience

The Upward Way

seemed more remote to her than it ever had. *Dear Father, may I submit to Thy own will, and be perfectly content in it,* she prayed earnestly.

Kneeling by her bed in the moonlight, a poem came to her, and she lit her lamp to write it down.

We should never forget to kneel in prayer
When we are pressed with temptation and care;
    Just hang on to God by the vital thread—
    He only can help as life's pathway we tread.
And also in joy, our thanks should arise,
Ascending to our Father above the skies.
    Sunshine and clouds make the Christian life sweet,
    There's nothing on earth can ever compete![24]

---

[24] This original poem was found in one of Ruth's journals.

Chapter Twelve

October 4, 1934, Thursday. Today is my twentieth birthday. I am out of my teens forever. How time does fly by. Life seems so short—God helping me, I want to become a more sincere Christian every day. Saw a beautiful yellow hornet's nest today. I did not work very hard, as I was not feeling the best, but did can some corn and picked more pears. Sent off some cards to my Pottstown Sunday school girls. Windy and cool today.

But back to summer . . .

Summer days passed as on the wings of breezes, and the cooler days of autumn blew in on summer's last whispers. Ruth rushed from one chore to another, full of the pluck and purpose of youth. The Clemmer's large truck patch would have been work enough to keep her busy. But besides that, there were the twice-daily barn chores, the extra market chores, and helping Ellen in her house up the hill. And last, but by no means *least*, was the important privilege of helping at times to care for tiny Ella Mae. As much as possible, Ruth made the drive to

The Upward Way

help Sarah with daily chores, also taking advantage of the opportunity to tend to her little niece's needs.

On a pleasantly cool Tuesday in the middle of September, Ruth was picking the last of the tomatoes from Sarah's small garden. "Three baskets," she said aloud. "These should give her a few more quarts of tomatoes for her canning shelves." One by one she lugged the heaping baskets to the back porch. Then she stepped inside the kitchen.

Sarah was relaxing there, holding Ella Mae while reading the mail. "Let me scrub the tomato stains off my hands, and then I'll relieve you of the baby," Ruth offered with a grin, knowing full well that Sarah was not looking to be "relieved." That little girl was her mother's greatest joy.

"You may hold her," Sarah laughed, "but only because I want to be kind and share my toys."

"Or you mean *joys*?" Ruth returned, holding out her arms for the precious bundle. She pulled the blanket back and gazed at her. "You know, I thought she looked so much like you at first. But she is looking more and more like Norman, isn't she?"

Sarah nodded. "Different people are saying that. She is fair-skinned like me. But she surely favors Norman otherwise, they say. Nose, forehead, chin, and mouth are like his, which I don't mind at all—I'm happy if she looks like her dear daddy." Sarah looked fondly at her baby in Ruth's arms.

The sisters chatted about the different friends that had been to see the baby, and then about things at home and other news in general.

The Upward Way

"Do you have any extra ground cherries?" Sarah asked after a while.

"Oh, I would think so." Ruth thought a bit. "We have at least six boxes half full of them, drying in the garage, and there is no way we need that many. Would you like some?"

"Oh, you know me!" Sarah laughed. "I always enjoyed ground-cherry pie. Norman isn't real fond of it, but he eats some when I make it."

"Okay. I'll try to remember to bring some over the next time I come." Ruth laid Ella Mae on her lap and unwrapped her tiny feet. She could never get over the marvel of such a perfect, tiny body.

"What are Mama and Dorcas doing today?" Sarah asked.

"Mama was making butter for market. And I think they were going to make grape juice. I picked nearly a bushel of grapes this morning at the other place before I came over here. They have yesterday's ironing to do too."

"How is Mark since he ran that nail through his foot?"

"Oh, I think he is better. But Roy was sick, and they took him to the doctor yesterday. I was helping Ellen do her washing yesterday because she spent so much time with Roy. He had a fever, and I think she was afraid he might get meningitis again. Mark had taken chickens to Philadelphia and wasn't home to help her."

Sarah got up slowly and got herself a drink at the pump. "Oh, how is Kore?" she asked as she set her tin cup down. "Wasn't he having some trouble with his hernia?"

Ruth nodded. "Mama and Papa took him to the doctor last week, and I think he will need surgery."

The Upward Way

"Poor boy! He won't like being down too well, will he? He will need to miss some school too."

Ruth laughed. "Well, he won't mind missing school. But I can't imagine he'll enjoy being in the hospital a week or two!"

"We'll have to be sure to visit him," Sarah said. "Will he be in over his birthday? That wouldn't be very nice."

Ruth shook her head. "Kore's birthday is on September 27, but his surgery is scheduled for later. I think Mama said they scheduled surgery for Monday, October 8, or something like that."

They shared more news of the community, but finally, Ruth laid Ella Mae back in her little bed, a bureau drawer lined with the softest and sweetest of blankets. "If I don't start working on those tomatoes, I'll never get finished!"

"Profound statement, to be sure," Sarah quipped.

Ruth laughed. "How would you like them done? Juice? Canned whole? Sauce?"

"Let's just can them whole," Sarah decided. "Norman was never used to drinking tomato juice for breakfast like we did at home. So we don't use much juice."

As Ruth drove home later, she reviewed the pleasant day in her mind. With interludes like these, life surely seemed more worthwhile. What a precious little one her sister was blessed with. Would such a privilege ever be her lot? She loved children, and how would she ever get through life without any of her own? Would she need to work in an orphanage to fulfill that longing for children?

Her thoughts went briefly to Charles. He had been home for a visit the end of August, before school started again at EMS in September. How good he had looked

The Upward Way

to her when he came to Grove Hill for Sunday evening young people's meeting, and what a temptation his being in the area had proven to be! Ruth shivered involuntarily as she thought of how he had asked for the privilege of taking her home. She recalled that visit in minutest detail. She had asked him about his spiritual condition, and he had freely admitted that nothing had changed from when he last talked with her. "But you can be a help to me, Ruth," he had pleaded. "Don't let me down like this!" By God's help, Ruth had stood firm. Even though it was hard to think about it, she was glad she had not given in to him.

But still, the longing for friendship was strong within her. *Dear heavenly Father, You know how much I desire a sincere Christian boyfriend,* she prayed now as she carefully maneuvered around the many curves. *Am I sinful to desire that? Isn't that normal for every young girl?* As she meditated and prayed, a voice seemed to speak within her, that she must give that desire to her faithful Lord. *Yes, dear Father, I want to submit to Thee. I know submission to Thy will is the only way to have true happiness and peace!* Joy again filled her heart as she recognized the peace that passes all understanding.

Then her thoughts turned to her Sunday school classes. What a joy those girls were! She had had the girls from her classes out to the farm in August. Thirteen of the girls from the Pottstown class were there one Thursday, and eight from her class at Grove Hill the week afterward on a Wednesday. Especially for her Pottstown scholars, it was a time of learning to know them in a new way. They were mostly community children, with little knowledge

The Upward Way

of a farm, and the farm had fascinated them. After a morning of introductions to the various farm animals, she had taken them for a hike along the creek to her special haven at its head, where they had eaten a picnic lunch. Then they had spent the afternoon in idyllic pleasure under the trees along the creek. When they had gone back to the house in late afternoon, Mama had served them with fresh homemade raspberry ice cream and pretzels, a special treat to these town girls.

Her class of sixteen- and seventeen-year-olds had also enjoyed their time, though in a different way. Some of them were her cousins, and all of them had been to the farm many times before. But even so, it was enjoyable, a time of sharing spiritually that they all seemed to appreciate.

"Thank you, Lord, for the fulfillment of teaching these dear ones," she prayed aloud as she turned onto Clemmer Road. "Help me to teach them the things I should. And above all, help me to be a faithful example. O Father, it is only by Thy help that I can make any difference in their lives."

Ruth parked the car in the garage and hurried to the house. *Home in time to do barn chores,* she thought, glancing at the clock.

No one was in the kitchen, and she peered around the door into the sitting room. Dorcas was sewing as usual. "Where are the rest?" Ruth asked, above the noise of the treadle.

The treadle stopped, and Dorcas turned around on her stool. "Papa and Mama are up at Mark's right now. There are some other visitors there—Bertha Emsweiler

221

The Upward Way

and her daughter, I think they said, and Henry Bechtel's and William Good's. I think some others too. I think Mama said Irvin's and Henry's will be here for supper."

"Irvin's?"

Dorcas nodded. "Irvin Kolb's. I think they and Papa and Mama need to talk this evening about what to do for Milton's."

"Well, I'd better start barn chores," Ruth said. "It doesn't sound as though Papa and Mark will give much help. And if we're having company for supper, the chores should be done on time." Ruth hurried up her garret stairs to change into barn clothes, hoping that Kore had already started with the chores.

More busy days passed—days of silo-filling between cool, rainy days, days of gathering in the remnants of garden crops before frost.

"Well, what do you have planned special for today?" Kore asked with a grin the morning of September 27.

Papa did not appear to see any humor in his question. "Well, for you, go to school," he returned. "Unless you'd rather stay home and fill silo."

"So, you're fourteen today," Mama said, picking up the conversation more amiably. She poured coffee into her cup and Papa's, the steam billowing up in soft vapors.

"And still growing," Ruth added, looking up at his nearly six-foot height beside her short five-two. She set the mush and a mug of molasses on the table.

"He's growing out of all his clothes something uncommon!" Mama exclaimed. "We're going to need to get him a new Sunday suit too. Maybe we can call that your birthday gift."

The Upward Way

"Time to eat," Papa said as he sat down.

After prayer, Mama continued her line of thought. "Would we have time, Papa, to take Kore for a new suit after school today. He does need one badly. His arms and legs are growing out of his old one so that he looks rather pitiful."

Papa looked at Kore. "If he needs it, we'll have to get him one I guess, though it'll likely cost as much as ten dollars."

"I need Sunday shoes too," Kore added. "I have to curl my toes to get my old ones on."

"What size are you in by now?" Dorcas asked, staring meaningfully at the big work shoes sitting by the cookstove. "What you're wearing now look like boats!"

Kore humphed in good humor. "Good for high water, hey?" he retorted. "Just like my pants are getting to be!"

"I guess we'll have to get shoes in town," Mama said, ignoring them. "We only have work shoes in the store upstairs."

Papa looked Kore up and down again. "Well, I guess if he needs clothes, we'll have to get them for him," he said. "But today? Maybe, if it rains."

It did rain. A shower came up about the same time that Kore burst into the house after school. Papa came in from chopping corn for the animals. "Well, boy, are you ready to go shopping?" he asked.

Mama came from the sitting room, carrying a piece of crocheting with her. "Is that what you're minded to do?" she asked. "If so, I should make a list of sewing things I need."

Soon they were off, and Ruth and Mark did the chores

The Upward Way

alone. Ruth did not mind. She always enjoyed times of working alone with Mark and the special opportunity to discuss things that were on her mind. This evening Roy was with them in the barn, following them around with his multitude of questions or sitting at the bottom of the straw funnel on a pile of straw with a kitten on his lap.

After the milking, Ruth went to feed the pigs. While she was shoveling corn out of the crib for the pigs, she uncovered a mouse nest with five very tiny pink babies in it. "Oh, look, Roy," she called out to the small boy, who was watching the pigs eating. "Look what Aunt Ruth found!" She carried the five wiggling babies to Roy, who cried with delight as he carefully took them on his own hand.

"Oh, they tickle," he cried. "Aren't they nice? I want to take them and show Mama and Robbie."

"Oh, Mama might not want them in the house," Ruth said, not eager to take time just now to go up the hill with him.

Roy looked amazed at that prospect, but readily gave in.

"Really, we should give them to the cats," Ruth suggested. "God made mice for food for kitties. And you know that Grandpa doesn't like mice in the corn."

Roy shook his head. "And I guess Mama doesn't like them in the house either," he said. "Sometimes they get in the food and chew stuff up. Mama doesn't like that."

He gingerly carried the wiggling babies to the barn, where he fed them one by one to his favorite kitten. Ruth watched him, trying to stifle the giggle that wanted to pop out as Roy stared mournfully after each disappearing mouse.

The Upward Way

Papa and Mama and Kore were back by suppertime, their arms full of boxes and pokes[25] of goods they had purchased. Kore carried a box with shoes.

"Where's your suit?" Ruth asked. "Did you find one that fits?"

Kore only nodded as he sat down to try on his new shoes again. "We found a nice one," Mama informed Ruth, "but it needed some altering. So we'll need to pick it up later."

The few remaining days of September passed, and then it was October. Before Ruth knew it, another birthday had come.

"Well, twenty years old," Dorcas greeted her when Ruth came in from the barn for breakfast. "You're catching up to me!"

"How does it feel to be twenty?" Kore asked from behind the *Farm Journal.*

"Not much different from being nineteen," Ruth returned. "Although it seems like a milestone. I think I read somewhere that character is basically formed by the time one is twenty," she added more soberly.

"Well, I guess you've lost your chance then," Kore said snidely.

"Kore, can't you be kind on her birthday at least?" Mama scolded from the cookstove, where she was stirring gravy for over the mush.

"I *am* being nice," Kore returned, acting stunned, his face peering around his magazine. "There was nothing at all un-nice about that, was there?"

---

[25] Mama usually called a bag a "poke," which usage comes from older English.

The Upward Way

"Well, you insinuated that Ruth has no character," Mama went on. "I certainly wouldn't call that being nice."

Kore shrugged and hid behind his magazine again.

What a way to start the day, Ruth thought as she helped finish the breakfast details. She hoped Kore was only teasing and did not actually mean what he had hinted at. But still, he was the one who worked the most with her—he should know how she really was, if anybody did! With that thought, some of the brightness of the day evaporated for her.

Papa came from the washhouse, and they all sat down to the table.

Ruth helped Mama can corn through the morning, and then she picked pears in the afternoon. The pears were hanging on thick this year, but were not as large as some years. She climbed up on a ladder to reach the highest limbs, sometimes needing to climb onto a limb to reach the pears hanging at the very ends of branches.

All the stretching and reaching pulled at Ruth's already sore back muscles. She rested briefly, kneeling on a broad limb and holding onto the branch above her head. Suddenly something caught her attention, and she hastily retreated to the ladder. Near the end of the branch to which she was clinging hung a huge paper nest, and at the hole at the bottom, she saw hornets busily flying in and out.

"That thing's more than half as big as a tomato basket!" she gasped aloud from the safety of the ladder. "I wish we could get it down and save it!" Later, she knew, the colony would break up for the winter, when the queen went into hibernation. But right now she did

The Upward Way

not want to trifle with it!

She decided to leave that branch and went to another part of the tree, soon busy again at plucking off the hard, green Kieffer pears. They always picked this kind of pears before they were ripe, and let them ripen slowly in the garage or shed where it was cool. Up and down the ladder, and up and down to empty her picking bag . . . "Oh, my back," she moaned aloud more than once. It had hurt when she had gotten up in the morning, probably from lifting heavy logs the day before. But she had not minded it much until now, with all the stretching and bending that picking required.

By midafternoon, her sore back had become a full-blown backache. Ruth left the twelve baskets of pears sitting in the orchard and went to the house. Mama was taking jars of corn out of the canner.

"My back is bothering me a lot, Mama," Ruth said. "I don't know if I lifted something too heavy or what. But it hurts so bad that pain is shooting down my legs and makes them feel almost paralyzed."

"Sciatic," Mama guessed. "Weren't you helping the men lift lumber around yesterday? I've told Papa that is no job for a woman! Why don't you go lie down till chore time? The pears don't have to be picked today."

"I left the baskets out in the orchard because I didn't think I wanted to lift them up onto the wagon to bring them in."

"I'll send Kore to bring them in when he gets home from school."

"Thanks, Mama," Ruth said gratefully, heading for her stairway.

The Upward Way

Squeak, squeak went her bed as she settled heavily onto it. "Oh, it hurts. I wish I could get relief," she murmured as she carefully changed her position. Finally, flat on her back on the floor, she got some relief from the pain. Very soon, weariness overwhelmed her in spite of her discomfort and the hard floor, and she was lost in sleep.

Ruth felt much better when she awoke some time later. But still, she wished she would not need to help chore that evening. Papa let her off from chores, and Ruth spent chore time getting cards ready to send to some of her Pottstown Sunday school girls.

Mama went out with Papa after supper to pull sweet corn for Amityville the next day. "I'm sorry that you need to do my work, Mama," Ruth apologized as Mama pulled on her shawl to go out.

"Tut, tut," Mama said with a smile. "Guess the exercise will do me good."

Ruth leaned against the window frame and watched as Mama and Papa went out the walk to the shed. Mama's shawl fluttered and flopped, and Papa was hanging on to his straw hat. The wind was whipping the treetops from side to side. Leaves fluttered down and scuttled across the yard. Ruth had not realized it had gotten so windy. "Wonder what the wind is going to blow in," she said to Dorcas, who was still putting food away from supper.

"Probably rain. But do you think you could help me wash these dishes? Or perhaps run these leftovers down to the cave, since the icebox is full? Or is your back too sore for that?"

"Sure, I'll help," Ruth said, sorry she had not thought of that herself.

The Upward Way

Dorcas was more talkative than usual as they did the dishes together. Dorcas washed in a dishpan on the table, and Ruth rinsed in another dishpan and put the dishes onto metal trays to drain. Then she dried the dishes with the usual feed-sack towels while Dorcas put them away in their places. Ruth was happy for the time to share with this sister whom she felt she barely knew. They so seldom did anything together—they hardly ever worked together, they did not sleep together, and when they went away, it was usually with others.

Maybe if we could have more times like this evening, Ruth thought as she later prepared for the night, *we could be closer as sisters. I surely wish we could be. Dorcas can be very nice when she wants to be. And after all, she is no doubt wanting to serve the Lord faithfully just as much as I am!*

The realization sweetened her thoughts, and she knelt by her bed with a special burden to try to be closer to Dorcas. *Lord, help me to understand how she must feel inside—the loneliness when most of her friends are married and having families, the frustration because of her inability to do the things that others can easily do . . .*

Outside, darkness had settled. She heard Papa and Mama come to the house and heard them talking in the kitchen for a while. She figured Kore must be working in the garage, when she heard the revving engine of one of the cars. After a while, she heard soft strains of hymns as Mama relaxed with a hymnal. " 'One sweetly solemn thought / Comes to me o'er and o'er: / Nearer my home, today, am I / Than e'er I've been before. . . .' " The words of this song especially penetrated Ruth's mind as she

The Upward Way

listened to the solemn tune.

"Another year of my life is past," she murmured as she slowly got to her feet. "Another year of service. But did I do all I could? Was God pleased with my life?" She walked to the window, where the wind was whistling through the cracks at the frame and gently whisking the curtains. "Lord, teach me to number my days, that I may apply my heart to wisdom," she prayed, in the words of David.

Chapter Thirteen

January 1, 1935, Tuesday. The beginning of another new year. We said good-bye to the old. Now we are one year nearer to eternity, and as each year passes, more and more responsibility rests upon us. How did I use the old year? Did I make the right use of my opportunities? The snow was slushy when we got up this morning. But now it is cold and icy again. I cracked walnuts, read some, and sewed awhile. Ellen went to Pottstown for some sewing circle work—I think to cut out dresses. We had Mark and the children here for dinner. My resolution this year was a strange one maybe—I resolved to put away a piece of silk material that Papa did not want me to make up. Not only did he not like it, but I felt convicted that it would be a poor example to my Sunday school scholars. We were at Pottstown this evening for services. John Leatherman preached.

But back to November . . .

Squeak, squeak! Ruth's bed groaned in protest. "Oh, ouch!" she also groaned in protest as she hit the wall in her haste. Then she sat suddenly back down on her bed and rubbed her head. "I guess I had better get out on the

The Upward Way

right side of bed," she muttered with amusement, reaching behind her to turn off the still-clanging alarm clock.

I must have gotten to bed too late last night, she thought, *to be up again at four o'clock this morning!* The evening before, Sunday, November 4, she had been to YPM at Grove Hill as usual. After church, she had stayed with Mark and Ellen's boys until Mark and Ellen came home from a special service at Rockhill, which was after eleven o'clock.

And now I start the week tired. Oh, well, it isn't the first time. Ruth laughed to herself. Lighting her oil lamp, she busied herself with getting dressed for the day. Then she knelt by her bed with her Bible.

Papa was already feeding the horses when she went to the barn an hour later. He did not wait in the house for her anymore, for which she was thankful. Maybe he was beginning to trust her to show up in the barn at the right time. She hoped that he could by now. She was already milking her second cow when Kore came slowly into the barn. Then Mahlon came from Mark's house. Mahlon was the new hired man, and he usually fed the cows and the young stock. Ruth was glad for Mahlon's help with the outside work. His help freed her from much of the heavy work of harvesting and cutting wood. Papa had hired him after her back began giving her problems a month or so ago, and she was so thankful for Papa's consideration—even though she was quite sure it went back to Mama's intercession for her.

As Ruth squirted the foaming milk into her bucket, she thought about the barn work. She missed working with Mark in the barn. But with four new chicken houses,

The Upward Way

which had added room for an additional two thousand chickens, Mark often did not help with the barn chores. The chickens took most of his time—what time he had left from the church work that called for his attention. *I don't mind the milking though,* she thought as she carried a full bucket to the milk house. If she had to choose among the farm chores, milking would still be her favorite job. She glanced briefly at the rows of Holsteins, arranged here and there in hastily added new additions to the barn. There were thirty-one cows now, with the new ones Papa had bought at auctions over the past year.

Papa came into the milking area sometime later. "Well, I'm going to the woods now for a little while," he announced. "I'll need to come back in time for board meeting at Souderton."

"I tended the other animals," he said, raising his voice to Mahlon. "Let the cows out into the barnyard after the milking." Ruth heard him give Mahlon some more instructions regarding the day's work.

Mahlon was working at the silo. "Okay," he said, beginning to shovel silage into a wheelbarrow.

"Mark is going out with me, Ruth," Papa added. "And he'll probably stay out much of the day. So you should husk corn, at least enough to chop for the cows tomorrow.

"And, Mahlon, Mark expects you to gather the eggs this morning and this afternoon. He says to just put them down in the cellar at their house, and Ellen will grade them as she has time."

It was still very dark outside, but very soon Ruth saw a bobbing lantern going out the field lane, with shadowy silhouettes of two figures toting guns, walking with it.

233

The Upward Way

Ruth milked twenty of the cows by the time Kore finished seven. He kindly offered to finish in the milk house, so she hurried to the house. The women and Kore ate breakfast alone, as Mama knew Papa would stay in the woods till the last minute. Then Kore hurried off to school.

When Papa came in from the woods a couple of hours later, he brought a nice pheasant rooster and four squirrels. "Game is running everywhere," he said cheerily. "It would have been nice to stay out there all day. Can you take care of the game, Ruth?" He hurried to dress for his board meeting. Mama and Dorcas planned to go along, but they were already dressed to go.

"Yes, clean the game, Ruth," Mama said, "and we'll have them for supper, and invite Mark's to join us."

"It's going to be a busy week," Ruth remarked as she found knives to skin the squirrels. "Tomorrow I have a dentist appointment." She grimaced as she thought about what lay ahead. "The dentist said I have fifteen cavities! He plans to fill seven of them tomorrow!"

"And Wednesday is sewing circle at Pottstown," Dorcas inserted.

Sudden hope rose up inside Ruth at that announcement. How she had always longed to go along with the other women to sewing circle. Since they now had another hired man, might she be able to go too? She turned suddenly to confront Mama. "I've never been to sewing circle. Do you think Papa would let me go?"

Mama looked at her kindly. "Tut, tut! Twenty years old, and never been to sewing circle. I'll see what Papa says."

Papa gave his consent, but not without some

The Upward Way

stipulations. "If you can milk your cows in time, and then husk enough corn for the hogs before time to go."

How Ruth hurried! She went to the barn at quarter till five to get an earlier start. Skipping breakfast, she stayed on the barn floor, husking corn until almost the last minute before Mildred Gogle would come to pick them up. Finally, she had a good-sized pile husked, and she rushed to the house to get ready. But before she was even out of her dirty clothes, she heard Mildred's Buick come down the road and stop at the sidewalk.

"Will you be ready soon?" Dorcas called up Ruth's stairway.

"Soon!" she returned. But then she had to hurry downstairs to the bathroom to wash thoroughly, and then back up the stairs to finish dressing. Tears came, and then began to run down her cheeks. *How thoughtless of me to make them wait so,* she thought with shame.

Finally, she was ready. Grabbing her coat, she rushed out the door.

"I'm sorry," she apologized. "I should have started sooner to get ready!"

"That's okay," Mildred returned, but Dorcas gave Ruth a look that told her she was not happy to be kept waiting.

As though Dorcas never makes us wait on her! Ruth's thoughts rose up in defense. But she quickly squelched them, trying hard to feel cheerful in spite of this unpropitious beginning to her first day at sewing circle.

Ruth did enjoy the time at sewing circle fully. Some of the fifty-seven women knotted comforts. Others sewed quilt patches together, while others quilted finished

The Upward Way

tops. Children played here and there, and at times Ruth stopped her sewing to entertain them for a short time. On the way home, they stopped at J. C. Penney's outside of Pottstown, where Mama allowed her to order a new coat. Then they headed home—home to pick up the pieces of unfinished work for the day.

Ruth worked very late, and fell into bed after eleven o'clock, very weary and broken-spirited. *O Father, please look down in pity on me. What a nerve-wracking day this has been. Maybe I should have just stayed home from sewing circle, but I did enjoy being with the other women. So much of my life seems like a man's life—with all the man's work. Help me, dear Lord. I don't want to pity myself!*

The next Tuesday, Ellen went with Ruth to pick up her coat at Penney's. But before that, they both had dentist appointments. Ruth needed to have the last eight teeth filled.

"Now listen, young lady," Dr. Prizer said with a meaningful nod of his head when he was finished, "you leave candy alone. You hear me? You'll not have any teeth left by the time you are forty at the rate you're going!" He bent over to write out her bill, while Ruth stood by, her ears burning at the rebuke. How well she knew she needed it! She surely did have a sweet tooth and could hardly leave sweet things alone!

"There you are," Dr. Prizer said, handing her the bill. "Eleven dollars, for the last time and for today."

Eleven dollars! What a lot! Ruth thought. She opened the metal snap on her purse and carefully counted out the money from her hard-earned savings. *But I guess it's my*

The Upward Way

own fault, she concluded.

Two weeks later, Mark and Ellen took Ruth along to Pottstown for the evening service. Pottstown was having a week of special meetings with Brother A. J. Weaver from Lancaster County. They went early enough for Ellen to keep another dentist appointment with Dr. Prizer. When it was time for the church service, Mark was feeling nauseated and decided to stay in the car.

"Can I sit with Aunt Rufie?" Roy pleaded when he saw that his father was not coming in for the service.

"You'd better sit with Mama, sonny. Maybe Robbie can sit with Aunt Ruth this time," Mark answered from the back seat, where he was already trying to rest. A basin, always carried along in case one of the children needed it, sat on the floor beside him.

Ruth thoroughly enjoyed the evangelistic message and listened intently, seeing new areas of need in her life and purposing by God's help to do better. She rejoiced to see the many who stood in response to the invitation, some being the parents of her Sunday school scholars.

But during the service, something else was going on outside that was less than enjoyable, at least to Mark. Later, he told Ellen and Ruth the story. He had fallen asleep and must have been sleeping soundly. Suddenly he awoke to someone raucously singing, "Oh, I wish I had a million dollars . . ." He realized the car was moving, and he jumped up—nausea notwithstanding—to ask what was going on. The young man who was driving the car stopped suddenly in the middle of the street, not realizing that someone had been sleeping in the back. He jumped out, and Mark jumped out after him, chasing him for a

The Upward Way

while. But when the man turned into an alley, Mark gave up the chase. He went back to the car and hunted his way back to the mission, where he stayed awake and alert until the service was over! "And I never thought again about the possibility of needing that basin!" he finished his report with a grin.

On Thanksgiving Day, the whole family and Norman's went to Reading for a special Thanksgiving Day service. "How many, many blessings and privileges we enjoy!" Ruth remarked to Sarah as they drove home. "Even if it's raining today, when we would have preferred sunshine!"

"Yes. And how thankful we should be," Sarah added. She gazed at little Ella Mae, and Ruth knew she considered her as one of her sweetest blessings.

Mama was wiping drips of seeping rainwater off the inside of her door with her handkerchief, but she smiled at them. "I was challenged by the message to be thankful 365 days of the year, rather than just one," she said.

"Even if the car leaks," Norman inserted with a grin. Then he added, "But that's a little thing, isn't it. We truly are blessed in this country—so much abundance, as well as so many liberties."

Ruth nodded in agreement, and then her thoughts took a devious turn. Uncle Claude's had also been there for the service, and just now she was remembering the smile that David Peachey had given her when they passed in the anteroom. Did he mean anything by it? Why could he not smile at Dorcas, instead of her? He was more her age.

Papa drove by Norman and Sarah's home and dropped them off before heading home. Slowly Papa drove up

The Upward Way

their muddy gravel road and parked in front of the garage. Wonder of wonders—Ruth looked again to be sure she was seeing right—Kore was already at the barn and starting with the feeding. Feeling very thankful, she hurried to the house to change into barn clothes and then went out to help with the milking. Only lately had Kore begun to help with the milking again, after his surgery in early October. And he seemed to be doing it more willingly.

As Ruth sat on her stool, pinging the streams of milk into her bucket, she sang the song they had sung that morning at the service at Reading.

" 'I am trusting in my Saviour,
    With a calm and steady light;
Hope is shining on my pathway,
    Making all things fair and bright.
I am trusting, trusting, trusting,
    I am trusting day by day;
I am trusting in my Saviour,
    To go with me all the way.' "

Kore smirked as he passed her on his way to the milk house, but she refused to let his mockery stop her song. What deep joy she felt in her heart for all God's goodness to her.

The next few weeks, Ruth got to see little Ella Mae and Sarah nearly every day. Norman was papering and repainting the Clemmers' downstairs rooms, and, of course, he brought the family along to work. Sarah and Ruth worked together almost like old times—*almost*, because now Sarah was a mother and was not quite as free to run around outside as she once was. Sometimes they helped Norman with the indoor work.

The Upward Way

One Friday, Ruth was feeling particularly jolly. She was helping hang wallpaper while Sarah tended her baby's needs. She laughed and laughed about every little thing, until finally Norman turned to her and said soberly, "Ruth, do you know the Bible says that 'as the crackling of thorns under a pot, so is the laughter of the fool'? Why don't you calm down?"

Feeling very smitten, Ruth turned and fled. Running outside to the cave, she broke into bitter tears. For some time she cried brokenheartedly. Finally, she realized that she had failed, not only in her actions around Norman but also in her present self-pity, and she freely confessed her failure to the Lord. Then the cold began to seep through, and she knew she must go back to the house. But how could she face her idolized brother-in-law? She cringed at the thought. Should she tell him she was sorry? How could she do that? Confessing needs and failures had not been a part of her training or parental example, and she shrank from the thought.

Instead, she went quietly to the washhouse, got her barn coat, and went to the barn. Only after Norman's had left for the day, and the milking was done, did she go to the house again. Sleep did not come easily for her that night as she rolled and tossed. *Squeak, squeak,* protested her bed, and *"You failed; you failed,"* protested her conscience. Only after she had finally promised the Lord to tell Norman she was sorry did she find a measure of peace and manage to get some sleep.

Tomorrow came—and so did Norman's again. True to her resolution, Ruth went promptly to Norman. "I'm sorry for being silly yesterday, Norman. I should know

The Upward Way

better, and I did appreciate your rebuke," she said, trying hard to keep her lips from quivering.

"Well, I felt bad too, Ruth," Norman said kindly. "Sarah can tell you I did." He looked at Sarah, who stood nearby with an understanding smile. "Perhaps I was too hard on you, and I'm sorry for that."

"Oh, no," Ruth protested. "I deserved it, and I'm glad for what you said."

After a few more moments of visiting, Ruth went happily to her Saturday work. How light her heart now felt. *Why is it so hard to say 'I'm sorry,'* she wondered. *It has to be pride, and Christians should be emptied of pride—which should make confessing failure very easy. Oh, why isn't it easier, dear Father? Please take away my pride, and help me to be truly Thy humble handmaid!*

For the next week, Ruth spent much time taking baskets of food to their many poor neighbors. How rewarded she felt at their sincere looks and words of gratitude, and the many happy tears, especially on the faces of the children! "Why, some of our neighbors, like the Lloyd's, hardly have anything to eat at their house!" she exclaimed to Mama on Saturday afternoon when she came back from there. "How do such people ever live?"

"We should do more for our poor neighbors,"[26] Mama said apologetically. "We get so involved in our own things and forget the needs of those around us."

"And we surely have plenty to eat ourselves," Ruth

---

[26] The social security program, begun after the Social Security Act of 1935, was not yet in effect. Most of these poor had no material assistance, other than through humanitarian programs such as churches.

The Upward Way

added. "We give perfectly good food to the horses and the hogs because we can't use it all!" She was thinking of all the produce that was not good enough to sell, and thus ended up being feed for the animals.

Many of the neighbors were well-to-do and often ordered fresh meat or cheese or garden vegetables. These Ruth continued to deliver, happy for the opportunities for neighborly contact and Christian witness. But as often as she walked with deliveries to such neighbors, she also carried along second-grade potatoes or turnips or some cheese that did not get "quite right," for the neighbors who were not able to pay. The poor neighbors, it always seemed to her, were the ones most ready to hear about a loving Saviour.

If there was any time to spare in the regular daily routines, Ruth spent it cracking black walnuts. The harvest last fall had been more than abundant, and she began to feel they should have left more for the squirrels, as hours of cracking them did not seem to noticeably diminish the pile. That was a job that Dorcas could help with, and even Kore and the rest of the family joined in during some of the long December evenings for some pleasant family times of picking nutmeats and singing together.

"Skinner took several feedbags of walnuts today," Papa began one evening as they shelled walnuts together. "He paid me $1.85 a bag for them, and seemed awfully glad to get them too."

Mama nodded happily. "That many less for us to bother with," she said. "I'm sure we could sell the nutmeats too."

"We should weigh some in pounds and put them

The Upward Way

in little paper sacks to sell along with the candies and things," Dorcas suggested. "We'll never use them all," she added emphatically.

Papa continued hammering a walnut he had placed on one of Mama's old flatirons. "Another one to pick out," he said as he handed the cracked nut to Mama. "Sure, we could sell some," he went on. "They'd be something else to take along to Amityville, now that produce is scarce."

And so, Ruth thought later, the nut-cracking evenings gradually became an enterprise, rather than a time of family enjoyment as they once had been.

The Friday before Christmas, Ruth got up to the softness of snow covering all the bleak landscape. Snow was still falling lightly as she tramped to the barn through several inches of the downy whiteness. A lantern was hung in the milking stable, and Mark, who did not often help with the milking anymore, was already there and ready to start.

"I hope the snow stays a while," Ruth said, and Mark looked up with a ready smile.

Papa passed them with a wheelbarrow of silage. "I wasn't ready for snow yet," he lamented. "I still need to get a lot more wood in and wanted to clean up the orchard too."

"It will melt again," Mark reminded him. "I wasn't exactly hoping for snow today either, but the Lord sent it, and we will thank Him for it."

"Oh, you were going to get those two chicken houses from Swartz's today, weren't you?" Ruth said.

Mark nodded as he sat down and began to milk his first cow. "We got those eight hundred chicks that the

The Upward Way

hatchery didn't know what to do with, you know. But we can feed them in the kitchen for a few more days!" He laughed. "The boys sure do enjoy them and won't mind that prospect!"

Ruth laughed in return. "You didn't say what Ellen thinks." She knew very well that Ellen had not wanted any chickens in her kitchen to begin with and had allowed them there only as a last resort.

Even if the others thought of the snow as a nuisance, Ruth loved it. She rejoiced for the opportunity to be out in it all morning, helping Papa and Mark cut wood and haul it in from the wood lot. In the house, Dorcas and Mama had mixed up numerous batches of cookie dough. When Ruth came in at noon, they were ready to spend the afternoon rolling out, cutting, and baking cookies.

"Do I get to help with baking cookies?" she asked as she came in, pink-cheeked and fresh from the cold.

Mama smiled at Ruth's eagerness. "I suppose. If Papa doesn't need your help. Sarah is coming to help too this afternoon, if Norman can get his Willys through the snow."

"Oh, wonderful!" Ruth exclaimed. "Maybe I'll keep Ella Mae happy while the rest of you bake!"

"Maybe I could baby-sit today," Dorcas returned with a grin. "Seems to me I hardly ever get that job."

Ruth thought, *I guess I do take that privilege away from Dorcas too much.* Aloud she said, "Sure. I'll bake this time, and you can entertain the baby. And I'll even share the cookies with you!"

Dorcas dimpled happily as she finished putting dinner on the table. She had been kinder, Ruth had often noticed,

The Upward Way

in the past months, especially since Ruth and Charles were no longer courting.

Papa had come into the kitchen and stood looking out the window toward the barn. "I guess Mark and I will work at whitewashing the new part of the barn this afternoon. I'm eager to try out that spray pump I got. It should save a lot of work."

Ruth laughed as she pulled out her chair at the table, remembering the many times she had helped to apply whitewash with an old broom. "It surely ought to go faster too!"

"It had better go fast!" Papa emphasized. "I heard the inspector has been in the neighborhood and might show up here any day. And since Pinchot is governor, farms have to be in apple-pie order."

"Oh, Papa," Mama remonstrated, "you shouldn't complain! You know Governor Pinchot has done a lot of good for us farmers since he's been in office. At least you often say that it's because of him that so many of the township roads have been paved, and things like that."

Papa nodded. "Yes, but he sure hasn't gotten to our road yet. Plus, he's awfully strict about some things that he hasn't any right to get his nose into, and a lot of the dairymen are looking forward to when he goes out of office at the end of '35." He stepped to the table, pulled out his chair, and sat down.

"Anyway, I hope the snow melts by tomorrow," Papa went on. "We need to haul those chicken houses for Mark home from Swartz's. And I wanted to fix the yard fence before winter settles in."

"Kore has off from school next week," Mama

The Upward Way

contributed. "Maybe you can get some extra things done then."

"Well, can we pray and eat?" Dorcas suddenly inserted. "We have all those cookies to bake this afternoon, and next thing you know Sarah will be here before we've even started eating."

Papa directed a look at Dorcas that told her he wasn't exactly happy with her comments. Then they bowed their heads for silent prayer.

After the cookies were baked late that afternoon, Ruth and Sarah put together tins of the different kinds for a number of their poor neighbors. "Maybe tomorrow we can deliver these," Ruth said.

"I wish I would be here to help," Sarah said. "I would enjoy visiting with Mrs. Cook again, and the Keely's, the Karl's, the Lloyd's, and some of the others."

"And they would be delighted to see you, especially if you took Ella Mae along," Ruth assured her.

"Why don't you take them now?" Mama asked from where she was watering her many violets. "Why don't all of you girls go? Take the car."

Ruth looked up eagerly. "You mean now, when it's about time to go to the barn? Who would milk my cows?"

"Well, Kore is here. And both Mark and Papa are out at the barn already. If they wonder where you are, I'll explain."

Dorcas had turned in her chair at the sewing machine and was watching them. "I'd like to go along, but I've got all these sewing orders that I need to have finished for Christmas. And besides, it's hard for me to get around—and in and out of the car so much—in this snow."

The Upward Way

Mama looked at Dorcas sympathetically as Sarah said, "I'm sure the neighbors would be glad to see you. But they'll not feel badly about it if you aren't along."

Even though Dorcas did not go along, the girls still decided to take the car so that they could take the baby along. Baby and tins of cookies were soon loaded. Everywhere they stopped, the people wanted to visit, so it was nearly six o'clock before they got home.

"Everyone was so grateful," Ruth burst out to Mama as she and Sarah shed their wraps in the warm kitchen. "It was so good to do this little bit of kindness for others!"

Ruth quickly changed and hurried in the darkness to the barn. Papa was not pleased about her absence, and she still had most of her cows to milk. Kore had grudgingly started milking her share, but he stalked off when she got there. Mark soon left as well, to go up the hill for his supper.

"I'm sorry to leave you to finish all this work. But we have all today's eggs to grade yet after supper," he explained.

"I was just glad you were here to help milk both this morning and evening," Ruth returned. "Do you want help to grade eggs this evening?"

"I don't think so. We can do it in a couple of hours, I think. Besides, you'll be here yet for a while, the way it looks. But thanks anyway."

Papa soon left to finish the feeding, and Ruth was left with her own thoughts as the milk zinged into the pails.

It was after seven o'clock by the time she finished milking, but thoughts of the well-spent afternoon sustained her. *It was worth it, to bring joy to so many*

247

The Upward Way

neighbors, she thought as she carried the last bucket of milk to the milk house. Kore came back into the barn with a smirk on his face as she was sweeping hay into the mangers.

"Hey, I've got a gift for you," he said. "This is to thank you for the extra work I had to do for you this evening." He held something in his hand, and he drew his arm back now, getting ready to throw it to her. "Catch!" he directed, sending it her way.

Instinctively she reached out to catch whatever it was. It was an egg, and when she caught it, it popped in her hand, splattering its foul-smelling contents all over her. What a horrible sulfur smell! "Oh, Kore! How can you be so mean!" she exclaimed as she hastily dropped the rotten egg. He laughed uproariously and made a quick exit. Sudden anger flashed up, and almost she ran after him with angry words. But instead, she turned and fled to the milk house where she beseeched the Lord's help, and tried her best to scrub off the awful smell.

Tuesday was Christmas Day, and the Clemmers spent the morning at Grove Hill for special services. The rest of the day until chore time they were at Uncle Jonas's, along with many of Mama's family as well. Ruth especially enjoyed the time with her cousin Grace, feeling that she and Grace were kindred spirits.

"How are you enjoying your two Sunday school classes by now?" Grace asked as both girls lay across Grace's bed. (No radiators or baseboard heat warmed the upstairs rooms in those days. But Grace did have a special blessing—the chimney from the wood stove downstairs in the living room went through her bedroom,

The Upward Way

making her room comfortable enough for visiting.)

"Oh, I am enjoying them," Ruth returned slowly. "I just hope my students are learning something!"

"I'll have to tell you what my sister Katherine told me—that should encourage you. You know, Mama and Papa visited in Lancaster County the other Sunday, at some church there—I forget the name of the church. When Katherine came home, she said, 'I can't believe how little the other girls in my Sunday school class knew about the Bible! I knew about most of the things because we have a good teacher here at Grove Hill.' " Grace smiled meaningfully at Ruth.

Thankfulness filled Ruth's heart. Maybe the girls were learning something. But if they were, it was because of God's help.

Before she could respond, the bedroom doorknob rattled. As both girls gazed toward the door, it opened slowly and a little yellow head appeared around it.

"Hi, Gerald," Ruth said with a laugh. "You may come in."

"This is where you is," the two-year-old lisped sweetly. "I can't fin' you downstairs."

"What do you want?" Grace questioned him.

"Paul wen' ou'side wif the big boys, an' I don't have anyone to pway wif."

"Come; you can be with us," Ruth offered, sitting up and making room for him on the bed with them.

Gladly he climbed up and began to entertain them with his stories, while the girls continued visiting over his head as they could.

"I saw Katherine started wearing a covering now,"

The Upward Way

Ruth said. "She looked so nice on Sunday, I thought."

Grace nodded. "Mama made her one after she became a Christian the other week. I thought, 'What a shame to put her beautiful hair under a covering!' "

Ruth looked questioningly at Grace.

"That's just what I mean," Grace went on. "She has such pretty, wavy blond hair, and now it's got to be all covered up."

"Covered up," Gerald said, looking at first one girl and then the other.

Ruth smiled at him and then turned back to Grace, a feeling of sadness in her heart. "Don't you feel the Bible teaches that a Christian woman is to be covered?"

Grace shrugged. "I guess. But you know Aunt Margaret thinks that teaching in 1 Corinthians is just Paul's teaching, not Christ's. She only wears a covering for church, and probably wouldn't then if she didn't have to. She was talking to Mama lately about it. You know, Aunt Margaret really knows her Bible, but Mama didn't agree with her at all. Mama insisted that that part of the Scripture is just as inspired as the rest of the Bible, and we have to believe it all or none. Mama was pretty fired up. I suppose your parents would have been too. But I like Aunt Margaret a lot. She's always so sweet."

Ruth nodded. She liked Aunt Margaret too. But she knew that Uncle Titus and Aunt Margaret did not agree with Papa and Mama about a lot of things. She knew that Uncle Titus would have liked to be involved in politics, but the church would not allow him to, and so he limited his involvement to serving on the local school board. She also knew that he usually wore a bow tie, even though

The Upward Way

many of the ministry, Papa included, felt very strongly about wearing a plain suit. And Aunt Margaret did not wear a cape dress. But they were members at Blooming Glen, which had always been one of the more progressive churches in their conference.

Suddenly Gerald slid off the bed, and was soon out the door and down the stairs.

"I guess we were boring company for him," Grace said with a laugh. "By the way," she added, "our mothers would have a fit if they knew we were sitting on a *bed!* Isn't that anathema to our good housekeeper mothers?"

"I suppose," Ruth agreed, "but where else are we to sit?"

"Oh, this is okay," Grace assured her. "Anyway, I was thinking about being at Uncle Titus's last Christmas. Remember how we girls opened the parlor door and they had a decorated Christmas tree in there?" She laughed heartily. "Aunt Margaret was horrified that your papa and mine found out about it! Then she tried to justify it 'because we always had a Christmas tree when we were children living in Virginia—and you know it, Vena and Jonas!' "

Ruth remembered all that, but she did not feel like laughing, because she had gone home feeling very badly about it. She still did. Why was simple, Bible obedience so often mocked, even among those who appeared to live it? She could not understand, but she did know that she wanted to be obedient, not only to the letter but also to the spirit of the Word.

Grace laughed again. "Remember how we liked to play with Aunt Margaret's dumbwaiter when we were younger?"

This time Ruth did laugh, recalling the time she had accidentally hit the button that dropped the dumbwaiter,

The Upward Way

loaded with food ready to go on the table, suddenly out of sight into the basement. "Uncle Titus was always handy at thinking up timesavers, wasn't he?" she said.

"But that time Aunt Margaret didn't think we girls were so handy to have around!" Grace returned merrily. "The old Good ire sparkled from her eyes, and we knew we'd better hustle out of her way for a while."

A chill slowly creeping over them, from the edges in, soon sent the girls downstairs to join the rest. Some of the uncles were dozing in the warmth by the wood stove. The aunts were visiting in the kitchen, discussing cheese, chickens, and children. Outside, lazy snowflakes were drifting down, and most of the younger set were out there, enjoying the fresh snow.

"Shall we go outside too?" Ruth asked. "Looks like more fun outside than in!"

"Sure," Grace returned. "I wish we'd have enough snow that we could get the sleigh out."

Soon Papa came out to drive the car up to the sidewalk, and Ruth knew it was time to go home and do chores.

Toward evening, the snow changed to rain. After chores were finished and supper over, Ruth curled up near the stove in the sitting room, eager to read the new book that her Grove Hill students had given her for Christmas: *Adoniram Judson, America's First Foreign Missionary.*

The Monday before New Year's Day was a very busy one. Papa was finally able to haul the two chicken houses home from Swartz's. The men worked at that most of the day, hauling them and setting them up, which left all the chores—milking, feeding, gathering eggs—for Ruth and Ellen.

The Upward Way

By the time Ruth had finished all the work that evening, it was after eleven o'clock. Mama was still reading in the sitting room. "Are you going to stay up to see the New Year in?" Ruth asked with a smile as she peered over Mama's shoulder to see what she was reading.

"I wasn't planning to. But I got started with this book, *Uganda's White Man of Work,* and decided to finish it." She chuckled. "Tut, tut! I'll pay for it tomorrow!"

"Is Papa still outside too?"

"He must be. I don't see how they have enough light to finish setting up those chicken houses, but he was determined to finish tonight."

"Well, who's helping him? Mark wasn't feeling well today when they got back from hauling the houses home, and he went in to bed."

"I think Kore is still out. And no doubt Mahlon is helping too."

"Oh, the poor fellows!" Ruth said. "I'm sure Kore isn't too happy about all this."

Ruth decided that if Mama stayed up, she may as well too. She would sing the New Year in. Opening the *Church and Sunday School Hymnal*, she began with "I'm Pressing on the Upward Way," singing all four verses. Song after song she sang, until finally Kore dragged himself disconsolately through the room and up the stairs. Soon afterward Papa also came in.

"What are you women still doing up?" he asked incredulously. "Nobody will feel like getting up tomorrow morning. And there's still work to do, holiday or no holiday."

The Upward Way

"I know it; I know it," Mama returned, laying her book aside.

"We wanted to see the New Year in," Ruth offered, glancing at the chime clock, which had just cleared its throat to strike the hour of midnight.

"Well, I'm going to bed. You can stay up all night if you wish to." And so saying, Papa headed for the stairs.

New Year's Day was markedly colder than the several previous mild days. Ruth sloshed through mud and soft snow to the barn at five-thirty. But by the time she came back in at seven-thirty, the temperature on the thermometer on the garage wall had dropped five degrees, and everything was beginning to solidify under her feet.

"Anybody game to go sledding today?" she gasped as she popped around the washhouse door into the kitchen. "The snow is getting a crust on top; and if it gets much colder, it will be good sledding weather."

Kore shivered beside the wood stove. "Br-r! Not if it gets as cold as the radio said it's to get."

Ruth looked questioningly at him. He had been home over Sunday. Did his mother have a radio? Perhaps she did. Ruth knew quite a few of their church members were getting them.

"How cold is it to get?" Mama asked. She was busy at the cookstove with some fizzing operation.

"They're talking about falling temperatures all through the day, and down to zero by tonight."

"Well, maybe I'll do some sewing today," Ruth decided. "At least if there isn't outside work." She turned to Mama. "I have that new piece of silk to make up that I got a couple of weeks ago. I'm eager to make and wear that one."

The Upward Way

Mama suddenly remembered something. "Oh, Ellen plans to help with some sewing circle work at Pottstown today, so she is hoping to leave the boys here."

"Good!" Ruth rejoiced.

"It would be a good day to crack more walnuts too," Mama added. "Roy can help with that. He likes to hammer the walnuts open."

"And hit his fingers, like he did the last time," Dorcas inserted. "And howl about how much they hurt the rest of the day."

"It wasn't quite that bad," Mama chided.

While the boys were napping in the afternoon, Ruth got out her soft silk material and spread it on the table to cut. It was shimmeringly beautiful, and Ruth admired it, thinking about herself swathed in such loveliness. Carefully she laid out her pattern, and carefully she cut. But the longer she cut, the more her conscience smote her. *Pride . . . it's just for pride's sake. . . . But Mama did not see anything wrong with it,* she justified herself. *And even Sarah said I would look beautiful in it.*

Some time later, Papa came through the room to his desk. Stopping suddenly by the sewing machine, he gazed silently for a bit. "What is that material for?" he asked finally.

"A dress for me," Ruth returned, quaking a bit. *Perhaps I should have asked Papa about it.*

"A dress for you?" he repeated. "All I can say is that it will tie your tongue."

"But it's so pretty," Ruth offered, attempting to justify her choice, "and Mama thought it was all right."

"It is too bright and shiny. I do not like it, and I do not

The Upward Way

think you should make it up. But since you are already sewing it, I will not say you positively may not."

Papa did not say anything more, and Ruth went on sewing. Other girls in their conference wore such fabrics, and some even worse! Even ministers' daughters did. Why couldn't she? But Papa's words kept going through her mind. *"It will tie your tongue. . . . It will tie your tongue. . . ."*

After some time, she carried the partially finished bodice to the bathroom and fit it on in front of the mirror. How the soft pink brought out the deep pink of her cheeks and the dark brown of her sparkling eyes and wavy hair. Turning herself, she gazed with fascination at her reflection. Suddenly, with stunning sharpness came the remembrance of a cartoon she had recently seen in a *Sword and Trumpet* magazine. It showed a young woman standing in front of a mirror admiring herself; and behind the mirror, and holding it, stood the devil. An inscription on the mirror said, "In vain shalt thou make thyself fair."

With new conviction, Ruth quickly took off the offending material and laid it aside. "Papa doesn't approve of it. He thought it would tie my tongue; and if it goes against his wishes, and ruins my example to my Sunday school scholars, I will not wear it! Besides, I'm afraid it will only feed my vanity." Ruth spoke under her breath, but her determination was as firm as though she had shouted it. She folded up the pieces and carefully put them all away in the storeroom bureau. "Maybe sometime I'll send it to sewing circle to cut up for quilt tops," she said, a great relief flooding her heart.

She went to the washhouse, where Mama, Dorcas,

The Upward Way

and Kore were cracking walnuts. A fire was crackling in the fireplace, making the room cozy despite the cold outdoors. "I guess I'll join the nutting crew," she said.

"Is your dress all finished?" Dorcas asked.

"No. Papa didn't like it when he saw it, and I decided it wasn't the thing for me to wear either." It was hard for her to express her real feelings about it, especially with Dorcas looking at her as though she thought Ruth had lost her senses.

"What a positive shame!" Kore exclaimed. "For once you get a dress that I like, and then you decide you don't want to wear it."

But Mama understood. "I wondered about it," she admitted. "But I know others have that kind of material and assumed it would be all right. I should have known that Papa wouldn't appreciate it." She shook her head as though regretting her lack of forethought. "Ruth, you made a wise decision, and God will honor you for it."

It was the evening for Pottstown's regular service. In spite of the wind and the frigid temperatures, the Clemmers all ventured out. Brother John Leatherman preached an inspiring sermon entitled "Looking Ahead to the New Year."

Ruth climbed into her squeaky bed that night with a happy heart. She had peace about the day, even though it had not gone as she had hoped, and there was no new and beautiful dress hanging in her wardrobe. "Father in heaven, thank You that I can be Your daughter. Help me always to hear Your voice and listen to Your gentle prods. How much I want to please You and do Your will," she whispered into the black stillness.

Chapter Fourteen

March 25, 1935, Momday. Today is my dear mama's birthday. She is 57 years old. I was burning brush along the creek bank. Helped Ellen transplant early tomato plants—she has 45 now in the cow stable windows! It was cloudy all day. Wondering about the future . . . James 4:7 was my theme for the day.

But first, back to winter . . .

The winter, Ruth thought, did not seem nearly as busy as previous winters had been. Maybe it was because Mahlon proved to be a good hired man, and his help freed Ruth from some of the outside work that she had been accustomed to doing for so long. Or maybe it was that she was more satisfied with her lot and more able to accomplish her tasks without such a wearisome physical and emotional drain.

Whatever the case, Ruth reveled in the new privilege of having time to read, time to sew, and even time to write now and then. She wrote a few stories and sent them off to the *Youth's Christian Companion,* as well as

The Upward Way

a couple to *Words of Cheer.*[27] Although one was returned as unusable, the rest were accepted, and her joy at finding a place of service in writing propelled her to new heights of satisfaction in her Christian life.

January was a month of cold, with many days of either sleet or snow.

"Is the cold what makes all the sickness?" Ruth asked one morning at breakfast in mid-February. She had been coughing for days, and Dorcas had had the next thing to pneumonia, Dr. Simpson had told her. Dorcas was still coughing harshly and did not try to do much. But Ruth had never been sick enough to stay in bed. "Yesterday Sarah called and said that Ella Mae is sick," Ruth added, "and now this morning at the barn, Mark said he had an awful sore throat. What is the matter anyway?"

Mama shrugged. "I don't know. Many others from church have been sick too. I guess it is just something that is going around. And I suppose all the cold and dampness doesn't help matters any. So Mark is sick," she added. "Won't be such a pleasant birthday for him."

"Oh, today is his birthday," Ruth remembered suddenly, "and I forgot to say anything about it."

"It was twelve below zero this morning," Kore contributed, apparently not impressed with birthdays. "The water cups for the cows were all frozen, and I had to haul water up from the spring for them. Mark brought a brooder stove down from one of the chicken houses to try to thaw out pipes."

---

[27] Both periodicals were produced by Herald Press at Scottdale, PA, and, along with *Beams of Light*, were used in most Mennonite Sunday schools at the time.

The Upward Way

Mama's thoughts must have still been on sickness, for soon she spoke again. "I never knew a winter with so many deaths. Why, tomorrow there will be two funerals at Grove Hill, and I don't remember such a thing ever happening before."

"So Hannah Good's and Aaron Funk's are going to be the same day?" Dorcas questioned. She began coughing harshly and got up from the table to take some more cough medicine.[28]

Mama looked after her pityingly and then said, "Yes, Hannah's is in the morning, and Aaron's in the afternoon."

Ruth decided to stay home the next day with Dorcas, since neither of them felt the best, while Papa and Mama went to the two funerals. Even though she would have felt best resting, Ruth decided to can the ground pork that was waiting in tubs in the washhouse. By using the big boiler on the cookstove, she was able to can thirty quarts by the time Papa and Mama came home at chore time.

"Tut, tut!" Mama exclaimed happily. "So you got some of the pork canned. Good for you." She bustled about with her bonnet and coat still on, counting jars. "Oh, by the way, Jessie Mack's are planning to be here for supper."

"So, were they at the funeral?" Ruth asked. "I guess he would be, since he was just ordained at Skippack, and ministers usually attend funerals in the district when they can."

Mama nodded. "We have plenty of food around to fix.

---

[28] This was probably a homemade mixture, possibly made with honey and vinegar.

The Upward Way

I'll get at it as soon as I have my coat off and my apron on. Is Dorcas resting?"

"She has been most of the day. I think I heard her at the sewing machine some, and she did come out to eat dinner with me. But most of the time, she's been resting."

"Where's Kore?" Papa asked, coming in just then.

"I haven't seen him all day," Ruth said. "Maybe he's up at Mark's; I don't know."

Just then an older model Chevy came slowly up the road. It pulled in at the garage and stopped there.

"Oh!" Mama exclaimed. "Are Jesse's here already? I had better hustle."

Ruth was looking out the window. "Jesse's wouldn't have such an old car, Mama." Then the person emerged from the car, and Ruth said in subdued excitement, "It's David Peachey, Papa! What is he doing here?"

Papa, still donned in his Sunday coat and hat, went back out through the washhouse and met David in front of the garage. Ruth watched them for a while as they stood in a patch of afternoon sunshine, wishing she'd know how to slip past and go to the barn. It was time to start the evening chores. Mama was bustling about the kitchen, but she had a mysterious twinkle in her eye, Ruth noticed.

"Mama, what do you know about this?" Ruth asked quietly. "Is he interested in Dorcas? Oh, I hope so!"

"I don't know," Mama confessed. "But I must admit, I would wish a nice young man like that would take an interest in her."

"So you think he is a nice young man?" Ruth inquired. "Does Dorcas think so too?"

The Upward Way

"I don't know how Dorcas feels," Mama admitted. "But I know Papa thinks he is about as fine a young man as ever came to our church."

"He puts our own young men to shame with his spiritual commitment, doesn't he?" Ruth continued sincerely. "But he is surely quiet. One doesn't hear much out of him."

" 'Still waters run deep,' the old saying goes," Mama said.

After nearly half an hour, Papa came back into the house, and the car went slowly down the gravel road. Not a hint of their conversation did Papa give, and Ruth was nearly bursting with curiosity. How she wished for Dorcas a faithful Christian companion! Sure, he was a little younger than Dorcas, but not that much—only several years!

Ruth's thoughts were suddenly interrupted by the jangling of the telephone. She hurried to answer it. It was Norman, and his voice, usually calm and gentle, now sounded frantic. "Can you tell Mama and Ellen to come right away?" he burst out.

"Oh, Norman, what is wrong?" Ruth managed to gasp.

"Ella Mae is not responding to us, and Sarah thinks she is in a coma. Oh, tell them to come quickly, if they possibly can. Dr. Simpson is coming too." And Norman hung up the telephone.

Ruth burst into sudden tears, hardly able to sob out the message. Dorcas came to the kitchen door, wanting to know what was going on, and Mama tried to tell her. "Run up to Ellen right away, Ruth, and see if she can be ready in a couple of minutes."

While Ruth was pulling on her coat, she heard Mama

The Upward Way

asking Dorcas if she felt well enough to get supper for Jesse's. Then Ruth was out the door and up the hill at breakneck speed.

In a few minutes, Mama and Ellen were ready to leave. After the Buick raced up the hill and out of sight, Ruth went to the barn, her heart so burdened that she hardly knew what she was doing. Somehow the cows got milked and the chores done. Jesse Mack's came, but when they heard what was happening, they kindly offered to go on home, which they did.

It was long past bedtime. Ruth had long ago tucked Roy and Robert in bed, and now their father had gone to bed as well. But still Ruth and Dorcas sat up, waiting expectantly for some word to come from Norman's. Finally the call came. Dear little Ella Mae had died peacefully in her mother's arms, never regaining consciousness. Mama and Ellen were going to spend the night with Sarah and Norman.

Ruth went to bed, but not to sleep. Between her tears and sobs, she prayed fervently for her dear sister and her husband. Mama had said that Dr. Simpson called it encephalitis, an inflammation of the brain usually caused by an infection somewhere else in the body. Ruth knew that Ella Mae had had a bad cold for more than a week, which none of their home remedies had seemed to help. And now she was dead. She was in heaven, but, oh, how empty Sarah's arms would be! How could they bear this loss! Over and over, Ruth committed them to the heavenly Father, whom she knew could comfort them in a way that no human being ever could.

The next days were taken up with funeral arrangements

The Upward Way

and the actual funeral. Ruth was numb with grief, and she knew that Norman and Sarah were also. She had gone to Sarah as soon as she had been able, and they had cried in each other's arms.

"Oh, my baby," Sarah had grieved. "How can I give her up like this?" For some time she had sobbed uncontrollably. Then she had quieted some and said softly and brokenly, "But I want to submit to the wisdom of our heavenly Father. I know He knows what is best, even though our hearts are breaking. He is good! I must remember that, and simply trust Him."

Somehow the following days returned to a kind of normalcy. Norman and Sarah spent a lot of time at the Clemmer home, and Ruth grieved to see how spiritless Sarah seemed. None of her former joys seemed to rouse her into any kind of response. Her appetite was gone, and had it not been for the support of her faith and her family, Ruth had no doubt but that the mother would have followed the little one in death. Norman seemed, though also deeply grieving, to be able to bear up somewhat better. He spent the days painting and finishing the upstairs bedrooms at Mark's house.

By the first of March, spring seemed truly to be in the air. The snow was all gone, and mud was everywhere. That day Ruth brought in the mail, stepping gingerly across the mud that was the road. "What is this?" she exclaimed aloud as she sorted through the various envelopes and fliers. "A letter from David Peachey—for *me*!" What would he be writing to her about? True, after David's talk with Papa that day a couple of weeks before, Ruth had waited eagerly for some word to come

The Upward Way

to Dorcas. But to her? There was some mistake!

Tucking the letter in her apron pocket, she sauntered into the house as nonchalantly as possible. No one need know about it, at least not until she had read it to see what it was about. And she was not about to read it until she was somewhere by herself with no possibility of being disturbed.

And so the letter waited until she was in her own room that night at ten o'clock. She lit her oil lamp and, with great trepidation, pulled the envelope out of her pocket and slit it with a penknife. It *was* addressed to her!

"Dear Ruth," it began. "Greetings in our worthy Master's Name. I have been observing you for some time and would appreciate the privilege of learning to know you better . . ."

The letter fell from Ruth's hand. Why, oh, why, did he ask her? She had no interest in him. Not one iota! All along she had interpreted the glances to be for Dorcas's benefit. Besides, he was all of five years older than she was.

She felt very inclined to write a positive *no* back right then. But that would not be fair to him, would it? *Oh, Father,* she prayed as she fell on her knees, *what am I to say to such a person to whom I feel no attraction whatever? What is Your will, Lord?* For a time she knelt silently. Like a whisper to her mind came the old time-proven words, *"Trust in the LORD with all thine heart; and lean not unto thine own understanding. In all thy ways acknowledge him, and he shall direct thy paths."*

For several hours, Ruth lay awake, struggling with the feelings in her own heart. Uppermost always was the plea that the Lord would spare her from someone

The Upward Way

whom she felt certain she could never love. She finally fell asleep, but not to sleep for long, before her alarm clock awakened her at four-thirty. Stiffly and wearily she got up to begin her day.

It did not take Mama long to realize that something was preying on Ruth's mind. "What has gotten into you, Ruth? You walk about like you are in a daze." Mama looked long at her, deep concern showing in her eyes. "Are you still grieving about little Ella Mae? You need to leave that with the Lord, and go on."

Ruth shook her head. "Not that. I have given that grief to the Lord." She looked around the kitchen hastily to be sure there were no prying ears or eyes. She heard the treadle of the sewing machine in the sitting room and figured Dorcas would not be able to hear above that.

"What else could be bothering you?" Mama probed.

"I had a letter from David Peachey yesterday." As soon as she said it, she realized that Mama probably already knew that such might be forthcoming. Is that what David had been talking to Papa about? Had they been talking about her, and not Dorcas after all, as she had surmised?

Mama's face lightened. "What is so terrible about that?" she asked. "David is a nice enough young man, I suppose, though as poor as a church mouse."

"And from the boondocks too, and his father is a drunk," Dorcas added, peering around the sitting room door.

Ruth turned quickly, startled at the sound of Dorcas's voice. She had not meant for Dorcas to know about this, at least not until she had sorted out her own feelings.

The Upward Way

But Dorcas had ears like a cat! How could she have forgotten that?

Mama looked at Dorcas. "We can't judge a young man by his parents, you know, although I'd want to be sure someone with a father like he has is what he claims to be."

"Well, all along I thought he was interested in Dorcas," Ruth said, figuring she might as well say it now that Dorcas was listening anyway.

Dorcas humphed emphatically. "Well, I guess he knew better than to try me. I wouldn't have anything to do with him, now or ten years from now!"

Ruth thought Mama should reprove Dorcas. She had thought that at times before, when Dorcas had displayed such uncharitable attitudes. But Mama very seldom had, and Ruth had never been able to understand why not.

All Mama said was, "All that we know about David Peachey is good, and we would have no problem with his wanting to court one of our girls. We just wouldn't want him to carry off our daughter to North Carolina."

"To live with the snakes and snapping turtles," Dorcas muttered. "I sure hope Ruth has more sense than to take up with such a nobody. He has no family background to be proud of, and no future to offer any girl either!" she added indignantly.

Mama looked as though she had been struck, but she did not speak. Was she perhaps regretting that she herself had been in the habit of making so much over her family history, so that she had possibly fostered an elitist pride in her oldest daughter? Ruth did not know, but she wondered about Mama's look for days afterward.

The Upward Way

Papa, when told about the letter, did not have much to say. "You have to know how you feel about him," he told Ruth. "Mama and I can't plan your future for you. He is a very fine young man, as far as anyone knows. And we appreciate his spiritual interests. But you have to know that he doesn't have any means of his own."

After thinking and praying about it for several weeks, Ruth finally sent David a letter. "I have nothing against you," she wrote, "but I just do not feel led of the Lord to pursue a relationship at this time."

But the letter being sent did not give Ruth the peace she expected, and the thought troubled her as she trimmed raspberries, or hauled manure, or butchered hogs the next few days. *Did You speak, Lord, and I was not willing to listen?* she questioned many times.

When Mama asked her what her answer had been, Ruth told her that she had said no. Mama looked disappointed, but she did not say much—only, "Well, I sure hope you have done the right thing."

Had she followed her own feelings, rather than give the Lord opportunity to lead in her life? Should she have asked counsel of others, like Uncle Claude's, or like Mark and Ellen? Why did her decision continue to haunt her? She had had no such qualms when turning down two others who had asked her since her break with Charles Derstine. But then, they did not have any kind of worthy character either, to appeal to her finer feelings. But David Peachey—kind, committed, and noble, whom nobody could find fault with in relation to his spiritual experience . . . Ruth could not decide whether she had followed God's leading or not. Finally, she was able to

The Upward Way

still her disquieting thoughts by enmeshing herself in continual activity.

Then on Sunday, her thoughts were once more thrown into turmoil. Who should have the topic at YPM that evening at Grove Hill other than David Peachey!

"Didn't David speak well?" Grace Good said after the service.

"Yes, he did," Ruth admitted freely.

"I wonder why he doesn't find a girlfriend among all the girls in our churches," Grace went on dreamily. "I imagine someone would have him."

Ruth looked quickly at Grace. "Would you?" she asked, truly wondering.

Grace shrugged, trying to feign unconcern. "I don't know. I haven't had any reason to make that decision."

Ruth had no desire to tell Grace that she had—and that she had turned him away. She thought about the sadness in his face as he was giving his topic, and she hoped that no one else had noticed it.

The girls ambled to the vestibule, where they got their coats. There stood David with the other young men; but as Ruth passed him, he purposely looked the other way. In a way, Ruth was relieved. And yet, in another way, she felt as though she had delivered a deathblow to some harmless creature.

The next day was Mama's birthday. Sarah and Norman came for the day, and Dorcas and Ruth planned that Mark's would also be there for supper. But before that, there was a lot of work to finish.

As soon as breakfast was over, Ruth planted the hotbed behind the house, with lettuce, radishes, onions, and red

The Upward Way

beets. Then she cleaned the yard, gathering up the winter's accumulation of debris. After cleaning up Mark and Ellen's yard, she carried Ellen's box full of thriving tomato seedlings to the barn where she helped Ellen replant them. As they worked, Roy and Robert bounced up and down the barn aisles, riding broom handles for horses.

"My horse is faster than yours, Robbie!" Roy teased, hopping faster and leaving his little brother behind.

"My hossie fas' too," Robert returned, trying hard to keep up.

Ruth and Ellen had to laugh at them as they watched them briefly. Then they went back to their tomato potting.

"What are you going to do with all these tomato plants?" Ruth asked as she set the clay pots up on windowsills in the barn.

"Why, pick tomatoes off them, I hope," Ellen returned gaily.

"If they do well, you'll have enough to supply an army," Ruth observed with a chuckle.

"That's no problem. I'll send the extras along to market." Ellen deftly firmed the last tomato into its pot. "There, that's the last one," she said as she set it on the window ledge and began cleaning up leftover pots and soil.

"Oh, when we asked Mama what she most wanted for dinner, she said dandelion," Ruth said later as she and Ellen and the boys left the barn. "Shall I get enough for your dinner too?"

"Sure, that would be good."

"Dande-lion?" Roy questioned. "What's that? Is it an animal?"

The Upward Way

Ruth laughed. "No, it's a plant. Something good to eat. Come along, and you can help Aunt Ruth find some."

When Ruth went to the house, Dorcas and Sarah were busy fixing dinner. Ruth quickly cleaned the dandelion, and Dorcas made the hot bacon dressing to go on it.

"Yum!" Sarah declared. "Maybe this is what I need to give me some pep once more. A spring tonic—don't they say that's what dandelion is?"

Ruth was relieved to find Sarah more like herself on this visit. Mama had said that time was a great healer, but Ruth knew that Sarah would grieve for a long time in her secret heart.

In the afternoon Ruth helped Kore and Papa clear brush away from the creek banks. What a mighty bonfire they had as they burned the great piles!

"We ought to roast hot dogs on one of these fires!" Kore exclaimed. "And bake potatoes in the fire. Have us a real picnic!"

Ruth listened with interest. "Should we, Papa? Would Mama enjoy that for her birthday? We don't have any frankfurters, but sausages would work."

Papa looked up, but he did not seem interested. "I don't know about that. Seems kind of cold for a picnic. Besides, it looks like it could rain any minute. Furthermore, I prefer to sit down at a table to eat my food."

Ruth looked up at the sky. It did look like rain. She had hardly noticed the overcast sky; the day had been so pleasant otherwise.

Ruth glanced at Kore. He appeared disappointed, but he did not say any more. *Maybe we ought to do things like that now and then,* she thought. *It would help Kore*

The Upward Way

to feel better about all the work.

The girls had made ice cream for supper, and with all the family there, it was an evening to be remembered. Ruth was relieved to notice that Sarah took nearly normal helpings of all the food. Perhaps being with her family in this way helped her and Norman to cope with their loss. She did not know how it would be to lose a child, but this she did know—that her heart had ached so much for her sister. Now some of the ache was lifted.

Ruth retreated to her garret later than usual that evening, her heart full of tender thoughts. It seemed the grief that had come to Norman and Sarah had drawn them together in an even closer bond of love. How Ruth longed for such a love in her life, in the form of a caring and loving husband. *Will such ever be my lot, dear Lord? You know, and I want to submit to Thee in this as well as in all else.* Her thoughts again drifted to David Peachey, and a certain sadness pervaded her consciousness. *O Father, did I do the wrong thing to turn away a godly young man, just because I thought he didn't suit me perfectly? What will become of him now? Will he leave the area so that he doesn't need to face me anymore?* Ruth felt badly to think of such a possibility. She thought he was a good influence among the young people, and she did not want him to go back to his people in North Carolina—back to an uncertain future and poverty.

Finally, sleep overcame her in spite of many searchings of heart.

Chapter Fifteen

May 20, 1935, Monday. Washed, ironed, scalded cheese, canned eleven quarts of poke (first canning of season). The men finished planting corn. This is truly a red-letter day—we had the wonderful privilege of gathering around the family altar again this evening, after years of absence! What all has transpired in the intervening years . . .

"What a glorious spring again!" Ruth declared on her way to the barn one fine April morning. The sun was already coming over the horizon, and all the indications were for a lovely day. Above her head the windmill blades were whirring and clacking in the fresh breezes. In the garden below the yard, she could see rows of peas beginning to show, and the flower beds around the house were full of the first blooms of spring.

Bird songs came from every direction, filling the morning with their courting calls. Roosters were crowing in the chicken house, and the guineas were adding their *buck-wheats* to the chorus of bird music. Morning was always the best time of day, Ruth thought with a glory in

273

The Upward Way

her soul, and spring was the best time of the year!

After breakfast, Ruth helped to take the sprouts off potatoes for the market at Amityville. The cave was nearly empty now, with only a few more potatoes—ones they were saving to plant—and a few more turnips. After Papa and Mama left for market, she and Kore began planting 650 Big Joe strawberry plants.

"Who's going to pick all these, is what I'd like to know!" Kore protested as they stuck plant after plant into the loose soil and firmed them in.

"I guess you and I," Ruth returned, not too worried about the picking just yet.

"And it's not only picking, but all the weeding till then." Kore stood up and straightened his back. "I get so tired of all the work."

"Well, what do you like?" Ruth asked. "You said you'd rather stay home today to help with the work than go to school."

"I'll tell you what I'd rather do. I'd rather go fishing or hunting. Or just walk in the woods. Or I'd rather go along with a bunch of fellows up to Ephrata again, like I did last Saturday! Didn't we have a good time, walking the streets and seeing all the girls, and eating ice cream at the soda shop! But, no, it's work, work, work, all the time, day in and day out."

"You weren't working last Saturday, were you?" Ruth reminded him. She could hardly believe that Papa had allowed him to go away with some of his church friends like that, but she guessed Papa felt he owed him a day off now and then. She would not have had a problem with his having a day off either, except for the kind of

The Upward Way

boys he was with, and the fact that Kore was only fourteen—hardly old enough to be running around, even with decent companions!

"But that was one day out of a million, believe me. And a grudgingly given one at that!"

Even though the exaggeration was obvious, Ruth could not deny the "grudgingly given" part, and so she kept quiet.

"Hey," Kore blurted out after a while, "did you hear Claude's hired man left him? The boys were talking about it on Saturday. Said he just up and left, hardly giving Claude any notice."

Ruth's heart almost stopped beating. "You mean, *Uncle* Claude?" she asked with bated breath.

Kore nodded as he troweled a hole for another strawberry plant. "Yeah, his hired man—that David Peachey, who didn't appreciate the fun things the young people did, and who drove around in that ancient Chevy. The boys were saying there's a rumor out that some girl turned him down," he went on, "and that he left because he was so heartbroken."

Sudden pain filled Ruth's heart. Was it really true? Had she hurt David Peachey—kind, gentle, and godly man that he was—like this? The light went out of the day for Ruth, and she finished planting berries with a heavy heart. The worst part of it all was that it seemed God was not sympathetic to her pleas for peace about her part in the situation. How she wished for time to go to her own secret retreat at the head of the creek and cry out her feelings to God. But there was not time for that. And so, silent tears fell on the freshly planted strawberries and watered them.

The Upward Way

After dinner, Ellen asked Ruth and Dorcas to go along with them to see the house in Pottstown that Norman and Sarah had just bought. Ruth went along eagerly, thankful for the diversion to take her mind off Kore's revelation of the morning.

Norman and Sarah were puttering around inside the house, trying to gather up the former owners' accumulated years of junk.

"Welcome!" Sarah called out as the women stepped onto the rickety porch. "Come in, if you can get in." She brushed blond curls off her face and left a black smudge in their place.

"We're coming," Ellen said. "But maybe we should have brought cleaning apparatus, rather than just coming for a tour."

"Maybe you can help clean later, after we get some order around here," Norman returned.

The sisters wound their way around boxes of junk, going from one room to the other. The tour was soon finished, as the house was not very big.

"Oh, what a cute little house!" Ruth exclaimed. "Well—at least it shows promise of being cute."

Sarah laughed. "Yes, you're right about the 'little' part. About the cute—well—once we get some fresh paint and paper on the walls and ceiling. And clean up the debris."

"It will be cute. It's so small and cozy," Ellen offered. "So much different from the big house you were used to."

"I know," Sarah agreed, carrying a box of old magazines to the porch to be thrown away. "And I didn't like to give up my roomy house. But you know," she added

The Upward Way

as she returned inside, "we wanted to transfer our membership back to Grove Hill, so we hoped to live closer. Pottstown will be closer to Norman's work too."

Ruth nodded. "And the house you lived in was a rented house too. It will be nice to have your own little nest with your own things."

"Here. Let me carry that for you, or at least help you with it," Ellen offered, taking a heavy box from Sarah.

"I won't refuse help," Sarah returned with a grin.

At least, Ruth thought gratefully, Sarah's cheerful spirit had returned in the last few weeks. She was sure Sarah still had many sleepless nights, grieving about the death of their little daughter. But through the day, she seemed almost like her old self.

Soon the sisters were all busy at various tasks. Dorcas was not able to haul out junk, but she could sweep it together on piles for the rest to clean up.

During the next two weeks, the Clemmers helped Norman and Sarah get their house ready whenever they had any spare time. Norman took a few days off from work and began the long job of painting and papering all the walls. By the beginning of May, their little house had taken on a new look, and they were eager to move their furniture. There were revivals at the Pottstown Mission the first week in May. So each evening that either Papa or Mark went, they took the truck and hauled a load of furniture to Norman's house. Norman's rented house had been mostly furnished. So as they had found good buys in furniture from time to time, they had bought it and stored it in a shed at the farm.

By Saturday, the furniture was all comfortably settled

277

The Upward Way

in Norman's new home. "Now we can put our feet under our own table, in our very own house!" Sarah exclaimed that evening. Mama and Dorcas had brought supper, and they all sat down together to eat after a busy day of moving. Mark and Ellen had helped them for most of the day. But Ruth had not been able to get over until the evening milking was done.

How often through the day she had thought of Norman's, wishing she could be there too. But Papa had wanted her help to plant a big patch of potatoes, and when that was finished, Mama had said she wanted the limas and more tomatoes planted, as well as the green beans. By that time it was too close to chore time to go to Norman's, so she had planted asters, petunias, and verbenas until time to milk.

"Well, we need to get on home," Mark stated soon after supper was over. "I hope Mahlon tended the chickens today. But even if he did, we still have eggs to grade when we get home."

Mama looked at Ruth. "And you have studying to do, no doubt," she said.

Ruth nodded as she gathered dirty dishes to wash in Sarah's tiny kitchen. She was still teaching two classes every Sunday—the younger youth girls on Sunday mornings and the junior girls at Pottstown Mission in the afternoons. "I wanted to study in the Bible doctrine book this evening, for my class tomorrow morning."

Papa got to his feet. "Then we'd better head on home. We've had a busy week."

Yes, it had been a busy week, Ruth thought, but with joy in her heart. On Thursday evening when she had been

The Upward Way

to the revivals at Pottstown, two of her thirteen-year-old Sunday school scholars had responded, Betty Sously and Mary Bauer. God had promised in His Word that seed sown would not return void, but would accomplish that for which it was sent. And now she was seeing results, however small, from her year of teaching this class. It gave her the needed encouragement to go on.

In her class at Pottstown the next day, Ruth proposed starting a fund to help missionaries. Their lesson was about Paul's first missionary journey, and Ruth had thought something like this could help her scholars understand better about the sacrifice missionaries need to make.

"This will be fun," Hazel Root said happily, her dark eyes sparkling. "My mom will give me a dime every Sunday, I think, if I tell her it's for the missionaries."

Ruth looked around her class to see other heads nodding vigorously. Most of the students, she knew, came from poor families. But they were willing to do what they could, and that was what blessed her heart right now.

When she went to YPM at Grove Hill that evening, Ruth could not help but furtively scan the benches across the aisle. Had David Peachey really gone home? He was not there, she finally concluded. A hurt and sorrow settled on her heart in earnest now. In vain did she plead with the heavenly Father to give her peace about her decision.

Week followed busy week—rainy days and sunny days, work in the garden and work in the barn, . . . But nothing seemed to penetrate the sadness that had settled over Ruth. She thought Mama eyed her occasionally, as though wanting to ask questions, but not knowing what to ask.

The Upward Way

It was Ellen who finally brought up the subject. She and Ruth were sticking onions together in the big produce patch, for a late crop of green onions for Amityville.

"You haven't seemed yourself for weeks, Ruth. What is the matter?" Ellen kindly questioned her.

Ruth shrugged, not sure herself exactly what was the matter. She just knew that a vague ache went with her wherever she went or whatever she did. Roy just then clattered up to them, pulling his wagon, and Ruth was spared an immediate answer.

"Hi, Mama. Hi, Aunt Rufie," he said. "See what I have on my wagon?" Ruth looked, and there, in a bed of straw, were three small kittens. "The kitties like a wagon ride," he assured Aunt Ruth, who must have looked doubtful.

"You had better take the kittens back to their mama, Roy," Ellen admonished him. "And then, can you stop by the house and listen if Robbie is awake. Then you may come and help Mama plant these onions."

"Okay," he said, starting off gaily, the wagon bumping and rattling along behind him.

Ellen turned once more to Ruth. "Tell me what's the matter. Are you missing Ella Mae, like the rest of us are?"

"Well, yes, that of course," Ruth said, wondering if perhaps that was all that was wrong with her. She had been really attached to that dear little girl. But certainly not more than her own mother had been, and Sarah was bearing up graciously and submissively.

"But I think it's more than that," Ellen persisted. "Mama said a couple of months ago that you got a letter from David Peachey. And that you told him no. Are you feeling bad about that?"

The Upward Way

Was she? Ruth hardly knew. She just knew that she greatly missed seeing him around. She missed the gentlemanly manners that seemed like a second nature to him. But more than all that, she missed his godly influence on the young people as they gathered for various functions. And it was because of her that he had gone away. Would she ever see him again? Would he ever come back?

Ruth looked up. Ellen was still watching her, kindness in her face. *I have to say something,* Ruth thought desperately. *But what? And how can I say I wish I wouldn't have told him what I did?* She stuck onions faster, hoping Ellen would not press for an answer. This seemed like something she could not even talk about with her dear sister-in-law.

Finally, Ellen settled back to her work. "Just remember, Ruth, that we are praying for you, whatever the trouble is," she said. "And if you ever want to share, we will be happy to listen."

After sticking half a bushel of onions, Ellen and Ruth planted late peas and several rows of corn. Then Ellen went to the house, and Ruth planted lima beans in several wooden flats to be transplanted later. She also replanted peppers, some yellow tomatoes, and some garden huckleberries into pots and carried them to the barn to join Ellen's tomato plants, which were now big enough to go into the garden.

The next Tuesday morning at breakfast, Papa scraped the last of his mush out of his bowl and leaned back in his chair. "I'm thinking I'd like to go to Bally to the mission meeting today," he said.

Dorcas looked on with interest. "I'd like to go too,"

The Upward Way

she asserted. Ruth looked on wistfully, but she had no hope of going away on a busy weekday.

"Aunt Emma asked on Sunday if we were going, and I said I didn't know yet," Mama added. "She and Jonas would be glad to go with us, if we go."

"Well, give her a call and let them know that we plan to go," Papa said. "The only thing is, I want to come back by that farm for sale near Royersville and look it over. They might not want to be bothered waiting around for us."

"*Another* farm, Papa?" Mama questioned, with exclamation points. "Don't we have enough work without another farm?"

Papa looked peeved. "I don't plan to work it. Just invest money there. We can rent it out, you know. Several young couples will soon be getting married and will need places to live."

"Well, seems to me," Mama persisted, "that if you are going to a mission meeting, you might be inspired to give more toward missions rather than to buy another farm!"

"Well, I can do both," Papa returned. "Investing in real estate is good business, and God expects us to use our money wisely, doesn't He?"

"Yes, if your god is money," Dorcas muttered under her breath, careful that Papa did not hear her.

"What about the verse that says, 'Having food and raiment let us be therewith content'?" Mama added. "Or 'Lay not up for yourselves treasures upon earth,' and all such verses? I would say that buying a fourth farm suggests more than a need."

Ruth glanced at Papa, and hoped that Mama would

The Upward Way

not say much more. Not that what she was saying was wrong, but Papa looked ready to burst out. He did speak but kept his voice under control. "The Bible certainly speaks of plenty of people who had wealth—like Job, Abraham, and Solomon. I surely don't see where God condemns it anywhere."

Mama chanced one more comment. "That was in the Old Testament. The New Testament teaching is this: 'For the love of money is the root of all evil: which while some coveted after, they have erred from the faith, and pierced themselves through with many sorrows.'"

"That verse says 'the *love* of money,'" Papa persisted, his voice raised. "You can have money and use it without loving it."

Ruth could have spoken. She could have said that perhaps Papa failed to see what others saw about him—that he seemed driven to get and possess and control. But she would not say that and risk his anger; she would only pray that Papa could see his need in God's eyes and repent before it was too late.

"Are you going to call Jonas's, Vena?" Papa asked, changing the subject.

"Oh—yes. I forgot that you had said I should." Mama got up from the table slowly, looking very burdened.

After the rest had gone and Ruth was doing the dishes, the telephone rang. It was Ellen. "Would you be interested in watching Roy and Robert this afternoon if we go to the mission meeting?" she asked.

Ruth thought quickly. She had been hoping to have the afternoon free to do some sewing while she was alone. But maybe she could still sew—especially if they took naps. And she would be glad for company, any company, on a lonely day. "Sure, I'll watch them," she said.

"Okay. Thanks."

So, soon after Ruth's lonely lunch, the boys came trooping to the washhouse door. "Here we are, Aunt Rufie," Roy called out.

"Here are!" Robert repeated as Ruth met them at the door. She waved to Ellen, who was standing in her doorway to be sure her boys arrived at their destination safely.

"Now, it's nap time," Ruth told them, after reading them several Bible stories.

"Oh, we must sing first," Roy pleaded.

"What would you like to sing?"

He looked up at Ruth sweetly. " 'Jesus, Help Me Be a Good Boy,' " he said. "I like that song."

Ruth tried hard not to laugh. "I'm afraid I don't know that song," she said.

"Well, then, 'Up From the Gravy Road,' " he suggested. "That's really my bestest song."

This time a chuckle did ripple out, but Ruth tried to cover it by saying, "Do you mean 'Up From the Grave He Arose'?"

"Yes, yes, that one." Roy clapped his hands. After singing that song and several simpler ones that Robert could help with, Ruth tucked them into makeshift beds on the parlor floor.

Ruth was glad for the sewing she was able to finish while the boys slept, because the next day was a busy one again, and she was not able to even think about such things as sewing. She spent most of the day cleaning out and whitewashing the cave at Papa's request. When that

The Upward Way

was finished, she began whitewashing the yard fence. That was Mama's request.

Mama and Dorcas had gone to the sewing circle, and many times throughout that lonely Wednesday, Ruth reconstructed the conversation from the day before. Why did Papa think he needed another farm? He had come home in the evening, declaring he liked it and was going to give the owner an offer for it. *If Papa paid his help better, he probably would not have money to buy another farm,* Ruth thought perversely. She knew Mark worked for much less than the going wages—that was why he kept getting more chickens, to try to make enough money to support his family and pay for his Buick. And for herself—why, Papa hardly paid her anything. She had to pretty much depend on what she could get for the few chickens and eggs and guineas she sold. Neither did Papa pay Kore anything in wages; he felt his room and board and the needed clothes was pay enough. That was another thing that made Kore bitter at times. *But then, he's not even sixteen,* Ruth thought. *I guess he doesn't need a man's pay—although he usually is expected to do a man's work. Probably Papa will pay Kore wages when he is older.*

Her struggle mostly lay with her own lack of funds. *Here I am, almost twenty-one, and have nothing to call my own! I wouldn't mind, if we were poor and Papa couldn't afford to pay me. But he can—but chooses not to.* Self-pity could soon have taken over in Ruth's heart as she splashed whitewash all that afternoon. And it did not help to be home without any of the women there—that is when she was more tempted to self-pitying thoughts.

285

The Upward Way

Especially since she would have been very happy to also go to sewing circle, but Papa thought there was too much work that needed to be done.

"I can't go on like this," she finally said aloud to the warbling birds around her. "I will sing!" And so she began singing, " 'I'm pressing on the upward way . . .' " Other songs came to her memory, and she sang on in the bright warmth of the afternoon.

By evening Ruth was very tired, but at peace with God and herself, having won the battle of resentment, discouragement, and self-pity. There was church that evening at Grove Hill, and she went along with the rest. Brother Samuel Rhoads was the speaker, speaking on "Personal Soul Winning."

The next week was rainy and cool. "I should set my tomatoes out," Ellen said on Saturday morning. "They are dying in the barn. But it is so cool, and I'm afraid they would die in the ground too."

"They might do better outdoors than in the barn," Ruth suggested. "Shall I help you plant them?" And so they planted, for better or for worse.

"If they need rain to start, they're getting that!" Ellen said laughingly as they worked in a steady drizzle.

"When we're finished here, I must mow the yard—rain or not!" Ruth added, not relishing the idea of pushing the mower around in the wet grass. But the grass was growing so fast, and if she waited for sunshine, who knew how tall the grass would be!

"I hope Mark and the boys get home with their chickens before too late," Ellen said. "He needs to preach tomorrow." He had gone to New Jersey for another five

The Upward Way

hundred laying hens.

Kore helped Ruth with the milking that evening, but he was unusually quiet. When she went up to feed her guineas, she noticed Kore and Papa talking at the machinery shed. Kore seemed much happier at the supper table than he had for weeks, or even months.

"Kore made a confession to me this evening," Papa said to Mama later, after Kore had gone upstairs to his room. Mama had been crocheting in the sitting room while Ruth relaxed in an armchair. Ruth looked up, all ears, eager to hear what Papa had to say. "He said he's sorry for some lies he told, and that he wants to do better," Papa added, sighing as he dropped into a stuffed chair.

"I'm glad to hear that," Mama said sincerely, her needle still and her eyes filling with tears.

Ruth did not say anything, but her heart was happy too, realizing the many struggles that Kore faced in his efforts to do right. *I need to remember to pray more for him,* she thought.

Finally the sun shone again, and the fields dried out in the spring warmth and breezes. The men spent every spare hour in the fields, planting corn. That left Ruth to do many of the barn chores. She worked long and hard, getting up early and going to bed late. *Lord, give me strength,* she pled often through the weary days. Sundays came, and with Sundays, the responsibility to teach her two classes. She did enjoy them very much, but when could she find the time to study? It seemed the Lord undertook for her and gave her special grace and strength through the busy weeks.

The Upward Way

Finally, on Saturday evening, May 18, the corn was all in. Mark came into the barn, looking dusty and tired but satisfied. "We're finished with the corn planting," he said. "Now we can think about something else!"

"Great!" Ruth returned earnestly. She carried her milk bucket and stool to the first cow in the row. "Move over, Bossie," she said, giving the cow a gentle shove. "It will be nice to have a reprieve from the hectic schedule around here." This she said to Mark as she began to milk.

Kore, who had just come on the scene, humphed. "*Reprieve*, did you say? That word isn't in anyone's vocabulary on this farm!"

"Well, at least maybe we'll have time to finish white-washing the fences and sheds, and things like that. Fun work, you know." She gave Kore an encouraging smile.

But Kore was in no mood for being cheered up. "And now Paul has bought another farm! I don't know what he wants with still more work." he complained.

"I guess he doesn't think he'll be working that farm," Ruth said.

Mark nodded. "He said Amos Detweiler's will be renting it." Mark headed toward the milk house for his milking bucket.

"Good!" Ruth said. "I didn't know how we'd have time for any more work around here. I'd be glad for more time off rather than more work."

"Same here!" Kore inserted. "Right now I'm just looking forward to a day off tomorrow." He disappeared around a corner of the barn.

Sunday was a wonderful "day off." Ruth taught her regular Sunday school classes, but then she decided to

The Upward Way

stay home in the evening from YPM and just go to bed early for a change. After a time of sweet fellowship with the Lord, she dropped off in a sweet and restful sleep.

Monday dawned fair and warm. "Spring is coming at last," she said to Kore as they milked together in the morning.

"It always does," Kore returned, but not unkindly.

"It's so nice out today," Ruth went on. "I hope to work at whitewashing the fences."

Kore groaned. "Whitewash and I don't get along very well. Guess I'll beg off."

Ruth broke into hearty laughter, remembering well the day last summer when Kore had whitewashed himself. "You can laugh—when it was all your fault!" Kore got up from his cow, a grin on his face, and carried his bucket to the milk house.

"By the way," he said, returning, "Paul said Vena wants to make cheese today. So we'll need to save a couple of cans for that."

"Okay." Ruth stripped the milk from her last cow and got up. If Mama was making cheese today, along with all the regular Monday work, she might not have time to do any whitewashing after all.

At breakfast, Papa had another chore to add to the already-busy schedule. "When we were planting corn in the field along the creek," he began, "I saw a patch of pokeweed[29] on the creek bank just the right size for eating."

"Oh, good!" Mama exclaimed. "We can gather some shoots for salad."

---

[29] While mature pokeweed is poisonous, the shoots of young plants are sometimes eaten like asparagus.

The Upward Way

"There were lots of nice young shoots," Papa added. "They're as good as asparagus any day!"

"Well, Ruth," Mama said, looking her way, "do you think you can gather a nice amount today—some to can, and some for salad."

Ruth nodded. She did not like pokeweed as well as Papa and Mama did, especially not canned, but it was good in the spring. "Shall I do that right after breakfast?"

"Maybe we should do some planting in the garden first," Mama suggested. "And I saw that the tomatoes and beans need to be dusted. But can you help get the washer going before you go out?"

Ruth pumped water to heat for washing. "I'll be back in to start the washer engine when the water is hot," she called into the kitchen. Then she rushed outside into the freshness of the morning. She raked diligently in the garden, smoothing the rich loam into deep brown softness. "There, that should be enough to plant four or five rows," she said to herself as she surveyed her work. "I doubt Mama needs more room than that for a few more things. And now to start the washer engine and fill the washer."

After the last boiler of water was emptied into the washer, Ruth hurried into the kitchen. "The washer is ready," she said to Mama, who was busily sorting through seeds. Dorcas came with a hamper full of wash. Several other full hampers were already waiting on the washhouse floor.

"Here; plant two rows of horticulture beans, and two more of Golden Bantam corn," Mama said, handing her the partially empty packets.

The day was so fragrantly lovely that Ruth dropped

The Upward Way

seeds with renewed zest. Now and then she stood still just to gaze into the blue canopy of sky above her head, dreaming as the cottony clouds floated by. Her thoughts were a prayer as she meditated on God's great power displayed in the heavens. Then her thoughts returned to the mundane, and she prayed for Norman and Sarah in their continuing grief. Now and then thoughts of Charles Derstine, somewhere in Virginia, would march across her consciousness. And she would breathe a prayer for him, yearning that he would return to the Lord. Thoughts of Charles always led to thoughts of David Peachey, and then the chronic sadness, which she had been trying so hard to shake, once more settled on her heart.

The garden work was soon finished, and Ruth loaded the wagon with some bushel baskets to go for a load of pokeweed. She wasted some time sitting on the creek bank, listening to the many birdcalls and trying to identify them. The oak and hickory trees around her were full of new leaves, and the squirrels were busy among them, now and then dropping a twig or a cluster of leaves near her. Chipmunks chattered and scolded as they ran here and there, darting in and out of holes, close to her.

"Time to get busy!" Ruth suddenly said aloud, jumping to her feet. Chipmunks scampered for their holes, and sudden silence descended as the birds stopped their songs mid-note. Ruth laughed. She knew everything would soon reverberate with life once more.

Soon she had gathered enough young, tender pokeweed shoots to satisfy even Papa. She started back toward the house, pulling her loaded wagon slowly behind her.

"Oh, they look nice," Mama said happily, coming out

The Upward Way

the washhouse door to examine Ruth's wagonload. "We'll fix some shoots for supper, with white sauce and hard-boiled eggs, over toasted bread. Won't that be good!"

"Sounds good to me," Ruth agreed.

"Dorcas is stirring the cheese. But you could go ahead and clean some of these shoots to can," Mama went on. "Just save enough out for supper."

After dinner, Ruth jarred the cleaned pokeweed shoots and put them in the wash boiler. The shoots filled eleven quarts. Mama was happy for the first jars of the season to put on her canning shelves.

That evening Papa was delighted to see pokeweed swimming in white sauce with hard-boiled eggs when he came to the table for supper. "Tut, tut! So we get some poke on toast for supper. What a treat!"

But the treat for Ruth came when she realized what Papa was carrying in his hand—his Bible! He was actually bringing his Bible to the table. Ruth looked on with surprise and delight. Was Papa really going to begin family worship again, after many years of feeling too busy? He was! Opening his Bible, he cleared his throat. "Mama and I have decided that we ought to begin having regular family worship again."

He paged a few pages and began reading from the Book of John, chapter one. The reading was a balm to Ruth's weary heart, and she knew it must also be a means of healing for all the other listeners as well.

Chapter Sixteen

September 29, 1935, Sunday. Went to Grove Hill as usual this morning. But something was not usual. . . . I soon noticed that D.P. was there, sitting where he had always sat before he went away last spring. I don't know how I got through my SS class. But the girls helped out. I had had them write compositions about their favorite Bible characters, and then they read those in class. That helped to pass the hour and cover for my nearly speechlessness. Then this evening, D.P. spoke out. Dear Lord, can it be . . .

Fall was definitely in the air. Ruth felt its unmistakable chill as she rushed to the house after the morning milking. But the day promised to be a nice one, and she was glad. The previous day had been a rainy one, but Sundays always seemed pleasanter when they were sunny.

"Where are you hurrying to?" called a plaintive voice after her.

Ruth stopped in her tracks and swung around. "I thought I would go in and do some studying," she told Kore, who was watching from the barn door.

The Upward Way

"Who's going to wash up the milk house?" he asked.

"I thought you might this morning."

"Well, if I have to," he returned, slumping sullenly away.

Oh, why does Kore have to act like that? Ruth asked herself once more. It always made her feel as though she was shirking her responsibilities—and yet, he could easily wash up this morning. The other barn chores were finished. Yesterday he had been moody too, and had given her a hard time about everything he did. There had been good times through the summer, when he had seemed to be doing better. But Ruth could never understand why he had such frequent relapses.

The table was set for breakfast when Ruth entered the kitchen a little later. "Please bring a jug of fresh grape juice up from the cellar," Mama said from where she was stuffing a chicken to go in the cookstove oven for dinner. "That will taste good with our breakfast this morning."

"Okay." Ruth clattered down the cellar stairs, retrieved a jug out of the cistern trough and ran back up the steps. After pouring herself a cup of the fresh juice, she headed toward the garret door.

"No breakfast this morning?" Mama asked, turning to look at her.

Ruth shook her head. "Not more than the grape juice. I need more time to study, if no one minds."

After Mama's okay, Ruth bounded up her garret stairs, eager for some quiet time before church. Her two classes each Sunday took a lot of time and study, but how dear her students had grown to her. And she found that she learned and grew right along with her scholars, perhaps more so!

The Upward Way

"Oh, that's right!" she exclaimed under her breath as she began going over her notes. "I assigned the Grove Hill girls compositions to write. If we read them in class today, I won't need to have as much prepared . . ."

She studied her lesson anyway, poring over the Bible passage until she felt reasonably prepared for the day. Glancing at her clock, she was happy to see it was only eight-thirty. "I'd have time to walk to church today," she said aloud. After telling Mama of her intentions, she was soon ready and on her way, stepping briskly out the road toward Spring City.

How lovely the surrounding woods were on this fresh morning. There had not yet been a killing frost, and the leaves were only gently changing to their fall colors. Ring-necked pheasants cackled in the overgrown fencerows, crows cawed above the cornfields, rabbits darted here and there along the roadside. In a little more than forty-five minutes, she had covered the four miles to church. As she walked up the short drive to the church, an old Chevy slowly pulled into the churchyard from the other direction.

Could it be . . . She hurried into the church, her heart filled with the conflicting emotions of trepidation and hope. Yes, it was David Peachey. He looked around with interest and then walked slowly to his usual place near the front of the church. Ruth cast furtive glances at him, so happy in her secret heart to see him once more. *He is actually handsome!* she acknowledged, wondering how she could have missed that fact before. He had acquired a healthy tan, and his blond hair looked lighter than ever. *Probably from a summer outdoors in the southern sun,* Ruth surmised.

295

The Upward Way

Grace Good came in and sat beside her. "Did you know David Peachey is back?" she whispered to Ruth. A little sting of jealousy twanged uncomfortably. Was her favorite cousin interested in David Peachey? Sometimes Ruth had wondered before, and now it seemed pretty obvious. Ruth hid her feelings and simply nodded, pointing with her chin toward where David was sitting.

"Papa stopped in with Uncle Claude's yesterday and talked with him there," Grace bubbled on quietly. "He said he's hoping to get his old job back, and I think Uncle Claude is planning to hire him again."

Ruth did not know what to say. Should she say "Good!" or "That's nice!" Or should she just be silent? She had never told anyone, except Mama and Papa, about his letter to her, so Grace would have no way of knowing how his being back affected her. She was spared an answer because Uncle Jonas got up then to announce the first song.

As soon as Ruth stood in front of her class of girls near the back of the auditorium, she realized what an awkward position she was in. There she stood facing David, who was sitting in the young men's class, at the back of the church. She sent a sudden and urgent plea heavenward for grace to take her place before the girls. As always, God was faithful and met her need. She was blessed by the contributions of the class that morning and thankful that no one seemed to notice her lack of coherent thought at times.

David was also with Uncle Claude's at the Pottstown service in the afternoon. But at least there, Ruth thought gratefully, she did not need to teach in his presence. By

The Upward Way

evening, she was emotionally exhausted and ready to spend a few quiet hours at home. But that was not to be. Papa insisted that she had no good reason to miss church, especially since Martin Heistand was going to be at Grove Hill with a message for the youth.

Ruth went with Mark's to church, holding their precious little Daniel, now just over two months old. How sweet he was, although Roy and Robert weren't so sure about him yet and seemed jealous of Aunt Ruth's attention to this noisy little stranger.

Although they were quite early, Mark's gathered their little ones and went into the church as soon as they arrived. Ruth stayed in the car, her mind busy with many thoughts. What had brought David Peachey back to Spring City? Had he found a girl at home, which made it easier for him to come back where one had rejected him? Surely he knew a lot of girls from his home church, and no doubt one of them would be happy to have someone as fine as he. Would he be here this evening, or would he choose to stay away? As she sat and thought, she tried to pray. Truly she wanted God's will for her life, but why did her prayers about this situation always seem to draw a blank?

Feeling almost frenetic in her helplessness, she bowed her head in her hands. *Oh, dear Father,* she prayed earnestly, *I want whatever is Your will for me.* The kaleidoscope of her thoughts suddenly seemed to take on form and substance. *Oh, God, I thought I didn't want him—could never love him. But now I realize how much I did care for him and how much I respected his spiritual convictions. And now he may have another girlfriend. At*

The Upward Way

least, he will likely never ask me again, after I turned him down so bluntly one time. Oh, God, help me to have the grace to live with my decision now, and to go on from here, happy in You—even though it means I may stay single all my life. And even though he may choose someone else from here—like my cousin Grace. . . .

Ruth spent a few more minutes in sober reflection and prayer, her heart now at peace, however the matter fell. Yes, she would rejoice with Grace, if that is what it came to. Glancing at her watch, she realized it was nearly starting time.

Ruth was no sooner out of Mark's car than she spotted David Peachey, only two cars away, also getting out of his. He came slowly toward her, looking pale and very nervous.

"Good evening, Ruth," he greeted her, his voice shaking.

Ruth, touched by his timidity, tried to respond in a way that would set him at ease. "And a good evening to you, David," she said gently. "We're glad to see you're back in the area."

"I am happy to be back," he replied, smiling weakly.

Ruth's eyes dropped to the ground, and in doing so could not help but notice his knees shaking inside his pant legs. *The poor man!* she thought in deep sympathy.

"I am wondering, Ruth, if"—he cleared his throat—"if maybe you have changed your mind since last spring. I came back, hoping that perhaps you had."

So he did still care! A great happiness filled Ruth's heart; somehow her world seemed to have turned right-side up again! *Thank You, Father in heaven,* she breathed.

The Upward Way

She looked up into his kind face. "Perhaps I have changed my mind, David. But I want to pray about this, and talk with my parents before I give you any answer. Is that all right?"

A great weight seemed to lift off David. His smile was ready and bright, and his blue eyes sparkled with a happy light. Gone also was his nervousness as he said, "I would want you to pray about it, Ruth." He glanced at his watch. "We had better go inside now," he added. "Please let me know when you have an answer for me."

"I'll do that," Ruth said softly as she started for the church.

Chapter Seventeen

May 11, 1938, Wednesday. Dear Journal, tomorrow is my wedding day! God has led us step by step, day by day, and my dear David and I, Lord willing, will be united as one tomorrow. I have not slept well for the past several nights, and probably won't sleep well tonight either. But I am so happy, happy, happy! Oh, God, dear heavenly Father—how can I express my deep gratitude to Thee!

"You could have chosen a less busy time of the year to get married, if you think you must get married," Dorcas stated at breakfast. Her smile for Ruth took the sting out of the words.

"Well," Papa spoke up, "I would say that Ruth has done her share to get things done."

"Oh, I didn't mean that she hadn't," Dorcas returned. "It's just that May is a busy time, as you all know. But I suppose things are coming along well—the fieldwork is caught up, the corn is all planted, and all that. And the garden is getting planted, along with all the extra things we needed to do."

The Upward Way

"And the flower beds are all planted," Mama added. "Plus a few more new ones that Ruth dug up this year. Everything looks in good shape to have a wedding here tomorrow."

"We still have cleaning to finish, and much of the food to prepare," Dorcas reminded them. "Cakes to bake and the ice cream to make, and whatnot else. That will take some time. But we won't be able to do the ice cream until tomorrow."

"Well, the potato salad is made, and the ham and the chicken is cooked and cut up, ready to serve. . . ."

"And everything's pretty good!" Kore inserted with a smirk. "Well, I didn't try the sweetheart salad you've got stashed away in the icebox."

Mama gave him a look that said he'd better stay out of the food, if he knew what was good for him. Then she went on, "All we need to do tomorrow for the first course is heat the green beans and brown the butter for them. I think everything is coming along really well."

"All the fences are whitewashed, and everything else that could be," Kore added. "And even some things that probably wouldn't have had to be—like the outhouse, and all the tree trunks around the house."

"Whitewashing sure goes faster with that sprayer," Papa asserted. "I'm glad I bought that thing a couple years back. It saves us a lot of time."

"Yes, that reminds me," Dorcas went on, "the porch needs a last good scrubbing today. That had to be saved for the last minute—with all the coming and going across it with dirty feet. . . . And the outhouse—that ought to be thoroughly washed down inside."

The Upward Way

Papa looked at Kore, who was shaking his head in protest. But Papa ignored his obvious disinterest and said, "I believe Kore can do both of those jobs. He doesn't have that much else to do after school today."

Kore sighed, rolled his eyes helplessly, and settled lower in his chair.

Ruth chuckled as she looked at him. She knew he was perfectly capable of including those few easy jobs with his regular chores, especially now that the fieldwork was finished. But he still often reverted to his "little-boy" responses when asked to do something, even though he was now seventeen. This was his last year of school. After he graduated, how would he ever handle the farm work full time? But that was not her worry, she decided.

She listened to the chatter and plans of the others with a satisfied heart as she slowly spooned up her bowl of mush and chicken gravy. It was hard to fathom that all this work was being done for *her*—that it was actually *she* who was going to be married. Her thoughts took her back four and a half years to Norman and Sarah's wedding. At that time, she had wondered how she would feel if she were the one for whom all the preparations were being made. And now she *was* the one.

"And the guests are all invited," Mama continued her train of thought.

"How will we get them all in the parlor?" Kore asked. "Some people might need to sit on the windowsills. Hey, I will—then I can slip out the window if I get too bored."

"There are only a few over thirty coming," Mama told him. "And I think we have plenty of chairs to seat that many."

The Upward Way

"Too bad." Kore shook his head in mock gravity. "At least I tried."

"Well, you surely wouldn't want to miss out on the eating part!" Dorcas exclaimed.

"I've already had a good dig at all there is to eat," Kore said behind his hand to her, enjoying tormenting her just as he always had Ruth.

"I was hoping to go to the woods and find dogwood today to decorate the parlor, Mama," Ruth said. "But will I have time? I know there is still a lot that you will need help with."

Mama nodded her head. "You should have time sometime today, especially if you can finish the cleaning this morning," she said. "Dorcas and I will do the cakes this afternoon and get the pudding ready and cooled for the ice cream tomorrow.

"But you may have to search long and hard to find dogwood that is still blooming nicely this late in the season," she added.

"I surely hope you plan to help with the cleaning," Dorcas inserted. "There is still a lot to finish."

"I want to," Ruth assured her with a smile. "I won't go out until everything is shining!"

All morning, Ruth and Dorcas cleaned. They rubbed and scrubbed and waxed the hardwood floors, polished furniture, and did all the other things that had been saved to the last minute. The windows had been washed the week before, and the muslin curtains washed, starched, and ironed. Mama blacked the cookstove and cleaned the kitchen thoroughly.

"It's only eleven o'clock," Ruth said, stretching

The Upward Way

happily after she had carried the last rag rugs from the porch rail to place on the waxed floors once more. "I'm going to scrub the porch and surprise Kore."

"Well, I'm not going to help with that," Dorcas returned. "I have enough else to do. And someone will need to prepare dinner for everyone around here." She limped to the kitchen, where Mama was still busy with polishing woodwork.

Ruth was almost finished with the wet, soapy porch-scrubbing job when Ellen and Sarah stopped by. But they came mostly to encourage, rather than to help. Ellen now had four little ones, Mark being only four months old. Norman and Sarah had John now, who was a year and a half and had helped very much to ease the sorrow of the loss of their first baby, dear little Ella Mae. David stopped by too, hardly able to stay away with all the activity going on for his sake. He stayed for dinner, but then he left to pick up his wedding suit at Sauder's—his first plain suit. Before, he had always worn a lapel suit, but usually without a tie, which was the practice in his home congregation at Holly Springs.

After the dinner dishes were done and Mama went to rest, Ruth took the market truck and drove to the woods. She parked on the woods lane and fought her way through the brush and undergrowth into the heart of the woods, stopping often to sniff and listen and look, enjoying as always the enchantment of the woods in the spring. Finally, where the stand of trees was the thickest, she found a copse of dogwood that still had fresh blooms. She cut armfuls and carried them back to the truck. After she had gathered as much as she could possibly need, she

The Upward Way

found a fallen log and sat down to think.

Happy thoughts filled her heart. Thankfulness to God overwhelmed her and made the tears start in her eyes. There was no one to hear, and she spoke aloud, pouring out her thanks to God. "Lord, You have been so good to me. How can I ever thank You? I praise You for giving me such a faithful, godly man to be my partner for life. Oh, Father, help us to be faithful to You, to walk in Your paths—wherever You may lead us. . . ."

Her thoughts hung up there for a time. *Wherever . . . ?* Was she really willing to go wherever God would lead? She knew David wanted to move back to his home area in North Carolina. Was that really where God wanted her to go? They had often talked about it, but Ruth was always reluctant. She did not want to leave her home and her family. Neither would she be able to take the taunting of her friends and cousins, who were already gloomily predicting that David would take her to the boondocks and scrub pines—just you wait and see! But she had not been able to tell David those things; she did not want to hurt him. And even if her friends had not mocked his background, she still could not live in such a place! It was the only real difference that she and David had ever faced, and she knew that it troubled him that she refused to give in.

"Ruth," he would say, "you know this area is not my home. And I do not feel at home here, because of the materialism and high-class living. Plus, there are already plenty of Mennonites here, while in the area I am from, many people have never heard the full Gospel. Won't you consider going back with me to North Carolina?"

305

The Upward Way

"But, David, your parents are so poor," Ruth would return, distressed. "Why, they don't even have an indoor bathroom or running water in the house. Your mother washes on a washboard out in the yard, and she has to carry all her water from the outdoor pump. And different times we visited, the chickens lived right under the house—and even the pigs sometimes. I am not used to that, and I don't see how I can give up the conveniences that I am used to, to live in such poverty."

"We wouldn't need to live quite so poorly," David would assure her. "You realize, don't you, that the poverty in my home was due partly to my father's drinking problem."

Ruth would always agree, and yet . . . "But everyone around there seems so poor," she would point out. "Not just your family."

Once Ruth got started, it was hard for her to see anything good about their "backward" way of life. But the thing that bothered her even more was David's home church. The people generally dressed quite simply, because many were poor by Pennsylvania standards, but they did not dress "plain" as she was used to. Very few wore cape dresses or plain suits. "And what about your church?" Ruth would point out.

David would nod his head. "I understand how you feel about the church," he had always agreed. "And I would be glad to see some things different too. But to me, our simple lifestyle there—even though not as regulated in attire—still is more Biblical than the materialism and greed and lack of spiritual interest and spiritual life that I see in most of your churches here."

The Upward Way

"But some among us have real spiritual interest," Ruth would return. "You appreciate Mark and Ellen a lot. And look at Norman and Sarah and other young couples like them, who have been willing to move and serve for the sake of city missions." Norman had been ordained on November 10, 1936, to serve as minister at the Norristown Mission. David had been with Ruth at that service, and together they had wept with Norman and Sarah at this new and awesome responsibility.

"I appreciate such as they," David was glad to tell her. "And the young men who started the Rocky Ridge outreach work a number of years ago. But they are so few among the many who don't seen to care about anything but having the newest and the latest. And the young people—are they concerned for anything other than having a good time? Sure, some are, but why so few? And why do so many wait until after they are married to settle down? I often wonder how many really do experience salvation."

Ruth could not deny what David saw in their churches. She had often seen it herself, and it grieved her. And the trends were growing worse. Young people came back from various colleges with "liberated" viewpoints, and even many older people were turning from the truths they had been taught and were looking to the world for answers to life's questions.

The radio, though taught against and discouraged in their circles, was becoming more and more a prominent feature in many homes. And with it came a flood of modernistic teaching and preaching, not to mention the world's songs and entertainment. Eternal security and other Calvinistic teachings were taking hold here and

The Upward Way

there, and Biblical doctrines that the Mennonite Church had always held dear were being discounted and scoffed at. How often Ruth had heard in the past year such statements as "All these peculiar Mennonite doctrines—why, it's just Paul's teaching." Not only did the plain suit and plain hat[30] come under attack, but so did the Christian woman's veiling, simplicity of dress, and even separation of church and state. And the ones who promoted such views were described as "winning," and "spiritual," or "well-read," or "tolerant and accepting." Along with this gradual undermining of Bible doctrine, Ruth also sensed a subtle intimidation toward those who chose to live according to the plain teaching of Scripture.

Many members who had never been content to submit to Biblical church authority were becoming more and more open with their influences. There was also much more openness about relating to and working with other community churches. All of these things hurt Ruth very much. But could not she and David continue to be good examples and show by holy lives that it is important to obey all the Scriptures?

David did not see it that way. He felt that eventually they themselves would be influenced to turn from truth. "I wish I could spare you, and the children God may give us, from the apostasy that is slowly but surely overtaking the churches here," David had pled more than once.

"Would you be content to live under another church

---

[30] Most men of this time wore hats for dress occasions, so direction was given in the discipline for a consistent hat for church members.

The Upward Way

conference? Say, Lancaster Conference?" Ruth had asked one time.

She could still remember how David had slowly shaken his head. "I haven't visited much in those churches, but what I have seen is almost worse than what we have here. At least as far as materialism and worldliness in business practices. And many of them grow tobacco for a cash crop, which seems like an awfully poor testimony to the world."

"But they are more conservative in dress, aren't they?" Ruth had ventured.

David had nodded, but reluctantly, it seemed to Ruth. "Yes, in some ways," he had admitted. "But for many, it is form without godliness. I have been appalled at the lack of Bible knowledge among them—especially among the young people I have met—and the lack of interest in spiritual things. Many leave the plain churches, which doesn't surprise me. They appear to be bleating sheep, longing for something they haven't found where they are. And if I don't miss my guess, they will shortly follow the same course that our conference here is taking."

Ruth was not sure she could fully agree with all that David was saying about Lancaster County, because she enjoyed the few friends she had from that area. And she had always appreciated the messages that she had heard ministers preach from that conference. But she understood why David felt the way he did. "David, you know that more than anything else I want to live in obedience to the Bible," Ruth had told him with an honest heart. "But I do not feel the need to live so far away from civilization."

And so David would drop the discussion for a time.

The Upward Way

Ruth thought about those times now, and her heart smote her. Was she being insubmissive? But she felt so strongly against it! If it were truly God's will for her to move to North Carolina, would not God make her willing?

Then Ruth's thoughts took a happier turn. She thought back to when David had asked her that evening two and a half years ago. She thought again of the great joy in knowing that he still cared. She had gone home with a happy heart to share with her mother. Then Papa wrote a letter to Brother Amos Kling, David's home pastor. Mama and Papa wanted to be sure about this man who came from such a faraway place and about whom they knew so little. Brother Amos wrote a long letter in return, with nothing but good to say for David. Yes, his father was not a faithful church member and he did have a drinking problem. But David was much like his mother— a faithful, godly woman who was a patient and uncomplaining saint. David's sisters appeared to be turning out well, and most of his brothers had chosen to walk with the Lord.

After several weeks of asking counsel and praying for wisdom, Ruth was ready to write David a letter of acceptance. Their courtship for the most part had been a happy one, although Ruth remembered times when she still was not sure she had made the right choice. David was so old-fashioned in many ways, and he was not at all the kind of young man that she had always dreamed of for a husband—a dashing, charming, rich, and talented sort of man. But then, she would get on her knees once more and plead with God for the humility she needed to be a true servant of His, one who would be willing to

The Upward Way

follow His will for her in everything.

Maybe I read too many of the wrong kind of books, Ruth mused now as she sat in the woods, listening to the myriads of birdcalls. *Maybe that is why I wasn't impressed for a while with such a lowly man as David. But I did stop reading the worst romance books because I thought they would do me no good.* She remembered giving several books back to their owners, not wanting to finish them or have them around to tempt her. *But there were the* Elsie *books that I just loved. I suppose they also fed the wrong spirit, although they were supposedly religious books.*

Ruth shifted on the log, and a wary chipmunk scolded and scurried off through the dry leaves. "And now we will be living next to Papa's, which David really was not eager to do," Ruth thought aloud. "He is afraid I will have to keep working as hard as I always did, if we live on the farm." Papa would have been glad to give David work, but David was planning to continue working for Uncle Claude, at least for now. Papa had built an addition onto their house, a separate apartment, and that was where David and Ruth would begin housekeeping.

Ruth thought about that now. . . . Had she insisted on her own way in that matter as well? "Dear Father," she murmured, "was I insubmissive to David? I didn't mean to be, but I thought it would be easier—at least for now—not to be so far from Mama and my family. And I was thinking of him. I really was, because I knew he had so little money saved to rent something else. . . ." David had given in to her wishes. How much fun it had been for them to help to build, and then to finally fix it up as

311

The Upward Way

their own little nest. All Ruth's things were moved into it now—all the simple little housekeeping things that she had been making for the past year, ever since she knew that someday she would be David's wife. Sheets, and tea towels made from flour sacks, quilts for which she had embroidered the patches, rugs she had crocheted from strips of old clothes sewn together . . . And together, she and David had scoured secondhand shops or stood at sales to buy the few pieces of furniture that they needed to begin housekeeping. It was all there now, and soon it would be hers and David's to use, together.

Happy tears came to Ruth's eyes and fell silently onto her lap as she thought of the precious words David had said to her last Sunday on the way home from Grove Hill. Ruth had taught her youth Sunday school class as usual and had commented on how much she enjoyed it.

"Oh, I hate to give up my classes for the weeks we'll be away on our trip," she had concluded, almost wailing.

David had looked at her fondly. "I have to tell you this, Ruth," he began. "The first time I saw you in front of that class at Grove Hill, I said to myself, 'There is my future wife.' It has taken a long time, but God willing, it will soon become a reality."

Ruth had been so touched. David had been so patient with her immaturity and had weathered so many storms because of her indecision! "If only I can make him truly happy from now on," she said softly. "He deserves it. 'Oh, God, help me to be a faithful and worthy helpmeet for this dear man.' "

Slowly, Ruth brought her mind back to the present; and slowly and stiffly, she got up from the log. "I must

The Upward Way

be getting old," she said with a chuckle as she stretched out the kinks in her back and legs. Scuffing through the old leaves, she headed toward the truck and then drove slowly back to the house.

David's car was parked again at the house, and he was waiting for her.

"So you found some nice dogwood yet," he observed with a smile as she came up the sidewalk with her arms full of it.

"Yes. But in the heart of the woods." Ruth returned the warm smile. "There's more in the truck if you want to help me bring it in."

"Now, don't drop leaves all over the clean floor," Dorcas warned from the table, where she was icing cakes.

"Oh, I'll be really careful," Ruth said. "And I'll clean up any mess I make. I promise!"

Together David and Ruth arranged vases full of the lovely sprays of green with their white blooms, setting them around artistically in the parlor. Then it was time to do chores, and David changed into chore clothes to help her with the milking. "Won't this be wonderful?" he remarked happily as they sat near each other directing warm streams of milk into their buckets. "To do this together as husband and wife?"

Ruth could hardly imagine the joy of living with the man she loved, but she surely did look forward to it. "God has been so good to us," she said.

After David had left for the evening, Ruth sang song after song. 'I'm pressing on the upward way,' she sang, truly desiring to gain the new heights she sang about.

Eventually Mama roused from her Bible reading to

The Upward Way

send Ruth to bed. "Tomorrow is your wedding day, Ruth. Go and get a good night of sleep."

"I'll go," Ruth returned, "but my heart is so full of happy thoughts that I doubt I'll sleep a wink!" She leaned over Mama's chair and planted a kiss on one soft cheek. "Thank you, Mama, for all you have done for me," she added softly, and then dashed for her garret stairway.

Squeak, squeak, went her bed as she sat on it to read her Bible. "The last time for you, you old bed," she said aloud, and the saying of it brought a queer ache to her heart. Why did last things always make you hurt so, she wondered wryly.

She opened her Bible to Matthew 28, where she had been reading. " 'Lo, I am with you alway, even unto the end of the world. Amen,' " she read with eager heart. "Thank you, Father," she breathed, "that You see and care, and that You will go with us. Please, bless our day tomorrow, and keep David and me in Your care always. . . ."

The night was long as she lay awake and watched the star-studded sky outside her window. But it was a night of prayer and petition, of giving thanks, and of spiritual yearnings.

Chapter Eighteen

February 25, 1939, Saturday. Dear Journal, you won't believe this. But I am a mother! Really and truly a mother—to a beautiful little daughter. She was born on the fifteenth, and today, Lord willing, I am to take her home from the hospital. I am waiting until dear David and Dorcas come to pick us up. I am so eager to be back in my own home . . . And now I am here. Ate dinner with Mama's but now came to our house to rest. David is such a good nurse, and such a wonderful papa.

"Are you comfortable, Mrs. Peachey?" the nurse asked as she gently laid little Arlene in Ruth's arms. "Shall I put another pillow behind your back?"

"If you don't mind," Ruth said, shifting forward a bit as the nurse carefully stuffed another pillow behind her back. "That feels better. Thank you!"

"If you need anything, just call me," the nurse said with a smile before turning to leave.

"Thank you. I will," Ruth responded. After the nurse left, Ruth gently pulled the blanket-wrapped bundle that

315

The Upward Way

was her daughter close to her, forming a kiss on her delicate forehead. "Ah, precious. How priceless you are!"

Little Arlene turned at her mother's voice. "Just a minute, wee one, and I will give you your breakfast," Ruth said tenderly.

How the medical staff had worked over that bit of humanity as David and Ruth fervently prayed. Finally, Arlene had taken a great gasp of air and burst into a loud cry. But had she been without oxygen for too long? Nobody knew for sure, and the doctor had warned the anxious parents of possible brain damage.

"Thank God, you surely don't appear brain-damaged, you dear little one," Ruth whispered as she hugged her. "We trust that you are completely all right. But if you aren't, we'll love you anyway!" Ruth shifted her position, trying to find a more comfortable way to relax.

"God did spare you to us, praise His Name," Ruth murmured now, hardly able to grasp what it would have been like to so soon say good-bye to this little stranger who had come to them.

Soon the nurse bustled cheerfully into the room again. "All finished?" she asked. "Why, she's a hungry little sweetheart, isn't she! Nothing wrong with her appetite!"

"No, and she's eating well," Ruth said happily.

"Well, good, good! And she'll be growing like a little bear." The nurse watched for a bit and then stepped back. "I'll stop back for the baby later."

"How soon will Dr. Simpson be in?" Ruth asked before the nurse went out the door.

The nurse looked at her watch. "Probably within the hour. Then you'll be out of here! Are you eager to go

The Upward Way

home?" She smiled at Ruth.

Ruth nodded happily. "It will be good to be home again, after ten days here. But you all were surely very kind to me, and I thank you!"

"You have been a good patient—so easy to look after—though you've had to endure much more than many."

"I thought of the Bible verse 'Weeping may endure for a night, but joy cometh in the morning.' " Ruth smiled at her. "It's easy to forget the stress when you have the dear little one to love and cuddle."

The nurse humphed as she stepped to the door. "I'll be back soon," was her only response.

Ruth carefully lifted Arlene to her shoulder, where she gently patted her back. Arlene's eyes soon fell shut, and she was sleeping when the nurse came back for her. "I'll take her back to the nursery for a little while. After the doctor checks her, we'll bring her back for you to dress to go home. Sound good?"

Ruth nodded. "It surely does!" She was eager to have her baby all the time. Especially now that she was feeling almost as good as new. *I can hardly wait to care for Arlene at home,* she thought, shifting to get out of bed for a break. Even though she had been the youngest in the family, she was thankful for all the experience she had gained with babies by helping to care for the nieces and nephews.

Sitting on the chair by the bed, Ruth opened her journal and began writing. *I'm glad David brought this in for me last evening,* she thought. *I really should catch up with everything that happened the past ten days—sometime!*

The Upward Way

Maybe I'll be too busy with the baby to keep a journal anymore.

Very soon, Ruth was on her way home with David. Dorcas had also come along and was just as happy about the new baby as Ruth could hope for. Fresh snow covered the landscape, and the Pottstown streets had patches of snow and ice here and there. David drove carefully and slowly.

"I sure am happy to be taking you home! Home is a lonely place without my wife," David said, smiling across the seat at Ruth.

"Well, the hospital was a lonely place too," Ruth responded, returning his smile. "But I'm glad for such places when we need them."

Dorcas spoke up from the back seat. "Papa took Mr. Reinart to the hospital last evening. He's been sick for the past week. Pneumonia, they said. And Mrs. Watkins has been sick too. Her daughter was over for some sewing supplies yesterday, and she said half the neighborhood is sick right now."

Ruth glanced fearfully at the baby on her lap. "I surely hope we can keep the baby well," she said.

"Oh, nursing babies don't get sick, they say," Dorcas told her. Dorcas went on talking about this and that, almost nonstop, until they turned onto Clemmer Road.

Once David glanced at Ruth with a little grin, and she thought she knew what he was thinking. He had often expressed to her that Dorcas talked too much—and that she usually had an answer for everything, whether she was asked or not. Ruth did not think Dorcas used to be that way, when she herself was still at home. Well, at

The Upward Way

least Dorcas was kind to David and had accepted him as part of the family, and for that Ruth was thankful. And Dorcas had certainly been kind to Ruth too since she was married.

"Shall we go to your folks first, Ruth?" David asked as they neared the buildings.

"Yes," Dorcas answered for Ruth. "Mama said to plan on dinner with us."

"That sounds lovely!" Ruth exclaimed. "I don't know if I know how to cook anymore!"

David pulled the car as close to the sidewalk as he could. Then he took the baby to the house before coming back to help Ruth up the icy sidewalk. Gratefully Ruth sank onto the kitchen sofa beside Mama, who was gently unwrapping the baby. Everything smelled so good, and home looked so inviting. The smell of the wood smoke from the cookstove smelled so wonderfully homey.

"Oh, isn't she sweet!" Mama cooed as she finally got to the baby inside all the blankets. "I'm sure she grew since I saw her at a day old."

"Well, she should—the way she eats," Ruth returned. "I'm so glad that she seems healthy and well."

David helped Ruth out of her coat and then took it to hang on the clothes tree in the sitting room. Dorcas also hung up her coat and then began to bustle around the kitchen to finish dinner preparations. Soon Papa and Kore came to the house. Kore slipped past Ruth and the baby with an embarrassed grin, but Papa took his turn admiring his newest granddaughter.

"Well, well," he said, "look at those dark eyes and that dark hair. She looks like her mama, does she?"

The Upward Way

Ruth smiled happily. "That's what the nurses said. But I wouldn't care if she looked like her dear daddy."

She turned to Kore, who had come back to the kitchen and was paging through a farm magazine. "Here, take a peek at this baby."

"Aw," he said, coming over for a look. "Babies all look alike to me. But, yes, maybe she does look a little like you"—his eyes took on a mischievous look—"short and round."

Ruth laughed good-naturedly. She knew she had gained too much weight, but she hoped she could lose it once she got back to work.

"Oh, it's too soon to tell who a baby is going to look like, at ten days old," Dorcas broke in from across the kitchen.

"Here, Grandpa, you must have a turn holding this baby." Mama handed Arlene to Papa and then huffed and puffed to get up from the sofa. Then she hurried to help Dorcas with dinner preparations.

Mama's dinner was delicious, as always. But Ruth was glad to get back to her own apartment, where she could have undivided time with her husband once again. David carefully tucked her into the overstuffed chair and then sat down across from her. Baby Arlene lay sleeping in her cradle nearby, close to the wood stove.

"Now, tell me about everything that has happened since I've been away," Ruth prodded, after David did not say anything for some time, but just sat looking at her fondly.

"I was just thanking God for my wife and baby," David said with some emotion. "How good it is to have

The Upward Way

you home, and to have our dear little one too, to hold and love."

Tears came to Ruth's eyes and ran down her cheeks—not sad tears, but grateful ones. Truly God had been good to them. David had proved to be all she could have ever hoped for in a husband—so kind and considerate of her, and a true spiritual leader in their home.

"Why the tears, dear?" David asked with concern.

Ruth dabbed at them with her handkerchief. "They're happy tears. I guess I'm more emotional than normal just now too. At least I've noticed that's how other new mothers often are." She blew her nose. "I'm okay," she assured him, smiling through her tears. "And very thankful."

Baby Arlene woke up then and David bent over the cradle lovingly. Little grunts came from her cradle. "Time for her mid-afternoon snack?" he asked, picking her up when she began to cry.

"She likely needs a diaper change first," Ruth said. "But I should do that, unless you really want to." She looked at him with a smile.

"Maybe I should watch how it's done before I give it a try," David conceded with a grin. "Where do I find a diaper?"

"On the bureau in our bedroom. I'll bring the stack out here to the dry sink later, once I get things organized properly."

David laid Arlene on Ruth's lap and then disappeared into the bedroom. Soon he came again with one of the three-dozen flannel diapers that Ruth had sewn the fall before. "These look awfully big for the mite of a girl that she is," he quipped.

The Upward Way

"I have to fold them up small," Ruth returned with a smile, demonstrating. She started undressing the baby and then stopped. "I may as well feed her first and then give her a bath. She didn't have one yet today," she decided.

"Good! Then I'll stay and watch the process," David said.

As Ruth fed the baby, David began to talk about his work of the past weeks. "Your uncle Claude told me last week that he's going to sell the farm; and so he won't have work for me for very long anymore," he said after a while.

"What a surprise!" Ruth exclaimed. "Has he been thinking about that for a while? What will you do?"

"Well, your father offered me work, but you know how that would go. It's been bad enough that you've had to work so hard for him since we're married."

Ruth nodded, remembering the often near-conflicts between her husband and her father over her needing to continue with nearly as heavy a work schedule as she had before she was married. David had talked with Papa about it, but Papa thought there was no reason she couldn't continue to work hard. "Hard work never hurt anyone!" he had declared emphatically.

"Perhaps not, in most cases," David had replied, trying to be careful not to irritate his father-in-law. "But Ruth is not always well and should not be expected to work as hard as she does. Besides that, she does need time to be a housewife."

But not until winter came had Ruth's work schedule changed much. She had been thankful that the cold

The Upward Way

weather always slowed down the outside work.

David spoke again. "I wonder how much Papa will expect from you now that you have a little one."

Ruth shrugged. She had thought about that too. But surely Mama would intercede for her.

"I don't want to say this unkindly or disrespectfully," David went on, "but your father reminds me of a slave driver at times. He is a hard worker and never seems to have a sick day in his life, so it seems he expects everyone else to function as well as he does."

Ruth nodded. How well she knew that. But on the other hand, she had been warmed by Papa's kinder treatment toward her since she was married. And how could she forget his words to her after she and David had been married last May? "Ruth, you have been a faithful daughter to us, and God will bless you for it," he had told her. And Ruth had actually seen tears glittering in his steel-blue eyes.

"I enjoy helping with what I can around the place," Ruth said honestly. "But I want my first duty to be to my husband and home. Of course that includes the baby now too." She looked fondly at the little one cuddled snugly to her.

"But I could wish that Papa would pay something for my work," Ruth went on after a while. "If he were poor, I would gladly work for nothing. But he isn't poor, and I'm sure my work was worth more than the rent for the house."

David nodded. "He put electric in for us, and he pays for that. And the water. And we get all the meat, milk, eggs, and vegetables we can possibly use. That

The Upward Way

all means something too."

"I know, and I am grateful. But I can see why you have always said that we would never be able to get ahead here."

"I wouldn't have the energy or the ambition to do all that your brother Mark does to make ends meet and to have a little extra," David agreed. "Furthermore, I don't want to develop the kind of work habits that your folks and your brother have. We need time for spiritual labors and for church and family. The Bible says that life is more than meat and raiment."

"And Jesus told His followers to seek first the kingdom of God and His righteousness, and then all we need will be given to us," Ruth added soberly. "Not that we are to be 'lilies of the field' and sit around and do nothing, but our work should take second place to serving the Lord."

"Your brother Mark told me that your papa is buying another farm, one that came up for sale next to his other one in Royersville."

"Still another farm?" Ruth gasped. "What does he think he wants with all these farms?"

David shook his head. "I'm sure I don't know. Your uncle Claude even suggested that he would likely buy his and then rent it out to some young couple."

"Wouldn't you want to rent from Papa?" Ruth asked, tilting her head questioningly.

"Well, your papa mentioned that, when I said I didn't want to work for him here," David said slowly. "But I really don't think that would work either. Do you think it would?"

The Upward Way

"Probably not. Since we are part of the family, he'd likely want to help us manage the farm. I don't think he interferes too much when others rent his properties, but I can see it would be different if we would."

Ruth was thoughtful for a bit. Then she said, "But what are you thinking about doing?"

David looked down at his hands and then back at Ruth. Then he said, "I've been watching the paper for farms to rent. You know, we've talked about wanting to rent our own place sometime, even before we knew Claude wanted to sell. In yesterday's paper I saw one up near Oley, in a little village called Yellow House. A man named Pentz owns it and was advertising to farm on shares. I wanted to wait until we could talk it over before I call for more information."

"Is it a dairy farm?"

David nodded. "A fairly large one, I gathered."

"Could you and I do all that work alone?"

"I assume the owner would help with the farming. But I don't know, Ruth. We'll need to pray about it and find out more. But it did sound like something we would both be interested in."

Ruth lifted the baby to her shoulder and gently patted her back. "It would be a challenge to run our own farm. But farming on shares would sort of break us in gradually, wouldn't it."

David nodded. "That's what I thought too. We wouldn't need to lay out money for equipment and cattle all at once."

"Well, this young lady is finished eating and is properly burped, so I guess I'll give her a bath now." Ruth

325

The Upward Way

gently laid Arlene across her lap and looked at David with a smile.

David jumped up. "How shall I help you?" he asked.

"I'll need a pan of warm water. Thankfully that comes automatically now from the spigot! And I'll get her a set of fresh clothes. You may run upstairs for a towel, if you will, please."

"Sure." David tenderly took Arlene from Ruth's lap and laid her on the dry sink turned into a dressing table. Then he helped Ruth out of her chair. As Ruth began gathering a clean undershirt and wrapper[31], David sprinted up the stairs for towels and washcloth.

Tenderly Ruth sorted through the piles of wrappers and tiny undershirts that she had sewn in her spare time. Then she got a fresh diaper and rubber pants and began undressing Arlene until David reappeared with towels from upstairs and a basin of warm water from the kitchen.

"I have to watch this operation," David said as he stood by. "I guess it's warm enough in here for such a tiny person."

"I think so. Surely feels warm enough to me anyway." Ruth took the tip of the washcloth and gently washed Arlene's face. Lifting the folds of skin around her neck, she washed there.

David watched in fascination. "This is a process I don't recall ever seeing before," he said tenderly. "I was second-to-youngest in my family, and of course didn't have the opportunity to care for nieces and nephews like you have."

---

[31] A wrapper was a loose-fitting gown, often secured with ties in the front, that many mothers of this time wore on small infants.

The Upward Way

"Isn't she a perfect miracle?" Ruth said reverently.

"She is. A wonderful gift from God. What a responsibility is ours to bring this little one up to love and serve God."

David continued to watch, at times taking the tiny fingers into his or stroking the wildly kicking little feet. But Ruth's thoughts took a devious turn, and soon she was performing her task mechanically. Somehow David's comments about their responsibility to their children took her mind back to his plea with her before marriage—to please consider moving with him back to North Carolina. To him, that was a much safer atmosphere spiritually to raise a family than here in affluent Pennsylvania. Was he thinking that now was the time? Was he thinking that if Uncle Claude no longer had work for him that they ought to consider that sort of major move? But he had not mentioned that. Did that mean he had given up the idea? Ruth did not know whether to feel relieved or guilty.

Chapter Nineteen

(October, 1940. No journal entries for some time. Perhaps Ruth was too busy now, with the care of a little child as well as spending time helping David on the farm.)

Brown leaves scudded across the yard in proliferation, driven by a brisk westerly breeze. The maples and oaks around the old-fashioned, clapboard-sided farmhouse had been gently dropping the red and yellow leaves of autumn, and now the yard was covered with them. Deep piles also rested against the barnyard fence. From below the yard came the sound of the creek as it rippled and gurgled over numerous rocks on its winding way to the Schuylkill River.

All these lovely manifestations of nature in fall were not lost on Ruth. She was out-of-doors now, as she always was if there was any excuse for it at all. Right now, in the garden behind the house, she was gathering pumpkins and acorn squash and laying them on piles beside the garden to be hauled later to store in the barn loft.

The Upward Way

Sitting in the coaster wagon nearby was a little girl, bundled up against the brisk autumn chill. "Ma-ma," she called now in her high-pitched voice.

"Mama is almost finished, Arlene dear," Ruth returned. "Are you getting hungry? You watch for Papa to come from the field."

Ruth pulled her scarf closer around her ears. That wind had a bite to it! Probably there would be frost during the night. She looked toward the leaf-strewn yard. "Oh, I wish I could have gotten those leaves raked before . . ." Ruth was thinking aloud, but did not finish the sentence. "Oh, well, maybe they will all blow across the pasture to the woods before anyone gets to them." She chuckled to herself. She well knew that if she did not get the job done, nobody else would either.

"Mama, . . . Papa come?" Arlene called again.

"Are you wondering if Papa is coming soon?" Ruth asked.

Arlene nodded. "Uh-huh. Papa come."

Ruth listened. "I believe I hear Papa coming now. Hear the tractor? *Putt-putt-putt.*"

Arlene looked toward the field lane, where very soon a green tractor came *putt-putting* to the barn. Ruth looked too. The Pennsylvania Dutch hex signs that brazenly adorned the barn called loudly for her attention. But they were Mr. Pentz's doings and not hers and David's, and she hoped everyone understood that. She quickly returned to the garden to gather the last several big orange pumpkins. As she pulled them off the vines and carried them one by one to the pile by the edge of the garden, she thought about David and his tractors. He

329

The Upward Way

enjoyed using them. But she missed farming with horses, as she was used to doing at home. Mr. Pentz had been farming for some years with tractors, and now David was finding that he saved a lot of time with them. Why, he could do in a day what it would have taken a week to do with horses.

But tractors do not have personalities, Ruth thought. *Like old Dick and all the other horses that Papa always had.*

Not only did David now farm with tractors, but he also had a full-time hired man, William Phillips. What a lift he gave David in the fields and in the barn. Very seldom did Ruth need to help with the fieldwork anymore, and only occasionally did she need to help with the milking. Usually that was when the men were extra busy in the fields, and then Ruth would take Arlene out with her. She would settle Arlene in the middle of some straw bales with some cats to play with, while she herself did the barn chores. Ruth chuckled to herself. She still was not used to modern milking machines. She would much rather milk by hand than with the modern De Laval milker system that Mr. Pentz had recently installed.

Ruth thought about all the little heifers in the shed beside the big barn. Usually it was her job to feed the calves morning and evening, especially if the men were busy. That was a job she knew how to do well, and one she felt comfortable with. She enjoyed it, and even when David offered to relieve her of it, she begged to be allowed to continue as long as she could.

The John Deere sputtered to a stop, and Ruth turned again to look toward the farm buildings. David had

The Upward Way

parked the wagonload of corn beside the corncrib, and soon he and William, who had been riding on the back of the tractor, came up the back sidewalk. Mr. Pentz, who usually worked with them, had been away for the morning. Ruth had heard his truck come home and then had seen him walk toward the barn half an hour ago, probably to check on the cows.

"Is dinner ready?" David called pleasantly when he saw Ruth still at the garden.

Ruth laid the last pumpkin on the pile with the others and began pulling the wagon toward the house. "Yes, everything is ready. I just decided to quickly gather the rest of these until you come from the field. They will soon freeze out here. Really, the outdoors was calling to me," she returned with a smile, "but we'll go in now and set dinner out."

"Pa-pa, pa-pa!" Arlene called delightedly.

David met Ruth coming across the yard and took the wagon handle from her. "Let me pull this to the house," he said kindly.

He looked down at Arlene, who smiled eagerly at him. "How's our girl?" he asked her. "Were you Mama's good helper?"

Arlene chattered happily to her papa in her own baby language. Ruth smiled lovingly at the happy scene as they walked toward the house.

Across the yard, Mrs. Pentz was hanging wash on her clothesline. She waved a hand as David parked the wagon by the porch and lifted Arlene out. "How are you all?" she called around the clothespins she had stuck in her mouth.

331

The Upward Way

Ruth stepped around the porch to talk briefly with her neighbor. She knew it would take the men a little time to wash up. The Pentzes, an elderly couple, owned the farm and lived on the other side of the huge double house. David and Mr. Pentz farmed on shares, and so far the arrangement was working out very well. Mr. Pentz provided the equipment and paid the bills. David's part was to do the farming, and then the total proceeds from the farm were split evenly between them. God was blessing their efforts to provide for the needs of their family, and Ruth often thanked the Lord for the plenty that they were enjoying.

How often Ruth had thought of the difference between working for this man of the world and working for her own father. Mr. Pentz was satisfied with his one farm and with the proceeds that it provided with a moderate amount of work. Why did her father, and many others like him in their own church circles, think they had to be working day and night and then buying and investing, in order to feel they were good farmers? Was it covetousness, as David claimed? Or was it good management, as her father claimed? She had to admit, she more and more agreed with David.

David and Ruth had moved here the spring after Arlene was born, nearly a year and a half ago, over the protestations of Mama and Papa. "It's too far away from us. We'll never get to see you or dear little Arlene," Mama had declared—though it was hardly thirty miles away. But it was true; since their move, they had not seen much of the rest of the Clemmer family. They rarely got back to Grove Hill since they were attending a small

The Upward Way

mission outside the little town of Oley, five or so miles north of them. Even though David had bought a better secondhand car, a 1936 Dodge, gas was expensive—too expensive to do a lot of running around.

When Ruth arrived in the kitchen ten minutes later, after a friendly chat with Mrs. Pentz, David had the water poured and was looking at a farm magazine. "Sorry I got held up," she said as she washed at the kitchen sink. "Mrs. Pentz was worrying to me about the war going on in Europe. Mr. Pentz had just picked up a newspaper in town, and she had been reading about it. She's afraid the United States is going to be pulled into it again, like it was during World War I. She remembers that so well and the horrors and deaths associated with it—the food shortages and then the sickness that followed the returning soldiers, even after the war was over. She talked about Hitler and his blitzkrieg. She seems worried that he will conquer America, the way he is mobilizing his forces in Europe and taking over countries."

"Well, we are in God's hands," David said as Ruth quickly took dishes out of the oven and set them on the table. "He sets up whom He will and puts down whom He will, the Book of Daniel says."

William, who was standing at the counter observing them, just nodded his head. He was not a Christian, but he seemed to be truly interested in learning what Christianity was all about. He was also very attentive during family worship each morning before breakfast.

David strapped Arlene in her high chair, and they all sat up to the table. As they bowed their heads to pray, David prayed audibly. But in her heart, Ruth especially

The Upward Way

remembered their country, praying that they could continue to live in freedom, the Lord willing. Mrs. Pentz's fears could almost shake Ruth's faith in the providence of God, if she would let them.

It was Wednesday, October 23, and once more Ruth was in the Pottstown hospital. Was it just on Monday that she had been working in the garden, gathering the last of the pumpkins? What a long time ago that now seemed! What a revelation of God's undergirding strength she had once more experienced! But joy truly comes "in the morning," her thoughts assured her once more.

Ruth bowed her head gratefully, letting her tears fall on the downy-covered head of the tiny infant clasped to her breast. "Thank You, God," she whispered. "And thank You for once more giving us a dear little one."

The infant squeaked in her arms. "Oh, you dear little Albert," Ruth crooned. "How your sister will love you."

The usual ten days passed before Ruth could even think of going home. But what a glad homecoming it was for her. David helped her to the house, where Mrs. Pentz was staying with Arlene until they came back. Arlene came running to her mama and begged to be held.

"See, Mama's arms are full right now," David explained kindly. He picked up Arlene and showed her the tiny bundle in Ruth's arms.

Ruth pulled back the blanket from his face so that Arlene could see her little brother. "See? Isn't our baby sweet?" Ruth said to the little girl. "You will need to be Mama's big girl now, and help Mama tend the little baby."

The Upward Way

Arlene just looked and looked, as though she could not grasp what it was that her mama was holding. A dolly, perhaps? But this one squeaked, and his tiny eyelids fluttered as he tried to open his eyes.

Soon after settling Ruth and the baby comfortably in the living room, David prepared to leave again. "He's going for Anna French," Ruth explained to Mrs. Pentz, who had just come pattering in from the kitchen. "She's a young woman from one of our churches who is coming to help me for several weeks."

Mrs. Pentz looked almost offended. "Well, my dear, I would have been so glad to help you," she said, "and you know that."

Ruth smiled at her. "I know. And you have been very kind to us. But David and I thought it best to have someone who could live in with us and help all the time."

"Well, I guess I could hardly do that." Mrs. Pentz looked relieved. "But I could have done your washing and things like that. And brought you some meals. And watched the little girl. She's so sweet and easy to care for."

Ruth knew very well that Mr. and Mrs. Pentz did not stick to the firm discipline that she and David believed the Bible taught for little ones, but she did not say that. "I know you would have done all you could. Now, just come look at this sweet little boy." She unwrapped his blankets and showed the little round, red face and the short, round body. Arlene crowded close too, and Ruth put an arm around her.

"Oh, what a precious little one," Mrs. Pentz said. "Now you have two babies. Why, Arlene isn't even two yet."

335

The Upward Way

"I know," Ruth agreed. "But think what great playmates these two will be in a couple of years."

"But what a world for them to grow up in!" Mrs. Pentz sadly shook her head. "Wars and what not. It doesn't look too good on the world scene."

"God is in control, Mrs. Pentz. He will care for His children," Ruth tried to comfort her. "You are His child, aren't you?"

"Well, I think so, though I don't go to the same church you do. Samuel and I do read the Bible and try to obey it, as much as we can."

"That's good. Keep reading, and keep your hearts open to what God says to you from the Bible. Then you can claim His promises of help and spiritual protection. God hasn't promised everything in this life to be easy, or the way we might like it. But we have the next life to look forward to, where there will be no more pain or sickness, no more war or trouble."

Tears came to Mrs. Pentz's eyes, and she dabbed at them with a handkerchief from out of her apron pocket. "God bless you, dear. You and David are such a comfort to Samuel and me."

Mrs. Pentz soon left, taking Arlene with her to her side of the house until David returned. "So that you can get some rest, dear," she told Ruth.

The weeks passed, busy weeks of harvest and fieldwork. Much of the activity Ruth watched from the windows in the house. She was feeling so lazy, with a good housekeeper to keep the everyday chores and the children cared for. And David had a good hired man to take care of the farm work. But it was a wonderful feeling, not to

The Upward Way

be driven for once to keep after all the daily chores, and she relaxed and found new joy in reading and studying the Scriptures.

Ruth also enjoyed visiting with young Anna French. Anna reminded Ruth very much of her own sister-in-law, Ellen, whom she had missed very much ever since moving here, near Oley. Anna enjoyed sharing with Ruth as well. One day, when Ruth was rocking Albert to sleep after his feeding, Anna came with a letter she had received that day.

"Now just you take a look at this," Anna said, blushing deeply but smiling as she handed the letter to Ruth.

Ruth smiled happily. "Do you have a good surprise?" she asked.

"Well, I don't know," Anna returned, sitting down close by. "Read it and tell me what you think."

Ruth carefully took the letter and glanced first at the signature. "Oh, from Ivan Houser!" She turned to look with eagerness at Anna. "What an outstanding young man he is! You know, he came into the church at Norristown, where my sister's husband is the pastor."

Anna nodded. "I learned to know him there somewhat because I was teaching Sunday school at Norristown for most of the past year. And all I know about him is good too. But I was so shocked to get a letter! I didn't know he ever thought about girls—I thought all he had on his mind was studying the Word!"

"Well, that surely sounds commendable," Ruth said seriously. "And I know I've heard Norman and Sarah speak very favorably about him." Ruth thought for a bit as she gazed at Anna. "So you were going to Norristown.

The Upward Way

My sister Sarah recommended you to help us when I asked her if she knew of a baby maid for us. But I didn't know how she had learned to know you so well."

Ruth quickly read the letter, almost feeling as though she were treading on holy ground to share this intimate moment with Anna. But Anna was eagerly waiting for Ruth's comments. "It's certainly a nice letter. How do you feel about it?"

Anna blushed again. "I have always thought he was the finest young man I ever met," she admitted.

"That sounds promising," Ruth said with a smile. "But you will want to pray about it and talk to your parents about it."

"And I'll talk to Brother Norman and Sister Sarah too," Anna finished.

When Anna left a month later, she was looking forward to her first visit from Ivan Houser that weekend. And Ruth rejoiced with her, seeing in those two young people a couple who would be faithful church builders.

Fall crops were harvested and stored before the howling winter winds descended on them. Then spring came, with its promise again of new life and beauty. Summer followed, and once again, Ruth planted a large garden. Sometimes Mama and Dorcas came to help her put up her garden things for winter. Sometimes Ellen or Sarah would spend a day, and precious times of sharing those days were. Then fall came once more, and with it, the busy weeks of harvest. And so, another year with its seasons had come and gone.

Mrs. Pentz had been right. Young Albert was just learning to toddle from Papa to Mama when the United

The Upward Way

States joined the Allies in what would be called World War II. It all began on December 7, 1941, when Japanese planes attacked the American naval base at Pearl Harbor, Hawaii, destroying many ships and planes. The United States responded on December 8 by declaring war on Japan.

Gasoline rationing began the next spring, on May 14, and on June 4, sugar also began to be rationed. As the war progressed, many other commodities were also rationed and in short supply. As were all other farmers, David was feeling the crunch from the war efforts. But with careful management and God's blessing, they were able to keep going profitably.

More often than Ruth liked to think about, David would mention the possibility of moving back to North Carolina. "I ought to be helping my parents," he said at times. "They are all alone since my youngest brother got married. And their health isn't all that good, especially Papa's."

Though Ruth felt sure she wanted to be willing to do anything God asked of her, she just could not feel good about moving to North Carolina. "God is blessing us here," Ruth would protest. "How could it be His will for us to move so far away?"

"Yes, God is blessing us," David would agree. "But whether we are receiving material blessing should not be the deciding factor in an issue like this. We need to be willing to go at God's call, whether or not it means a sacrifice financially."

Then Ruth would try another angle. "Just think, David. If we were so far away from my family, we couldn't even

339

The Upward Way

go to my cousins' and friends' weddings. I would miss that so much."

David just looked at her.

So Ruth hurried on. "Just like next week, on June 13, Kore is to be married. I would surely not want to miss his wedding. Why, he was like a brother to me, as he was growing up. And he is marrying Uncle Henry's Ethel."

"We can thank the Lord that Kore grew up to be a respectable young man," David said after a while. "I used to wonder what would become of him, as I observed him as a young fellow at Grove Hill."

Ruth nodded. So had almost everyone else. But she and David had continued to pray for him often. And now he appeared to be taking life more seriously.

The wedding, held at the Grove Hill church, was a wonderful opportunity for Ruth to again enjoy her friends and cousins. It also provided valuable family time once more with Mark's and Norman's and Papa and Mama. Those times seemed to be getting fewer and farther between as their own family and work increased.

Three months later, on September 23, 1942, Anna Mae joined the Peachey family. She was another blue-eyed, fair-complexioned baby, much like Albert, who was now almost three. Ruth would have loved to have Anna French for her maid once again, but now Anna was Mrs. Ivan Houser. And so, while Ruth was in the hospital for this ten-day stay, Arlene and Albert went to stay with a neighboring Mennonite family, the Mast Stauffer's, with whom David and Ruth had developed a very close friendship over the past several years. After Ruth and the baby came home, Mrs. Pentz willingly helped with

The Upward Way

the housework from time to time, and the older children could often be outside with David.

Winter came again, on the heels of a rainy fall. That winter was a cold, damp one, with snow or rain more days than sun. Sickness was rampant, and many older people in the neighborhood succumbed to the various influenzas sweeping the country, no doubt carried back by the many returning soldiers. Unfortunately, Mr. Pentz was one of those. Mrs. Pentz cared for him with all the kindness of her loving and giving nature; but after several weeks of growing weaker and weaker, Mr. Pentz lost the battle.

David was thankful for the opportunity to read Scripture to him and pray with him on several occasions. Mr. Pentz appeared to die a saved man, which was a great comfort to Mrs. Pentz as well as to David and Ruth.

Through the time of Mr. Pentz's sickness and death, they often wondered when they would need to be uprooted once more. Again, David mentioned his wish to move south, but again Ruth begged for more time to consider such a life-changing move.

Then new clouds rose on their horizon, clouds that threatened to turn the light of day into the darkness of deepest night. Albert suddenly became very sick, complaining of sore throat and a headache and wanting only to be held. Dr. Fedder came out to check him and left aspirins to bring his fever down. But Albert seemed to grow worse rather than better. Soon he broke out in a red rash on his chest and abdomen. When he cried for Mama, Ruth noticed his tongue. "How strange," she murmured aloud in deep fear. "His tongue is covered with a whitish

341

The Upward Way

film, and yet there is red showing through, which makes it look almost like a strawberry." In spite of the cost of a call, she called her faithful sister-in-law Ellen. "Our little Albert is sick," she said, explaining his symptoms. "I don't know what to do for him."

"Are you sure it's not typhoid fever?" Ellen questioned in a concerned voice. "Have you been drinking water contaminated with animal waste? Or is your milk contaminated? The coated tongue makes me think of that. You had better call the doctor!"

Dr. Fedder came again and very carefully examined the very sick boy. "He doesn't show all the symptoms of typhoid," he decided after Ruth told him Ellen's verdict.

"Scarlet fever," Dr. Fedder finally pronounced after further perusal. "And that means you will have to keep him in isolation. Wash all his dishes and clothes separate from the rest of the family." He then explained careful disinfecting procedures as well as his care. "You had better hire a private nurse to come in and care for him. Aren't you caring for a tiny baby?"

Ruth nodded, her heart breaking. How could she bear not to care for her own sick child? But bear it she must, and with God's help she somehow made it through the next several weeks while Albert's life hung in the balance.[32] Those days when she felt she could bear no more, Ruth would bundle up warmly and tramp down to the creek, to a place under a large, spreading oak tree, where she had often poured out her deepest burdens to the Lord. There, with no one to hear but the chickadees and the

---

[32] Since the development of antibiotics, scarlet fever is not a feared disease, and very few people die from it.

The Upward Way

bluebirds, she poured out her anguish to God. "Oh, God, you know how I long to hold our dear little boy one more time," she cried from a heart wrung with pain. "Spare him to us, Father. Nevertheless, he is Thy child, first of all, and surely You love Him best of all." And then, from the depths of her being, she prayed, "Thy will be done."

What a day of relief when Dr. Fedder announced a turn for the better, and that Albert—barring any setback—was on the way to recovery! But the days were still long for Ruth, and the nights even longer as she was kept from the presence of her little son. How it hurt to the innermost depths of her heart to hear Albert plaintively call for his mother and to know she could not go to him! More closely than ever she clung to the Lord, and to David, who had sorrowed nearly as deeply as she had.

After Mr. Pentz's funeral, Mrs. Pentz had offered to sell the farm to the Peacheys. But Ruth was not keen about settling down permanently so far from her parents. David thought the farm was too big for him to handle alone; besides, he would rather have bought a farm in North Carolina. When she knew David and Ruth did not want it, Mrs. Pentz put the farm up for sale. With many sad farewells, she went to live with her daughter near Reading.

"What are we going to do now?" Ruth asked tearfully. She was still physically rundown and emotionally spent from the long weeks of concern and sleepless nights over Albert, and every change and decision looked major to her.

"We'll need to find another place, dear," David said, "but the Lord will provide for us."

The Upward Way

"What about William? He has been such a good worker."

David smiled. "I think he is thinking thoughts about a place of his own," he said.

Ruth nodded and then wiped the tears from her face. William had become a Christian almost two years before. Soon after he had joined the church at Oley, he had begun courting a fine Christian girl.

"In fact," David went on, "he told me just this morning that he is planning to be married this spring."

"Oh, I'm glad for him and Barbara," Ruth said, with a smile in her heart that soon broke out on her face. "She is a sweet girl and will make him a wonderful wife. Where will they settle? Does he want to farm?"

"They're thinking about moving to the new outreach work in Vermont," David said. He shivered. "Rather him than me! Up there with the bears and with the frigid temperatures. And snow nearly every day all winter long! It's bad enough here. I'd rather go south than north!"

"Oh, but they say it is beautiful there in the spring and the fall. I guess especially in the fall, when all those sugar maples turn red. I'd love to see it."

"Well, who knows? Maybe sometime we can go to visit them if they move to Vermont."

"We wouldn't be able to, if we live very far away—like in North Carolina—would we?" Ruth asked with a teasing smile.

David's look changed from jovial to serious, and he did not reply for some time. "Ruth, I have to be honest and say that the burden never leaves me that we should move where life is simpler. And not just because I was

The Upward Way

from the south. So many things in the churches around here cause me great concern. I fear for our growing children. What future do they have in a church where most of the young people have more interest in the things of the world than in the things of God? And so many changes are coming into our churches. Simple Bible obedience is being mocked as out-of-date and only for ignorant people. Church rules are scorned, and those who choose to obey them are intimidated and made fun of.

"You know yourself how Grove Hill has changed just in the five years since we left there. Coverings are smaller. Many members no longer dress plain. That wouldn't be so terrible, perhaps, if the change from "plain" would not instantly become an adopting of the world's styles, which is exactly what does happen. You know too that the radio is common among the members; and along with it, much of mainline Protestant theology is creeping in. Many members see no wrong in serving in public office or in voting, and some are beginning to take out various insurances, even life insurance, and to join the labor unions."

"But Uncle Amos was ordained bishop, and he is a conservative man. And Papa and Mark and . . . well, Papa and Mark are still preaching the Word and holding to the old ways."

"But Norman and Sarah?"

Ruth winced with an inner pang that made her want to cry. More and more when they visited Norman and Sarah and the Norristown Mission, Ruth heard things like "We have to be like them to win them. When we are so different from the world, we drive them away."

The Upward Way

"You know how Norman's are only voicing the feelings of many who are in the mission churches. And the contrary voices are even louder from those coming home from our colleges."

David looked kindly at Ruth. "You mentioned 'old ways.' Ruth, my dear, we need more than old ways to make it to heaven. We need Bible truth and people committed at all costs to living what the Bible teaches. The Pharisees did very well at keeping the old ways. But Christ had no good to say about them. Sometimes I think that is part of the problem with historic plain churches—they get so intent on keeping the old ways that they lose sight of the real goals! Surely, to keep the old ways is right and good, if they are applications of Scriptural principle and if they do not violate the commands of God in any way. Jesus said to the Pharisees, 'Ye . . . have omitted the weightier matters of the law, judgment, mercy, and faith: these ought ye to have done, and not to leave the other undone.' Jesus was not condemning their keeping of the Law, but rather that they made that an end in itself, neglecting the deeper fruits of righteousness.

"Keeping the old ways in our conference became an offense to many, and you know that. Things like using wine for Communion, the insistence by some to use German in worship services, and the opposition to Sunday school and revival meetings, growing tobacco for a cash crop, or the low courtship standards. But these things changed awfully hard—because they were the old ways. And how many souls were lost, especially young people, because of it. How much we need to know the Word and do the will of God!"

The Upward Way

Ruth nodded soberly. David had talked about things like this before, and she knew the Scriptures well enough herself to appreciate his concern. She knew very well that there were many scattered throughout their churches—like her father—who stuck to traditional ways judiciously, but whose lives left much to be desired in showing mercy and true love to others, in practical holiness and right living. Somewhere there was a right course—not in the ditch on the left and not in the ditch on the right—on which she and David wanted to lead their family heavenward. And David felt they could more easily find such a course where there were not so many different groups of Mennonites, all claiming to be faithful followers of God.

But to leave home and move four hundred miles away . . .

"Oh, David," Ruth said, tears beginning to fall again, "you know that I want to follow God's leading for us. But you feel so strongly that we ought to move south, and I feel so strongly that we ought to stay with our churches here and do what we can to help them." She fumbled for a handkerchief to wipe her eyes.

"I don't mean to make you cry, Ruth," David said tenderly. "We will continue to pray about it. I'm sure that if we truly want God's will for us, He will show us unmistakably what His will is."

Ruth truly appreciated David's kind consideration for her feelings. But still within her was a growing sense of failure on her part. Was God displeased with her that she would not submit to her husband's wishes in this one area?

Chapter Twenty

November, 1949 . . .

It was a deliciously balmy Saturday in November, one of those rare days in which fall delivers one last remembrance of summer's warmth and beauty before winter descends with a vengeance. Unable to bear the indoors on such a day as this, Ruth was outside with her growing family.

She looked around her now—at the old, mountain-stone cottage that she and David had called home for the past five years. The woodwork was clean and white in fresh paint; David was always good at keeping after little chores like that. The tin roof, that sounded so musical during rainfalls, glowed silver in the bright sunshine. Tall maples and oaks graced the yard. Ruth always loved the cool shade in the summertime. But right now, the leaves were mostly all off, and stark branches jutted skyward. The yard was full of the restless leaves, and Ruth had been eager for the opportunity and the perfect day to rake

The Upward Way

them together and haul them to the garden.

Today was such a day, and with the help of ten-year-old Arlene, Ruth had made good progress in cleaning the yard. Anna Mae and Jean Elaine romped happily in her raked piles. From time to time they ran to the baby coach, parked nearby on the porch, to check on six-month-old Vena Grace.

Somewhere in the distance, Ruth heard the *putt, putt* of the tractor. David and Albert were fixing the fence in one of the back fields, where the cows had broken out the day before. For a time, Ruth leaned on her rake as the children called and shouted around her. Her mind drifted back over the recent years.

While the Pentz farm had been for sale, she and David had watched the papers and scouted the area closer to her parents for farms for sale. Then Papa had found one outside of Royersville, just on the other side of the Schuylkill from Grove Hill. The farm was already fixed for dairying, and it was just the size that she and David were looking for. When the owner accepted their offer, they were ready to settle in. With the good help of Mark and his boys and Papa, they had made the move from Yellow House to this farm, and very soon they were feeling at home.

But David still was not quite happy. Ruth could sense that without any great difficulty. They once again had moved their membership to Grove Hill, and David saw all the accumulated changes that had taken place over the past fifteen years. She knew he did not feel at home in their church. She could understand that, and yet these were her relatives. That made the situation even more

The Upward Way

complicated, for she knew in her heart that it would be very easy for her to make the little changes along with others, in order to fit in.

Little changes... Ruth mused. Not all were little, she had to admit. Recently they had begun omitting kneeling prayers. Now they stood for prayer or simply bowed their heads. But, she had reasoned to David, kneeling was not very practical now since they no longer practiced segregated seating. While she could understand David's concern about courting couples sitting together for services, she saw nothing wrong if some chose to sit together as families. But David felt it was just one more step on the route to being "just another community church." He felt that segregated seating was a practice from the past that encouraged modesty, reserve between men and women, and better congregational singing. He felt that it was a tradition that ought to be held on to. Most families now carried insurance—much against the teaching of previous decades that such a practice was a denial of trust in the overruling power of an almighty God. But that was only the beginning of all the other little changes—the trend toward smaller and smaller headship veilings, or none at all, cut hair, worldly styles of dress . . .

I appreciate the preaching, Ruth thought as she absently watched the girls chasing their friendly chickens from the front yard. *Our ministers are still preaching the Word. But the preaching—just as David says—is more about love and tolerance, while the deeper concepts, such as discipleship and cross bearing and obedience and commitment, seem to be missing.* She continued to muse. *Something else seems different too. I can't quite think*

The Upward Way

what it is. Is it a more take-it-or-leave-it approach to the Word—as though if we want to obey, that's okay, but if it doesn't quite suit, why, God will overlook it because He loves us so much?

She thought about Scriptures that spoke of obedience as a necessity to enter heaven and wondered how such obvious truth could be overlooked. But then she remembered David's comment recently—that God will let people believe what they want to believe and then finally give them over to deception when they choose that course. "It worked that way during the time of the minor prophets," he had said. "Just read any of those books; God's so-called people were sure they were doing right and could not understand why the prophets kept crying their words of doom! But the problem was that they were not living in obedience to God's Word—and it is the same thing today. God will finally send judgment on any who do not live in obedience to truth, no matter how glowing their testimony." Then he had quoted the verses from 2 Thessalonians 2 about those who "received not the love of the truth. . . . And for this cause God shall send them strong delusion, that they should believe a lie."

"Mama! Look, we got the chickens all back in their pen," Anna Mae said as she came panting up to her mother.

Ruth was suddenly awakened from her reverie, and she looked across the yard to the chicken house. "I see you did. Good for you," she praised the little girl.

"Me help too," Jean Elaine said, prancing up on sturdy legs.

"We didn't get the mother hen," Anna Mae added.

351

The Upward Way

"She went under the corncrib with her chicks."

"That's okay," Ruth said with a smile for the girls. "The mother hen will take care of her babies."

"Another hen is setting in the feed room," Arlene contributed. "I saw her when I fed the chickens last night."

Hm-m-m, I'll have to watch for them to hatch, and pen them up before the weather gets too cold, Ruth thought. She loved to set eggs for her many ducks and chickens. But usually she only set them in the spring, so that the little ones would have the warm summer to grow up in. *Oh, well, I guess the chickens do things their own way sometimes!*

A cry came from Vena Grace in the coach on the porch.

"Arlene, would you go rock the baby a bit and see if you can get her to sleep?"

"*I* will, Mama; *I* will," Anna Mae volunteered, quickly starting on the run to the porch.

Arlene just stood grinning as she watched her go. "She loves her little sister, doesn't she, Arlene," Ruth said with a smile for her oldest daughter. "You don't get much of an opportunity to tend to her needs, do you?"

Arlene shook her head. "Well, at least I get to bathe and change her because Anna Mae can't do that yet." She got her rake and continued her job, while Ruth's thoughts went to their precious, youngest child.

Thank You, God, for sparing my life. Her thoughts were a prayer as she remembered the blood clot that had passed through her heart and lodged in her lung.

"Only a miracle of God will save your wife," Dr. Sutter had told David when Ruth was still vacillating between life and death.

The Upward Way

David had gone to his car, he told Ruth later, looking for a private place where he could cry out the anguish of his soul to God. There he had pled with God for mercy, finally committing Ruth's life to God and to His will.

But still, as Ruth slowly recovered, they often had talked over what David should do if she would not make it. "David, if you marry again, make sure it is someone Arlene loves," Ruth had whispered one time from her hospital bed. "She is such a sensitive child."

God chose to spare my life, Ruth thought now. *I was ready to go, and in many ways—except to leave my dear husband and children—the going would have been welcome! Oh, to see my dear Saviour face to face! But I guess He still has a work for me to do, and I want to be faithful in it.*

Thank You, Father, for my precious five! And thank You that my health is almost as good as ever. Truly You are a miracle-working God. Ruth picked up her yard rake and carried it to the garage. The girls were all running around and playing now, jumping in the leaf piles and having great fun. She should be keeping them busy! Except Jean Elaine. Where was she?

Ruth looked slowly around the yard. Oh, there she was, climbing up the maple tree. "That girl is such a climber!" Ruth exclaimed under her breath as she hurried across the yard to the tree. She would never forget the day last fall, when Jean Elaine was only a year and a half old, that David had come to the house trembling, carrying a chastened-looking Jean Elaine. "She was all the way to the top of the silo ladder," he had told Ruth, his voice still shaking. "Forty feet off the ground! When

353

The Upward Way

I saw her, I hurried up the ladder after her. She called down to me, 'I hold tight, Papa; I hold tight! Don't 'pank; Papa, don't 'pank.' But I did when I got her down. She can't try tricks like that!"

Ruth called up into the tree. "Come down, Jean Elaine. You'll ruin your dress, if you don't fall out of the tree first!" she said, frustration edging her voice. "Why did you go up there anyway?"

"Oh, Mama, I saw the prettiest little bird. It was coming down the tree head first, and I wanted to see where it flew to." Jean Elaine was already clambering from branch to branch on her way down.

"My dear child, you can't catch a bird by climbing a tree!" Ruth assured her. "Now come down."

"I am, Mama," Jean Elaine said, wrapping her legs and arms around the trunk and sliding the last ten feet to the ground.

Ruth wiped dirt off the little girl's face. "Girls shouldn't climb around like that," Ruth admonished her. "God teaches us to be modest. That means that we keep our dresses down. And little girls climbing in trees can't keep themselves very modest, can they?"

Jean Elaine looked up at Ruth with big brown eyes. "I should wear pants like Albert does. Then I could climb trees," she ventured.

How many girls from our churches has she seen in pants, Ruth wondered soberly. *No doubt quite a few, especially little girls. What should I say?*

Ruth's thoughts were a puzzle as she stooped for a moment, absently brushing bark and stems and dirt off Jean Elaine's dress. "The Bible teaches us that God does

The Upward Way

not want women and little girls to dress as men do. God wants women to look different from men."

Jean Elaine's eyes brightened. "I have pigtails, but you cut Albert's and Papa's hair," she said happily.

"That's right," Ruth agreed, deciding not to carry the discussion any further at this point.

"Come, girls," she said, marshaling their forces. "Let's load these leaves on the cart and take them to the garden." After dozens of cartloads of leaves had been hauled to the garden and dumped there to make humus for next year's vegetables, Ruth took the little ones and headed toward the house to make dinner.

Anna Mae ran to the baby coach on the porch. "I'll bring Vena Grace in," she said, reaching down and releasing the brake as she had often seen her mother do.

"Be care—" Ruth began, but took off on a run as the coach careened across the sloping porch floor. "Oh, no!" she exclaimed, her heart in her throat. She was not quite fast enough, and the coach dropped off the edge of the porch, dumping over into the yard. Baby and blankets landed with a plop in the grass.

Vena Grace set up a wail, and Ruth hurried to her. "Thank God, she can cry!" Ruth declared as she gathered the distraught baby in her arms and tried to comfort her. "Anna Mae, you must be more careful. The baby could have been hurt badly," Ruth said, turning to her, unaccustomed harshness in her tones.

Anna Mae stood silently by, her lips quivering. Ruth's heart smote her. *The poor child did not mean it. Furthermore, I sounded more like my own father than I would like to admit! Oh, God, help me to be a patient mother!*

355

The Upward Way

Ruth went to Anna Mae and spoke more gently. "I'm sorry, Anna Mae. Mama should not have been so harsh with you. Vena Grace is all right, and I know you didn't mean to do it."

At this Anna Mae burst into tears. "No, Mama. I just wanted to help," she cried disconsolately.

Ruth drew her close and gently brushed the hair out of her eyes. "It's okay, Anna Mae. Everything is all right. We'll just try to be more careful the next time. Let's stop crying now and go get some dinner for Papa and the rest."

Finally, the small girl was comforted, and she followed the others into the house. Ruth quickly peeled sweet potatoes and sliced them to fry. They were one of David's favorite dishes. Then she made gravy with the sausage left from supper the night before. "Now, what shall we have for a vegetable?" she asked Arlene, who was busily setting the table.

Arlene thought a bit. "Is there still broccoli in the garden? I think I saw some."

"Good! Can you take a pan"—Ruth rooted in the cupboard for a small, stainless steel bowl—"and bring in enough for dinner?"

"Okay." Arlene was out the door on flying feet. Soon she returned.

"Now you girls may set the bread and butter on and pour the water," Ruth directed. "Papa will soon be in."

"May I go for the mail, Mama?" Arlene asked after the table was ready. "I saw the mailman go when I was getting the broccoli."

"Sure. But be careful, and don't go close to the road," Ruth reminded her. She was busily cutting garden lettuce

The Upward Way

for a salad. Then she added a tomato and grated a carrot over the top.

"Oh, look, Mama. A letter from Grandma Peachey!" Arlene entered the kitchen a little later, taking an envelope from the stack of mail and showing it to her mother.

"Good! We'll read it when Papa comes for dinner. Shall we?"

David and Albert soon came stomping up the back path, and the growing family sat down to a table laden with good things from the farm and garden. Ruth looked around happily and gratefully at their growing family as they hungrily cleaned up their food. God had been so good to them! And all the children were healthy and well. Such a blessing was hers.

"What's for dessert, Mama?" Albert asked. "Just applesauce?"

David looked at him kindly. "That's enough for this time, my boy," he said. "Mama had a delicious dinner, and we all had plenty to eat."

"But I like pie and cake," he insisted. "Like we get at Grammy Clemmer's. Why, she even has pie or cake for breakfast!"

"That's all right if she does that, and we often have pie and cake too," Ruth said. "But everything is eaten up, and we didn't do the baking yet today." Her thoughts took her back to David's kind suggestion soon after they were married that she did not need to serve pie or cake for him every meal. He was not used to it, and he thought it probably was not that good for him anyway. Ruth had been relieved, and yet she did still enjoy having her sweets at times.

The Upward Way

"This afternoon we want to bake," Arlene added. She was becoming quite good at baking cakes and cookies and following simple recipes.

After everyone was finished eating, Ruth read the letter from David's mother as the children listened eagerly. One part in particular, the older children caught—Grandma's invitation to come for Thanksgiving.

After Ruth was finished reading, David looked over Jean Elaine's head to Ruth. "What do you think about going to my home? The children have off for several days from school. And probably we could get your nephews to do the work for the weekend."

Inwardly Ruth cringed. Not that she did not love her mother-in-law, but would such a visit only intensify David's longing to move back? She knew how these visits always went. But it *had* been almost a year since they had been home for a visit. . . . "We haven't been down there since last Christmas," Ruth said. "It would be nice to go again, especially for Grandma's sake. I'm sure she gets very lonely since Grandpa is gone. And she hardly knows our children."

"And we hardly know Grandma," Arlene said.

"Yes, she gets very lonely, living there alone since Grandpa died," David added. "I wish we were close enough to help her out now and then."

"Well, your brothers are nearby," Ruth objected. "They could help her with various things."

David nodded. "I'm sure they do."

Albert's eyes gleamed. It was obvious he was thinking about a trip to North Carolina. He loved to go places, especially for long trips. "Yes, let's go!" he begged.

The Upward Way

And so the trip was planned, even though Ruth did not feel quite willing, and the day finally came to leave.

"Any more suitcases, Albert?" David asked as Albert came lugging one more.

"Mama said this is the last one."

"Well, then, let's get loaded up! Where's Mama?"

"She said to tell you she'll be here in a couple of minutes."

Soon Ruth hurried out, Vena Grace in her arms. Arlene carried the diaper bag, and the other two hurried along with their favorite dolls.

"Hop in, everyone," David said. Ruth hopped in quickly. She knew that when David wanted to go somewhere, he did not have much patience for stragglers!

The weather in North Carolina was balmy on Thanksgiving Day. Most of the Peachey family was home for the day, and Grandma Peachey had her hands full with all the grandchildren running in and out. Screen doors banged, and children called and shouted to each other.

As the others visited animatedly, Ruth looked around her in quiet observation. How could she ever live in such poverty? Sure, since Grandpa had died several years ago from a strangulated hernia, Grandma's circumstances had improved somewhat. The older children had seen to it that she had electricity installed when the power company had finally strung the lines along the road in front of the house. An indoor bathroom and hot and cold water at the kitchen sink soon followed. But still . . . Ruth looked almost with disgust at the chickens roosting on the clothesline posts and the pigs rooting happily in what was once the garden. There was really no yard; it

The Upward Way

was just mud and animal dirt! She cringed as she saw the evidence of small feet tracking it into the house all day.

The Friday after Thanksgiving was quieter. Ruth spent the morning helping Grandma with the task of cleaning up while David fixed a barn door and put up a fence that would hopefully keep the pigs in a confined area.

"I would enjoy going to the water again," David said after dinner. He pushed his chair back from the table far enough to take Vena Grace on his lap. "There wouldn't be so many people around either this time of year."

Grandma looked up with interest. "Well, I would enjoy that too. I haven't been to Batchelor Bay since Pop died. He liked to go fishing there, as you boys all know."

"Shall we all load up in the station wagon and go for a drive?" David asked.

"Yes, yes!" came from all sides as the children voiced their feelings and clapped in anticipation.

"Let's help Grandma clean up the kitchen, and then we'll see if we can find our way there," David said. Handing Vena Grace to Ruth, he stood up and began clearing the table.

Soon they were on their way. They drove through pine barrens and marshland, acres of cleared ground from which sweet potatoes and peanuts had been harvested, and more marshland. Here and there were dairy farms, with mostly Jersey or Guernsey cattle grazing in rye fields.

"Look there, Ruth," David suddenly said, braking the car and pointing to the left at a well-maintained dairy farm. A realtor's sign stood at the end of a long lane, advertising that the farm was for sale.

The Upward Way

Ruth did look. Poplar trees bordered a long, sandy lane that led to a large farmhouse, set behind a hedge with huge maple trees all about it. A windmill sat to the side, near an outbuilding. She thought she could see a dairy barn behind the house, and, yes, there were cows in a pasture near the barn. *I just know what David is thinking,* she thought, her whole being cringing at the idea. *And yet . . . it does appear to be a decent farm, so that we wouldn't need to live totally like backwoodsmen!* She knew she shouldn't feel like that, but still she did. If David so much felt they should move to his home area, why should she have such negative feelings about it?

David quickly pulled to a stop and backed up close to the lane. "I'd like to get that realtor's number," he explained, quickly rooting to find paper and pencil. "Just in case we have further interest."

Ruth turned to see Grandma Peachey smiling happily. But she did not feel like smiling. To come to visit here once a year—well, that was okay—but to live here—never! Why, it was just sand and pine trees and marsh, and all so uninterestingly flat!

David did not say more just then. Perhaps he sensed Ruth's conflict. But he did bring it up in their bedroom at Grandma's that evening. He was bent over, unlacing his shoes. "Well, Ruth, what did you think of that dairy farm we saw on the way to the bay?"

Ruth's answer was guarded. "It was nice enough, at least considering how a lot of places look in this area," she said.

"What would you think about buying a place like that?"

The Upward Way

"Isn't it sort of far from Holly Springs and from your family?"

"I thought of that. But that area is known to be better farming area. And we'd have only about twenty-five miles to church." He looked at Ruth with longing in his eyes. "Why don't we pray about it?" he suggested finally, when Ruth did not say any more.

After spending time in prayer, they continued to talk while Ruth fed Vena Grace and got her settled for the night. "David, if it is God's will for us to move here, I truly want to be willing," Ruth said finally, tears filling her eyes. "But how to know God's will—that is the question."

David was silent for some time, apparently deep in thought. "Is it ever right to ask for a sign?" he asked finally.

"I was thinking of that too," Ruth said as she laid Vena Grace carefully in the crib. She wiped her eyes and blew her nose. "Gideon asked for a sign, and God did not condemn him for that. I know we hear teaching that God directs us in our day without signs—through the Word, through open and closed doors, and through the counsel of the church. But we have been getting such contrary signals, it seems to me."

David nodded. "I was thinking about that too. Here at Holly Springs the brethren say one thing. Your family and the others at Grove Hill say exactly the opposite. And I feel strongly one way, and you feel strongly the other."

The tears started again as Ruth looked at David's drawn face. "My dear husband," she said earnestly, "I do want to submit to you in all things. Why is this so hard for me? I used to wonder why it seemed so hard for

The Upward Way

Mama to submit to Papa, and now it seems I follow her example too much."

David pulled a tablet out of his pocket. "This is what we can do. Let's write 'yes' on two pieces of paper and 'no' on two others and put them in a box. Then we will pray about it. We will pray that if God wants us to move to North Carolina, we will both pull a 'yes' from the box."

"But what if one of us pulls a 'yes' and one a 'no'?" Ruth asked doubtfully.

"We will pray and trust God to give clear direction," David said.

On two slips of paper, David lettered a big "yes." On two others, he lettered a big "no." Then he put them into a container on the bureau, shaking them up well. "Now, let's commit this to God," he said, "and trust Him to show us what His will is."

Again they knelt by the bed to pray. Ruth was in tears, the whole fabric of her well-ordered life in danger of unraveling any moment. But she prayed from a full heart, beseeching the Lord for a submissive heart to His will. Then David drew a slip. It said "yes." Then Ruth did. It also said "yes."

"Can we do it once more, David, to be sure?" Ruth pled.

Again they drew, with the same results.

And again, Ruth begged, "Just once more?"

Again, they both drew a "yes." [33]

---

[33] Although this is a true account, we do not endorse it as a Scriptural method of finding God's will. Had both openly considered the situation in which they found themselves and the Scriptural principles involved, God would have shown His will without the sign. God was indeed merciful to them.

The Upward Way

That was a holy moment for both of them, as confessions were made and aspirations were shared and considered.

The next morning, David called the realtor, and they were able to schedule an appointment to see the place.

"I think I could be happy here," Ruth conceded, after seeing the home with all the amenities of the time.

"The barn is fixed adequately too for a dairy," David said. "I guess we will decide finally if this is for us if the owner accepts our offer."

After the long, traumatic weekend, Ruth was ready to head the many miles back to Pennsylvania on Monday morning. Somehow she felt the need for un-pressured time to think, to sort out her feelings and to come to grips with such a move as obviously being God's will.

Their own stone cottage looked so good when they drove up to it late that night. "How glad I am to be home once again," Ruth stated, crawling stiffly out of the car.

"Thank God for safety," David added, to which Ruth nodded sober agreement.

The children spilled out, not too tired to check out their favorite haunts. David changed his clothes and went to the barn to be sure all was in order there.

On Tuesday morning, the children needed to go back to school. Arlene and Albert picked up their lunch boxes and started for the door, but Anna Mae came to Ruth crying.

"Why, Anna Mae," Ruth said to her little daughter, "what is the matter?"

Arlene stepped back from the door. "I think I know, Mama," she said. "When some big boys get on the bus,

The Upward Way

they tease her and make her cry."

Oh, if only they wouldn't need to ride the bus to school, Ruth thought. She didn't know what all might be happening on that bus to influence her dear children away from God.

Anna Mae stood looking up at her with tear-stained face. "Just be kind to them," Ruth encouraged her, gently smoothing her blond hair. "And maybe they won't tease you anymore."

Albert was waiting impatiently at the door. "I hear the bus coming around the bend," he said. "We'd better run for it!"

Soon the children were out the door and on the run to the end of the lane. Ruth turned back to the duties of the day, of which there were plenty—loads of laundry to do after a four-day trip, the house to clean up, and whatever else comes up in the course of a day for a busy wife and mother. But there was a peace in her heart, a peace she had not experienced for years. Ever since—was it ever since the first time she had refused to consider David's plea to move to North Carolina? "Dear Father in heaven," she prayed aloud as she gathered piles of laundry from the children's bedrooms, "I'm sorry for failing You. I didn't know I was doing wrong. But I guess I should have known, because Your Word teaches that the wife is to submit to her husband in all things. . . ."

A few days later that week, the realtor called with the word that the farm owner had accepted their offer. "He said," the realtor told David over the telephone, "that he knows your offer is a lot less than the list price. But he was happy that Plain People wanted to buy it, because

365

The Upward Way

he knew they would keep up the place."

David turned happily from the telephone. "There's our answer, Ruth," he said after repeating the realtor's words to her.

The moment was bittersweet for Ruth. Obviously this was God's will; it seemed there could no longer be any doubt. And she could now sincerely rejoice with David. But how should she break the news to her family and her many friends?

Before she had the opportunity to do that, another experience came to them that threatened to shatter their rest in God's leading and leave them with a new wave of doubts and fears.

"The realtor called and wants to set up an appointment for settlement as soon as we can work in another trip south," David told Ruth early the next week.

Ruth gasped. She had not thought about the possibility of another trip so soon. "Would we take the children out of school? And who would do the work? And how would I explain to my parents why we need to go back again?"

"Aren't you going to tell them about our plans to move?" David asked, incredulity in his voice. "Should we go over this evening and talk to them?"

"I want to sometime," Ruth hedged. "But I haven't gotten up enough nerve yet to tell them. I just know how they will try to talk us out of it. I figured once we've made settlement on a place, there isn't much they can do to change it."

David looked as though he did not agree that her plan was the best way to manage things. "Well," he said slowly, "we will need to ask someone to do the work.

The Upward Way

And somebody would need to stay here with the older children, I suppose, so that they can go to school."

Mark and Ellen were understanding when David and Ruth told them in confidence of their plans, and they did not contribute anything in a negative way. In fact, Mark had this to offer: "I have been distressed with the continuing trends away from Gospel obedience and simplicity among our church families. Maybe this will be an answer for you and your family, to stay conservative. I can't very well move, since I am ordained as deacon here."

Mark's offered to keep quiet until David and Ruth could tell Papa and Mama themselves about their planned move. Ellen suggested that she could stay with the children for the several days they would be gone, and Roy and Robert would do the barn chores.

With everything so well taken care of, David and Ruth and the two younger children left with eager hearts, heading south. All went well until Wednesday, the second day of their stay. David's younger brother burst into Grandma Peachey's house right after they were finished with supper. "Your brother-in-law called and wants you to call him right back," Emory said. "It sounded urgent. I can take you over in my car."

Ruth waited in great anxiety until David returned. What had gone wrong? Had one of the children been hurt? or even killed? Was someone sick? Papa or Mama? She tried to pray, and Grandma Peachey stood by, offering comfort in her own way.

Soon David returned, and Ruth saw at a glance that something was terribly wrong. David's face was white and drawn as he stepped in the door. "We've lost our

The Upward Way

barn," he gasped. "It burned to the ground this evening."

"Our barn? You mean at Royersville?" Ruth blurted out. "Are the children okay?"

"Yes, thank God, they are. They were in the barn when it started. Mark said the neighbor boy, Delbert, had come over to play with the children, and he thinks Delbert may have been playing with matches. It appears that he threw one into a pile of straw when it burned down to his finger. Anna Mae was there with the boys when the straw pile caught fire. Arlene came on the scene and pulled the dazed children to safety."

Ruth burst into tears. "Oh, why did we leave them?" she cried. "Have we not been in God's will? Have we done something wrong that God has brought this upon us?"

David put an arm about her. "Ruth, we can't feel this way. Whom the Lord loves, He chastens, and we must not question what God allows. Just submit. We can be truly thankful that the children are safe."

"Yes, I am," Ruth said through her tears. "And I want to trust God in all these things."

"Mark said the boys were milking when they smelled smoke and realized there was a fire," David went on. "They were able to get the cows out, but the pigs and chickens were all lost."

"How must this make the children feel? And Delbert too," Ruth said, still wiping tears. "He knew better. And usually we didn't even let him play with the children unless we were around."

David nodded soberly. "I know. But we won't press any charges."

"I didn't think you would. But still—our children.

The Upward Way

Shouldn't we start home right away?"

"Yes, we should," David agreed. "At least we have finished what we came to do."

Grandma Peachey stood up quickly. "Let me fix you some coffee," she said. "It will hearten you up. And then I'll pack some sandwiches for this evening while you travel."

All the way home, Ruth dreaded what they would find when they arrived. It was very dark when they reached home well past midnight, but the next morning revealed the sad state of affairs. Ruth remembered how their barn at the homeplace had burned when she was a teenager. All the horrors she had felt then were revived as she stood silently by David's side, viewing the destruction. The children all gathered close to them, and Ruth pulled them protectively to her. "At least you are all safe," she said with quaking voice. "Thank God for sparing your lives."

Albert burst into tears and flung himself into his father's arms. "Oh, Papa. I told Delbert we aren't allowed to play with matches," he sobbed out. "But he wouldn't listen to me. I was so scared we'd be all burned up!"

Somehow the next days passed. The cows were at the neighbors and being milked there, so David and Ruth had little to do but try to pick up the pieces of their lives. After the barn debris had cooled enough, David hired a crew with bulldozers to come in and push everything together to finish burning. He would not plan to build again but would let the new owners—if they could sell the place—decide on the kind of structure they wanted.

Over and over, Ruth's heart was hurt as she heard people discussing their plight. "Well, they should have

The Upward Way

had insurance. Then they wouldn't have had such a big loss right now—and just when they were planning to sell the place too. Too bad." Or, "They should realize that God is speaking to them, telling them that their plan to move to the boondocks is a wild notion." After each fresh cut from someone, Ruth fell to her knees, pleading with God to give her grace to overlook and forgive. God did give grace, but the strain of those weeks was almost overwhelming.

"How far we have moved from true compassion among us," David said one evening as Ruth was rehearsing a church sister's telephone call from the day. "What a sad plight when God's people can no longer be recognized by their love for each other."

Ruth nodded tearfully, knowing that David was referring to the verse that says, "By this shall all men know that ye are my disciples, if ye have love one to another."

"It wasn't that we expected help or anything," she said. "And yet, I remember a little more than twenty years ago when Papa had his barn fire. There was a totally different feeling about such calamities, and people were there for us!"

David laughed ruefully. "Well, somebody gave us a pig," he said. Then he added, "But even though friends let us down, God never will. And we can trust His care."

Over the next weeks, David arranged for the sale of the cows. At the same time, they were packing for their move to North Carolina. Though Papa and Mama had not been pleased when told about David and Ruth's decision to move, Mama and Dorcas were there almost every day, helping Ruth to pack and clean.

The Upward Way

Close friends offered to drive trucks loaded with goods to their new home in North Carolina. Before Christmas, a caravan of vehicles started out early, David leading with their truck and Amos Bechtel following next in line.[34]

An eager group of workers was waiting at the farm when the weary caravan arrived late in the afternoon. Among them were some of David's sisters, who had spent the last several days papering the upstairs bedrooms. Willing church sisters from Holly Springs had also cleaned the whole house. Brethren were waiting in the barn and yard, ready to unload farm machinery and set up furniture.

Ruth entered the house to the fresh smell of soap and wallpaper paste. A kettle of thick stew bubbled on the stove, giving an inviting, lived-in smell to the roomy kitchen. "Thank you, everyone," she said gratefully as sisters-in-law and helpful church sisters came to greet the weary travelers.

By late evening, nearly everything was in place, and the helpful workers from the area and the faithful friends from Pennsylvania had all gone their ways. David and Ruth sat in the spacious living room, their family gathered around them. After a time of Bible reading and prayer, they just sat enjoying each other and the cozy fire burning in the fireplace. Soon David began singing, and the rest all joined in as they could.

" 'God hath not promised skies always blue,
    Flower-strewn pathways all our lives through;
God hath not promised sun without rain,
    Joy without sorrow, peace without pain.

---

[34] This move took place on December 15, 1949.

The Upward Way

> But God hath promised strength for the day,
> Rest for the labor, light for the way,
> Grace for the trials, help from above,
> Unfailing sympathy, undying love.' "

"What a promise," Ruth said with tears in her eyes.

David smiled at her. "All day the verse was going through my mind: 'My presence shall go with thee, and I will give thee rest.' Just another of God's promises, and we can trust them all!"

"I like this place," Albert said happily. "I took a bike ride to the woods today. It's just full of pine trees! I'm going to love going there to find pine cones and moss!"

"I like the house. It's so big and homey," Arlene said. "I feel at home already."

Ruth looked across the living room to a motto that someone had hung up there for them today: *"Home is where the heart is."*

"Yes, I feel at home too," Ruth said, smiling at the children. "My family is here, and God is here. That is all we need to have real joy!"

Chapter Twenty-one

Spring, 1954 . . .

From the chicken house came the happy songs of the leghorn hens. Ruth stopped for a moment to listen, a smile in her heart. *David must be in there feeding them,* she thought, *with the way they're going on.* She snapped another towel and hung it on the clothesline. Then she looked around her gratefully. God had been so good to them. In the four years that they had been living here in Rawlins, North Carolina, Ruth had grown to love the area. But more than that, she had grown to love the people and was realizing more and more the mission field right at their own door.

All around them lived people who were searching for truth—black people and white people, poor people and rich people. Mennonites were new in this community. And nearly every day, someone came to the door for some reason or other, and she or David were able to give them a Christian witness. Often on a weekday evening,

The Upward Way

either she and David or the whole family would go to visit some seeking or elderly people in the community. They would sing for them or read the Scriptures. Their station wagon had usually been packed full when they had gone to Holly Springs for Sunday morning worship services. And now still, David went out early each Sunday morning to gather in those from the community who wished to worship with them.

Sweet scents of lilacs drifted to Ruth from the several blooming bushes along the white farmyard fence. Above her head, the maple buds were bursting with the new life of spring. And around her flew the ever-busy birds—robins, mockingbirds, sparrows, bluebirds, and crows—calling and singing and letting everyone know that spring was here once more.

David came up the walk then, with almost-five-year-old Vena Grace trotting determinedly beside him. "I helped feed the chickens, Mama," she stated happily. "And I want to gather the eggs now. Papa said I may help him."

All the other children were in school, and Ruth was thankful for this one at home to keep her company through the long days. But so often, at least if David was around the buildings, Vena was out with her papa.

"Papa needs to make a telephone call, Vena, and then I will be out again," David told her. He looked at Ruth with a smile and then back to Vena. "Maybe you and Mama can go gather the eggs in the meantime."

"I was about ready to," Ruth returned. "I just wanted to finish hanging up the towels." Soon Ruth took Vena by the hand, and together they went to the chicken house.

The Upward Way

How Ruth enjoyed her chickens. She moved among them now, talking to them and gently shoving them out of her path, and the happy hens sang so loudly that the tumult almost hurt her ears. David often declared good-humoredly that their eggs did not pay for the feed they ate, but he enjoyed taking care of them as much as Ruth did. He had fixed up the old horse barn to use as a chicken house, putting a second level in the haymow to keep chickens on two levels.

Ruth carried one basket along with her, lifting the eggs out of the many nesting boxes. Vena carefully retrieved a few too. Always now, before Ruth stuck her hand into the nest boxes, she looked carefully first. She would never forget her fright when one day last summer she had put her hand into a nest box to grasp the leathery coil of a curled up black rat snake! She laughed now. But it hadn't been funny then! She had left her egg baskets and had gone on the run for David. He returned with his .22 and had soon dispatched the snake, which had been carefully guarding its accumulated food supply. The snake had measured over six feet long, and even their feisty rat terriers had not wanted to go near it.

Ruth laughed again, and Vena turned to her. "What's funny, Mama?"

"I was thinking about that snake we found in a nest box last summer and was hoping there wouldn't be another one."

Vena's eyes got big. "I hate snakes," she declared. "I was with Papa and Albert when they found one in the bunny hutches last summer. It scared me! It stuck its tongue out at me, like this." The little girl demonstrated.

The Upward Way

"That is how snakes can sense what is happening," Ruth explained. "They aren't sticking out their tongues, but just trying to find out if they are safe or not."

"Oh." Vena thought for a bit. "But I still don't like them."

"We had a lot of snakes around last summer, didn't we," Ruth said. "We found one on a duck nest, and one when we were picking peas in the garden. And we found some in the cow barn and here in the chicken barn—all great big fellows! Black snakes are good for killing mice and rats, but I don't like when they come around where we want to be, or bother the things that we want!"

"Like eggs and bunnies," Vena added.

Soon Ruth and Vena had filled one basket. Ruth set that one outside the pen door and got the second one. After the two baskets were full, Ruth carried them to the utility room in the house, where she would clean and grade them later.

And so the day passed. Once more at three-thirty, the big yellow school bus stopped at the end of the lane, and the four schoolchildren jumped off and bounded in the lane, book bags and lunch boxes bumping against their legs. Ruth watched them come with mixed feelings. If only they had a Christian school. Each morning, she and David prayed with the children before they went off to school, and she knew God could keep them. But what a stress it was, to continually counter the world's influences to keep them thinking right about godly things. The songs they came home with, the games they played, the worldly language, the pressure to dress like the other children and to go to the after-school functions, the pressure of school-time shows

The Upward Way

and dramas, and the dances and sports . . . These and much more kept David and Ruth praying for the privilege of a way to teach their children without needing to send them to public school.

Jean Elaine was the last one in the door; and by the time she got there, the rest had had their say. "Mama," she said eagerly, "tomorrow is field day. And we get to play games the whole day. And today was Patsy Sherman's birthday, and we all drew a picture of her, and the children chose mine as the best to hang up on the blackboard. And I got 100 percent on my spelling test. And Mrs. Smack said—"

"Are you going to talk all night?" Albert asked, from where he was paging through a farm magazine that had come in the mail that day.

"It's nice you got 100 percent," Ruth told her, "and that your picture got chosen. But we don't want you to boast. That shows pride, and we don't want our little girl to be proud."

"What is 'proud,' Mama?" Jean Elaine asked.

"It is when we think we are smarter or better than other people," Ruth said. "The Bible says that we should not think more highly of ourselves than we ought to think. That means that we can do some things well, but there are many things that others can do better than we can."

"Oh." Jean Elaine seemed to understand. "Some of the others can run faster than I can at recess."

"Today we had an air-raid drill," Arlene contributed. She was in eighth grade this year.

"What do you do then?" Ruth asked.

"We crawl under our desks," Anna Mae said.

The Upward Way

"We go out in the hall and kneel with our heads down and our arms folded over our heads," Arlene added.

"It's always so scary," Anna Mae went on. "I don't like air-raid drills. They're even worse than fire drills."

"Well," their mother encouraged them, "you can always remember that God is with you, no matter what happens. Just keep trusting in Him." But while she spoke, she wondered why such fears of nuclear attack needed to be implanted into tender young hearts.

Albert went to the cookie jar and noisily took off the lid, looking at Mama with a grin. She noticed and responded just as he had expected her to. "Change your clothes first. Then you can have a snack. But hurry! It will soon be time to bring in the cows and start milking."

Saturday came again, and the children were all home for the day. David helped for the morning, and together they planted the "patch." (Ruth had earlier planted her backyard garden.)

"One thing I know," declared Arlene, "I sure like planting in this sand better than among the rocks we had when we lived in Pennsylvania! I still remember picking rocks!"

"Believe it or not, I like planting in the sand too, Arlene," Ruth said, smiling at her. "I've learned to love gardening without rocks."

"And digging potatoes with our toes," added Albert with a grin.

At the dinner table, David pushed back his chair. "Is the house all ready for church here tomorrow?" he asked with twinkling eyes.

Anna Mae clapped her hands while Arlene spoke up.

The Upward Way

"Mama and I were cleaning in the evenings this week to get ready," she said.

"I get tired of having church in our house," Albert stated. "I wish we'd always go to Holly Springs." He enjoyed his friends at Holly Springs and had not been happy, Ruth knew, to partially sever those ties last year when they had started having church here at Rawlins.

"When several new families moved into our area during the last year or two," David explained, "our bishop thought we could begin having services here. And also, we wanted to hold to a more Biblical standard of practice than what Holly Springs has."

Arlene nodded. "All the families who attend here are young families, and there isn't anybody my age. But anyway, I don't care. I'm just glad not to need to be with the young people at Holly Springs so much. Some are nice, but some are so worldly in the things they do."

Ruth gazed fondly at her oldest daughter. At fifteen, Arlene was a growing Christian, developing firm convictions of her own. She was also considered old enough to be with the young people. But the things that went on at the gatherings were not always the most upbuilding. Arlene had told her mother just after the last one that she was never going to go again. "They paired off everyone for games," Arlene had declared, "even us younger ones. And I had to be with Kenneth Russell—and I can't stand him!"

"You need to be careful with your attitude toward him," Ruth admonished her young daughter. "But I agree that it isn't right for you young teenagers to think about boyfriends and girlfriends."

The Upward Way

"I know, Mama, and that's why I don't want to go again. It seems the wildest ones are the ones that plan the evenings and tell everybody what to do. And usually the games are the kind that I don't feel right playing—games that involve boys and girls holding hands, and other foolish things like that."

Ruth groaned in her spirit now as she thought about the church at Holly Springs. It seemed the same influences were coming in there that were touching plain churches everywhere—the surge toward freedom from any kind of restraints or standards. Just as the cry had been at Grove Hill, so the Bible-based standards here were being labeled as legalism. The young people, influenced by public schools, the radio, and worldly neighbors, were taking on the practices of the ungodly around them. Those in authority seemed powerless, or else unmotivated, to stem the tide of liberalism. How disappointed David was. And yet he had never regretted the move south, to the slower pace of life where there was contentment without the push for material gain and prosperity.

"We're thankful for the few families from Holly Springs who have been coming over here," David said. "These families want to maintain a conservative practice just as we do. We've usually had a nice-sized group. Brother Ira has been suggesting that maybe we should be thinking about building a church soon."

The next morning was busy as Ruth prepared to teach Sunday school, along with finishing preparation for several dishes for the noon meal. Others would be bringing food too, but it was always Ruth's responsibility to see

The Upward Way

that everything went smoothly as the meal was served. David and the older children helped to set up chairs in their large living room. French doors opened into an equally large dining room, so chairs were also set there, in case more room was needed.

Soon after nine-o'clock, eager worshipers began to arrive. Ruth noted with pleasure that Brother Allen Rohrer, from a sister church in Maryland, was visiting for the day. No doubt he would preach. Quite a few community people were there, some having been personally invited by David or Ruth or by one of the other families new in the area. David had brought some of them in his faithful station wagon.

"We're glad for each one who has come this morning," David said as he got up to open the service. "We're especially glad for Brother Allen's presence. He will be bringing us the message after Sunday school."

The morning service was a blessing and a challenge to all. Ruth's heart was blessed and thrilled as she noted the oneness of heart and spirit among the gathered group. *Thank You, God, for continuing to lead us in Your way. Continue to lead us in the upward way, the only way that leads to You.*

The other sisters all helped to set out the potluck lunch, and after a time of fellowship, the worshipers separated to their own homes. That evening they would again meet for worship at the Peacheys, which they did on the first, third, and fifth Sundays of each month. On the second and fourth Sunday evenings, they all attended at Holly Springs.

"Time for naps," Ruth said to the younger children.

The Upward Way

Arlene and Albert were reading in the living room—Arlene ladylike in a stuffed chair and Albert spread out on the sofa. Anna Mae was putting a puzzle together on the dining room table, and Vena Grace was helping her find the pieces.

Jean Elaine was sprawled on the floor in front of the fireplace with a book. She sat up now and looked at her mother with puzzlement on her face. "Mama, I heard Papa say that Brother Allen brought presents. I waited all during church, but he didn't give us any presents. And he said he would have a message. I thought the message would be about the presents."

Arlene and Albert both looked up and began to laugh, and Anna Mae giggled from the dining room. Ruth tried hard to stifle the chuckle that wanted to rise up within her. No doubt Jean Elaine had misunderstood something, she thought. Well, yes, David would have talked about presence. How was a little girl to know the difference between *presents* and *presence*?

"He didn't mean gifts," Albert began in a belittling tone.

Ruth looked at him reprovingly, and he turned his eyes down again at his book. Then Ruth turned to Jean Elaine. "You didn't understand quite what Papa was saying," she began. "Papa was saying that he was glad that Brother Allen was *present,* or here at the service."

Jean Elaine's face registered understanding as she said, "Oh." Then she added, "But I really did want to see those presents."

"I just hope we can soon build a church here," Arlene said.

The Upward Way

"I think there is talk about that," Ruth told her. "Papa said that the bishop would like to see us build before another year."

"Oh, another year? I wish it would be before that!"

"We don't mind having church in our house. Thank the Lord that we have a big house."

"Today there were forty-six here," Albert contributed. "I counted them while Emory was taking the offering."

Ruth nodded. "We already have a nice-sized congregation." But what she appreciated most was the unity of the spirit among them, and the love that was freely shown from one to the other.

"You know what I wish," Arlene broke in suddenly. "I wish Grandpa and Grandma Clemmer would come sometime for a church service here. I think they would appreciate our church."

"No doubt they would," Ruth agreed, thinking how Grandma in her letters often expressed their disappointment with how things were going in their churches.

"They were here when we were still going to Holly Springs," Albert said. "They were here a couple of times, weren't they?"

"Yes," Ruth said, "and your uncles Norman and Mark were here too with their families. They have come once each summer."

"And your Uncle Amos from Virginia, and your Uncle John and Aunt Lydia," Arlene contributed. "We've had lots of company since we moved here. I couldn't begin to name everyone. Sometimes we have company every weekend, and even through the week!"

Ruth nodded. "Most of my aunts and uncles have been

The Upward Way

here." Suddenly, she laughed. "I guess they wanted to make sure we weren't getting too uncivilized down here in the boondocks!"

Arlene laughed with her, understanding the reference. But Albert just looked on, puzzled. "We don't live in the boondocks," he said. "I know what that word means, because some of the cousins tormented me about it and I looked it up. It isn't nice to say we do, is it, Mama?"

"No, not really, Albert. But we'll just let them talk, and laugh with them. God led us here, and we're happy here, and that is all that really matters."

Albert nodded, apparently satisfied.

David popped his head around the living room door. "I'd like to walk to the woods," he said. "Anybody want to go with me?" He looked invitingly at Ruth.

"I'd love to," she said. Turning to Jean Elaine and then Vena Grace, she reminded them, "You girls should go for naps now."

"Okay," Jean Elaine said, closing her book and laying it on the fireplace mantel. Vena Grace hopped off her chair in the dining room, and soon both girls were racing up the stairs.

"I'd rather read than go for a walk," Arlene said.

"And I'd rather do my puzzle," Anna Mae added.

"Okay," Ruth agreed. "Arlene, could you please watch out for the younger children? Why don't you go upstairs with them until they settle down for naps."

Arlene nodded.

"I'd like to go for a bike ride," Albert said, standing up and stretching. "I get too bored just sitting and reading all Sunday afternoon!"

The Upward Way

"I don't mind if you ride your bike, Albert," David consented, "but be sure to stay on our land, and don't ride on the road."

"Okay," Albert agreed. "I have lots of field lanes to ride on. I really like to ride my bike here at this farm. There aren't any hills to worry about like our farm in Pennsylvania had!"

"So you still remember the hills?" David asked with a chuckle.

"I sure do!" And Albert slammed the back door.

Soon David and Ruth were walking slowly across the yard. Hearing a flicker call, Ruth looked to the top of the nearby windmill. "Up there it is," she said, pointing. As soon as she spoke, the flicker took off for the woods, dipping and soaring in its characteristic flight. Ruth sighed. "It's good Jean Elaine didn't hear that bird. She'd have been up there after it."

David nodded. "No doubt," he agreed. "But what more can we do for that girl? She is such a climber. We took the bottom two sections of ladder off the windmill when we moved here, because she was always climbing up there after the birds' nests at the top."

"Then she soon learned to just climb up the metal framing."

"And no matter how or how much we discipline, we just can't seem to break her of it."

"She's still at it," Ruth added. "This past winter she'd climb the rafters to the barn roof and pull out the sparrows that had crawled in the spaces between the wood framing and the tin. She'd put them in her coat pockets and bring them downstairs in the barn to play with them."

385

The Upward Way

"And trees, and silos, and barn roofs, and shed roofs... What will be the end of that girl? Why can't we help her?"

By now, they were walking out the field lane. Albert was riding his bike back and forth past them. Then he rode the other direction, going out the field lane toward the hay fields to the west.

"And her vivid imagination!" Ruth added. "It's a wonder she hasn't broken every bone in her body for all the times she has jumped off roofs, sure that she'll be able to fly like the birds!"

David chuckled dryly. "And the only hurt she's ever suffered from her trying to fly is the time she happened to come down on a garden rake that someone left lying in the grass."

"Her foot took a lot of stitches to close it up that time, and I thought surely that would be the end of her trying to fly."

"But it wasn't?"

Ruth shook her head. "I'm afraid not. I was taking in the dry wash one day just last week and saw her sailing out the upstairs barn door. Vena Grace was standing in the doorway, watching her go, but didn't have the nerve to follow, apparently."

"Well, we'll have to keep working at guiding her right. I guess she is a normal child, just more curious and imaginative than some. I just hope and pray she doesn't mortally injure herself before she grows out of some of these things!"

"At least she's not destructive like she was for a while," David added. "Remember that day, soon after we moved here, when I came in from the field for dinner.

The Upward Way

You were standing outside the pantry door crying, Vena Grace was in her playpen crying, and Jean Elaine was standing at the door with egg all over her and tears running down her cheeks."

"Do you think I'll ever forget?" Ruth returned. "I couldn't believe a child of ours could ever be so awful. She had thrown eggs all over the room, stuffed them into cupboard drawers, dropped them behind shelves and into empty canning jars, put them on the floor and stamped on them. . . . I didn't know what to do. And so many other things she did! I would just like to forget." She sighed. "Sometimes I'm at my wits' end to know what to do for her. And I cry out to God for wisdom."

"Well, all children have sinful natures. And we can never expect to get through life without finding that out. You're right. We can't expect to find the right way through these experiences without the wisdom and help of God."

"I guess such revelations of the fallen 'angels' we've produced help to keep us humble," Ruth concluded.

The Jersey cows came to the fence, curious as to what was happening. Feeling unusually frisky, they cavorted along the fence, keeping pace with David and Ruth all the way to the woods.

"What a happy herd of cattle!" Ruth laughed.

David chuckled with her. "They surely are friendly. I've had to get used to little Jerseys and Guernseys, rather than the big Holsteins that we milked for years in Pennsylvania." He reached over to pet the nose of one who had stretched across the fence. "But the milk companies down here put a premium on milk fat, which we get a lot

387

The Upward Way

more of from these little producers."

"I had a hard time getting used to them too," Ruth agreed. "But now I like how tame they are and easy to handle. And the calves are so cute."

"And they make good 'horses' for the children to ride around on," David added with a dry chuckle.

Ruth looked at him and returned a laugh. "Leave it up to Jean Elaine. That was probably her idea too!"

David tramped along silently for a while. Ruth knew he was thinking at times like this, and she did not interrupt. She just looked around at all the fresh greenery of spring. Most of the forest ahead of them was pine trees, but here and there among them was the colorful addition of newly leafing deciduous trees.

As they entered the woods, David looked about him with enjoyment. "Ruth, isn't this all wonderful?" he asked, his blue eyes alight.

Ruth nodded, her heart in perfect agreement. She had always loved the solitude of the woods, where nothing could be seen or heard but that which God had made.

"But mostly, I'm happy to be here, where God wants us, doing what God has led us to do," he went on after a bit.

"I'm happy here too," Ruth said, gladly acknowledging the peace that she had felt since the move to North Carolina. "I feel our move here has been a real blessing to me spiritually, as well as to our family."

"Especially since we have had church here at Rawlins," David added with feeling. "The Lord has provided a faithful church family for us, and I can never thank Him enough."

The Upward Way

"Oh, look!" Ruth exclaimed quietly. "There goes a red fox."

David looked where she was pointing, to see the sly creature slinking through a copse of holly trees. "It probably has a den with cubs somewhere back in there," David said. "I used to enjoy hunting out such, when I was young!" He went on to tell about a young fox cub that he and his brothers had found and tamed.

Ruth looked at him, enjoying the animation on his face. *David has been so happy since our move south,* she thought. *I never saw this side of him like I have in the past couple of years. I guess I really never knew him before! What a wonderful Papa he always was, and a dear husband to me, but even more so in the past several years! Why am I so blessed? But then, why didn't I consent to his wish to move, long ago? I'm so glad the Lord patiently led me step by step and didn't give up on me. Thank You, Father in heaven!*

389

Chapter Twenty-two

Spring ,1955 . . .

Ruth paused in watering her violets to gaze out the east windows. Across the field, up in the corner of their woodland, their new church was fast taking shape. David was there working today, and even now she could see men like ants crawling on the roof, putting on shingles.

"Mama, how soon will the new church be finished?" Vena Grace suddenly asked, at her elbow.

"Oh, I didn't know you came in." Ruth laughed, startled. "Weren't you out playing with Tootsie?"

"I was," Vena Grace replied. "And I was watching Papa and the other men work at the church. Then Tootsie saw a cat coming across the yard and jumped off my lap to chase it. So I came in to find you."

Ruth chuckled. "Dogs like to chase cats, don't they!" She looked again across the freshly plowed field, where, sometime within the next month, David would want to plant corn. "It looks like the brethren will soon have the

The Upward Way

roof all shingled. I think Papa said they hope to begin having services in the church in one month," she added.

"How soon is one month?" Vena asked, looking puzzled.

"It will be after about four more Sundays."

"Oh." Vena nodded.

Ruth carefully watered the plants on the last table. She enjoyed her violets. *Just like my mother always did,* she thought.

"Mama, you sure have lots of flowers!" Vena said suddenly. "Yesterday I counted this kind"—she pointed to the violets—"and you have 117 pots of them!"

"I do?" Ruth was surprised, not so much at the amount of violets, but that Vena could count them. She knew that the little girl had been counting eggs and anything else that she handled, but Ruth had not realized she could count that high. She smoothed Vena's hair. "You're eager to go to school next year, aren't you?"

Vena Grace giggled and ran to the door. Soon Ruth saw her again sitting in the yard, the little black terrier in her lap, watching the men at work.

How my mother always enjoyed her violets, Ruth thought as she continued watering the many pots. *My mother . . .* Ruth's thoughts suddenly took a sad turn. Mama had had a cough she could not throw off and so had gone to the doctor. He had discovered two suspicious lumps. A biopsy had revealed what the family had all feared—cancer. Now Mama was staying with Sarah, in her home in Norristown, where she was getting treatment at a nearby hospital. But what would be the end?

And, dear Father, my own needs . . . For the past month, she had not been very well. And now she was

391

The Upward Way

quite sure another little one would be coming to their home. Along with that, she had been experiencing times of such weakness that she could hardly do her own work. Dear young Arlene had been picking up much of the responsibility of homelife as Ruth struggled to stay on top of the nausea and the heart spells that sometimes confined her to a chair for most of a day.

"I just wish I could go help my sisters to care for Mama," Ruth murmured aloud as she carried the watering can back to the kitchen. "Maybe I'll feel better in a few weeks. I pray so. But right now I feel like I must rest again." She sank into her favorite chair with a sigh.

David found her there when he came home for lunch two hours later. She awoke to his concerned face looking into hers. "Are you all right, dear?" he asked gently.

"Just tired," she said. "But I feel better now. I'm sorry, I don't have lunch ready. And where is Vena Grace?" She pulled herself forward suddenly.

"She came to meet me when I drove in and said that Mama's sleeping, and that she set the table and got 'supper,'" David said with a smile. "She does have the table set, but her 'supper' consists of bread and butter and jelly and pickles." He had to laugh in spite of himself. "But she was real pleased with herself."

"Bless her heart," Ruth said, smiling. "I'll go warm some leftovers." She stood up quickly, and almost as soon sank back into the chair.

David's smile changed to concern once more. "Are you okay?"

Ruth nodded. "I just felt like I was going to faint. I have to get up more slowly, I guess."

The Upward Way

"I think you should be seeing a doctor again, Ruth," David said. "I think Dr. Lambert should know about this weakness of your heart."

"I did tell him, the last time I was there," Ruth assured David. "And I told him about how my mother also had spells with her heart, which would sometimes send her to bed for a day. He thinks it is probably the same thing; in which case, he assured me, it is not life-threatening."

"And now this other . . ." David's eyes twinkled happily in spite of everything.

Ruth nodded again, also feeling great joy. "But now I must get some lunch." Ruth struggled again to get up.

"You stay sitting, dear. Vena and I will find something to fix and bring it to you here."

"Please, I want to do my own work, if I possibly can," Ruth begged.

"Then, give me your hand, queen of my heart and home," David said cheerfully, his blue eyes twinkling. His strong arms soon had pulled her to her feet, and Ruth hurried to the kitchen to find Vena already pouring the water.

Vena giggled happily, not caring that there was water slopped around every cup. Ruth did not care either. *Dear child. Will she someday be motherless? . . .*

That night was especially long. Ruth lay awake, gazing out into the bright, starlit March night. *I must be sleeping too much during the day that I can't sleep at night,* she thought ruefully. *But what should I be doing differently? I get so tired, and feel like I just have to rest.* After spending time in prayer for each of her loved ones, for their church family, and for many other needs that

The Upward Way

came to mind, Ruth finally fell into a restful sleep.

But the next night was a repeat, and the next night, for the next week.

I know why I can't sleep tonight, Ruth thought grimly as she once again lay awake in bed. She had been to Dr. Lambert again the day before yesterday. Just today he had come out to the farm and sat in the living room with her and David.

"I don't like to tell you this, Mrs. Peachey," he had said, hesitating as he cleared his throat with his characteristic *huh-hum.* "Your test results show that for some reason your heart is very weak. I would recommend that you get yourself a good maid and just take it easy."

"But how can a mother take it easy?" Ruth had protested. "I have my family to care for. And I ought to go see my mother, who has cancer, and even help to care for her."

Dr. Lambert had looked very firm. "If you want to be here to care for your own family five years from now, you had better listen," he had said decidedly. "With the condition your heart is in, any exertion could take you. Am I being plain enough?"

Ruth had nodded as tears came to her eyes, and David had looked stricken. What tenderness he had shown to her as he oversaw her care the rest of the day.

And now, here she lay in bed, once more wide-awake, her mind reliving all the experiences of the past few days. Once again, she turned her cares and fears over to her heavenly Father. *Dear Father, it isn't that I don't want to be with You. But my family needs me so. I would like to be here with them at least until they are grown. But,*

The Upward Way

Lord, You know what is best. I do long to do Your will, and to be all that you want me to be . . .

Ruth suddenly awakened. It was like a voice had spoken to her. "Why don't you ask for anointing?" She turned to look at David, beside her in bed. But he was sleeping soundly and peacefully. He had not spoken to her. She must have imagined it. After some time, she drifted off to sleep again, only to be awakened by the same feeling or thought, as of an audible voice, "Why don't you ask for anointing?"

This time Ruth lay fully awake. *Did you speak, Father? Should I ask to be anointed? But nobody does that anymore. I have never witnessed an anointing service. . . .* She carefully rolled over in bed and turned on her small bed lamp. Finding her Bible, she flipped the pages to James 5, where she knew the account about anointing with oil was recorded. Carefully and thoughtfully she read the Scripture, and then she reread it. *It surely does sound as though it is something Christians should be practicing,* she concluded.

David suddenly awakened and turned to her. "Are you all right?" he asked, concern mirrored in his eyes.

Ruth told him about her experience. "What do you think it was?" she asked. "Do you think it was actually the Spirit of God speaking to me? But why would God tell me that? I don't remember ever being in a service where someone was anointed with oil to be healed."

David thought about that for a time. "Anointing with oil is certainly a teaching of the Scriptures," he said. "And it is included in the ordinances that we profess to practice. But, as you say, it is seldom done anymore. I

The Upward Way

don't know why. Shall I call Brother Ira in the morning, and ask him what he thinks?"

Ruth nodded. "I would be glad if you would talk to our bishop. He would give good advice."

With peace in her heart, Ruth settled once more to sleep.

Brother Ira was happy to come at their request and administer this ordinance. A time was set for the Sunday following, on April 2. Those days seemed long to Ruth as she battled the thrusts of Satan. Physically, she seemed to be weaker each day until by Saturday, she could not even lift her arms to comb her hair. David did that for her, as gently as any woman. Arlene had stayed home from school for a couple of days to help with the many household duties. By Sunday, Ruth was not able to be on her feet for more than five minutes without the weakness and pain that let her know it was time to sit down again and rest.

"How can I ever get through a worship service?" Ruth mourned to David on Sunday morning after he had helped her to prepare for the day.

"Why don't you just stay in your chair," David told her kindly, "and the ministry can come in here to have the service."

Ruth nodded, thankful for her husband's kind care.

Most of the worship service she was able to hear and understand. The singing was especially meaningful to her as each song seemed to speak to her own special need. After a Sunday school lesson on the courage of Caleb, Brother Ira preached on the ministry of suffering. "Suffering is one means God uses to draw us closer to

The Upward Way

Him," he said near the end of his message. "God does not bring trouble to us because He likes to see us suffer, but because He is interested in our eternal salvation." Ruth was blessed as she picked up gems of truth from her chair in her makeshift, downstairs bedroom. David led her favorite song at the end of the service. But how it did fit with the theme of the morning message: "I'm Pressing on the Upward Way."

" 'I want to scale the utmost height, / And catch a gleam of glory bright; / But still I'll pray till heav'n I've found, / "Lord, lead me on to higher ground.' " Tears filled Ruth's eyes as she softly sang along. Would she soon be realizing the higher ground of heaven, with its gleams of bright glory? She did not know. She only knew she wanted to be faithful until that time, whenever it would be.

Several of the sisters spent time with her as they shared lunch together. After lunch many of the people left, to go home and pray for the service that was soon to take place in the Peachey home.

Then it was time for the special anointing service. The ministry and their wives and several others of David and Ruth's closest friends gathered in the room with Ruth. After a time of singing and testimonies, the gathered worshipers spent time on their knees, praying. In her heart, Ruth joined in their prayer for her healing. *According to Your will, O my Father!* she prayed, truly desiring to be submitted to God's will, whatever the cost.

Then Brother Ira administered the ordinance. Such a feeling of peace and rest flooded Ruth's heart. God was so good! Whatever His will, truly that was best—whether

The Upward Way

in life or in death.

When the service was over, Ruth got up to greet the sisters and to visit briefly. After some time of visiting, she realized she had not felt any weakness at all. She turned to Sister Anna. "I feel stronger than I have for months," she stated with conviction. "Does that mean the Lord has healed me?"

Sister Anna looked at her with surprise and happiness in her eyes. "It surely would seem that way!"

Soon the anointing service had turned into a praise service as everyone rejoiced with Ruth and David. In the days that followed, Ruth took up her former duties with great joy, caring for her family and working outside in the beauty of the returning springtime.

The next week, Dr. Lambert stopped by for a regular house call and to pick up several dozen eggs. He found Ruth outside working in her flower beds. His eyes opened like saucers. "Just what are you doing out here, young lady?" he demanded.

Ruth brushed the loose sand off her hands as she stood up, full of her usual vigor. "It's a story I have to tell you. Come in and sit down. David is working at his desk, and he will join us."

As they sat around the kitchen table, each with a cup of tea, Dr. Lambert followed the story with great interest. "And so, you feel God has healed you?" he asked reverently, when the story of her anointing and subsequent healing had been told.

"Yes, I do. And God gets all the glory."

Dr. Lambert reached for his satchel and pulled out his stethoscope. After listening to her heart for some

The Upward Way

time, he took her blood pressure. Then he listened to her heart again. "Your blood pressure is good, and your heart sounds completely normal." He shook his head as though he could hardly believe what he was hearing.

"All I can say is that I have to believe your story," he said finally. "You appear to be a well woman, when before I wouldn't have given two cents for your chances!" His voice quavered, but he stood up to leave with his usual professional air. "Just keep serving the God that is able to do such wonderful things!" he added.

"We surely mean to," David said sincerely, and Ruth nodded in heartfelt agreement.

"I must be getting back to the office. It looks to me as though I won't need to make any more house calls here. But do take care!" He picked up his satchel.

"Don't forget your eggs," Ruth called gaily after him as he started out the front door.

"Oh, yes." He turned around suddenly and then shook his head.

David and Ruth stood together at the front door as they watched Dr. Lambert drive out the lane. Then Ruth turned to David eagerly. "He said I'm a well woman. Do you think that means I could spend some time with Mama?"

David thought for a while before returning fondly, "I think you owe it to your mother and your family to do that. But the rest of us will surely miss you."

"If I took Vena Grace with me, you wouldn't need to mind her through the day," Ruth offered. "I'm sure she'd be happy to play with the cousins there."

Ruth was able to find her way north with Brother Ira

The Upward Way

and Sister Anna, who were still in the area from the previous weekend. With fond good-byes, she left her family early Friday morning.

"How will you get back home?" Sister Anna asked in the midst of their visiting as they traveled north.

"David thought he could bring the family and come for me next week," Ruth said. "We would need to take the children out of school."

"Have you heard lately how your mother is doing?"

"My sister Sarah or my sister-in-law Ellen keep me informed every few days by telephone. Sarah called yesterday. Mama had been staying with her in Norristown for a while, but now she is home. Maybe you knew that. Anyway, Sarah said she is getting weaker every day, and the doctor is not sure what to do for her anymore. My maiden sister, Dorcas, is at home, and she gives most of Mama's care. But the others help all they can."

"I'm sure you're glad to be able to go and spend time with her, especially if her days are numbered."

Ruth nodded. "Yes, I am! It was so hard for me when I knew how sick Mama was and that I was not able to stand the trip to be with her at all."

"How old is your mother?"

Vena Grace, on the back seat with Ruth, gently patted her arm. "Mama, Grammy just had a birthday," she whispered. "Remember, we children made her cards."

Ruth smiled at her little daughter. "That's right," she said. "Mama just had a birthday on March 25. She was born in 1878, so that would make her seventy-seven."

"Then she has had a long life," Brother Ira said comfortingly. "And a fruitful one."

The Upward Way

"Yes, she has. And I don't grieve for her going to be with the Lord. How could I! I only grieve for how we will all miss her."

Mark and Ellen met Ruth at Brother Ira's home in Morgantown to take her and Vena Grace back to Spring City. On the way, they caught up with much that had happened in Ruth's life, and then in general with the family. Then they tried to prepare Ruth for how poorly Mama was actually doing.

"I don't think we'll have her long," Mark concluded.

Ellen sadly nodded her head in agreement. "She has gone back so fast since she was diagnosed with cancer."

"I'm just so thankful that I will be able to spend a little time with her yet," Ruth said with tears. "I have missed Mama so much in the years since we've moved."

"Mama and Papa have gotten to your place a few times, which is nice," Mark said. "They talked a lot about how much they enjoyed their week with you when they were there last fall. Papa liked the wide-open fields and even said maybe he ought to buy a farm down there." Mark chuckled a little.

"And Mama loved going to the ocean with you," Ellen added. "She seemed to enjoy seeing the majesty and the power of the waves."

Ruth nodded, smiling. "I was surprised how they both seemed impressed by the ocean. I don't know if they had ever seen it before."

"Mama really enjoyed worshiping with you, even if your church was in your home," Mark went on. "And Papa appreciated the conservative group."

Ruth thought back to the once-a-year visits that Papa

The Upward Way

and Mama had made. She was thankful that they had finally accepted their move to North Carolina and could rejoice with them. Mark's and Norman's had also visited at least once a year. David's had not been able to do as well in return, having only gotten back to Pennsylvania twice since their move south.

Soon Ruth's thoughts were interrupted by a pat on her arm. She looked down to see Vena Grace's big brown eyes turned on her. "Mama, is Grammy going to die?" she asked solemnly.

Ruth drew the child to her. Maybe they had been talking too freely in front of her. And yet, Vena Grace was old enough to understand about sickness and death. "Grammy is very sick, Vena Grace," Ruth told her now. "And Jesus may come to take her home to be with Him."

Vena Grace said no more, only nodded soberly, as though understanding.

How glad Ruth was to finally arrive at Papa's house. She and Vena Grace walked with some trepidation into the small downstairs bedroom in the apartment where she and David had first lived. Mama welcomed Ruth and her little granddaughter with a glad light in her eyes, but Ruth could hardly believe how frail and thin her dear mother looked as she lay propped up in bed. Kneeling by her bed, Ruth kissed her, and then fought to hold back the tears until she could escape and cry, out of Mama's presence. Vena Grace came close to Grammy's bed too, looking on very soberly.

Grammy reached out a hand and gently patted Vena Grace's arm. "You look so much like your mother did at this age," she said slowly, catching her breath between

The Upward Way

every few words. "I'm so glad you could come with your mama."

Then she slowly turned her eyes to Ruth. "I'm so glad you're here, Ruth," she said, panting to get her breath. "You've had a hard time of it yourself."

Ruth nodded, hardly trusting herself to speak.

For the next days and nights, Ruth spent as much time as possible in her mother's room. Each day, Mama was noticeably weaker, and Ruth knew instinctively that she could not last much longer. Vena Grace was often with her mother in the room with Grammy. Sometimes she sat on a small rocker, rocking one of Grammy's dolls. Other times she just sat, watching soberly, her big brown eyes full of questions.

On Monday night as her mother lay wakeful, Ruth sat by her bed, reading from the Psalms. Mama put out her hand, and Ruth stopped reading to look at her fondly. "Ruth," Mama panted, "I have to say this to you.... God has forgiven ... me all my sins.... I know I'm going to Him, and I'm so eager!" She stopped to gasp for breath. Finally, she went on. "But I've been ... too proud. I was so conscious of ... social status, and I was ... proud of Papa's wealth." She stopped again to gasp for breath. "Those things ... are nothing ... when you ... come ... to die. Nothing ... Thank ... God, He has ... forgiven me."

Ruth laid her cheek against her mother's sallow one, and the tears fell in spite of her efforts to hold them back. "Oh, Mama, you have been a good mother to me, and I love you."

"Sing ... to me. Sing ... 'Jesus, Keep Me ... Near ...'"

"Do you mean 'Jesus, Keep Me Near the Cross'?"

The Upward Way

Ruth asked, wondering how she could ever sing.

Mama nodded weakly. Ruth began to sing, her voice gaining strength as she sang through all the verses.

That was the last that anyone heard Mama speak. Soon afterward, she slipped into a coma, and the next morning, April 12, she passed away. Papa and Mark and all the girls were by Mama's bedside as the time between each breath got longer and longer. Then Ellen laid her ear against Mama's chest. "Her heart is just fluttering," she said with tears. After a short time, she added, "And now it is silent."

Softly she stood up and drew the cover over Mama's face. Papa dropped his head on his hands and broke into heavy sobs. Mark went to call the doctor and the undertaker. Ruth fled to the room where she had been staying and gave way to a flood of tears. "O God," she cried after her grief had somewhat subsided, "how weak we poor mortals are! And death makes us so aware of our own mortality and how fleeting life is! Keep us faithful to You so that we can all meet Mama again in heaven some day." She was recalled to the present by a hand on her arm. As she turned, there stood Vena Grace, a doll clutched in her arm and tears running down her face.

"Oh, dear child, I'm sorry I forgot about you for a bit. Grammy went to be with Jesus, and Mama is sad."

"Why are you sad, Mama, if Grammy is with Jesus?"

Ruth drew the child to herself. "Because we will miss Grammy. We won't be able to talk to her anymore. And I am sad for Grandpa because he will miss Grammy too."

"And Grammy won't be able to come visit us anymore. She's all died up."

The Upward Way

"You mean, she died," Ruth corrected gently. "That means the part of her that sees and talks and hears has gone to be with God. All that we see is her body. After a few days, we will have a funeral, and Grammy's body will be put into the ground. But we can still know that the real Grammy is up in heaven with God."

"And she's happy there!" Vena Grace concluded with a smile.

Ruth called David and told him the sad news. He made plans to come with the other children as soon as possible. The next days were filled with the coming and going of friends and relatives and with making plans and preparations. Then came the viewing and the funeral, with all the related emotional stress and loss of rest.

David and Ruth helped their children go to bed early on Saturday evening, hoping themselves to be able to get a good night of rest. Dorcas had already gone to her room, where no doubt she was dealing with her own grief alone, as she was more apt to do.

But Papa wanted to talk. "Just sit down in here and talk awhile," he begged, indicating the living room. "I probably won't be able to sleep anyway."

He sat down heavily in his favorite chair. "Oh, what will I do, all alone?" He shook with silent sobs for a time; then he seemed to brace up again. "Well, Mama was ready to go, and that is such a comfort."

"And you have Dorcas here to keep house for you, Papa," Ruth reminded him gently. "You won't be all alone, like many would be."

Papa was finally able to contain his grief as they talked over the events of the last few days. Then his

The Upward Way

thoughts seemed to turn to other avenues. "I have to tell you, David. I was upset when you took your family to North Carolina. But now when I see how far our churches have drifted, I can't help admiring you for the move you made." He shook his head sadly. "And I have to appreciate what you are trying to maintain in your family. I know Mark means to do well too, but it's so hard when almost everyone else just follows the current downstream. Nobody wants to keep the old ways anymore."

Ruth glanced at David. *Will he remind Papa of his own needs just now? Papa seems so mellow. Or might Papa have come to God in true repentance and made things right with Mama before she died? Wouldn't that be wonderful—an answer to our years of prayer! But then, wouldn't he acknowledge those failures now, if he had?*

"I appreciated the funeral service today," David told Papa. "Uncle Amos had a powerful message, preached not to the dead but to those of us who still need to be faithful till death. I feel sure that Mama is with the Lord. The only way we can hope to meet her over there is if we have met the conditions—if our sins are forgiven, and we maintain a daily walk with the Lord in true holiness and righteousness."

"Yes, of course," Papa agreed.

David just looked at Papa with grief in the look. Ruth did not say anything. They surely did not want to judge Papa falsely, but still, if the fruits of his life had not changed, could he be right with God?

Papa did not say more, and so her thoughts went back to the service.

Yes, the service had been a blessing to her, but her

The Upward Way

heart had nearly broken to see how many changes had come into the church since they had been there last. And how sad she had felt when she met Kore and his wife, her cousin Ethel, and realized that neither of them placed any value anymore on the Biblical practices they had once been taught.

Papa seemed to awake from his reverie. "Yes, Amos had a good message today, but that is usually as far as it goes. People hear, but they do not listen."

Ruth looked up at Papa, wondering—hoping that he had seen the needs in his own life. His concerns for Biblical conservatism were right, truly; but it took so much more to be right with God than to hold tenaciously to a set of right standards.

But Papa was going on. "I have to tell you, you will be disappointed if you go to Grove Hill tomorrow morning. Things just aren't the same. Women song leaders, women teachers, women study group leaders, women speakers for Sunday evening topics. And many of those same women have cut hair and no coverings."

Ruth looked at David aghast. That must have come just since they moved away, although—well, occasionally some women were doing some of those things before they left. How could they overlook the very obvious teaching of Scripture that women are to keep silence in the church?

"You might want to visit Bridgetown tomorrow morning for worship," Papa went on. "You remember that young man, Ivan Houser, that came into the Norristown Mission in its early years?"

"Oh, yes," Ruth said. "He married Anna French, who

The Upward Way

helped us out when Albert was born."

"Well, anyway, Ivan has been ordained minister at Bridgetown, and he is a conservative man. He can really preach too."

"Oh, I'd enjoy going there. I'd love to see Anna again," Ruth burst out. "Could we, David? Would you want to go along, Papa? you and Dorcas?"

"Well, now, I'd enjoy that, but people would wonder if I wasn't at Grove Hill."

"We were to Grove Hill today for services," David said slowly, "so I suppose it would be in order for us to worship at Bridgetown tomorrow. I would enjoy meeting Ivan Houser again."

Anna was surprised and delighted to see the Peacheys the next morning at church. She and Ivan would not hear of anything but to have David's stay with them for lunch and the afternoon. "We always need to be ready for visitors, and we have plenty for everyone," Anna assured them.

"Well, we shouldn't stay long, should we?" Ruth said in an aside to David. "It wouldn't seem fair to my family—which is who we really came to Pennsylvania to see."

"That's right," David returned with a smile. "We can visit long enough that they don't feel we're hurrying off."

Ruth enjoyed learning to know Anna again, and learning to know their family. Their oldest daughter was close to Anna Mae's age, with a number of children younger.

After lunch, while the children played quietly with toys or with games around the kitchen table, the older people sat and visited in the living room. It did not take David and Ruth long to realize that Brother Ivan had many deep concerns for the church as they discussed various issues.

The Upward Way

"I came into the Mennonite Church to get away from the world," he said after a while, "and now the world is coming into the Mennonite Church."

"Did you know that divorce and remarriage is being tolerated in some of our churches?" Anna went on to say. "I never thought the Mennonite Church would follow the world in accepting that."

"It is just one more way that people are making room for themselves, to try to serve the Lord without needing to give up their sins," David added thoughtfully. "I think we see more and more what Paul warned against—people using grace as a license to sin."

"Brother David," Ivan began, "if you met many of the young people from our churches through the week, you would not even recognize them as being Christian. Many of our women appear in public dressed like men, and many go without any kind of headship veiling through the week. Only some of the older women still wear traditional plain clothes, but even many of those welcome home their sons and daughters from the colleges, or wherever, dressed in the world's latest styles. It is all so sad and bewildering to me. I came to the church, longing for a holy church, longing for a place where Christianity showed itself in every area by a disciplined, Biblical lifestyle."

Brother Ivan shook his head sadly. "I came into the church at the Norristown Mission. There your brother-in-law took me over the Eighteen Articles of Faith. Now I don't know if he even believes them anymore. I asked him about something lately—I think it was wedding rings that he is allowing in his church—and he stated that he

The Upward Way

has been 'enlightened' since he taught me that the wearing of 'gold and pearls' was forbidden by the Scriptures."

How sad such words made Ruth feel, and yet she knew Brother Ivan spoke the truth. Although she still dearly loved her sister Sarah, something had sadly changed in the last twenty years. No longer did they see eye to eye on many spiritual issues. Although Sarah herself had not changed so much in the way she appeared, she had changed in what she tolerated and accepted. And rather than the sweet, humble girl Ruth had known her to be, she now carried herself regally and responded to others with the world's charm rather than with Christian grace.

"I suppose you haven't visited much in our churches lately," Brother Ivan went on after a while. "But you would be shocked at all that goes on in the name of Christianity. Didn't Paul say in 1 Corinthians 1 that God has chosen by the 'foolishness of preaching' to save those that believe? Well, now we have anything from skits and plays to movies and musical shows. These were first introduced in the young people's meetings, because the leaders felt they had to keep the young people entertained to keep them in the church. Well, it doesn't work that way—it just takes more and more, and finally that doesn't satisfy either. When people are born again, they don't need to be entertained. Anyway, it didn't take long till entertainment became part of regular Sunday morning worship services too. It is not unusual even to have guitarists to entertain on a Sunday morning."

David and Ruth looked at each other in disbelief. Could things really have drifted that far? "What do people do with Jesus' words, 'They that worship him must

The Upward Way

worship him in spirit and in truth'?" David asked. "And Paul speaks of 'teaching and admonishing one another in psalms and hymns and spiritual songs, singing with grace in your hearts to the Lord.' "

"It seems to Anna and me," Ivan said, "that Christianity has become a system of beliefs where *you* do the way you feel like doing and *I* do the way I feel like doing, and it really doesn't matter to God—just as long as we believe in Him—and we'll all get to heaven after a while."

"And the Bible is just a nice book, a book of good things to read and talk about, but not necessarily to live by," Anna added.

"I think the problem," David began slowly, "is that people have lost sight of a holy God. They are trying to reduce God to their level, where He is just a nice friend, and they can do as they please and He won't do more than slap their hands if they get really bad."

"God is a God of love, and that is all the emphasis we hear," Brother Ivan agreed. "But sadly, many are overlooking that God is also a God of justice—and that the Scriptures speak more of God's justice and judgment than of His love. If we believe the Bible at all, we had better believe that God will not dismiss disobedience, nor will He overlook the willfulness of people deciding on their own code of conduct!"

"Oh, but 'the Bible is an outdated book—at least Paul's writings are!' " Anna injected. "I hear that so much at sewing circle among the sisters. I wonder, if the Bible is outdated, exactly what then do they base their salvation on? If the headship veiling was just for the Corinthians,

411

The Upward Way

as they claim, then why practice Communion? Wasn't that just for the Corinthians too?"

Brother Ivan shook his head. "That is how apostasy works, as I read church history. People decide that simple obedience to the Word is outdated, and they concoct a religion that is easy on the flesh and go happily on their way. People tell me—in our own church circles, mind you—that I'm out of step with the world. Well, I tell them I surely hope I am, because I'm listening to a different drumbeat!"

David smiled, a sad smile. Then he said, "I've done some reading from church history too. I think of the Dutch Mennonites, and even the Russian Mennonites in more recent history. It was when they became 'rich, and increased with goods' that they started down the road of apostasy. And yet our people see no threat at all in riches."

Brother Ivan humphed. "I agree with you 100 percent. But we can't follow that thinking in this conference. People think you've taken leave of your senses! To not be rich? Why, that is what life is all about to many, and riches have become their god. No, they don't know it; or if they do, they would never admit it! And all the time, the devil is having a heyday with souls."

"Well, there is hope," David said. "Jesus said that there will always be a faithful remnant. And they will be those who have forsaken all to follow Him."

Ruth nodded, thinking how often those verses had been a comfort to her after she had finally been willing to leave family and friends and go with her husband to serve where the Lord wanted them.

The Upward Way

"We have hope! Brother Ivan," David said suddenly. "I appreciated so much your message this morning, 'The Riches of the Resurrection.' Paul likens the sowing of a seed, and the new growth that comes forth, to Christ's death and resurrection. Then he proceeds with an extremely important truth—that without death, there will be no life. And that death, according to many New Testament verses, is death to self. Only as self dies can a 'new plant' grow that is able to bear resurrection fruits—love, joy, peace, longsuffering, gentleness, goodness, faith, meekness, and temperance."

Ivan was gently nodding. "You caught my burden," he said. "Without death to self, there is no life in God."

"And that is what the new birth encompasses," David said reverently.

Ruth looked from one to the other, her heart full of thanksgiving to God for the few faithful ones that they were finding here and there. But then she thought of Mark, and how he had stood and talked a long time with her and David in the barn on Thursday evening. He felt so burdened by all that was coming into the church, but Ellen did not share his views, which was a grief to him. She rather encouraged him to be tolerant, Mark had said, because she was very sure most of their church people really did want to serve the Lord.

Monday morning dawned, another lovely, fresh spring morning. Ruth knelt at the open window of what had used to be her and David's bedroom when they had lived in Papa's apartment. David had gone to the barn to help with the milking, and Ruth had the room to herself. She looked across the brightening meadow to the creek

The Upward Way

meandering between the oak trees along the bottoms. From time to time, she heard calves bawling, chickens cackling, pigs squealing, or a horse whinnying. How familiar everything seemed—and yet how different.

Many memories crowded into her mind . . . How the years had passed, and now here she was, a forty-year-old mother with five children of her own! God had been faithful through every circumstance of life. Surely He had been overruling in leading them to North Carolina, where they could raise their children away from the overwhelming influences of apostate Christianity. "Thank You, Father," she whispered. "As I look back, I truly see Your hand of love in all your leading. Had we stayed here, I could never have stood up to the pressures and influences that came on so subtly and gradually. Thank You for Your faithfulness in taking us one step at a time, and for Your kind patience when I balked at Your will. . . ."

For many years, Ruth had continued her practice of getting up early for private time with God. But how she still longed to know Him better, to be all that He wanted her to be, to be a continual godly influence to those who followed her.

She bowed her head on her arms. "Father, I am ever Your handmaid. Continue to guide me in the way that leads to You."

Epilogue

"Let us hear the conclusion of the whole matter: Fear God, and keep his commandments: for this is the whole duty of man. For God shall bring every work into judgment, with every secret thing, whether it be good, or whether it be evil" (Ecclesiastes 12:13, 14).

As Papa had lived, so he died. His older years only magnified the "weaknesses" of his healthy and useful years. Blindness coupled with some senility left him a powerless and unhappy old man. When Dorcas and others of the family could no longer manage his care at home, he was taken to the Souderton Home, where he had served on the board for most of his years. There, in desperation and bitterness, he took his own life, on March 11, 1965, at the age of eighty-one.

David and Ruth continued to walk with God, submitting to the good experiences along with the bad, knowing they all came from a merciful heavenly Father. Their last child was born in the late fall of 1955 with no health challenges to Ruth despite the dire predictions of the doctor

The Upward Way

after Vena Grace's birth. Some years later, they again needed to face a very hard change in church life. This time they moved to another part of the state and became members in a newly established "fellowship" church.

Ruth, after her miraculous healing, never again suffered heart trouble. For many years of her life, she read the Bible through every year. She continued to teach Sunday school until a muscle condition confined her to a wheelchair. She died late in 1988 at the age of seventy-four, due to complications from her worsening muscle condition.

David lived alone after Ruth's death until senility finally made it necessary to be moved into the home of a daughter. There he lived for a year and a half until he died of congestive heart failure in 1995, at the age of eighty-six. David's favorite verse was "God is our refuge and strength, a very present help in trouble." Often, even after senility caused him to forget who his children were, he lay awake at night, singing in his bed, songs of praise and hope and victory—songs he had loved in the past. He was usually sweet and cheerful, even in his senility. As he had lived, so he died.